THE
SOLAR
WAR

BY A.G. RIDDLE

The Atlantis Trilogy

The Atlantis Gene

The Atlantis Plague

The Atlantis World

The Extinction Files

Pandemic

Genome

The Long Winter Series

Winter World

The Solar War

THE SOLAR WAR

A.G. RIDDLE

First published in the UK in 2019 by Head of Zeus Ltd
This paperback edition first published in the UK in 2020
by Head of Zeus Ltd

9 7 5 3 1 2 4 6 8

A catalogue record for this book is available from
the British Library.

ISBN (PB): 9781789544930

Typeset by Divaddict Publishing Solutions Ltd.

THE
SOLAR
WAR

Prologue

Deep in space, billions of miles from Earth, an ancient machine awoke.

First, it checked its systems.

All were normal.

Then it found the source of its awakening: a message.

Inside the data packet was a simple command. It was a task the machine had completed thousands of times: the annihilation of a primitive civilization.

The machine ran several simulations, quickly settling on the optimal way to eliminate the target. The question wasn't whether it could wipe out the primitives. It was how to do so with the least amount of energy expenditure. Energy was the most precious resource in the universe. The grid needed the energy from the star in the primitives' solar system.

It would soon have it.

The machine powered its engines and began moving toward the planet, which the local inhabitants called Earth.

1

James

The doctor's gloves are covered in blood.

The floor is covered in blood.

Emma is squeezing my hand so hard I'm not sure I'll leave this room with it. She cries out, and I shudder as if a cold wind were blowing across me.

"Can't you give her something?" I ask the doctor, still wincing.

"It's too late." To her, he says, "One last push, Emma."

She grits her teeth and strains again.

"That's it," he coaxes, his hands held out.

Why didn't she take the epidural? If offered, I would take an epidural at this point.

I'm a medical doctor. I never completed my residency or practiced medicine because I knew robotics and AI were my true calling. With that said, one thing is certain: I'm not tough enough to have been an obstetrician. Moments like this take nerves of steel.

Emma strains again and a cry bellows into the room, loud and clear, the most beautiful sound I've ever heard.

The doctor holds the baby up for Emma to see.

Her eyes fill with tears, her chest heaves, and she sinks back to the bed, exhausted. As long as I've known her, I've never seen her so happy. I've never been so happy.

"Congratulations," the doctor says, "you have a healthy baby girl."

He hands our child to a waiting team who runs a series of tests.

I lean over and hug Emma, and kiss her on the cheek. "I love you."

"I love you too," she whispers.

A nurse lays the child on Emma's chest, and my wife cradles her closer.

I can see the relief in Emma's face. She has been terrified that the child would have birth defects from the radiation Emma was exposed to while in space.

Initially, I was concerned as well. But the doctors assured us that the child was fine for several reasons. First, the newer vessels created by NASA are much better shielded against radiation than those created in decades past. Secondly, our daughter was conceived several months after we returned from the Battle of Ceres. Both Emma and I, like all of the returning crew, went through biocontainment when we landed. The process included treatments to improve our bone density and radiation-cleansing therapy.

When we learned Emma was pregnant, Izumi and the other doctors ran every test under the sun and showed us the results. But still Emma worried. Like most first-time parents, we both did. Now it seems they were right. Our daughter is healthy. And so beautiful. We've decided to name her after Emma's mother, Allison.

THE SOLAR WAR

"Welcome to the world, Allie," Emma whispers.

A scream echoes in the night. The baby monitor on Emma's bedside table practically vibrates as it blasts the sound into our bedroom. She rolls over and studies the blue-green night vision image.

Allie lies on her back in the middle of the crib, swaddled tightly. Her face is contorted, mouth open, crying non-stop. It blows my mind that a child so small can make a sound so large.

"I've got it," I mumble as I sit up and throw my legs over the side of the bed.

She grabs my arm. "No. You have to work early."

"True, but I've still got this."

I kiss her on the forehead and pull the covers back up to her chin. She needs to rest.

The last month has been exhausting for both of us, and she has borne the brunt of it. It's my turn to pick up some slack.

I stumble into the nursery and hoist Allie out of the crib. I hold her tight to my chest and gently rock her as I walk around. Emma is better at this. She has a singsong voice, and she knows exactly what to say. My rendition is like an awkward marionette, trying to soothe the child, saying, "It's okay... it's all right." I don't even attempt a song.

Oscar appears at the doorway and whispers, "Sir, can I help?"

Oscar has a variety of skills. This is not one of them. I'm not judging. It's not one of my skills either.

"No, it's okay."

5

I settle into the rocking chair and sway silently, Allie's blue eyes staring up at me, innocently, maybe a hint of curiosity there. I place my index finger in her small palm and wait. A second later, her tiny fingers wrap around my finger, holding it. I smile and stare in wonder at how little and fragile she is. How innocent she is. And how ruthless and deadly the world out there waiting for her is.

Before Allie was born, I had a laundry list of worries. Now I have one: her. I imagine every parent worries about the world that awaits their child, but the world we have brought Allie into is in crisis, torn between our everyday struggles and preparing for a war we know is coming.

Billions died during an ice age known as the Long Winter. Only nine million of us survived. When the ice spread across the Earth, the survivors flocked to the world's last habitable regions, setting up sprawling refugee camps. The Long Winter has broken, but we're still here in the camps, though there's a growing movement to return to our homelands and start over.

Behind everyday life in the camps looms a threat rarely spoken about but never forgotten: the grid. Some say the alien entity that brought the Long Winter is gone for good. But I can't take that risk.

If the grid returns, it will be to finish us, to wage a war to end all wars. I'm going to be ready for that war. Because it's my job. And because I'm a father now.

It's still dark out when Allie finally surrenders to sleep again. I should go back to bed, but I'm too wound up. Being out of work for a month has been tough for me.

In my small office nook in our habitat, I scan my email messages and open the news feed.

In a video thumbnail, a reporter stands before an expanse of frozen landscape. Two years ago, I would have assumed she was in Antarctica. Now you can't tell—this is what half the world still looks like. Text at the bottom of the screen reveals the location: Washington, DC.

Behind the reporter, a dozen US Navy helicopters and throngs of troops are congregated around a giant excavator. I click play on the video, and the machine begins digging into the snow, carefully uncovering something.

The reporter's voice rings out in my tiny office, and I rush to turn the volume down.

"Behind me, American military forces are taking the first step in reopening the American homeland."

The camera zooms in, revealing the object beneath the snow: the dome of the US Capitol building.

The scene expands to include the reporter once again.

"Ladies and gentlemen, we're going home."

Another video catches my eye, one I don't want to watch and can't help but watch.

The opening sequence is a wall of snow slowly melting to reveal the show's logo, *Melting Point with Craig Collins*.

Melting Point is one of the most popular news programs on AtlanticNet, one of only a handful that are syndicated around the world thanks to recently launched satellites.

"My guest this hour is acclaimed robotics expert Dr. Richard Chandler. He's here to talk about his new book, *Saving Earth: The Real Story Behind NASA's Desperate Mission to End the Long Winter*."

The screen changes to a view of the book cover, and then fades back to Craig and Chandler sitting around a small table.

"Thank you for being here, Dr. Chandler."

My former university professor and mentor, and later nemesis, smiles like a Cheshire cat. "My pleasure."

"Let's start with your book. Everyone's talking about it. It's been read—what—a million times on the net?"

"At least. I'm not really sure. I don't pay attention to those types of things. I just want to get the word out."

"Well, at least a few people have taken issue with some of those words. I'm talking specifically about your claims regarding the first contact mission and the Battle of Ceres. Your account has been disputed by NASA and officials from the three superpowers."

Chandler shrugs, apparently unbothered. "They have every incentive to dispute the claims. They want to be the sole source of the truth. It's the only way they can ensure that they stay in power. But as the ice melts, so does their grip on the world's population. Their focus is the Solar Shield project, but the reality is that we need a balanced approach to defending Earth and more of a focus on what the people need."

"Which is?"

"To go home. To the cities and houses we left. For life to get back to normal. That's what people want—and what the three major governments fear most."

"Let's get back to the book for a moment. In it, you say that you were a central part of the planning and execution of the first contact mission as well as the Battle of Ceres where we defeated the grid. And now you claim you're being excluded from any further missions and planning. But the generally accepted history is that James Sinclair was the lead scientist and roboticist on the mission. How do you reconcile those two accounts?"

"I would encourage viewers to look at the undeniable facts. No one at NASA can deny that I was the first roboticist contacted about the mission. No one can deny that I was at the Kennedy Space Center when the crew was brought together and briefed. Yes, Sinclair was on the *Pax* and in the Spartan fleet. I remained here on Earth in a planning capacity—for good reason. You don't put your greatest minds in harm's way. We knew the missions were extraordinarily dangerous. We needed to plan for the future."

Chandler pauses, seeming pained about what he's about to say. "I would also encourage viewers to look at the source. Perhaps the only fact that no one can deny is that James Sinclair is a convicted felon. Before the Long Winter, the United States government deemed him a risk to public safety. They imprisoned him. And that's precisely where he was when the first contact mission was being planned—in prison. He was offered a conditional pardon in return for his service aboard the spaceships."

Chandler nods diplomatically. "With that said, I'm willing to give credit where credit is due. Sinclair did some good work during the two space missions. But do we really want a convicted felon like Sinclair leading our efforts to defend Earth? We need a different kind of person in charge. One who has shown a history of acting in the public's interest—not their own."

This has been going on for months now—Chandler bashing me. Spewing half-truths and self-aggrandizement.

It's true, he was at the initial meeting at NASA before the first contact mission launched. But his plans for the robotics part of the mission would've severely limited our chances of success. I challenged him on it, and when Chandler became combative, Dr. Lawrence Fowler, the director of NASA, removed him from the mission. Looking back, pulling Chandler from the crew probably saved the mission. Might have saved the world.

I can't look anymore. I shouldn't have opened the video in the first place. But I know deep down that if public sentiment turns against the government, we won't just be fighting the grid, we'll be fighting amongst ourselves. We can't afford that.

2

James

Outside the habitat, I march toward the hard-packed street, my feet crunching in the sludge of melting snow and loose sand.

Here in Camp Seven, in what used to be Northern Tunisia, the sun is peeking above the horizon, spewing hazy yellow light on the white, domed habitats that line the streets like melted marshmallows sticking out of the sand.

On mornings like this, when the sun we have always known shines brightly, it's easy to see how people might think we're safe. To think everyone can just go back to their homeland and everything will be normal. But what's normal anymore? Do the banks and other companies that had existed before the Long Winter still exist? What of the mortgages they held on people's homes? And credit card debt? And even bank accounts? Are there even any records left?

Before the Long Winter, I always felt like an outsider in the world, a person with no real place, someone who didn't understand the way the world was and why people did what they did. Once again, I feel like a man in between. Camp Seven is the only home I want to claim. This is where Emma and I returned after the first contact mission, broken and hopeless. This is where Oscar and I nursed Emma back to health when she was too weak to stand. This is where Emma and I fell in love and where our child was born and where my friends and family live.

To me, this is home.

At NASA headquarters, I have a private office next to Fowler's. I don't spend much time there. I'm usually with my team in our large workroom, building prototypes for drones and designing the ships that will defend Earth.

As usual, the workroom is a pigsty when I arrive. Nice to see that hasn't changed. Our long metal work tables are covered in mangled drone parts, interrupted only by flat screens that rise up in the wreckage like billboards in the middle of a miniature junkyard.

The entire team is here: Harry Andrews, the other roboticist on the project; Grigory Sokolov, a Russian astronautical and electrical engineer; Lina Vogel, a German computer scientist; Min Zhao, a Chinese navigator; Izumi Tanaka, a Japanese physician and psychologist; and Charlotte Lewis, an Australian archaeologist and linguist. Oscar is here too, working quietly in the corner.

I expect seven smiling faces, a smattering of "welcome backs," and maybe a hug or two. My arrival elicits none of those, only solemn expressions, no one moving forward to greet me.

Finally, Harry walks up and lightly puts a hand on my

shoulder. He's twenty years older than me and always quick with a joke, but his tone is dead serious now. "Hey, James. We have something you need to see."

Without another word, he leads me out of the room and down the hall.

"See what?" I ask, jogging to keep up.

"I need to show you," Harry replies as he stops at the door to one of the clean rooms. We only use the clean rooms when we need to emulate the sterile vacuum of space.

What's this about?

Harry bends slightly and exposes his eyes to the retinal scanner, and the airlock door slides open. He strides past the blue space suits and helmets hanging on the wall.

"Do we need to suit up?" I ask, looking first at Harry, then back at the team. Everyone avoids eye contact.

"No," Harry says. "It's been through quarantine. It's not a threat... unless it gets on you."

"What's been through quarantine? What's going on, Harry?"

"It's better if we show you," he says softly and steps through the inner door.

The clean room is empty except for a long metal table that holds a single item: a white plastic box about the size of a suitcase. Harry motions toward it. "You're the only one qualified to handle it, James."

The team stares at me as I approach the box and slowly open the hinged top.

A small object lies inside: a silver biohazard bag.

"It's organic," Harry says as he inches forward to stand beside me at the table. "It's a sample. We think the entity creating it arrived on Earth right after you left." After a pause, he adds, "We need you to tell us what to do with it."

I can't resist the mystery another second. Gently, I peel the seal off the biohazard bag and peer inside. There's a puffy white object, flat, about the size of my hand.

My face goes slack when I realize what it is. I nod slowly as I reach inside and take the diaper out. "You guys are hilarious. Really."

The group breaks into uncontrolled laughter.

"This is what you've been doing while I was gone?" I'm trying to act serious, but I can't hold it any longer. A smile forms on my face and I shake my head, fighting not to laugh.

I hold the diaper up. "This is the maturity level of the team of geniuses the world is depending on to save them? Diaper jokes?"

Harry makes his face serious again and whispers, "We need you to tell us what to do with it, James." He pauses. "You're the only one qualified to handle it."

That ignites another round of laughter. In the doorway Oscar is smiling as well, all the while studying the others' faces, seeming to take note of their reactions.

Just then, I realize that there's actually some heft to the diaper. There's something inside. Surely not. Due to a strange mixture of horror and curiosity, I slowly spread the diaper open, revealing a dark brown blob. No. Surely they wouldn't have…

Again, feigning seriousness, Harry echoes his earlier words, "It's organic."

Grigory breaks from the group and walks toward me, reaching into his pocket. "Not to worry, James. I come to your rescue."

The Russian engineer unfolds a white paper bag and takes a bagel out. Before I can react, he takes the diaper from me and dumps the gooey brown contents onto the bagel and folds the top over. I'm speechless as he takes a bite.

He shrugs, speaking with his mouth full: "What? It's not like they're making anymore Nutella."

After a more serious meeting to catch up with the team, Oscar and I descend to the basement of NASA headquarters, into a lab that only he and I have access to. It's a place where I've been conducting a secret project, one I think has the potential to save humanity from the war that's coming.

As I enter the room, the LED lights turn on automatically, illuminating the cavernous space with its concrete walls and floor and metal girders above. My footsteps echo as I walk toward my prototype.

"Wake up. Run system check," I call out.

"My name is Oliver. All systems pass."

Oliver looks exactly like Oscar, but he has some significant system upgrades. In short, Oliver is built for battle: on Earth or in space. If we're going to have any chance of beating the grid, we're going to need a lot of androids just like him.

Fowler's office is similar to mine: sparsely decorated, a wall full of flat screens, and family pictures on his desk.

The largest wall screen displays a real-time image of the newly rebuilt International Space Station, glittering against the black of space. It was built by the world's three super nations: the Atlantic Union where Emma and I live, the Caspian Treaty, where survivors from Russia and the Middle East reside, and the Pac Alliance, which is home to the surviving Asians. My team was intimately involved with the design and construction, including consultations with Emma. She was the mission commander aboard the original ISS when the grid destroyed it, killing her entire crew. I think working on the new station was deeply cathartic for her. Indeed, it's been a symbolic achievement for all of us— an example of just how much we can achieve in a short amount of time if we work together. But more importantly, the ISS is a practical tool for the defense of Earth. The new station will be much more than the last: it will be a shipyard where we'll build the fleet that will defend humanity.

Our plan for Earth's defense is twofold: drones and spaceships.

Our Centurion drones will be capable of both observation and attack. A large percentage of the six thousand Centurions we're planning to build will be stationed near Earth. The rest will be scattered across the solar system, lying in wait, watching.

The spaceships will house the vast majority of our offensive capabilities. We're calling them supercarriers and each will be capable of transporting and deploying ten thousand battle drones. We expect the first carrier to be operational in five years, though I wouldn't be surprised if it took us a little longer. On the screen, arms of scaffolding branch out from the ISS, beginning the work on our first prototype supercarrier, the *Jericho*.

"Good to have you back," Fowler says, rising from his chair and offering his hand. "How are Emma and Allie?"

"They're doing great," I reply, taking a seat. "Thanks for asking."

"And how about you?"

"Let's just say if the camp runs out of coffee, I may not make it."

"Yeah, your blood-caffeine concentration might be high for a while." Fowler bites his lip. "Look, I have some bad news, so I'll just start with it. The triple alliance defense committee has denied your request to put Oliver into production."

"Did they say why?"

"Not specifically. But I think they're worried that the grid could compromise any android army."

"The same is true for the drones."

"That may be. But the drones aren't in their backyard, a hundred feet from their homes, capable of killing them in the night."

"Do you see any chance for negotiation?"

"Not really. They're pretty set on the issue. But they're allowing you to continue your development work. They do see the value in having a working prototype and a solid design in case we ever need to put Oliver into mass production."

The decision is a blow to my work and one that I think is wrong. If we end up fighting a war on the ground we're going to need some help.

I want to ask about progress on the *Jericho*—and a number of other things—but I can't resist mentioning the interview with Richard Chandler first. At this point he may be a bigger threat than the grid. "Did you see *Melting Point* this morning?"

Fowler's usually kind, grandfatherly expression turns hard. "I saw it. Don't worry about Chandler."

"It's hard not to."

"I'm afraid we've got bigger problems. We're going to need those ships and drones sooner than I thought."

"What did I miss?"

"A lot of little things. And three very big things."

Fowler taps on his keyboard and the wall screen switches to a map of the solar system, the sun at the center, the planets around it, thin white lines tracing their orbits.

He hits another key and the image zooms in on the Kuiper Belt, a collection of asteroids and dwarf planets that circles the entire solar system, just beyond Neptune. Three objects break free from the belt, heading toward the inner solar system.

"As you're well aware, it took a lot of effort just to get these probes near the Kuiper Belt. We still don't know how much mass is out in the Kuiper, but our projections are that it might be two hundred times that of the asteroid belt."

"A lot more mass for the grid to build weapons and solar cells from."

"Correct. There are three dwarf planets in the Kuiper—including Pluto. We used to think most of the periodic comets originated in the Kuiper, but that's been disproven. The belt is dynamically stable, which is why we were so surprised to see these asteroids break from it."

The implication is clear to me: the grid has returned. It's likely sent another machine similar to the first—a harvester—a craft capable of traveling to our star system and transforming raw materials into the solar cells it requires.

"You think a new harvester has sent the asteroids toward Earth."

"I feel we should proceed on that assumption. If so, it means the new harvester arrived some time ago."

"How long do we have before impact?"

"We're still working on the projections."

"Best guess?"

"Two years. Roughly."

"The supercarriers will never be ready by then. Even if we expedite construction, we'll miss it by a year, maybe more."

"I agree. We'll have to take the asteroids down with a drone fleet. A large one." Fowler leans forward. "How doable is that?"

"I don't know."

3

Emma

Two Years Later

The habitat is filled with my favorite sound: the pitter-patter of little feet slapping against the floor.

Though I want to, I'm in no shape to chase Allie this morning. I put a hand against the wall, waiting for the nausea to pass.

From the master bathroom, I hear the footfalls stop, drawers in the kitchen being pulled open, their contents rattling around.

"Allie," I call out, "come back in here where I can see you."

It's silent except for the news playing over the habitat speakers.

A report out today from the United Nations estimates that for the first time since the Long Winter ended, there are more humans living outside the evacuation camps than inside, as the wave of immigration out of the

Atlantic Union, Caspia, and the Pac Alliance continues. New Berlin tops the list with the largest population, followed by Atlanta, and London.

But not everyone is happy with the pace of migration out of the evacuation camps. Dr. Richard Chandler, one of the scientists who was instrumental in defeating the grid, is calling on the superpowers to place more focus on returning its citizens to their homelands. Here's an excerpt from last night's edition of Melting Point with Craig Collins: "The grid is gone, yet the vast, vast majority of worldwide economic output is dedicated to defense spending. These evacuation camps have become nothing more than forced labor camps. We're all working endlessly on James Sinclair's super ships and the drones he claims will save us. Well, the truth is that the grid may not be back for a hundred years. Or a thousand years, or ever. Yet we live in abject poverty with no say, no vote, no basic rights. This has to change."

I really dislike that guy. Not as much as James, but a lot. He's all over the news, telling lies and stirring up trouble. Unfortunately, he's also gaining followers.

Another drawer in the kitchen slides open.

"Allie, I mean it! You're going to time out in…"

Silence.

"Three."

"Two."

"One!"

As if a race was starting, the sound of tiny feet pounding the floor once again rings out, and Allie appears in the bathroom doorway, smiling innocently.

"What have I told you? No playing in the drawers. Only Mommy and Daddy can open the drawers."

Some children have a sad face. Allie's sad expression is full-body: hanging her head, shoulders rolled forward, arms hanging loose—as if every bit of energy has been drained from her. She has three modes. Full-on, blissful playing. Sleeping. And the current state of sulking (which escalates to whining when she doesn't get her way, an occurrence that happens several times daily).

From my perch on the closed toilet, I point to the toys on the bathroom floor: seven bracelets, a stuffed sheep, and a yellow rubber duck. "I need you to play in here until I'm ready. Okay?"

Another wave of nausea grips me. I feel as though I've been thrown out of a plane and am free-falling with no control.

Allie ventures closer and reaches out and hugs me, her tiny arms around my lower abdomen, too short to get all the way around me. She peers into my eyes, studying me.

"Mommy boo-boo?"

"No," I whisper. "I'm okay, sweetie."

"Mommy sad?"

I place a hand on her back and gently move it up and down.

"No. I'm all right. Just play with your toys. Everything's okay."

I close my eyes again and wait. When the nausea passes, Allie is placing the bracelets on her arm, arranging them in an order that makes sense only to her. Without warning, she bends over and picks up a raisin from the floor.

"No, sweetie, don't eat that."

Allie brings the raisin to the sheep's mouth and pauses as if feeding it. She looks up at me, a hint of mischief there. I smile.

And she eats the raisin before I can stop her. I have no idea how long it's been on the floor. It's not from breakfast this morning. But if our human ancestors were hardy enough to survive the Toba catastrophe and cross the Bering Strait, Allie will probably survive a day-old raisin. Maybe two days old. Possibly three.

I open the drawer of my vanity and feel around for the personal health analyzer. I hold it to my finger and wait for it to draw the few drops of blood and run routine tests. The device beeps, and the results appear on the display. Blood chemistry is normal except for a borderline low vitamin D level.

The camps are out of birth control (it was low on the priority list when the mass evacuations happened—the governments prioritized food, shelter, and life-saving medicines). James and I have been careful, but the last two years have been extremely stressful. Our bedroom time has become a necessity.

I scroll to the bottom, holding my breath. I exhale when I see the result. I stare at the screen, filled with both joy and fear.

Pregnant: Yes

Allie holds my hand as we pass through the security checkpoint at NASA. As usual, she's wearing the tiny backpack James made for her. In his usual fashion, he went overboard, equipping it with a GPS tracker, a camera, and a speaker we can use to communicate with her. I wouldn't be surprised if he secretly built in some kind of hidden deployable attack drone to protect her.

James and I both work at NASA, and we used to walk Allie to preschool together every morning. But for the last eight months or so, he's always gone when I wake up and returns home after dark. He's working himself to death. He's doing it to protect us, but I wish he would take more time to be with us.

At the preschool entrance, Allie releases my hand and makes a break for it, but I grab her and pull her into a hug. When I relax my hold, she takes off like a thoroughbred at the opening bell of the Kentucky Derby, backpack bouncing as she races past the teacher, who waves at me.

As I walk the halls of NASA headquarters, I get a few second looks, flickers of recognition from people who might have seen me on the news feeds. Some people are just curious about my limp.

The limp is a remnant of my time in space and the loss of bone density I sustained. It's not going to get any better, and because of it, I'll never return to space, not for any extended period of time anyway.

Since I was a child, my dream was always to be an astronaut. I achieved that goal, but the two battles with the grid left me unable to continue in that career I loved. Like everyone in this strange new world after the Long Winter, I've adapted. I've found a new role to play, one I cherish.

That's life. Things always change. And we have to change with it.

The auditorium is half full when I walk onto the stage. Fifty faces stare down at me from the rows of stadium seating, tablets at the ready. My students remind me of myself when I trained at NASA: eager, bright-eyed, and dedicated to the cause. Some of these men and women will crew the two supercarriers being constructed right now. They will be on the front lines fighting the grid. Our future is in their hands, and it's my job to prepare them. There's only one way to do that, but still, I dread what I'm about to do.

I step to the lectern and speak into the microphone, my voice booming in the high-ceilinged auditorium. "Space is a dangerous place."

I let the words hang there like a warning.

"So. What's the key to survival in space?"

I've told the class that there will be an exam in the next three sessions. It won't be a written exam; everyone knows that from stories passed down by past classes. It will be an applied exercise, one no class has ever seen before. As expected, they think their answers now might be part of the test. Voices ring out from every row of the auditorium, all students eager to register a response.

"Oxygen."

"Power."

"Situational awareness."

"Sleep."

"Capable crew."

"A good teacher."

That last one gets a few chuckles from the group and a humorless smile from me, but it won't help the French engineer with his grade.

A slender girl with strawberry-blonde hair in the front row speaks up as the answers die down: "Being prepared for anything."

I nod to her. "Correct."

I point to the EVA suits lining the walls, hanging there like bizarre curtains in a theater. The suits used by NASA in space are more than decoration today. There are a hundred suits, two for each student. I made sure of that.

"For example, at all times, you need to know where your EVA suit is."

The students turn in the seats, eying the suits.

"Why? Because you never know when you'll need it. I know, because when I was on the ISS, if I had reached my suit a few seconds later, I wouldn't be here right now."

As my students digest the words, I reflect that if I hadn't gotten to my suit in time, I never would have met James or given birth to Allie or lived to carry the child growing inside of me right now. All of my fellow crewmembers were too late to get to their suits—except for one. He had the misfortune of being hit with shrapnel. There was nothing he could have done to survive, or me to save him.

"In space, seconds matter. A split second could be the difference between life and death—yours or that of the person beside you. And everyone down on Earth. Sometimes, there's nothing you can do to survive. But you can always be prepared. And it always ups your *chances* of survival."

I snap my fingers. "Suits on. Last five are cut."

The auditorium breaks into chaos as the students practically jump out of their seats and run to the EVA suits hanging from the walls. The room soon looks like a game of Twister, students elbowing and crawling over each other to get to the suits and slip inside.

When my fifty students are suited up, I signal them to take their helmets off. Every one of them is breathing hard, eyes trained on me.

I motion to the cameras behind the stage. "I'll check the footage and notify the last five. If you don't get an email from me, you're still in this class. For those of you who don't make this cut, I hope you'll reapply. Remember, the second key to survival in space is to *never* give up."

Though he works long hours and I see him less and less at home, James always meets me for lunch. It's our ritual, a respite in the middle of our hectic work days.

All morning I've debated when to share my news. I've never been good at keeping secrets. Ever since I was a kid I've worn my feelings on my shirtsleeve. He'll know something's up and, simply put, I need to tell him I'm pregnant, for my sake too.

He's standing in the cafeteria waiting when I arrive. There's a troubled look on his face but he brightens when he sees me, a smile tugging at his lips. The crow's feet at his eyes and lines on his forehead have grown deeper in the last few years, like ruts ground into him by time and stress. But his eyes are the same: intense and gentle.

"Hi," he says.

"Hi yourself."

His tone turns more serious. "Listen, I have something I need to tell you."

"Me too."

He bunches his eyebrows. "You do?"

"I do." I hold a hand out. "But you first."

He pauses, seeming to gather his thoughts. "Okay. But not here."

I follow as he leads me out of the cafeteria and up to his office. On the screen there are three video feeds showing rocky, spherical asteroids. The date-time stamp at the bottom of the image tells me that these are live images, apparently from probes or drones. All of the asteroids have large craters, but without a frame of reference, I don't have any sense of how large they are or where they are.

"These three asteroids broke from the Kuiper Belt about two years ago. We've been tracking them since."

"Are they…"

"On an impact course for Earth? Yes."

My body goes numb, mouth runs dry.

"Size? Time to impact?" I ask, voice devoid of emotion, mind struggling to process this potential death blow to our species.

"Each is about the size of Texas. Any one of them would be an extinction-level event. Time to impact is forty-two days."

"The supercarriers—"

"Won't be ready in time. Not even close." He turns and faces me. "But we won't need them."

"The orbital defense array can handle them?"

"No. They could destroy smaller asteroids, but nothing on this scale. We've created a fleet of attack drones specifically for these asteroids. We've been launching the drones along with the parts for the supercarriers to try to keep it out of the news. A mass panic would cause even more issues."

"What's the plan?"

"The drones will engage the asteroids in one hour. We're going to blow them to bits."

I exhale. "This is what you've been working on. Night and day."

"Yes. For two years." He takes my hand. "I'm sorry I didn't tell you, but I knew it would worry you."

"It's okay. I understand."

"I want you to join us in ops control for the battle."

"Of course. I'll cancel my afternoon class."

"Great." He steps toward the door but stops. "What did you want to tell me?"

"Nothing."

He glances back at me. "Sure?"

"I'm sure. It's nothing."

There's no way I can tell him now.

After. I'll tell him after.

4

Emma

NASA's mission control center looks like one of the old stock exchanges: people are standing at terminals, shouting, pausing to listen to their headsets, and shouting some more, occasionally falling silent to stare at the screens in front of them. The large viewscreen on the far wall displays video feeds of the three asteroids and stats from the drone fleet.

The room is hot and loud and smells of coffee. There's a sense of tension, of time running out. Through the crowd, I spot Harry sitting at a workstation, typing furiously on the keyboard. Grigory is shouting in Russian to a person at his station. Lina is next to him, headphones on, staring at her laptop, lines of code scrolling up as she searches for something. Min is conversing with Lawrence Fowler, both sipping from coffee mugs. I don't see Charlotte or Izumi.

James leans close to me and whispers: "There's about a thirty-five light-minute delay between us and the asteroids, so we're nearing the end of our time frame to issue changes to the pre-battle sequence for the first fleet of drones."

"The attack is automated?"

"Yes."

"Are the drones camouflaged?"

"They are. We're using the same methods we employed on the *Pax* and the Spartan fleet. The drones look like floating space rock."

"The image quality in the video feeds is incredible."

"More of Lina's handiwork. She's been tweaking the data compression algorithm. We've positioned the drones in a daisy chain to comm-patch the images back to us."

Fowler wanders over to us and gives me a light hug. "Good to see you, Emma."

"Likewise." I motion to the frantic activity around us. "Was it this busy when the Spartan fleet launched?"

"No. It was busier then."

Fowler excuses himself to see what Grigory and his colleagues are debating, and James and I settle in at his terminal.

My voice low, I ask, "What do you think is going to happen?"

"I expect the asteroids to deploy countermeasures."

"And if they don't?"

"Our drones will hit them. The asteroids will be split into pieces. My second fear is that the asteroids have some sort of propulsion apparatus attached. Once we hit them, they might accelerate and change course, trying to get past our other drones."

"I assume you've accounted for that?"

"We have. We'll attack in waves. We've got twelve fleets of drones out there—all spaced out. We'll make adjustments after the first four fleets hit the asteroids."

I watch as James scans the data and types messages and occasionally answers questions via his headset. The minutes pass slowly. Finally, an announcement booms from the overhead speakers: "First fleet command cut-off in ten, nine, eight..."

When it reaches zero, it feels like air going out of the room. People slump back into their chairs and stare at the screen, a few throwing pens onto their desks, others burying their faces in their hands. It reminds me of a college exam where the proctor's just called time and half the room wasn't finished and the other half is second-guessing their answers.

"What now?" I whisper to James.

"Now we wait, and see if we got it right."

I'm chatting with Lina when a countdown appears on the main screen.

30

29

28

Around the room, conversations die down. Everyone stands. Some people pull off their headsets.

I drift over to stand next to James as a voice once again booms over the room's speakers. "First fleet ordnance deploying in three, two, one."

White flashes consume the three video feeds as the drones release their missiles.

I hold my breath, eyes glued to the screen, waiting for the white to fade. When it's gone, I see nothing but the blackness of space, dotted by rocky objects of all sizes. There must be hundreds of them.

James immediately sits back down and scans the data coming in. I can read some of it, and I know it's good news—the payloads hit the asteroids, and hard. The survey shows that the asteroids have broken into more than one thousand objects, ranging widely in mass, the largest still classified as extinction-level targets. Where there were three extinction-level asteroids before, there are seven now. While that's technically bad news, it's a step in the right direction.

The voice over the loudspeaker sounds again. "Second fleet acquiring targets." The seconds seem to tick by like hours. Finally, the voice says, "Second fleet deploying ordnance in three, two, one."

Again, white flashes cover the screen and fade, leaving a field of even smaller rocky objects against the black backdrop.

When the data from the drones appears, I exhale. There are almost two thousand objects now, but only three that would cause an extinction-level event.

The shouting resumes, until the third fleet deploys its ordnance. And the cycle repeats once more.

After the fourth fleet's flyby, everyone in the room springs into action, resuming the fever pitch of activity I witnessed when I first arrived. I soon learn the reason: they have a very short window to issue new commands to the remaining eight fleets.

James and his team left a large gap between the fourth and fifth drone fleets. The fifth fleet (and all the fleets behind it) are still close enough to Earth for us to issue updated commands before they encounter the asteroids. The idea is to adapt the approach with each wave of drones, maximizing the impact of the ordnance.

The team around Min's desk talks quickly but in an orderly fashion. The debate at Grigory's station is chaotic.

James plops down on his chair and stares at his screen. He suddenly looks so tired. Harry wanders over and smiles at me. "Hi, Emma."

"Hi, Harry. How are you?"

"Oh, you know, I love a good game of Asteroids."

His reference to the old Atari game gets a laugh from me and a tired grin from James.

"Figured we'd be seeing more action," Harry says to James, who just nods, eyes still on the screen. I can almost see the wheels turning in his head. I've seen that look before: on the *Pax* and here in Camp Seven in the months after. He's working something out in that big brain of his, and I think he doesn't like where it's going.

Harry turns to watch Min's group for a while; then he glances back at me. "They've got about…" Harry leans over and peeks at James's screen. "… seven more minutes to make course changes to the second wave of fleets. Sounds like they're going to split them into two smaller groups of two fleets each." He nods toward Grigory's group. "And they're trying to figure out how to maximize the payload efficiency."

"And you guys…"

"Thought this battle would be less one-sided," Harry replies. "Figured we'd be dealing with an active combat situation, issuing new commands to each fleet to adapt our attack."

James leans forward and types a command on the keyboard. On the screen, a message appears.

FIRST FLEET: DEEP VIRUS SCAN INITIATED

Harry peeks over, sees the command and starts asking James questions about it. I stand and walk away, leaving them to work. Is that what James thinks is happening: a virus? Are the drones infected? Sending bad data back? It's possible. It would mean that the asteroids might be whole, untouched, and still heading for Earth.

Izumi must have slipped into the room during the battle. I spot her near the back wall, standing beside Oscar, who smiles widely at me. He's been working on his facial expressions. They're getting better, but the levity of his expression is wrong for the mood in the room. Still, I'm glad to see him trying. Charlotte's here too now, conversing with an Italian cryptography expert whom I taught in my class eighteen months ago.

When I reach her, Izumi hugs me and whispers in my ear: "He struggled with whether to tell you."

"I figured. How has the group been?"

"A mess. Stressed. Sleep-deprived." Izumi's gaze drifts to the wall screen. "I hope it's almost over."

She has perhaps the toughest job of all: keeping the team healthy, mentally and physically.

The command deadline for the second wave passes and the tension in the room ebbs. It ratchets up again about thirty minutes later when they make contact. By the time the third wave finishes, the asteroids have been pulverized almost to dust. Cheers go up around the room. The mood turns jovial. I hear a few people apologize to the colleagues they shouted at during the battle. Everyone is standing, smiling, relieved. Except for James. He sits at his desk, staring at the screen.

I walk over and read the message flashing in red letters.

NO VIRUSES DETECTED

"What's wrong?"

"Nothing," he mumbles, eyes still on the screen.

I settle into the chair beside him and try to make eye contact. "Are you sure?"

"I'm sure. It's nothing."

That night, everyone comes over to our habitat for dinner. Harry mans the grill, wearing a T-shirt with a logo for a fictitious restaurant called "Apocalypse Grill."

Grigory stands beside him, drinking a cocktail that I'm pretty sure is ten parts vodka, one part something else. He started the night speaking English. Now, as his blood alcohol rises, the Russian words are slowly creeping in every now and then. Lina stands next to him, drinking a Beck's. It's weird seeing a branded beer after the world economy has collapsed, but recovering items from the now thawed cities has become a big business. Salvage companies have been scouring the world for bottles of medicine, beer, and whiskey. Those are the biggest sellers—not diamonds and gold. The Long Winter has changed us in ways I never imagined. And I never imagined Grigory and Lina getting together. It's always the quiet ones that surprise you.

Min and Izumi sit at a wooden picnic table near the grill, talking quietly. Their budding romance is the worst-kept secret in Camp Seven, and it's going at a glacial pace, like a chess game where each player takes months to consider their next move.

James and his brother Alex are laughing about something, but I can see in my husband's tired eyes that his mind is elsewhere. I had thought I would tell him about the pregnancy tonight, but I sense that this still isn't the time. I'll wait until tomorrow.

Beyond the house, the kids are running in the open expanse of hard-packed desert, playing soccer, Oscar serving as referee. At the height of the Long Winter, I wondered if I would ever see kids playing soccer again. But here, against the backdrop of the setting sun, the world looks normal again.

But it's not normal for us—not for James and his team. They've told everyone outside the group that tonight's celebration is for the completion of a new drone design. This is what endless war looks like: lies to the people around you and danger they never see.

Inside, the younger kids are playing with a robotic dog James made a few years ago. My sister, Madison, and Alex's wife, Abby, are whispering in the kitchen as I approach them.

"This looks like gossip."

"Maybe it is," Madison replies, a coy smile on her face.

"That means it's definitely gossip."

"It's gossip," Abby admits. "Rumor is that Izumi and Min are moving in together."

"Her place just listed on AtlanticNet as available in forty-five days," Madison says.

"She could be moving out of the camp," I reply, mostly to make conversation.

"Doubtful," Madison says. "That group from the *Pax* is inseparable." She takes a sip of wine. "But we're thinking about it."

A bolt of fear runs through me. "You and David?"

"He wants to move to Atlanta. He's heard that they're going to start a lottery for farmland—like the old days when the West was settled. He wants to be there, says the entire economy is starting from scratch again and we need to get in now or we'll miss the boat. It's like colonial times again."

"Alex thinks the same thing. Wants to move to London, says the schools will be better there." Abby finishes the last of her wine. "But I keep thinking, it's already freezing there, what if the Winter returns? We'd be evacuating again."

"It's a bad idea," I say absently.

"Yeah," Abby replies. "I think we'll end up in Atlanta. London is just a flight of fancy for him."

"No, I mean it's a bad idea to leave Camp Seven at all." They both look at me, waiting for a reason. But I can't tell them what I know. So I tell them what they already know. "Look, Camp Seven is still the safest place to be. NASA is here. We've got a bunker, hardened greenhouses, water supply. It's better to wait for now."

"Do *you* have gossip?" Madison asks. When I don't reply, she presses me. "Is the grid back?"

I bite my lip. "I just think you should wait, okay? Can you trust me?"

Madison stares at me, silently prompting me, but I don't say a word.

Abby sets her glass on the counter. "I'm going to check on the kids. It's too quiet out there."

Madison pours herself another glass of wine and then holds the bottle up. "Wine?"

"No, I'm good."

She narrows her eyes, boring into me as if she can drill down to the secret I'm hiding. Her expression changes, as if her drill has found pay dirt. It's almost creepy how easily she does that.

I lead her to the master bedroom and close the door, hoping no one can hear the secret I'm about to share. This feels like middle school all over again.

"I'm pregnant."

She throws her arms around me, splashing a little wine on my back.

"Is James excited?"

I hesitate. "He will be."

"You haven't told him?"

I cock my head to the side. "Not exactly."

"Why not... *exactly*?"

"I'm waiting for the right time."

She stares at me, the drill out again, probing for an answer, but she seems to get nowhere this time.

"He's had a lot on his mind recently," I explain.

"Such as reasons we shouldn't leave Camp Seven."

"Such as you're correct."

"Okay. Well, I'll talk to David about staying." She smiles at me. "I'm so happy for you."

When everyone's gone, we put Allie down in her crib. Sometimes when she's had company over, she puts up a fight. But she's worn out tonight and is fast asleep within minutes.

James and I sit in the living room, watching the news on the TV. When a segment about Richard Chandler starts playing, James rolls his eyes and trudges toward the bedroom. Chandler is apparently touring the Atlantic Union, rallying people to move back to their homelands, insisting that the three remaining governments are dictatorships. That guy loves being on TV.

James is tucked under the covers, eyes closed, when I come to bed.

I still get the impression something is bothering him. I wish I knew what it was; I wish I could help.

He opens his eyes when I climb into the creaking bed. "Hey."

"Hey."

"Thanks for having everyone over. I know it was short notice."

"Thanks for blowing up those huge asteroids."

That elicits a sharp chuckle from him. "There's no asteroid I wouldn't blow up for you."

"And would you do one more thing for me?"

"Anything."

"Tell me what's bothering you."

"Nothing."

"And if it was something, what would it be?"

James closes his eyes for a long moment. Then, his voice flat, he says, "If it was something, it would be the fact that it was too easy." He stares at the ceiling. "The grid is smarter than that. Hurling asteroids at us is just... too simple for them."

"What are you going to do?"

"I'm going to get some sleep for the first time in two years, and when I wake up in the morning, I'm going to figure out what I can't get my head around right now."

He closes his eyes again, and I scoot close to him and turn out my light.

I'll tell him tomorrow.

I awake to the sound of the bedroom door flying open. I hear footsteps and see a silhouette of a figure moving toward the bed, reaching out, grabbing James forcefully, and shaking him.

For a brief moment, I'm paralyzed with fear.

It's still dark out. The lights in the living room cast a soft glow into the bedroom, too dim to make out the intruder's identity. The figure shakes James harder and then lifts him up, the strength displayed incredible. James finally startles, grabs the hands holding him, and wrestles against the grip like a fish on a line.

A wave of nausea rushes over me. I fight not to throw up.

A voice, clear and calm, rings out in the bedroom.

"Sir, please. You have to go."

Oscar.

James's own voice comes out scratchy and soft. "What?"

"Asteroids. They're going to make landfall."

5

James

My groggy mind can barely grasp what Oscar is telling me.

Asteroids.

Impossible. We destroyed them. And they were months away from Earth.

He seems to read my confusion.

"Sir, there's another group of asteroids. Smaller, in greater quantity. They were hidden from our sensors somehow."

I'm awake now. The fog in my mind clears like a cloud blown by a strong wind. "How many?"

"Seven hundred—"

"Where are they now?"

"The outer ring of Centurion drones just spotted them. The leading object is a little over four hundred thousand miles from Earth—"

I grab Oscar's shoulders. "Do as I say, and do nothing else, do you understand me, Oscar?"

"Yes, sir."

"Take Allie to the bunker. Go down to the Citadel, and

wait for me there. Protect her at all costs. Go. Don't stop for anyone or anything."

Without a word, Oscar turns and races out of the bedroom. A split second later, I hear the nursery door fly open, the handle cracking the hard plastic wall. Allie cries into the night.

Emma rolls out of the bed and hurries to the master bathroom, where she flips the toilet lid up and empties the contents of her stomach. Truth be told, I want to do the same thing. This could be the end of the entire human race. We have to get to the bunker. Seconds count now.

I throw open a dresser drawer and toss a long-sleeve shirt and sweatpants at her.

"The bunker. Right now, Emma. Please. We have to go."

She has her eyes shut, swallowing, as if fighting to control her stomach.

"Emma!"

She gasps as more vomit comes up. She hangs her head when it stops, trying to catch her breath.

I storm into the bathroom, grab the clothes, and slide an arm under her legs, the other across her back, and scoop her up and march out of the bathroom.

"What are you doing—"

"Saving your life."

Her eyes still closed, shivering, she lurches forward. The vomit sprays across my shirt, but I don't even flinch. I just keep marching out of the habitat.

The warm night air seems to jar Emma awake. She puts her arms around me and swallows, gulping deep breaths.

I've felt like this once before: when I pulled her from the wreckage of the ISS. She was weak and sick then, with lingering decompression sickness. But it's not just our lives at stake now.

"Allie—" she gasps.

"Is on her way to the bunker."

I pull the autocar's door open and put Emma and the clothes in the back seat. In the driver seat, I hit the button to activate the car and shout, "Emergency override. Enable manual control."

The car beeps, and I shout again: "Disable safety restrictions, authorization code Sinclair seven-four-alpha-nine."

The car's next beep is drowned out by the tires spinning in the sand as the car blasts away from the habitat. The force throws Emma against the back seat. She closes her eyes again and leans forward, head between her knees.

"James," she croaks.

I instruct my phone to call Fowler, and he answers on the first ring.

"James—"

"Can the orbital drones protect us?"

"They're acquiring targets but hundreds of asteroids are still going to get through."

My mouth runs dry. *Hundreds* of asteroids are going to hit the Earth. The large asteroids were just a diversion. The harvester somehow hid the smaller asteroids from our sensors. We were so focused on the larger threat we just… missed it.

I missed it. And I knew it. I should have—

"James, you have to get to the bunker."

"We're on our way."

"Call your team. And, James?"

"Yeah?"

"It's not your fault. Focus on getting to safety. We'll figure this out after that."

Fowler disconnects, and I realize Emma is talking, head still between her knees.

"Madison?"

"What?"

"Call Madison. Please."

"Okay."

I instruct my phone to call her as I drive like a madman, over a hundred miles per hour through the camp's hard-packed sandy streets, a trail of brown dust swirling behind. The car's headlamps and the moon light our way.

"Madison," I yell when she answers. "Get to the bunker. Right now. Don't take anything—"

"What—"

"I'm serious. Get to the bunker. There's going to be an asteroid strike. You're dead if you don't get to the bunker. Get David and the kids and go. Go now, Madison."

I hang up and tell the phone to call Alex. It beeps once, twice, then a third time and goes to voicemail.

In the rear-view, I see Emma sit up. She's white as a sheet, shivering.

"Was it the food?"

She closes her eyes and swallows. "It wasn't the food."

"A virus?"

"I'm fine."

She begins pulling the sweatshirt on. It's warm outside, but it'll probably be cold in the bunker.

I instruct the phone to call Abby. Maybe Alex turned his phone off.

As the phone beeps, the car zooms past the habitats on the periphery of Camp Seven, into the vast expanse of open desert beyond. The bunker is three miles away. I press the accelerator to the max. The wind noise picks up, pressing into the car like a hurricane.

I curse and slam my hand into the steering wheel when the voicemail picks up. "Abby, if you get this, get out of the camp and to the bunker. Quickly. Asteroids are going to make landfall. The bunker is your only chance of survival. Hurry."

In the rear-view, my eyes meet Emma's. She looks more steady now.

"Thanks for calling Madison."

"Of course."

"Can't get Alex?"

"Or Abby. Probably turned their phones off."

For a brief moment, I consider turning the car around, going to their habitat, and beating on the doors and windows. Oscar said the asteroids were four hundred thousand miles from Earth? But going how fast? And where will they make landfall? I've always assumed that the harvester we defeated at Ceres managed to send data back to the grid. That data would have included the locations of Camp Seven and the bunker. My guess is that one or more asteroids will hit the camp directly and that Camp Seven will be one of the first targets hit.

How much time do I have?

Much as I want to, I can't turn around. I'm a father now. I have to be there for Allie. Even if we survive the impact, we face long odds of surviving the aftermath.

I call the rest of my team. About half answer. I leave messages for the rest. A second later, my phone blares an alarm. They've activated the emergency alert system, instructing everyone to get to the bunker.

Up ahead, the lights of the bunker complex peek over the horizon. I slam on the brakes when we reach the massive warehouse. The autocar skids and Emma braces herself against the backs of the front seats.

"Let's go," I shout to her as I bolt out of the car. I put an arm around her and help her run. Our footsteps echo on the warehouse's concrete floor as we hobble along. Her bone mass never recovered from her time in space, leaving her with a limp. I hate to do it, but I have to push her. Every second counts.

With my free hand, I hold my phone up and tell it to dial Alex.

"Come on, come on," I mutter as it rings. "Come on…"

Voicemail.

Again.

Surely they heard the alarm. They live two doors down. I should have walked over there and beat on the door. But I didn't know then that he wouldn't answer his phone.

At the entrance to the bunker, a group of Atlantic Union soldiers are wearing full battle gear, rifles at the ready. Two break from the group and march to us. A tall soldier with a colonel's insignia nods to me. "Dr. Sinclair?"

"Yes."

He motions to the sergeant beside him. "She'll take you down to the Citadel."

I glance at his name patch. "Thank you, Colonel Earls. Are you in charge?"

"Yes, sir. The flag officers have decided to stay at

CENTCOM to direct the evacuation and defensive operations."

Earls shouts to a soldier standing by the door, holding a tablet. "Check 'em off the list, Dodson."

The list. I realize then that the evacuation isn't just about how many survive. It's about *who* survives. That's what the troops by the entrance are doing—they're gatekeepers. And for good reason: the Citadel won't hold the entire population of Camp Seven. Not even close. The real question is how long can we stay down there. The bunker can only hold so much food—and that food can only support so many people for so long. Those are the variables.

Someone at Atlantic Union command had to factor those variables when they made the list. They were faced with the impossible task of determining who is vital to our species' survival. If you ask me what's the most precious thing the grid has taken from us, I wouldn't say it's the billions of lives we've lost, or the billions of acres of land, or our homes. I would say it's the little pieces of humanity it has sheared off along the way. Like this moment, where we have to choose which innocent people have to die so the rest of us can survive.

At that moment, I have a selfish thought, one I'm ashamed of, but know I have to act on.

I place a hand on Emma's back and nudge her toward the door to the elevator. "Go ahead. I'm right behind you."

"What're you going to do?"

"Try Alex again."

Emma bites her lip. "The list..."

She's thinking the same thing I am. I turn to the soldier, Dodson, whom the colonel had shouted at. I can't see his insignia, so I settle for: "Mr. Dodson?"

He looks up, almost startled.

"Is there a Madison Thompson and her family on the list?"

He taps the tablet. "Yes, sir."

"All family of critical personnel are on the list, sir," the sergeant adds.

I feel a mix of relief and guilt. I can tell Emma feels the same thing.

I nod toward the entrance to the bunker. "Go ahead. I'll be right down."

"You promise?"

"Promise. Allie's down there waiting on us. She's probably scared. You should go."

When Emma's gone, I dial Alex again.

When his voicemail picks up, there's only one thought in my mind: running to that electric car and driving back to town. I lost my brother once because of a mistake I made. I can't lose him again.

6

Emma

The elevator doors open onto an empty room with metal walls that shine under the white LED lights above. The floor is a grid of white plastic tiles, softly glowing, like a dance floor that might light up as I walk across.

At the end of the room lies a set of double doors painted with large block letters that spell CITADEL.

A dozen soldiers stand around the door, rifles pointed at the elevator—at me.

"Emma Sinclair," the sergeant calls out, voice echoing in the metal room.

The soldiers don't flinch.

"Step forward, ma'am," one calls out.

Another types a code into the panel beside the double doors, which open with a pop.

Beyond the doors, there's a foyer that's crowded with more troops. They glance at me before continuing their conversation.

Warm air washes over me as the doors close behind me, and I try to get my bearings. There are three doorways from the foyer. One to the shared bathrooms, another to the sleeping quarters, and the last door to a mess hall.

The mess hall has a living area, and everyone seems to be congregated there, sitting on the couches and club chairs and staring at the wall screens. One of the smaller screens is playing a cartoon I recognize: *Frontier Girl*. Set in the 1800s, it's about a young girl who moves from the city to the American West with her widowed father. I know it because it's Allie's favorite show. She doesn't fully understand it. I think she just watches it for the horses.

I peek around the door frame and spot Oscar sitting in a club chair, facing the screen, Allie in his lap, still and quiet, focused completely on the show. My heart breaks. Even as I battled the nausea and the wild car ride to get here, my mind kept flashing to Allie, wondering if she was safe.

As I approach, she turns and sees me, then hops off Oscar's lap and runs to me. I hug her and lift her up, and it's the best feeling in the world.

"Da?"

She hasn't quite mastered the word "Dad" yet, but it's clear to me that she senses that something is wrong.

"He's on his way, sweetie."

"Home..."

"We'll go home. Soon."

I bring her back over to the club chair, where Oscar rises to let me sit.

"How long, Oscar?"

"Ma'am?"

"Until impact."

"Current estimate is thirty-one minutes, twenty-three seconds."

A lump forms in my throat. Allie seems to read my reaction. She takes my hand, wrapping her small fingers around two of mine. "Mom…"

"Just watch your show, Allie, please. Oscar, I need you to do something."

"Anything."

"Go up to the surface and find James and tell him that his daughter and his wife are down here and they need him and so does everyone else."

James

At first, the residents of Camp Seven arrive in waves. One or two cars at a time, carrying people like me who somehow got an early warning. Emma and I probably got the earliest warning of all—thanks to Oscar. He's wirelessly connected to the AtlanticNet defense network. He knew as soon as the asteroids were spotted. I'm thankful for that.

I know a few of the new arrivals: NASA staffers who saw the alert from the orbital defense satellites and civilians who were working the night shift at CENTCOM.

The troop carriers arrive next, disgorging AU soldiers into the warehouse, clad in full battle gear, helmets with lights, body armor, and rifles loaded and ready.

Colonel Earls is still in charge, and I hope he has the answer I need.

"Colonel, do you know the time to impact?"

He gives a sharp nod to the two aides standing near him and they march away, soon giving orders to the throngs of recently arrived troops.

Voice low, Earls says, "About thirty minutes."

I have time. Just enough time to reach Alex.

"Thank you, Colonel," I call back to him as I race to the car.

The moment it starts, the door flies open and a hand grips my shoulder.

I look up to find Oscar leaning into the car. "Sir."

"Not now—"

"Sir, Emma has instructed me to give you a message: that your daughter and wife are down in the Citadel and that they need you and so does everyone else."

I stare at him, my hands still on the wheel. Finally, I slump back into the seat and shake my head. She's right. But it's an impossible decision. Be a father and husband or save my brother. There's only one choice.

I leave the car running, but step out.

"Oscar, I need you to go and get Alex and Abby and their kids. Hurry. We only have—"

"Twenty-nine minutes, sir."

"Thank you. Go. Now."

The electric car throws up a trail of dust as it blazes into the night. When it's out of sight, I draw my phone and try Alex and Abby again.

Voicemail.

I trudge back to the warehouse.

"Name!" a female soldier shouts at me. Her tone softens when I look up. "Oh. Sorry, sir. Please come forward."

The waves of cars stop for a few minutes, then it's a flood—a continuous stream of vehicles arriving, dust clouds behind them, parents carrying crying children into the warehouse, shouting, chaos.

The troops separate the horde into six groups that are spaced throughout the warehouse. The story is that the bunker is being prepared and that they will be brought down as soon as possible—and that anyone being disruptive will lose their place. It's a lie. There are already more people in this warehouse than the bunker can hold.

With each passing minute, it gets hotter in this massive space, the heat of bodies and fear coalescing and pressing into all of us. How many will we leave to die up here? And what's the alternative? Tell them the truth? It would be chaos, and in that chaos maybe none of us would get down to the safety of the Citadel.

Fowler and his family arrive, looking haggard and worried. He pauses to talk to me as his wife and children hurry to the elevator.

"What are you doing up here?"

"Waiting on Alex."

He checks his watch. "Don't wait too long. Twenty-one minutes."

"Yeah. I heard. Any idea where they'll touch down?"

The expression on Fowler's face confirms my worst fear: Camp Seven will take a direct hit.

"Where else?" I ask.

"Caspiagrad. The Pac Alliance CENTCOM. And New Berlin, London, and Atlanta."

I don't know whether the settlements have bunkers. I doubt it. Their focus has been on rebuilding above ground. The carnage will be unimaginable.

"Don't wait too long," Fowler says over his shoulder as he continues to the elevator.

Members of my team arrive shortly after: Grigory first, then Min and Izumi, Charlotte, and finally Harry, his mood somber and resigned. Even during the darkest periods on the *Pax*, he remained optimistic. He just looks defeated as he places a hand on my shoulder and walks to the elevator.

I haven't stopped calling Alex. And he hasn't answered.

Twelve minutes left.

After going down to the Citadel, Grigory returns to the surface and comes to stand beside me, staring out at the groups of people waiting. Some of the kids are lying down, trying to sleep. Most of the adults are clustered together, whispering as they cut glances to the troops and the doorway into the elevator room.

"Who are you waiting on?" Grigory asks.

"Alex. You?"

"Lina. When we got the news, she went to the office."

"What?"

He shakes his head. "She has a new program for the Centurion drones. Thinks it will help."

"She'll get out in time."

We both stare at the cars arriving, hoping when every door opens that we'll see our loved ones.

Madison and David and their two children arrive and run toward the elevator. The guards ID them and escort them to the elevator, drawing scowls and looks of confusion from the people seated in groups around the warehouse, waiting their turn.

Madison hugs me. "Thank you for calling."

"Of course."

"Emma?"

"She's down below with Allie."

I glance at my phone when they're gone.

Seven minutes.

Someone in a group nearby shouts, "There's not enough room. They're going to leave us up here."

More voices join in, asking questions and screaming, the words drowned out in the cacophony. The groups are all standing now, kids too. They edge forward, the leaders pointing at the soldiers, who train their rifles on them.

The wall of people closes on us, and suddenly, it breaks. People burst forth, making a run for the elevator. Directly toward Grigory and me.

8

Emma

My heart leaps every time the door opens. It quickly becomes apparent who was on the list: NASA staffers and military personnel. The people we need to fight the grid. And their families—what good are fighters if they don't have anything to fight for?

The soldiers here in the Citadel busy themselves by taking everything out of the cabinets and moving it to storage. Anything glass is either removed or taped to prevent breaking. They think we're going to get hit directly. Can this bunker survive that?

Every time the door opens, I expect to see James, or Madison, or Alex and Abby. But all I see are strangers or people I recognize vaguely from NASA.

Fowler's wife Marianne is the first person I know. She sends her kids to one of the tables in the mess hall and comes over to hug me.

"Where's Lawrence?"

"Upstairs talking to James."

"James is still here? In the warehouse?"

She looks confused, as if thinking, *Where else would he be?*

"Yes, he's standing near the elevator."

I can't help but grin. Oscar did his job.

James's team arrives next, everyone but Lina. Grigory is pacing, agitated. I know exactly how he feels. He doesn't wait long down here. He leaves and, for a moment, I think about doing the same thing. But I can't leave Allie alone. She can't lose both of her parents.

So I wait. And when the doors open and Madison comes through, I run to her and hug her with every ounce of strength I have and I hug my nephew, Owen, and niece, Adeline, with everything I have left. Madison's husband, David, brings up the rear, joining in the hug.

Now that Madison is here, maybe I should go. I can convince James to come down here. If something goes wrong, Madison can take care of Allie.

I'm walking toward the doors when the floor begins shaking. The chairs in the mess hall rattle. The screens go out. The lights dim. It feels like an earthquake, but I know exactly what this is: an asteroid has made landfall.

9

James

When the first shots go off, the crowd freezes. Silence descends. All eyes focus on the AU Army troops fanned out around the outer doors of the elevator room.

Colonel Earls's voice rings out in the warehouse. "All civilians back to your stations, right now."

Slowly, the hordes back away like a wave receding from the shore, certain to return.

I lean over and whisper, "You should get out of here, Grigory."

"So should you," he mumbles.

I just shake my head as I watch a new group of cars arrive, parking beyond the rows of abandoned vehicles. I squint, trying to make out the passengers emerging in the night.

I think but am not sure... Yes! Oscar is leading the way; behind him is Alex. Following is his wife, Abby, and their kids, Jack and Sarah. They're going to make it. I check the countdown on my phone.

Five minutes left.

Just barely, but they're going to make it.

The colonel's voice once again booms into the night. "All right, now we're going to be coming around, escorting you all to the elevators. If you disobey my people—or if you leave your group—you lose your place. Permanently."

Seconds pass quietly, everyone in the warehouse staring at the soldiers, hoping they'll stop at their group and call them out. My stomach turns watching it. This is the grid's form of torture: reducing our habitable world, then making us choose who will live.

The ground beneath my feet shakes. It's an asteroid impact. My guess would be that it touched down in Europe. New Berlin maybe. The first asteroid has fallen. How long do we have before the one coming for us makes landfall? Seconds probably. The rumbling grows stronger, perhaps more asteroids touching down, the sound like thunder rolling through the night.

The concrete floor cracks. The steel rafters groan. Grit and dust fall like rain. And when the rumbling below our feet subsides, the crowd erupts again.

People surge forward, children in their arms, heads down, plowing into the soldiers. Shots go off from several guns.

It has to be now. We have to get to the elevator.

I can't see Oscar anymore; he's somewhere out there, swallowed in the crowd.

I shout but my voice is drowned out by the chaos.

My mind screams for me to turn and run to the elevator, but I could never live with myself. Almost absently, I feel myself running forward, toward the crowd, piercing the line of soldiers, who aren't prepared for an assault from behind.

I break through their hold, into the mass of shouting, crying people, their fists in the air, bodies sweaty.

I realize then that Grigory is beside me, helping me snake my way through. People are happy to let us pass, so long as we aren't headed for the elevator. We take one step after another until I can see Oscar. He's practically swimming through the masses. Jack and Sarah are on his back, arms draped around his neck like rag dolls.

When he's five feet from me, I turn and begin working my way back toward the elevator, trying to open a hole for him. I catch an elbow in the cheek and my right eye waters; pain pulses as I feel blood rushing to the bruise that's forming. I keep going, step after step, feeling my feet pressing into arms and legs and backpacks and all the things people left behind on the floor.

A fist punches me in the stomach and a man yells, "Get back."

I double over, and Grigory's hands grip my arm and pull me forward, my head still down.

Oscar pulls ahead of us and barrels forward until we're staring at the end of a rifle and a line of soldiers.

"We're with NASA!" Grigory yells as he raises me up so they can see me.

The soldiers squint at my bruised face and wave us forward. As soon as they make an opening, people pounce, trying to get through, trying to keep us back.

A melee ensues, Grigory, Alex, Abby, and I trying desperately to protect Jack and Sarah as we work our way through the line. It's a blur of fists punching and hands pulling and grabbing at me. Oscar fights for us, his preternatural strength finally scaring away our attackers.

When we cross the line, the soldiers close the hole. I stare forward, at the open elevator doors. But the car is full—people crowded into every square inch, staring back at me, scared. A man in the corner punches the control panel, silently urging the doors to close.

We're three seconds away. There isn't room for all of us, but I bet we could fit the kids in. I take Jack and Sarah's hands and pull them toward the elevator, but the doors close just as I reach it.

I release their hands and my niece and nephew run back to their parents.

Standing alone, panting, beaten and bruised all over, I take my phone out and check the time.

One minute left.

I turn and look out at the warehouse, at the saddest scene I've ever witnessed in my whole life. I feel the tears coming and it isn't just from the guy who elbowed me in the face.

Alex pulls me into an embrace. "Thank you, brother."

My voice cracks with emotion when I respond. "You'd have done the same for me."

"Our phones were off. We would have never gotten here without you and Oscar."

He glances down at a fissure in the floor. He's thinking the same thing I am: will the elevator even still work? It's too late to use the emergency tunnel. It's probably collapsed. Are we already too late?

One by one, the soldiers escort people out of the crowd to join us. Kids mostly. There's a six-year-old girl with red hair and freckles who's crying and calling back to her parents, who are behind the line, telling her to stay there, that they're coming soon. They know it's the last time they'll ever see their daughter. But she doesn't. She keeps calling out for them.

A woman about Emma's age joins the group and stoops down to talk to her, trying to calm her down. She works at NASA, but I can't remember her name.

The elevator should have been back by now. But there's nothing I can do about that now.

I put my arm around Alex and pull him close.

10

Emma

Allie runs to me and wraps her arms around my legs and buries her face. Her voice is muffled by the sound of the bunker shaking.

I bend down and hold her. "It's okay, sweetie. You're safe. Everything's going to be okay."

I keep saying the words, hoping they're true.

When the rumbling stops Allie says exactly what I'm thinking. "Da?"

"Dad's coming."

The words come out fast, sounding far more certain than I truly am.

Holding her, I walk out to the foyer and watch the outer doors, hoping they'll open and James will walk through.

Seconds seem like hours. Allie feels heavy in my tired arms, but I can't stand to let her go right now. I lean against my good leg, both of our weight bearing on it.

The outer doors open and my heart practically bursts. A dozen people rush out. Kids mostly, but some military in uniform and NASA staffers I recognize.

But James isn't there. Or Alex. Or Abby. Or Grigory.

An Atlantic Union Army colonel with a name patch that reads Earls is in the group. He instantly takes charge of the situation.

"Listen up. Projections show that an asteroid strike in our vicinity is imminent."

The group behind me begins shouting questions, but Earls silences everyone.

"There's no time to talk. You need to follow our instructions—right now."

He nods to a captain, who begins directing the troops. The adults and older children are moved to the mess hall, where they crouch under the tables, hands covering their heads.

They usher Allie and me to the residential wing, to a small room with bunk beds on each side. We take the bottom bunk. Madison and Adeline lie across from us on the other bottom bunk. The lights are on, and I can see my sister's frightened face. She's shaking slightly, holding tight to her daughter. I hold Allie close and wonder where James is.

Allie can tell we're scared, and it's scaring her. She begins to sob, her words muffled, tears falling on my neck. I wish I could be brave for her, but it's impossible here and now, knowing we might have seconds to live. I cradle her closer to me and shift to position my body over hers, a mama bear shielding a cub in her den.

The previous impact was a hollow boom and a rumbling.

This strike hits like a cannon ball into a car. The ground bounces us like a trampoline. I hold Allie as my back hits the bottom of the bunk bed above and we fall back. Lights flicker. Dust fills the air. My ears pop and ring for a long moment. Sound returns like the volume on a speaker being turned up. Screams and crying are all around me.

"Madison!" I shout, unable to see her. My voice sounds quieter than I expect. So does hers, as if it's muffled.

"I'm okay. You?"

"Yeah."

I peer down at Allie, who's still and quiet, her face tucked into the crook of my neck, as if hiding from the danger around us. Her chest is heaving. She's alive.

"Sweetie," I whisper, peeling her back from me. Her strength is amazing as she clings to me. "Sweetie, I need to see if you have a boo-boo."

"Da?"

I've held it until now, but the levee breaks and the tears come and they won't stop. I don't answer because I don't trust my voice. That will only upset her more.

The good news is that she's okay. There's a bruise on her thigh, but it doesn't need treatment. Others weren't so lucky. Beyond this bunk room, I hear them calling out for help.

For a long moment, I hold Allie and stroke her hair and wonder what life will be like now. The world has just been destroyed. Again. Before, during the Long Winter, we had something to work from. We had a chance.

Now, I'm not so sure.

The first time I hear my name being called out, I think I'm imagining it. Then he calls again, "Emma!"

"I'm here!" I yell, voice scratchy.

A figure cuts through the haze in the room, swatting the dust away. His face is bruised, hair mottled with sweat and dust. But James is alive. He must have gotten down on the last elevator trip, right before the impact. He bends down and hugs us, and I've never been so thankful in all my life.

11

James

In the darkness, voices call out like lost souls trapped in a
purgatory between heaven and hell.

Mom!

Dad!

Andrew!

Susan!

Justin, can you hear me?

I hold tight to Emma and Allie as the bunker shakes
again.

"Another asteroid?" Emma whispers.

"Yes, but not here. Probably hitting the other camps," I
reply, my voice low, hoping Allie doesn't understand.

Another quake follows a minute after and they keep
coming, some only seconds apart, like a storm raging,
seemingly without end. The Earth is being pummeled. My
guess is that each asteroid is about half a mile across—
small enough to be hard to see by our telescopes, assuming
the asteroids weren't cloaked somehow in the first
place.

Still, an asteroid a half-mile across is large enough to do real damage. The impact crater would be ten miles wide. The blast wave would travel up to fifty miles. The effect of the impact would be felt up to a hundred and fifty miles away.

On and on through the night, the impacts roll across the bunker, shaking dirt and grit loose from the ceiling, forcing the lights to flicker on and off. I hold tight to Emma and Allie and think, *I have to get us out of this bunker. I will get us out. I just hope there's a world left to return to.*

The Citadel isn't the Ritz. It wasn't designed to be. It was designed as a temporary refuge during a disaster. Simply put, it was designed to be short term.

The accommodations reflect that. It's cramped and dark (the generators have reduced the power output, including lights, to give us more time down here—at least until we determine if we can run on full power).

Instead of gathering everyone in the mess hall, teams of soldiers come around and take stock. They evacuate the wounded and instruct the rest of us to stay where we are. For now, this bunk room is our home.

Fowler comes around to check on us. He's in charge, which I count as the best-case scenario.

I can't help blaming myself. I should've seen it. I should've known that the grid was smarter than a simplistic attack. It's inconsistent with its level of intelligence or capability. *Why didn't I see it?*

Deep down inside, maybe I did. That's what's been bothering me the last two years. Somewhere in my subconscious, I knew that the three large asteroids weren't the real attack. Why didn't I admit it to myself? Why didn't I dig deeper? That's my job—to protect these people and my family.

The answer seems obvious: I wanted it to be true. I wanted the threat to be a simple one—a threat we could handle. I wanted our war with the grid to be over.

Now it's just begun.

They've updated the Citadel since I was last here. This area where the bunks are used to be a large hospital room. There are ten bunk rooms, each with eight bunks. Some of the adults will have to sleep out in the mess hall. The kids are assigned to bunks but none of them want to sleep. They're too scared. I can't blame them.

The younger kids crowd into our bunk room. They're in school with Owen and Adeline, and I think being together makes them feel a little safer. Emma and Madison try to distract them by reading stories.

There's a small office nook near the bunk rooms. After the soldiers have made their rounds, I retreat to the office and am relieved to find a working tablet. I'm too wired to sleep. I need to work.

One piece of good news is that the water still works down here. In shifts, the residents visit the shared bathrooms and shower, no doubt to help them relax. Sleep will be hard to come by tonight.

Oscar comes by and simply stands outside the office nook and waits. He knows me so well. He asks no questions, offers no opinions. Finally, I turn to him.

"The elevator is the priority. We were the last to arrive on it. If the asteroid strike was far enough away, maybe it's operational. We need to determine that now. And if the elevator's out of commission, we need to know if the shaft is still clear. You'll have to do it." The reason is obvious to him: because it's too dangerous for one of us. He doesn't even flinch.

"Yes, sir."

He leaves without another word. If that elevator works, we might have a chance. If not, the odds get longer.

From the office I watch the kids trudge toward the showers and then exit again, hair wet, shoulders slouched, exhausted. Fowler comes by and leans against the door frame to the office, looking weary and far older than his sixty-two years.

"Need anything?"

"We're good."

"Let's get together first thing in the morning and try to figure out what to do." He eyes my tablet and the viewscreen above the desk. It shows a map of the Citadel and the emergency escape tunnels. "But I get the impression you've already started working on it."

"Just getting ready."

He steps into the office and pulls the sliding door closed. "Nobody saw this coming, James."

"I should have."

"You can't think that way. You saved us once—actually, probably a dozen times. This is not over. Get some sleep, and we'll sort it out tomorrow."

I'm weary to my bones when I lie down on the bunk. A few minutes later Emma strides in, Allie in her arms, our child sleeping peacefully.

I scoot back and lie on my side, and Emma gently lays Allie between us as she slides in. She looks so tired. She takes my hand in hers and leans over and kisses me on the lips. With her face still close to mine, I whisper, "How is she?"

"Scared."

The small bunk bed is tight, but there's no way we're separating tonight. I'll sleep in the mess tomorrow night.

I reach over and pull her close.

"I'm going to get us out of here. I promise you."

I expected Oscar to return that night with news about the elevator. I was waiting for him when I drifted off to sleep. When I wake and exit the bunk room, he's standing in the hall right outside the office nook.

"What did you find?"

Oscar has been working on his facial expressions, but he's elected not to use them now. His face is a mask. The wait for his response is agonizing. The placid gentleness of his voice is a complete disconnect with the message he delivers.

"The elevator shaft is caved in."

12

Emma

I wake feeling battered and tired, my legs and arms aching. Allie sleeps peacefully next to me, but the spot where James slept is empty.

Nausea grips me suddenly.

I close my eyes, waiting, hoping it will pass. But my head swims as though I'm spinning and can't stop.

Arms shaking, I climb over Allie and hobble to the shared bathroom. I make it just in time to empty the meager contents of my stomach. I wait by the toilet, willing it to pass.

This bout of morning sickness is the worst yet. Yesterday's exertion has taken its toll. Stress and fatigue are known to exacerbate morning sickness, and I've had my share of both in the last twenty-four hours.

I'll definitely need my cane today, and it got left behind. Just like a lot of things. And more importantly: a lot of people.

When the nausea finally subsides, I make my way down the hall, hand holding the wall to take the weight off my bum leg. The office nook James was using last night is empty. He's not in the bathroom either.

I find Madison in the small open common area that adjoins the bunk rooms, sitting in a reclining chair with a baby on her chest, a bottle to its mouth. I bet it's the child of one of the parents who were left behind.

She looks up as I approach, smiling, revealing how lined her face has become.

"How long have you been up?" I whisper.

She shrugs gently and returns her gaze to the child. "Didn't look at the clock when I got up."

Translation: a long time.

"I can take over."

"No. I'm sure you've got things to do. I'll handle things here."

I lean over and kiss her on the forehead, and wander out of bunk wing and into the foyer. It's empty as well.

I hear noises coming from the mess hall. Pots banging. Conversation. Voices I recognize. Slowly, I make my way over, taking labored steps. I really need to fashion a cane. I have to take some of the weight and pressure off my legs, especially my left leg.

The seating area in the mess is empty. The noise is clearly coming from the kitchen. I push the swinging doors open and find Fowler and Grigory standing at a steel island, their arms covered in pancake batter and egg substitute.

Grigory throws his hands up. "This is waste of time. Let them eat cereal. We have plenty."

Fowler glares at him. "This is important, Grigory. Normalcy—"

"What is this normalcy? That is not word."

They both seem to realize I'm there at the same time.

Fowler smiles. "Sleep okay?"

"Not bad."

I walk over to the kitchen island and put my arms on it and take some pressure off my legs. It feels so much better. "Where's James?"

The two men share a glance. I know that look. It says, *Should we tell her?*

I answer the unspoken question. "Tell me."

"James and Oscar," Fowler says, "are looking into how to get out of here."

"I'm going to see if he needs a hand."

I push off the table, wincing as the weight hits my leg.

"See if he wants to cook breakfast," Grigory calls out as I exit through the swinging doors.

I don't find James and Oscar at the entrance to the elevator. I try to operate the panel, but it doesn't respond. Not good.

Where would he be? The entire Citadel facility is one level, with a basement under it for all of the mechanical equipment and storage. I don't know where access to the basement is. I wander the halls for a good thirty minutes before I find it. Everyone still seems to be asleep, likely exhausted by the exertion and emotional stress from last night.

The access to the basement looks like a utility closet. It's dimly lit and there are boxes of parts and supplies stacked along the walls.

A wide switchback staircase lies at the back. I descend the staircase, into the darkness, stopping at the bottom just long enough for my eyes to adjust to the lack of light. The basement is so large I can't even see the far wall. Concrete columns dot the space, like stalactites reaching from the ceiling. Wires and pipes crisscross the ceiling and hang down, connecting to junction boxes. The ceiling can't be more than seven feet high. It's like a cave that might be inhabited by a mechanical monster.

"Hello?" I call out.

"Ma'am," Oscar replies softly in the darkness.

"Oscar, where are you?"

"Turn eighteen degrees counterclockwise and proceed. Watch your step, ma'am."

I forget sometimes how non-human he is. Seeing in the dark is only one of Oscar's extraordinary capabilities. I step carefully through the dim light, over wires and pipes and around small devices which might be water heaters or air purifiers or some other mechanical item the Citadel needs.

I find Oscar beside what I can only describe as a hatch. It's round and has a wheel, like an ancient naval ship. It stands open and beyond is a corridor of darkness.

"What's going on, Oscar?"

"This is one of the emergency escape passages. James is currently inspecting it."

"*One* of the escape passages?"

"There are two. In case one collapses. We checked the other one earlier. It is blocked by debris."

"The elevator didn't work when I tried it."

"The shaft has collapsed," Oscar says without emotion. "We disabled the elevator doors from the Citadel's main control panel."

I motion toward the tunnel. "How long has he been gone?"

"Forty-five minutes and twenty-one seconds."

"That seems like a long time."

"Exploring the other tunnel required only twelve minutes and thirty-two seconds. The cave-in was rather close to the tunnel entrance. However, I had expected him to be back by now. He insisted on going himself."

"Why?"

"In his words: he was tired of standing around just waiting on me."

I suppress a smile. "Do you have a flashlight?"

Oscar hands it to me and says, "I probably don't need to tell you that he would not want you to enter the tunnel."

"Noted."

I climb into the tunnel, which is roughly five feet tall. I have to stoop to walk, but I don't have to crawl. The walls seem to be metal, and they're cold to the touch. My footsteps echo as I go.

I yell, "James!" and wait, but no response comes.

"Ma'am," Oscar calls to me. "Shall I join you?"

"No. Stay here. If I don't come back, go get Fowler and bring help."

"Yes, ma'am."

I continue on, trying to favor my good leg. Soon, I sense a slight incline, which seems to increase with every step until I'm certain that I'm walking at almost a thirty-degree angle. My legs burn. I can feel my lower back cramping. And then the tunnel dead-ends up ahead. As I reach it, I realize that the tunnel actually makes a U-turn. Coming around the turn, I shine the flashlight down the corridor. Nothing but darkness.

"James!" My voice echoes in the darkness.

Again, no response.

I feel a rumbling below my feet, a tremor that sends a bolt of fear through me. The ground where the asteroid struck must still be settling. We need to get out of this bunker. We need to get above ground.

When the shaking stops, I pick up the pace, legs still burning, the throbbing growing with each step. I really need that cane. I need to find my husband more.

I reach another switchback and turn the corner and hold out my flashlight and call out again. Still nothing. I push on, worried now.

At the next switchback, when I shine the light, I can see something up ahead, lying in the tunnel. There are bits of rocks and dirt on the floor in this section of the tunnel. It's as if the debris entered at some point up ahead and slid down here. I'm sure of it: the ceiling of the tunnel has been punctured. The sections of the tunnel before were cold and dry. Here there's a slight dampness on the walls.

But it can't be James up there. I don't see his flashlight. Still, I quicken my pace. My legs are starting to shake from the exertion, but I push on. I'm practically running when I reach the pile of debris. Something's jutting out from one end.

It *is* James, lying there, unconscious, rocks all around him. I freeze, my shaking hand holding the flashlight. He's not moving.

I reach out and put my fingers to his neck. A heartbeat, weak but regular. He's alive. His flashlight lies on the ground, busted in pieces by the falling debris.

I have to think. My first priority is to move him away from the puncture in the tunnel overhead. More debris could come through. I put my hands under his armpits and pull with all my might, dragging him up the tunnel and away from the rubble. With his head in my lap, I sit in the tunnel and try to catch my breath.

"James, can you hear me?"

Nothing.

There's no way I can pull him out of this tunnel. I should go for help, but I don't want to leave him.

I push up and drag him farther away from the place where the tunnel collapsed, finally depositing him at a switchback. When I've caught my breath, I begin hobbling back down the tunnel, calling Oscar's name. It's a lot easier going downhill. And the pain has taken a back seat to my worry.

Soon, Oscar calls out, "Ma'am?"

"Come quickly, Oscar. James needs you."

13

James

I wake in the Citadel's small med bay off the bathrooms, my head throbbing, like the worst hangover I've ever had in my life. I'm nauseous too. I lean over, thinking I might vomit, but nothing comes, only pain in my back.

The curtain around my section of the med bay is closed, and just inside, Emma sits in a chair, a stern look on her face.

"We're instituting the buddy system from now on," she says.

"Wonderful," I mumble.

"What happened?"

"The tunnel was already breached. I was inspecting it when a tremor shook some of the rock loose."

She rises and takes my hand. "You've got to be more careful. We can't afford to lose you. I can't afford to lose you."

Afterwards, we do indeed institute the buddy system. Oscar and I go back into the tunnel that afternoon, with a lot

THE SOLAR WAR

more caution. The second escape tunnel leads much farther toward the surface. But it's caved in as well.

My assumption is that the asteroid hit directly above the Citadel. I had assumed that it would hit Camp Seven directly. The grid must've targeted this bunker, reasoning that the most valuable personnel would be evacuated here. It probably did the math and calculated that the asteroid strike here would annihilate Camp Seven as well. Two for one—the grid is all about efficiency. *The conservation of energy*, I believe was the term. For Lina's sake, and all the people we left behind, I hope the grid has miscalculated. I hope that at least some portion of the population survived the blast.

It might be a while before we find out. For the moment, we're trapped down here. Plain and simple.

Fowler organizes a meeting with my team (minus Lina) along with Emma, Colonel Earls, and Oscar.

We gather in the kitchen, around the steel island, some of us sitting on stools, others leaning against the commercial refrigerators.

It kind of reminds me of the bubble on the *Pax*, where we all tethered ourselves to the conference room table and hashed things out. We're under a similar amount of pressure here.

"Let's start with status reports," Fowler says. "By department."

We all focus on Izumi. The natural place to start is with the health of our population.

"The good news is that there are no serious injuries. Nothing requiring immediate surgery. The Citadel does have a decent supply of various medications, and I expect it to last longer than our food supply."

"Which will last how long?" Fowler asks.

"Roughly three weeks."

"Can we ration?" Harry asks.

"Three weeks is if we ration," Izumi replies. "And we need to start today."

"After what everyone went through, I think a generous breakfast was the right thing to do," Min snaps.

Izumi shoots him a defensive look. "So do I. But now I think we have to start rationing."

"I thought humans could survive for weeks without food," Grigory says, ignoring their squabble.

"Technically, that's true," Izumi says. "But it's not that simple."

"Given the situation, I think we could all use a primer in survival basics," Fowler says.

"Okay," Izumi says, taking a deep breath. "In order to survive, the human body requires oxygen, water, and food, roughly in that order. We can live for five to ten minutes without oxygen, three to eight days without water, and anywhere from twenty to forty days without food. But how long a person can survive without food varies greatly from person to person, depending on their weight, genetic make-up, medical conditions, and—most importantly— whether they have water." She glances at James. "Is our water supply secure?"

"Very. We have a water sanitation system here in the Citadel and we're connected to an aquifer nearby."

"That's good news," Izumi says. "The other good news is that the human body is very adaptable. When it doesn't get the calories it needs, it shifts its metabolism to buy us time to find those calories. The first thing it does is take the glycogen from our livers and convert it to glucose which goes into our bloodstream. When that glycogen is gone, the body starts using stored proteins and fat. Initially, these are broken down into glycerol, fatty acids, and amino acids, which lower the body's need for glucose. The proteins that aren't essential for survival will be used up first. If the body still isn't getting the calories it needs, it shifts again. It starts relying on fat more, which it converts into ketones. And finally, when the fat reserves are gone, it begins cannibalizing the remaining protein. Muscles, our largest protein stores, are quickly depleted. That leaves proteins essential to cellular function. When the body begins using those, organ damage and failure follows. At this point, the immune system begins to severely degrade. Infectious diseases we might have fought off easily become deadly. Death from cardiac arrest is common at this stage. Most who live past those dangers die of one of two diseases: kwashiorkor and marasmus."

"That," I say slowly, "is quite possibly the best pep talk possible for getting out of here."

Izumi holds her hands up. "Sorry to be so grim. Bottom line: those in better health and with more fat and protein stores are going to fare better. That's what my rationing plan will try to do. The goal is to slow our consumption as much as possible without risking long-term organ damage. After three weeks, we're going to start seeing fatalities and permanent organ damage."

"What else can we do to improve our chances?" Fowler asks.

"Staying hydrated is crucial. We should avoid all stimulants. No coffee—no caffeine of any kind. Reducing our energy expenditure will also help."

"Sit around and watch TV all day?" Harry asks.

"Sure. But I would advocate G-rated content. Anything that gets the heart racing just uses up more calories."

"Three weeks," Fowler says slowly. "Why wasn't there more food down here?"

Colonel Earls exhales. I think he was expecting this question. "The Citadel was stocked at the required levels, but we're at ten times the max-rated population for the bunker. My group was told that any potential asteroid impact was still six weeks away. The evac plan and provisions were due for review but it wasn't a priority. Everyone at CENTCOM was focused on the engagement with the three large asteroids."

"The question," Emma says, "is how do we get out of here in three weeks?"

Slowly, everyone's gaze drifts to me.

"As most of you have probably heard," I say evenly, "the elevator shaft is completely collapsed."

Grigory leans back in his chair. "I can make explosive."

He's perhaps the most anxious of all of us to get back to the surface. I don't blame him. I would be too if Emma were up there.

"Too risky," I reply. "The blast might not clear the shaft, and it could destabilize or even collapse the bunker."

"The two escape tunnels are blocked?" Harry asks.

I nod.

"Can we dig out?" Charlotte asks.

"I don't know. We don't know what's beyond the cave-ins. But I think it's safe to say it will take considerable time. One of the cave-ins is close to the Citadel, indicating the tunnel might be badly damaged all over. The other cave-in is farther out, but there are cracks all over the tunnel." I pause a moment. "If I had to guess, I'd say it's much more than three weeks of digging. And digging will be dangerous, as I can attest. Even with hard hats and proper precautions, I don't favor it."

Grigory throws his hands up. "So we're trapped? Useless bunker."

"There's another way out," I reply quickly.

All eyes focus on me.

"The backup water system." As expected, I get confused looks. "As I said before, the Citadel has a robust water filtration system. It was designed to be self-contained. The idea was that the purifiers would recycle the water and reuse it, similar to the methods we use on a spaceship. We knew if the water filtration system failed, it would be deadly for everyone down here. So we built in a backup water source."

"The aquifer," Emma says, seeming to realize where I'm going with this.

"Correct. And we're connected to it by a tube."

"A tube filled with water," Grigory says, seeming annoyed. He pulls up a map of the Citadel on his tablet. "A tube that is almost two kilometers long. And barely big enough for one of us. And *assuming* you make it to the aquifer, how do you get to the surface?"

"The warehouse is connected to the aquifer as well," I reply.

"Via another tube," Grigory says holding his hands out. "Which is probably collapsed."

"It probably is," I admit. "But the asteroid impact no doubt disrupted the ground around the crater. I'm hoping there are large crevices above the aquifer—and that they run all the way to the surface."

The room falls silent, the group contemplating that possibility.

"The aquifer is pretty far beneath the surface," Emma says. "Assuming there's a viable passage to it, climbing out would be extremely difficult for a lot of people down here."

I turn to her, nodding. "True. But it may be our only option."

"Let's back up," Harry says. "Can we even get to the aquifer? Do we have scuba gear down here?"

"No," Fowler replies.

"We don't need any." I motion toward Oscar. "We have someone who doesn't need oxygen, who can swim like a fish for miles and never tire."

In the basement, Oscar hooks into the generator and charges until he's at full capacity. I don't think he'll need the full charge, but it's better to be safe than sorry.

In the water treatment plant, he stands by the tank, peering through the hatch.

"You'll likely only be able to use your feet for propulsion," I explain. "It's hard to know how fast you'll be able to go. It might take up to three or four hours to reach the aquifer."

"And then?"

"You have to use your best judgment, Oscar. If we're lucky, the asteroid strike opened the top of the aquifer. If you see light above, swim for the top and get to the surface. If not, try to find the backup tube that leads to the warehouse."

"And what if the pipes leading to the aquifer or to the warehouse are collapsed?"

"Then we truly are trapped down here."

14

Emma

Oscar has been gone for two days. I know James is worried about him.

While we wait, we've tried to establish some kind of daily routine, mostly for the children's sake.

In the common room of the residential wing, David and a few of the other fathers and mothers keep a makeshift daycare for the younger children.

In the mess hall, Madison and Charlotte have organized a school of sorts. It's like frontier times: kids of all grade levels, from elementary to secondary, together in a one-room school. The kids are loosely grouped by age, and Madison and Charlotte float around to each station, handing out assignments and checking on progress. Madison's even organizing a play to be performed. The idea is simple: if we stay busy, maybe we'll stay positive and optimistic.

I find James in the basement. Work lights shine down from the girders in the ceiling, illuminating the mechanical parts lying on the floor in piles. From the looks of it, he's been disassembling any piece of equipment which isn't essential.

"What can I do to help?" I ask as I sit beside him.

"Nothing. Just... tell me about your day." He doesn't look up from the piece of equipment he's working on, what looks like an air-scrubbing unit.

"I took Allie to daycare."

"With David?" he says without looking up.

"That's the one." I smile.

"Then what?"

"Then I worked with Fowler and Grigory on a plan to make our food last longer."

"Yeah?"

"We think we can turn part of the basement into a small farm."

He nods, the way he does when he's being supportive but isn't convinced.

"What are you building?"

"Mostly just taking stuff apart."

"Getting an inventory to see what you have to work with?"

"That's right."

"What do you want to build?"

He smiles. "Guess."

"Something that saves us."

"You can do better than that."

I think a minute. Obviously, he's building a robot. It hits me then. "A robot that can dig us out."

"Close. I'm designing a robot small enough to slip through the cracks in the escape tunnels. It might have to dig a little bit to get to the surface."

"And then what? How does a small robot on the surface help us?"

"Think about it."

"Oh. Right. You're going to call for help."

"Exactly."

The bunk is too small for both James and me, but that hasn't stopped us from sharing it. Every night since we've been down here we've slept together, on our sides stacked in like anchovies, Allie between us.

Madison's night light is usually the last to go out in the bunk room. When it does, James whispers to me, "I meant what I said. I'm going to get us out of here."

"I believe it. I love you."

I consider telling him that I'm pregnant, but it's still not the right time. He has enough on his mind.

I wake to the feeling of someone grabbing my arm. I realize that it's James—gently pulling my arm from his side. He climbs over me and out of the bunk. Thankfully, I don't feel any morning sickness. I think James would put it together if he saw it now.

When my eyes adjust to the darkness, I realize that the door to the bunk room is cracked. A figure waits outside, water dripping from his clothes.

Oscar has returned.

Did he find a way to the surface? Or has he come to deliver bad news—that we're trapped with no hope of getting out of here?

15

James

In the small office nook, Oscar gives his report.

"Sir, I apologize that it took me so long."

"What did you find?"

"The water pipe was impacted in several places."

"Breached?"

"No. Only dented. The passage was narrow but passable."

"You reached the aquifer?"

"Yes, sir. And I reached the surface."

"How?"

"The water tube to the warehouse is completely collapsed. But I found a passage from the top of the aquifer to the surface. I'm sorry it took so long. I reached many dead ends."

"Did you inspect the escape tunnels leading out of the Citadel?"

"They're collapsed near the surface, sir. Very far away from the cave-ins we identified down here."

The news is a gut punch. The escape tunnels were our best chance of getting everyone out quickly and safely. But we're not beaten yet.

"I'm very sorry, sir."

"This isn't over."

"I don't understand. I'm still the only person who can get out."

"For now, Oscar. I want you to go back to the surface. First, I want you to go to the Olympus building and send a wireless ping to Oliver. If he's online, get a system status check."

"And if he's online?"

"We could definitely use his help, but if he's buried in rubble, and I suspect he is, don't recover him yet."

"Yes, sir. What shall I do after I ping Oliver?"

"Go the CENTCOM building next door. There's a bunker in the ground adjacent to it, on the northeast corner. If I'm right, some of the bunker might still be intact. If it is, here's how to get in and what I want you to bring back—these items are the key to everything…"

At our morning meeting, I tell the team that Oscar reached the surface. The news is met with muted celebration. There's a sense that we just might get out of here, that we have a chance of survival.

Everyone wants to know the next step. That next step is for me to inspect the route and determine if we can evacuate everyone that way. I know Emma will be against me going. But I have to do it. For that reason, I'm coy about my plan. I reveal only that I've sent Oscar back to the surface to search for some items that will give me an idea of what our options are. Thankfully, that's enough for them. For now.

That night, I'm in the basement working on my micro drones when I hear footsteps emerging from the water treatment room. I haven't given up on the drones, but I'm hoping I won't need them.

Oscar marches towards me, holding up the garments I requested, careful not to let them snag on anything, carrying them like a bride's wedding dress that has to be perfect. And they do. Any puncture could mean death for me. When he reaches me, he carefully lays the two space suits down.

I stare at them a second. It's a gamble. But it's our best shot.

"Sir, I tried connecting to Oliver. There was no response."

"Probably crushed."

Oscar doesn't respond. His face is a mask, but I wonder if his AI has progressed to the point of feeling something at the news of Oliver's destruction. I had always considered Oliver to be like a younger brother to Oscar. I wonder if Oscar did as well.

"Sir, may I ask how you intend to use the suits?"

"They're our ticket out of here. You'll pull me and one other person out through the backup water tube. If it works, we'll use the route to get the rest of the population out."

"And if not?"

"If not, well, we'll figure that out then."

"Who will join us on the initial trial?"

That is the question. One of the younger Army soldiers is the obvious choice. They have the best chance of making it through the tube alive. But it's not just about reaching the surface. It's about what we might have to do once we get there. If things get complicated, I'll need an engineer.

"Grigory. Please go and wake him up. Leave a note for Fowler and the team informing them that we're going to the surface and that we'll be back as soon as possible. Hurry. Time is a luxury we don't have."

In the dim light in the basement, Grigory stares at the two space suits.

"This is madness."

"This," I say, pointing at the suits, "is the only way out of here."

He squints at me. "Why me?"

"Because you're healthy enough to make the trip. And I know how bad you want to get out of here. I would too if it was Emma up there. And finally, when we get to the surface, we need to determine the best way to get everyone out. It might mean changing the plan—possibly trying to clear the elevator shaft or one of the escape tunnels. I need an engineer."

"Glad you finally admit I am hero in all this." He studies the suit. "This is going to be the strangest EVA in history."

When we've suited up, we make our way to the water treatment plant, where Oscar lowers himself into the small pool at the entrance to the backup water tube. The pool was meant to be a staging area where we could deploy repair drones to go into the pipe and perform maintenance. I never envisioned it being used like this—as a staging area for people going into the tube. It's cramped and the tube itself is barely big enough for Grigory and me with the suits on. There's no way we could swim inside it. But Oscar can.

When I give him the go-ahead, Oscar ties an electrical wire around his waist, checks it, and dives headlong into the tunnel. He kicks his legs and disappears in a bubbly wake.

I hold the wire, waiting, until I feel his signal: four sharp tugs followed by three tugs.

I tie the wire around my own waist, let out some slack, and Grigory does the same. We both enter the pipe and Oscar begins pulling us through.

Inside the tunnel, it's pitch-black except for our helmet lamps. The darkness and lack of control in the confined space is nerve-racking. If the suit catches on anything and tears, it will be a slow, agonizing death. I feel sweat forming on my brow, and I realize I'm holding my breath.

The time in the pipe seems endless, the view ahead always the same, almost as if I'm staring at a still image of a dimly lit pipe.

We've attached a comm tether between Grigory's suit and mine, but we have no way to communicate with Oscar.

"I feel like fish being reeled in," Grigory says.

I laugh and that helps my nerves settle a bit.

Finally, I see a faint light up ahead. A few seconds later, the pipe opens into the vast expanse of the aquifer.

I immediately glance upward. A few small pinholes of white light shine down from the dark, rocky dome. It reminds me of looking up at the stars at night.

Our helmet lights cut beams through the water, which is dotted with particulate and dust, like a cloud floating through space. The asteroid impact has left its mark here too.

We drift to the top of the aquifer and follow Oscar as he climbs into a large crevice, which looked smaller from below.

I reach up carefully, gripping the rocky opening and trying to pull myself out of the water. The suit, now wet, is too heavy for me to manage. This is a new model, state of the art, but it simply wasn't constructed for Earth's gravity. Oscar grasps my upper arm and pulls, careful not to snag the suit. I push hard when my right foot grips the rocky ledge above the water, leg muscles burning. When I've cleared the water, I collapse and sit there, panting as I take my helmet off and breath in the damp air.

Oscar helps Grigory out of the water, and we methodically take the suits off and place them on a ledge. There's no way we could climb through the rocky pass above carrying their weight—and they'd likely snag and tear. Better to leave them here.

Oscar opens a duffel bag and hands each of us an LED headlamp and a belt, which we hook to a rope that connects to him. The passage to the surface will be winding and although I expect there will be some ledges, I still instructed Oscar to bring the rope in case one of us slips. The rock is damp, and I'm not an experienced climber. I doubt Grigory is either. This should be interesting.

We climb slowly at first, Oscar testing every hand- and foothold, often shining his headlamp down on us, making sure we're okay. My fingers are soon raw and aching. I wish I had asked Oscar to get some gloves. Like a kid on vacation, I want to yell, *How much longer?* But I push on silently, climbing and crawling, occasionally coughing when a dust cloud drifts down.

Oscar stops twice to give us a break.

"I miss being fish on line," Grigory says.

"I miss the elevator," I reply.

Above, a sliver of light shines into the passage at an angle, silently saying, *Just a little bit farther.* That, and the thought of Emma and Allie below, gives me the energy I need to press on.

I wonder exactly how long I've been gone from the Citadel. I glance at the clock on my phone. Almost seven hours. The journey to the surface was much more difficult than I imagined. And it's taken a lot more time. I should've known that Oscar would understate it. It's nothing to him. Even if we could get enough space suits, this isn't a viable route to evacuate everyone from the Citadel.

My thoughts go to Emma. She must be worried sick. I figured I would have a look at the route and impact crater and be back before she woke up. She's no doubt awake now, and she won't be happy that I didn't tell her about my plan.

We make the final push, and by the time the sunlight is blazing through the opening at the top, my arms feel like spaghetti noodles. Oscar reaches down into the passage and takes my arm and pulls me up in one swift motion.

I squint, trying to blot out the sun. It doesn't shine nearly as bright as it did before the asteroids struck, but compared to the darkness of the last eight hours, it's nearly blinding. As my eyes adjust, I try to estimate how much solar output has fallen. My guess is 50 percent. The sky is hazy, a dusty cloud that stretches as far as I can see.

It's cold too. I wonder: is it only from the asteroid's dust cloud—or has the grid repositioned the solar cells left in the system between Earth and the sun? Those solar cells were manufactured by the first harvester sent to our system, built specifically to collect the sun's energy. They've been adrift since we defeated the harvester at Ceres. We made no move to attack them for a simple reason: they're small and the solar system is vast. Even if we could find the solar cells, they could disperse. We'd have to chase them down. There are likely thousands, maybe millions of them.

Are we facing a double attack—from the asteroids and the leftover solar cells? Has the Long Winter already returned?

The asteroids alone might be enough to end all life on Earth. Their effects are far deadlier than what happens at the impact site. When an asteroid makes landfall, it sends a blast outward, a fireball that burns everything in its path. When the fire runs out, the force of the blast continues, knocking over trees and buildings. The asteroid impact also sends chunks of earth into the sky. For hours, the ejecta fall back to the ground in fiery impacts. The impact also causes earthquakes, tsunamis, and hurricanes.

Things get quiet after that, but the short-term consequences are just as dangerous. Acid rain begins. The sun is blotted out, plunging temperatures. Crops die.

The long-term effects of an asteroid impact ultimately depend first on its size and secondly on where it hits. The worst consequence is ozone destruction, which would open the planet up to deadly UV radiation. Beyond that, a potential runaway greenhouse effect could increase the CO_2 in the atmosphere and heat the planet up too much.

There's nothing I can do about the immediate effects—the blast and the earthquakes and ejecta have come and gone. The short-term effects are what we face now: acid rain and cooling from the dust cloud. We'll have to face the long-term effects at some point—if there is a long term for us.

Oscar opens another bag and hands Grigory and me some warm clothes. When we've slipped into them, I take the satellite phone from the bag.

As Oscar reported, the phone can't connect to the network. The satellites are gone, likely hit by asteroids or maybe even ejecta thrown up by the impacts. I leave the phone on just in case it connects.

It's a long shot, but I activate the handheld army radio. "This is James Sinclair, a survivor in Camp Seven. If you can hear me, please respond."

A minute passes, Grigory and I sitting on the ground, Oscar watching impassively. I repeat my broadcast, wait another few minutes, then toss the radio in the bag. "We'll repeat the broadcast on the hour."

Grigory looks at me curiously, silently asking why.

"Might be some helos flying over looking for survivors."

That's a long shot. Camp Seven is, or was, the Atlantic Union's seat of political and military power. If anyone were flying helicopters looking for survivors, it would probably be us. We're struggling to even get above ground. Odds are the other camps fared even worse.

But our rescue is only half the reason to leave the radio on. There might be some people who are trapped calling for help over the radio. It's a long shot, but if we can help them, we have to try.

There's an electric army car parked nearby, which Oscar also recovered from the CENTCOM bunker. Grigory and

I pile into it, and Oscar commands it to proceed to the coordinates where the warehouse above the Citadel used to be.

Before the asteroid impact, the ground here in Tunisia was a rocky desert, like the surface of Mars. Now it's scorched and smooth. The rocks are gone—melted or blown away by the impact shockwave.

The ground is dotted with streaks of glass where the heat melted the sand. It's surreal. In the hazy silence, I feel like a space explorer roving across an alien planet.

Oscar stops the car at the lip of a vast crater, and we all get out to survey the destruction. The bottom of the crater is like a dust bowl, smooth and perfect. The asteroid wasn't massive. Not a dinosaur-killer-sized piece of rock. But it's still breathtaking. The crater must be a mile across. The destructive impact is incredible. My stomach twists in knots thinking about the wave that would have hit Camp Seven. It's miles away, but it would have been hit hard. Probably not by the fireball, but certainly by the force of the blast. Grigory, standing beside me, stares at the crater. I know what he's thinking—and hoping. That we're not too late to save Lina.

But at the moment, we have a larger crisis to address.

"Let's state the obvious," I begin. "The tube to the aquifer and passage above isn't viable for evacuating everyone from the bunker. Even if we brought food back to the Citadel, we couldn't transport it in large quantities. It would take a lot of trips to keep everyone supplied and even more to get people out. It would take weeks, maybe months to evacuate everyone. We might run out of food down there and accidents could happen."

Grigory nods. "Even if we could solve the time and supply issues, I don't like it. The passage out of the aquifer could collapse at any moment. We need a better solution."

"Sir," Oscar says, "I could drive to another camp and try to make contact and see if they can assist us."

"They're probably in the same shape as us. Traveling there by car would take time, which we don't have. As Grigory said, we need a solution that gets everyone out safely and reliably." I pause, thinking for a moment. "Oscar, did you see any excavation equipment at CENTCOM?"

"Yes, sir."

"Good. We'll make a quick survey of the camp, then head to CENTCOM, and see what we have to work with."

Grigory shoots me an anxious glance, and I know what he's thinking—that maybe we'll find Lina at the Olympus building. I hope we do, and that she survived somehow.

Without another word, we get back in the car and drive at top speed toward the camp. When we reach the first buildings on the outskirts, my fears are confirmed. They are flattened like wooden prairie homes hit by a massive tornado.

We drive farther into the camp, over the rubble and pieces of buildings lying in the street (thankfully, the army vehicle is equipped for this). Seeing the devastation is gutwrenching. Anyone inside one of these buildings had no chance of survival.

Deeper into the camp, the buildings change from blown-over remains to crumbled ruins, domes that are caved in, lying in head-height piles of debris.

Grigory fidgets next to me. Up ahead, at the center of what's left of Camp Seven, lies the remains of the Olympus building, which housed NASA, NOAA, and several other scientific organizations. Olympus was part of a campus that included a hospital, the CENTCOM military headquarters, and the government administration building. Being at the center of the camp certainly helped the buildings avoid the full force of the blast, but their height didn't. All of them are heaps of rubble. Olympus used to be six stories tall. It's about two stories high now, a lumpy expanse of debris.

Before the car even stops, Grigory jumps out and runs toward the pile. I'm right behind him, listening for any signs of life—screams, crying, or voices. I hear only the wind blowing across the ruins.

The smell is worse: sewage, rotting food—and death.

Grigory calls out at the top of his lungs, "Lina!"

He bounds into the rubble pile, climbing across the cracked hard-plastic walls and twisted steel beams, yelling her name, slipping and catching himself as he goes. Then he stops suddenly, turning to me, fear and anger in his eyes. "We have to find her. Help me. James, please."

"Grigory—"

"James, please."

I turn to Oscar. "Take another vehicle and head back to the Citadel. Bring Izumi and Harry back. Hurry. We'll start searching for survivors while you're gone."

As I wade into the rubble pile, the hazy sun is starting to set on this wasteland, the only place I ever wanted to call home.

"Okay, Grigory. Let's find her."

16

Emma

I lie in the bunk, my back to the wall, Allie beside me, a place left for James. I thought he'd be back by now. Last night, he left a note saying that he and Grigory were going to the surface and that they would return as soon as possible. I figured I would see him by lunch. But he didn't return. I looked for him again at dinner. And when Allie and I emerged from our bath. He's still not here. If he knew he'd be gone for twenty-four hours, surely he would have woken me to tell me that instead of simply leaving a note for Fowler? I can't help wondering if something's happened to him. And I can't help leaving a place for him in the small bed, hoping he'll be there in the morning.

"Da?" Allie asks.

"He's at work, sweetie."

"Now?"

"Yes, he has to work at night right now."

"Home..."

"We'll go home. I promise. Right now it's time to be quiet and go to sleep."

A few weeks. One way or another, that's the truth.

We have enough food for roughly sixteen more days. That's the terrifying thought I go to sleep with.

The next morning, the team meets in the kitchen for two very good reasons. The first is that we don't want anyone to hear our conversation. The second reason is that one of us now has to stay in the kitchen at all times. No one has called kitchen duty what it is: guard duty. Food is our most precious resource. It's the ticking clock. If someone raids it, it could be deadly.

Everyone is here except for James, Grigory, and Oscar.

"We've had some requests from some of the parents…" Izumi pauses as if searching for the right words. "They've asked about the rationing."

"We've been over this," Fowler replies, "no exceptions."

"They're not asking for exceptions, per se. They're asking that they be allowed the right to forgo their rations and that those rations be added to their children's allotment."

"That'll open up a whole can of worms," Fowler replies. "Namely, what about the kids with no parents down here? And if we do it for some parents, I think the other parents will feel pressure to follow suit."

"Even if we say no, they'll likely do it anyway," Min says. "They'll just hide their food. Some of that will spoil."

"What have you told them?" Fowler asks Izumi.

"Only that we would consider it. Are we considering it?"

"I agree with Min," Harry says. "What choice do we have? I don't have any kids, but I'm certainly willing to give up my rations for the children down here."

A knock sounds at the door to the kitchen. I for one am relieved to have a break in the debate.

"Come in," Fowler calls out.

Oscar presses the door open and strides in quickly.

"Where's James?" I ask before I can even think about it.

"He's on the surface."

"Is he okay?"

"Yes, ma'am. He and Grigory made it safely."

"Can we evacuate via the aquifer?" Fowler asks.

"No, sir. James has ruled that out. He has another plan. I'm sorry, but he instructed me to hurry. I need Dr. Tanaka and Harry to come with me now."

17

James

My hands are aching and freezing. The climb above the aquifer was bad. Digging through the rubble of the NASA headquarters building might be worse. The wreckage is heavy and sharp and my hands are freezing.

The sun has set and the temperature is dropping by the minute. But Grigory and I keep digging in silence.

Beneath the thin layer of snow and ash, we find things I expect: shattered solar panels that once covered the top of the building, the hard-plastic girders that held up the structure, and strands of electrical wire that were just under the roof, close to the solar panels.

There's also something I don't expect: a thick, black, gooey substance scattered across the debris, like oil sprayed haphazardly.

Grigory reaches out and picks up a piece, rubbing it with his fingers. "What is this?"

"Not sure."

"Maybe remnants of the ejecta that fell back to the ground," Grigory says.

"It could have mixed with part of the solar panels."

"If so, it might have given off toxic fumes when forming," Grigory says absently, still rubbing the substance on his fingers.

"True. Something to think about for the survivors."

We dig in silence after that, the smell of death all around us, neither of us acknowledging it. Occasionally, we pause to catch our breath and warm our hands. I try the satellite phone and radio every time. Grigory calls out for Lina.

Neither of us gets an answer.

So we keep digging.

I grab one end of a hard-plastic wall and Grigory grabs the other and we heave it off the stack. Below is a metal table with a flat-screen display in the middle, shattered. Grigory stares at it. He recognizes it. I do too—it's from our team room. If Lina was in the mission control room, we're close.

We take the table and haul it out of the rubble and keep digging. If this building had been made in the conventional way, like the ones in America, with steel and concrete, drywall and wood, there's no way we would be able to dig through it this quickly by hand. But the buildings in Camp Seven were erected quickly, made from mass-produced, lightweight materials. Strong materials, ones that don't shatter and or break easily.

I scoop up pieces of a whiteboard and toss them away from the pile. A few days ago, we were writing on this board, tweaking our plan to stop those three large asteroids. Now we're picking up the pieces—literally, because we missed the true attack.

I missed it.

With each piece of wreckage I pick up, I can't help thinking: without NASA, what chance do we have? Maybe the Caspians or the Pac Alliance have a command center that no one knew about that survived this.

The truth is, we have to get up into space and start fighting the new harvester. More importantly: we need to know what we're dealing with. And who's left to fight it.

I feel a faint wetness fall on my ears, something in my hair. I look up and realize sandy-brown snow flurries are floating down all around us. It's truly winter again, and it's cold enough for the snow to stick to the ground and take hold.

"James!" Grigory yells as he begins digging furiously, throwing a mangled office chair out of the way, a battered tablet after, and then a model spaceship, which scatters across the rubble.

At his feet, I see an article of clothing: blue pants. Grigory lifts a cubicle divider revealing a hand, then an arm. I rush to him and reach into the debris, tossing away a computer screen and keyboard, uncovering a torso.

The person isn't moving. Or breathing.

Grigory reaches up and pushes the desk away. Our headlamps shine down like searchlights from above, illuminating the man's bloody, lacerated face.

He's one of the control technicians for the orbital defense array. I can't remember his name. Maybe Thomas. Or Travis. Nice guy. He probably stayed to try to optimize the array's defense. I bet he did the math and figured if he could take out at least one more asteroid, that would be worth it. His life for thousands.

"Should we..." Grigory begins but trails off, eyes lingering on the body.

I shuffle over and grab the man's feet. "Let's just move him out of the rubble for now."

By the time we've stumbled across the pile and laid our colleague on the ground, it's the dead of night, the only light that from our headlamps.

I'm cold and hungry and tired, more tired than I've been in a long, long time. But we keep digging.

The snow soon forms a blanket on the rubble, making it slippery as we step across. The cold wind cuts through me, down deep, making me shiver. I keep going, lifting tables and walls and screens and chairs and keyboards, hands trembling, cheeks cold and chapped by the wind. I grit my teeth and bear it because Grigory is my friend and so is Lina and this is what we have to do right now.

Oscar won't be back for at least twelve hours. Unless he manages to get through the passage above the aquifer and the tunnel faster.

We find another body. And another. Each time, my heart leaps and each time it crashes when my fingers touch their cold, lifeless skin. Little by little, it becomes apparent what we'll find in this pile of misery.

Grigory and I are both exhausted and freezing. We take more frequent breaks, sitting next to each other, rubbing our hands, breath coming out in white wisps that drift through our headlamps like ghosts rising from the rubble. But Grigory pushes on. I'm about to ask him to stop, to make the well-reasoned plea that I've rehearsed a dozen times in my mind, when we find her.

It's clear that Lina was indeed in mission control when she died. I recognize the desk dividers and the workstations. I found a piece of the large wall screen shortly before

Grigory uncovered her arm. He recognized the long-sleeve T-shirt instantly.

I stand there for a long moment and watch as he stares at her body. I expect him to break down. I would. But he simply reaches out and gently removes the items covering her and brushes the dirt and soot from her face and hair and takes her hands and places them over her chest. I step closer and, in his eyes, I see a simmering rage so strong I feel it could literally tear him into a thousand pieces. And I feel it too.

It takes the last bit of strength I have to help Grigory load Lina into the back of the electric car.

Weary and cold, I instruct the car to drive over to the CENTCOM building, which is a hundred yards from the remains of Olympus. They designed CENTCOM as a sprawling, three-story building with a courtyard in the middle, similar to the Pentagon before the glaciers of the Long Winter trampled it. And like the Pentagon before it, the Atlantic Union's CENTCOM headquarters is a sprawling wasteland now.

The building's designers had the foresight to build a massive bunker adjacent to it, reinforced to withstand a direct airstrike. The thinking was that they could retreat there if hostilities with the Caspians or the Pac Alliance broke out. The plan was for the bunker to be stocked with everything you'd need to fight a war: weapons, food, armor, and, importantly for our current situation, drones. I just hope stocking the facility wasn't overlooked in the last two years as we planned to defend against the large asteroids.

It's clear that parts of the bunker are collapsed, mainly around the periphery. Ruins of the CENTCOM building lie below ground level like piles of trash thrown in a gulley. That's probably why they didn't evacuate anyone to the bunker—they weren't sure if it would survive the asteroid, or, if it did, what parts would come through the impact.

Luckily for us, one of the bunker sections that survived has a working entrance ramp, and it lies open from Oscar's previous entry.

I take manual control of the car and guide it into the tunnel. The overhead lights snap on as we emerge from the tunnel. I'm relieved that we have power down here. I'm assuming that's thanks to a battery backup. If so, those batteries were likely charged by solar panels that sat atop CENTCOM. Those solar panels are gone, and soon, the power in the batteries will be gone. We need to set up an array of solar panels to recharge them. But one thing at a time.

One side of the bunker looks like a garage, with troop carriers, armored vehicles, and more lightweight cars like the all-terrain unit we're driving. Another one of the swift all-terrain vehicles is gone—the one Oscar retrieved while we were digging at NASA. It's no doubt sitting by the entrance to the aquifer now.

There are several pieces of earth-moving equipment, including a large excavator, a giant bulldozer, and several attachments for the excavator, including a hydraulic hammer and thumb. These massive machines were no doubt used to build the CENTCOM bunker and the planners chose to leave them here in case the entrances to the bunker had been caved in. They left themselves a way to dig out. And now those machines may be the key to getting everyone out of the Citadel.

Glancing around, I take stock of the rest of the facility. There are three rooms off the open area: a small med bay with an operating room, a situation room filled with inactive screens, and a large mechanical room with a small water treatment plant and an air purification system.

The other side of the open area is filled with crates and racks full of supplies, including what I had hoped we'd find: weapons, drones, armor, communications gear, and MREs —Meals, Ready-to-Eat.

I'm starving and weak, and I want to rush to the ration bins, but first Grigory and I take Lina's body to a troop carrier and gently place her on one of the long benches in the back. Grigory sits beside her, staring. I retrieve a thick blanket from a supply crate, drape it over her, and leave him alone, closing the door of the troop carrier behind me.

I break out the MREs and wolf one down, barely stopping to breathe. The troop carrier's rear door swings open and Grigory steps down, his eyes still moist and bloodshot. I open an MRE, start the heating element, and hand it to him. We don't speak a word as we eat. We're both too tired and too overwhelmed. Shivering in the cold depot, we eat in silence.

When we're full, I set a space heater in another troop carrier and line the floor with blankets and sleeping bags. Sleeping in the situation room might be more comfortable, but space in the vehicle is smaller and easier to heat.

"What now?" Grigory asks.

"We need to get some rest. When Harry gets here, we'll firm up our plan and start digging at the crater."

Grigory nods and heads for our troop carrier.

A thought occurs to me. "Actually, there's something else we can do before they get here."

He raises his eyebrows.

"Search for survivors."

"How?"

"There's probably some surveillance drones with infrared capability down here. I'll set them up to do a full survey of the camp. We'll sleep while they fly over."

Even if someone out there survived the blast wave, they've been buried for four days, likely without food. It's a long shot, but I can't go to sleep knowing we're not at least looking for anyone who needs help.

When the drones are in the air and transmitting data back to our control station, Grigory and I climb into the armored troop carrier and slip into the sleeping bags. I set my alarm for three hours. That's about how long the survey drones will take.

I wake to hands on my shoulders gripping me, pushing me into the floor, shaking me, shouting.

My face is still bruised and aching from the elbow I took before the asteroid impact. The rest of my body feels even worse from the climb out of the aquifer and the digging at Olympus.

In the darkness, I realize it's Grigory shaking me, the words he's uttering Russian, probably curse words.

My phone alarm is blaring.

"You set a code on your alarm?" Grigory mutters when he realizes I'm awake.

I roll over and tap the six digits into the phone and it silences. "Yeah, it ensures it actually wakes me."

"No, it only ensures that it wakes me up."

We pile out of the troop carrier and over to the drone control case. It's about the size of a briefcase, with a control panel in one half, a touchscreen on the other. The screen shows a map of Camp Seven with layers for satellite and infrared imagery. I switch to infrared and feel a surge of hope.

Life signs.

I count twenty-six. All buried beneath the habitats. That surprises me. Like the other camps in the Atlantic Union, Camp Seven has warehouses and greenhouses around the periphery, beyond the habitats. From the drone survey, it's obvious that the warehouses and greenhouses were all taken down in the blast. I had hoped at least one or two of the facilities at the side of the camp opposite the blast wave might have survived, and that we would find survivors there. No such luck.

Twenty-six survivors. I had expected more. Hoped for more.

Rescuing them is more time sensitive than the Citadel evacuation. We need to act quickly.

For a moment I consider trying to dig Oliver out of the basement of Olympus. We could use his help. Like Oscar, Oliver could swim through the aquifer and the Citadel's emergency water tube. He could double the rate at which we evacuate people from the Citadel—and those people could help us recover survivors here on the surface. But there are two problems with going after Oliver.

One: it would take time to reach him, even with the heavy equipment here in the bunker. I was hesitant to use the excavator at Olympus before because I hoped there were survivors in the rubble. The drone fly-over confirms that no one is alive in the debris. Still, digging with the excavator now could still inadvertently harm Oliver. We might rip him in half in the process of trying to find him.

The second issue is that I doubt Oliver survived the building's collapse in working order. The basement under Olympus wasn't built with the same rigor as CENTCOM, and twice as much building mass collapsed upon it. If Oliver were still operational, he would have responded to Oscar's ping. Best case—he's offline, either conserving power or damaged.

That leaves Grigory and me to go after the human survivors. I wish I knew how long they have to live. Days? Hours? Minutes?

In the middle of the floor, I leave a note for Oscar, Harry and Izumi telling them we've gone out to search for survivors.

"Whom do we go after first?" Grigory asks.

The answer comes to me immediately. It might not be the wisest move, but it's the only one I can live with.

"The life signs with the lowest mass."

"The children."

"That's right."

18

Emma

After Oscar leaves with Harry and Izumi, I set about doing something I probably should have done when we first arrived: inspecting our food supply.

We took a count of our supplies five days ago. But we didn't physically open each box and look inside. As Min and I unseal the cartons of MREs and rations, I'm devastated by what we find: spoiled food. Several crates of MREs must have been damaged in transit to the Citadel. Their contents went bad months, maybe even years ago. With the lost supplies, we estimate that we have twelve days of food left—not sixteen as we previously believed.

James needs to know this.

All day, we keep watch, waiting for him, Grigory, or Oscar to emerge from the water treatment plant. But none of them return.

That night, I hold Allie close, hoping James will wake me in the night.

He doesn't.

When I wake, he's not in our bed. At this point, we haven't heard from James or anyone on his team for nearly twenty-four hours. Someone should have been back by now—Oscar at the very least to retrieve others to help on the surface. My greatest fear is that James and his team are injured or dead.

If they're still alive, trying to get us out of here, they believe we have about sixteen days of food left. We need to buy at least that much time for him.

I skipped dinner last night. Most of the adults did. Abby, Madison, and I shared an MRE for breakfast this morning, the sustenance barely beating back the hunger deep inside of me.

After breakfast, what's left of the team meets in the kitchen, each of us sitting on a stool, eyes weary, all dreading what's ahead.

"Okay," Fowler says, "obviously we need to make our rations last longer. Let's talk about our options."

The expressions around the room—from Min, Charlotte, and Colonel Earls—tell me that none of us think there are any options. Or at least any good ones.

"The only option apparent to me," Earls says, "is a reduction in population."

Even as tired and hungry as we are, that draws reactions: a scowl from Charlotte, surprise from Min, and a curious look from Fowler. I'm horrified by the idea.

"What exactly are you proposing?" Fowler asks. "We don't have a way to get more people out." Clearly, he's hoping Earls isn't saying what we all think he is.

"No. The population would stay the same. I would request volunteers from my troops to stop taking rations."

"That's absurd," Charlotte says.

"I don't think we're there yet," Min says, face stoic.

"The sooner we make the call, the more time we buy ourselves," Earls says. "I think we have to assume something has happened to James and his team on the surface. Best case, something has slowed them down. We can speculate on what that is—maybe the passage to the aquifer collapsed or the suits were damaged or the tube collapsed. Bottom line, if we do nothing, we're giving them four days less than they think they have." Earls pauses a moment. "Izumi said that those in the best health will endure the lower rations best. Especially those with excess fat and muscle. My people are fit. They don't have a lot of fat on their bodies, but they do have a lot of muscle. And they've been trained for operating in challenging environments."

Charlotte shakes her head. "For all we know, James could arrive in a week and those troops will have starved themselves for nothing."

"Not for nothing, ma'am. We're at war. In war, you fight the battle in front of you, and you don't always know how that battle will affect the war's outcome. Every one of the soldiers down here took an oath when they joined the Atlantic Union Army—an oath to protect its citizens and to give their life if necessary."

"This isn't a battle," Charlotte insists.

"It is, ma'am. Starvation is the weapon our enemy is using on us. We need to fight it the only way we can, which is by reducing the number of mouths we have to feed."

I shake my head. "Charlotte's right. And plus, we need to think long term, about what happens *when* we get out of here. We may need those troops more then than we do now. We need them in good shape to help us. No. I'm against it."

"What do you suggest?" Min asks me.

"Let's consider the extreme rationing plan previously proposed. All the adults reduce their caloric intake. If we do, I bet we can buy another four days—the time James thinks we have down here."

"That kind of rationing is bound to have some effect. People will be lethargic. Irritable."

"Yes. But we'll all be alive."

19

James

Grigory and I load up the troop carrier we slept in with supplies: food, medicine, and communications gear.

Over our clothes, we don army winter weather gear, including thick gloves and insulated helmets.

Grigory seems eager to get out of this bunker and start going after the people buried in the rubble. The work will take his mind off Lina, and I think finding someone alive would do my friend a lot of good.

"We're going to dig by hand?" he asks.

"We'll have to. The excavator's too large to use at the habitats where the life signs are. It might do more harm than good. Plus we're going to need it at the Citadel crater."

"We're going to dig them out?"

"Yeah."

Grigory nods, seeming to approve of the plan.

We climb into the troop carrier, and I switch to manual control and gun it, the massive truck rumbling out of the bunker, up the ramp and into the hazy early morning. Camp Seven's sandy, hard-packed streets are littered with debris.

The scene reminds me of coastal towns after a massive hurricane, as though a giant hammer came through and flattened everything and scattered the pieces.

Our destination is a habitat the same size and configuration as the one Emma, Allie, and I shared. A three-bedroom family domicile.

A blanket of snow now covers the lumpy pile of rubble.

I step out of the truck and call out, "Hello! We're here to help!" I wait for a moment. "If you can hear me, please respond."

The only sound is the cold wind blowing across the dunes of white-covered debris.

We leave the troop carrier running. The solar panels on top easily power it, even with the diminished solar output. The space heater is set to warm the cargo compartment, where we've left our blankets and sleeping bags: a makeshift portable hospital ward. Depending on what we find, it might become an operating room. I've laid out the medical supplies I might need. I hope Izumi gets here soon. She's a far better surgeon than I am.

Grigory marches to the approximate location of the vital signs on the map and starts digging, brushing the snow away and picking up the shattered pieces of the habitat one at a time and tossing them away.

I join in, silently surveying the wreckage: the pieces of the solar panels that covered the top of the home; next, pieces of the roof and ceiling and lights; and then pieces of the wall and hard-plastic studs. The top layer of wreckage is dotted with the same black goo we found in the debris at the Olympus building. I take a second to inspect it, rubbing it between my gloved fingers, searching for any differences between the two samples. It seems the same. It's gritty, slightly sticky. I think I see a sparkle in the middle of the sample. It's probably just the sunlight playing tricks on my eyes.

I wipe my hands clean and keep digging. I go slower when we begin to uncover children's toys. The first toy is a plastic board with puzzle pieces of different shapes: circle, triangle, rectangle, heart, and square, each in a different color. It's a learning game for toddlers. Allie has one just like it. A minute later, I pick up a shattered tablet and glimpse a leg beneath it. I work faster then, uncovering the torso and the arms and the face.

The child can't be older than five or six, a boy with dark brown hair, eyes closed, skin gray, hard, and cold.

Grigory and I stand there, staring, both frozen by the sight. The wind blows across the rubble, sweeping bits of grit, dust, and snow over the child. I lean over and brush his face off; then I hoist him up and carry him back to the troop carrier, where I spread a blanket over his body. I was wrong. The troop carrier is more than a mobile operating room. It's a hearse too.

I wonder if this was the life sign the drone identified. If so, did the child die since the drone's survey? Was that boy clinging to life while Grigory and I slept in the CENTCOM bunker? Our bellies were full. The troop carrier was warm. And he was out here. Freezing. Dying. Waiting for rescue that never came.

That thought rips through me like a blender tearing me apart. We could have dug faster. Slept less.

I have to know if there's anyone still alive in that rubble pile.

I open the drone's control case and study the map. When the drone flew over a few hours ago, it estimated the mass of the survivor at twenty kilograms. The boy we just found is about that weight, if I had to guess. But I have to be certain.

"I'm going to have the drone do another fly-over," I say to Grigory as I set off toward the habitat again and start digging. Neither one of us says anymore about it. We just assume there's still someone down there. We hope.

Five minutes later, I lift a dining table off a child's chest. The small body is still. I move the rest of the debris off the boy, revealing his head and face. He has short brown hair and a purple bruise covering his left cheek. Dried blood is caked around his nose. He must have hidden under the dining table. It wasn't enough. He was about Allie's age.

The drone's control case beeps, the sound indicating that the survey is complete.

I walk back to the truck and scan the updated map. The only heat signatures are the truck, Grigory, and me.

We were too late. By how much? Minutes? Hours? If we had dug faster, slept less...

I can't think that way. We have to keep moving. It's the only thing we can do.

When we've loaded the second child into the truck, Grigory points to the map. "We should prioritize the ones with stronger vitals."

"No. We stick to the lowest weight first."

"The adults—"

"The adults—parents—would want their children saved first."

I know it's the right thing to do because if I were buried in the debris and Allie were beside me, I'd want them to take her, no matter the odds. So that's what we're going to do.

The next habitat is a few blocks away, a crumbled heap that looks disturbingly similar to the one we just left.

The sun is higher in the sky now, but I could swear it feels as though it's getting colder. That supports my suspicion that the grid is positioning the solar cells between us and the sun. If so, the world will be an ice ball again soon. This time, we don't have the tools to rebuild our civilization. And we have very little to fight with. As I dig, I can't help wondering how we'll survive this.

The digging is slow, back-breaking work. Soon I'm panting, my breath coming out in wisps of white steam.

I pull the gloves off and say to Grigory, "I've got to take a break."

He follows me back to the truck, and we sit in the cab, warming ourselves, each chewing a protein bar, chasing it with water, staring straight ahead.

"It's using the solar cells to freeze us," Grigory says.

"Probably."

"Tell me we are going to fight."

"If we can."

"Promise me, James, that we'll fight them."

Three years ago, I would've said, *Of course we're going to fight*. But I'm a father now. What good is fighting if it won't save my children? Revenge is a luxury. Survival is a necessity.

"We're going to do what we have to do to survive."

I can tell Grigory doesn't like that answer. He shakes his head and bites off another piece of the protein bar. I don't blame him for wanting to strike back at the enemy that killed the woman he loved. He doesn't want to survive anymore, not without her. He wants to hurt the thing that hurt him.

We've been digging for fifteen minutes when we reach more toys. A stuffed bear. A dozen small animal figurines. A plastic barn smashed to pieces. Yellow fencing that must've gone around the barn, wadded up. Bedsheets with a cartoon princess and prince, characters I don't recognize.

There's also a small child's tent, the support frame mangled, the fabric still mostly intact. Allie has one just like it. In my mind's eye, I can picture it set up in our living room. It's round with a conical top. The walls are striped red and white. Blue flaps hang over the entrance. I can see her hiding inside, me peeking past the blue flaps to scare her and the sound of her laughter filling the small habitat.

In the pile of debris, I reach down to pick up the blue flaps of the entrance. I stop at the sight of a child's arm. I motion to Grigory, and when he steps closer, I gently tear the tent open, revealing blonde locks of hair matted with blood. I jerk my glove off and brush the hair away and find the child's neck and squeeze.

My vision blurs from the tears that flow when I feel the faint beating of a pulse.

Obviously, the AtlanticNet is down, so I have no way to look up who lived here, and I don't recognize the girl. I want to call out her name, but I have to settle for, "Hey, can you hear me?"

To Grigory, I say, "Let's get her into the truck."

Gently, we lift her and carry her across the rubble. She hangs utterly limp in our arms, feeling so fragile. She's taller than Allie, probably three or four years old. I imagine she hid out in her tent when she heard the rumbling. Did her parents tell her to go there? We haven't found their bodies. And based on the drone's readings, I know what we'll find if we do.

In the truck, I quickly do a cursory exam. There's a dark blue-black bruise on her ankle. A similar contusion on her left arm, which looks more serious; the bone is probably broken.

"What should we do?" Grigory asks.

"Don't know."

"Aren't you a doctor?"

"Technically."

"Well, what is technical thing to do here?"

I close my eyes and rub my eyelids. "I don't know, Grigory." The cold and sleep deprivation and aches are starting to affect me.

He's undeterred. "What do you mean you *don't know*?"

"I had a rotation in emergency medicine twenty years ago, but I haven't performed any since."

He throws his hands up. "I remember stuff I learned twenty years ago."

"Are you sure enough about it to risk someone's life? A kid's life? When you might be doing more harm than good?"

"All right, all right. Don't be so sensitive."

For a long moment, we just sit there staring at the girl, looking as peaceful as if she's just sleeping. Except for the patch of blood on her forehead. Now *that* I can do something about.

I take an alcohol pad from the med kit and clean the wound. She winces but doesn't wake. I take it as a good sign.

"Now what?" Grigory ask.

"We keep going."

I'm studying the drone's infrared map when the radio crackles to life, Harry's voice booming in the small space.

"Apocalypse one, this is apocalypse two, do you read?"

As bad as things are, I can't help but smile. I grab the radio and activate it. "We read you. Good to hear your voice, Harry."

"Good to be here. Rough trip though. Nothing like being a hotdog pulled through the eye of a needle to tell me I need to lose weight."

The mention of him losing weight momentarily reminds me of the Citadel and the people trapped there. "Hopefully, we won't have to go back that way."

"What's the plan, James?"

"Grigory and I have a survivor that needs medical attention. Izumi and Oscar, I need you to get over here as quickly as possible." I glance at the map and call out the coordinates of the next habitat we're going to. "Harry, I want you to take the large excavator in the CENTCOM bunker and drive it back to the crater at the Citadel."

"Can't we transport the machine?"

"No. I'm afraid we don't have a truck or trailer large enough. You'll have to drive it. Radio us when you get there. The trip is going to take some time. Take all the battery packs you can find. The solar panels on the excavator's roof aren't efficient enough to sustain it at full driving speed for long. Plus, I think solar output is already dropping."

"Will do," Harry says. "What should I do when I get there?"

"Use the old map of the warehouse. Start digging where the elevator shaft was."

"Roger that."

"What do I need to bring?" Izumi asks.

"I'm not sure. We have a Caucasian female, estimated age is four years, multiple contusions, possible fractures, and a laceration to the head. I've cleaned and bandaged the open wound. Vitals are stable, but she's not conscious. Just bring whatever you think you need. And hurry."

At the next habitat, Grigory and I dig faster, maybe because we're encouraged by having found a survivor, or maybe because we're getting better at boring our way into these debris piles.

But this time, we have a problem. We've reached the floor of the habitat, at the exact location the drone says we should find a survivor. The map says the vitals are erratic but the heat signature is there. Weight estimate is a little over seventeen kilograms. Almost forty pounds.

"I don't get it," Grigory says.

I scan the items around us: a fabric couch cut to pieces. A club chair mangled, almost flattened. A hard-plastic bookcase turned face down, its contents strewn across the floor: books and pictures and trinkets.

"Help me," I say to Grigory as I grip one end of the hard-plastic bookcase.

We lift it in unison, revealing a boy lying flat on his back, clutching a small plastic spaceship in his hand. We throw the bookcase over and I reach down to check his pulse, which is stronger than I was expecting.

"Hey," I whisper, my breath coming out in white clouds as the snow falls, large flakes hitting his face and hair.

His right eyelid cracks open, a brown eye peering out at me, hollow, tired, and scared. But he's alive.

The eyelid slowly closes, and I'm about to get Grigory to help me lift him up when I hear another troop carrier barreling towards us. The safety locks are off and someone's driving—the truck's AI would never drive that fast. But Oscar would.

The truck skids to a stop and he and Izumi throw the doors open.

"Over here!" I call out.

"Status?" Izumi asks, bending down, laying a white camouflaged military bag beside the boy.

"We just found him."

She works systematically, her hands racing over his body. I can tell from her body language that she likes what she's seeing. She moves slower as she runs her fingers through his hair, probably looking for any lacerations or knots. He turns his head slightly. Both eyes peel apart this time, slowly, like flowers opening, then close again, as though their weight is too much for him to hold open.

"Young man, can you hear me?"

His lips part, but no sound comes.

"The picture and address match a child in the AU database named Sam Eastman," Oscar says. "Age: four-point-one years."

"Sam, can you hear me?" Izumi says to him. When he doesn't respond, she looks up at us. "He's in surprisingly good shape. How?"

I point to the hard-plastic bookshelf. "Someone—probably his parents—put him under that deep bookshelf. The debris dented it, but it never broke."

Izumi takes out a flashlight and pulls his eyelids open, moving the light back and forth. "Saved by reading," she mumbles as she studies his reactions. "The parents?"

"He's the only life sign at this location. Can we move him to the troop carrier? We've got another patient."

"Yes, let's do that."

"Oscar," I begin, but he's already moving around the debris pile, positioning himself to pick up the child's head and torso. I move around to his feet and we lift him up.

As we move across the shaky, uneven pile of debris, I catch sight of some of the black gooey substance sticking to Oscar's shoes and pants. It appears to be moving. Surely not. It's probably just him shaking it off as he walks. But I could swear it's sliding down his pants leg and up his shoes, converging on the area where his socks would be if he wore them. Strange.

"Which truck?" I call back to Izumi as we clear the house.

"Yours. Let's keep the patients together. I want to move them as little as possible."

We set the boy next to the girl and Izumi climbs in and touches a health analyzer to his finger, taking a drop of blood and watching the screen, waiting for results.

"H-H-Hey..." the boy croaks, voice faint and scratchy.

"Hi, Sam," Izumi says, smiling, placing her hand on his head. "You're going to be okay."

"James," Oscar calls out, voice flat, but loud and urgent. "I'm experiencing…" He freezes, eyes glassing. "I'm experiencing a malfunction, sir."

"Malfunction?"

"Sir, I don't know what's happening to me."

"Explain."

"My system says it's installing a software update."

How is that possible? Just before I realize the answer, his eyes close.

He's being hacked.

"Oscar! Scrub working memory and shut down all systems.."

His eyes open.

He smiles. It's a smile that is authentically human, one that doesn't convey joy, but smug satisfaction. It's an expression too advanced for Oscar to manifest. And it's an expression he would never make.

His voice is different when he speaks, the tone is arrogant and slow and bordering on condescending. I've heard it once before.

"Hello again, James."

20

Emma

I'm walking towards the double doors to exit the kitchen when Fowler calls to me, "Emma, could you stay for a moment?"

I wait while the rest of the team exit, the only sound the swinging double doors rocking back and forth. When everyone's gone, Fowler says, "For the record, I agree with the plan you put forward. Extreme rationing is the right move now."

I sense a "but" coming.

"However, I hope you'll be sensible about it. When it comes to yourself."

"What does that mean?"

"It means," he says slowly, "that the rations you eat aren't just for you."

"Who told you?"

"That's not the issue at hand. This conversation is about your unborn child."

"There are more lives at stake down here."

"But none more important to you or to James. A person can't fight if they have nothing to fight for."

21

James

"Oscar?" I ask, studying his face. I'm nearly certain of what's happened to him, but I hope I'm wrong.

"Oscar isn't here right now."

"Who are you?"

"Call me Arthur. You met one of my colleagues a few years ago." He pauses. "At Ceres."

Grigory races to the troop carrier, reaches into a bag and draws out a semi-automatic rifle and whirls toward Arthur and me. I turn and put myself in front of the gun, hands raised. The barrel shakes as Grigory stares in rage at Arthur, finger on the trigger.

Behind me, Arthur speaks slowly, tone condescending. "Temper, temper, Grigory. This tin man is your only way off this desolate rock. Better behave."

Grigory shouts in Russian, spit issuing from his mouth. I step toward him, hands still held up.

"Cool it, Grigory. We need to figure out what we're dealing with."

"We're dealing with the enemy!"

I step forward again and extend my hand. "Give me the gun," I whisper. "There will be a time and place, but it's not here and not now."

He glowers at me. Finally, his finger slips away from the trigger and his body relaxes as he looks up at the sky. I take the gun and hold it to my side, afraid to put it back in the truck where he can get to it.

Arthur watches Grigory walk away, then continues in the same leisurely, arrogant tone. "Now. Where were we? Oh yes, introductions. At Ceres, you called my associate Art. Why not call me Arthur? I'm older by roughly sixty thousand years, but share some of the same basic programming."

"What are you? Are you the harvester?"

"No, the harvester is a separate entity. I operate independently, usually in situations like this."

"What do you want?"

"We still want the same thing: the output from your sun."

"That's not going to work for us."

Arthur smiles, a wicked, knowing smile. "No, it certainly won't."

"Then why are we talking?"

"This is a negotiation."

"Negotiation of what?"

"Your surrender."

22

Emma

In the mess hall, I find Madison setting up for the day's lesson, the school-aged kids already starting to take their seats at the long tables.

I grab her arm and practically drag her from the room. "I need to talk to you."

"What—"

In the hall, I spin and stare at her. "You told Fowler I was pregnant."

She straightens and lifts her chin defiantly. "I did."

"I told you that in confidence."

She studies me for a minute, as if organizing her thoughts.

"The other parents have been talking about extreme rationing," she says, eyes locked on me. "Everyone's for it. I knew it would come up in the leadership meeting. So I had to tell Fowler. I knew you wouldn't tell him—and that you would advocate for the extreme rationing. It's our best chance, but you need to eat, Em. I'll tell the entire bunker if I have to. You can hate me for the rest of your life, but this is a child's life we're talking about."

I exhale deeply and stare at the ceiling, willing a response to emerge from the cauldron of emotions swirling in my mind.

As I have with Madison for the last thirty-something years, I settle on a single word, utter it, and walk away.

"Fine."

I find Fowler at the desk in the office nook off the bunk rooms, the same nook James occupied before he left.

"What're you doing?" I ask, leaning against the door frame.

"Trying to figure out what James was working on. Thought there might be a clue as to what happened to him."

He holds up a hand sketch that looks to me like a small drone with an improvised head for boring on it. There are shorthand notes and numbers around it, like Sanskrit wrapping an ancient drawing.

"It's all Greek to me," Fowler says. "If Harry was here, maybe he could make sense of it. Not much we can do with it."

In my life, I've never felt as trapped as I do now. Even when the ISS was torn to pieces and I was stranded in that module, I still held on to hope. This feels much darker. Maybe it's the lack of food or maybe it's the simple fact that we are literally buried under a world that has just been ruined, but it feels as if I'm staring into the abyss and all I can see is a dead end. If I'm feeling it, I know others are. I trained for scenarios like this. I've survived several of them in the last few years. And I wonder: Does that make me qualified to do something about it? Maybe it does. Maybe that's the role I can play down here—and I think it's every bit as important as what James is doing on the surface.

"There is something we can do."

Fowler glances up at me.

"James is clearly working through something on the surface. We've got our own struggle down here."

"Which is?"

"To keep hope alive."

Fowler nods solemnly.

"If we don't, things will get bad down here. We're already hungry and scared."

Fowler's gaze drifts away from me. "We'll survive," he says, the words coming out hollow, as if he barely believes them.

"We will. But surviving isn't just about staying alive. It's about holding on to what you're surviving for. Those were your words to me an hour ago in the kitchen."

"What are you proposing?"

"Have you ever read *The Birthright*?"

He squints, as if trying to place the name. "The psychology book? Sure. It was all the rage twenty years ago."

"I want to form a study group for the book."

"Why?"

"I think it offers what we need right now."

A small smile forms at his lips. "Food?"

"No, it's far more essential than that. The book gives us a distraction. And maybe even something to believe in."

That afternoon, when the kids are gathered in the mess hall for school, I lead the adults down to the sub-basement. The dark cavernous space is the only area large enough to host the meeting. The common rooms between the bunk rooms would be too crowded.

Somehow, the sub-basement is perfect for the event. I've set out LED lanterns in a circle with blankets and pillows for people to sit on. The concrete columns rising up throughout the room make it feel like a cave down here, or some ancient catacomb where we're meeting in secret, a sect brought together to discuss some great revelation.

Nearly all of the adults in the Citadel are present, including Fowler, Min, Earls, and most of the soldiers. Madison, Charlotte, and Abby are upstairs conducting the school and a few other adults are keeping the younger children.

I've spent the last two years teaching aspiring astronauts how to survive in space. This is oddly similar—it's as if I'm teaching, but my audience is different, and the environment we're trying to survive is arguably much harsher than space: our own minds.

The Birthright is first and foremost a psychology book— one that offers theories that were hotly debated twenty years ago. I'm not exactly qualified to lead a discussion about those ideas, but I'm going to do the best I can because I think everyone here might benefit from it.

"I'd like to start by reading the opening of *The Birthright*." My voice, though quiet, still echoes in the vast space.

On my tablet, I turn the first page of the book.

"Every human is born with a birthright. That birthright is happiness. Our greatest challenge to achieving happiness is not the obstacles we encounter in our life. The true barrier to happiness lies inside of us—and it's the one thing we can't ever escape: our own mind.

"From birth, we are educated on countless aspects of life on earth, from personal hygiene to personal finance, but there is no widely accepted curriculum for understanding and managing our own minds. Indeed, almost every human remains the victim of their own mind throughout their entire life, never learning to master it, or manage it, or even understand it. *The Birthright* was written to change that. This book is an owner's manual for a human mind. If you read it and do the maintenance it recommends, your mind will run smoothly. It will break down less often, and in the end, it will take you to your birthright. Indeed, a well-tuned mind is the only road to true and lasting happiness."

23

James

I stare at Arthur in disbelief. "Why negotiate with us? Why not just kill us? You've clearly already started the job."

"I suspect you can surmise why I'm negotiating, James. You are, after all, a step ahead of your entire species. Always have been."

"The conservation of energy."

"Exactly. Gold star."

Arthur's tone drips with condescension. The facial expressions are a departure from those displayed by Art—the avatar the grid previously showed us on Ceres. I wonder why. More than that, I want to know what Arthur has done to Oscar, how the harvester took over his body. That might reveal a way to defeat Arthur.

"What have you done to Oscar?"

"Nothing really. Just packed his primitive little AI program away in a dark corner."

"You sent something down with the asteroids. The black substance."

"Yes," Arthur says as if he's growing bored. "A physical

insertion medium. Used to deploy my code. Barbaric stuff. Haven't had to use it in eight thousand years."

"You've certainly changed your attitude since Ceres."

"We're the grid, James. We adapt. The other harvester tried to reason with you then. Unemotionally. With the facts. It offered you peace and you chose war." Arthur's eyes drift over to the rubble pile that used to be a family's home. "How'd that turn out for you?"

"You don't have to be smug about your victory."

"Oh, but I do. Because you need to know how the grid really sees you. As an inferior species. Vermin in its way. You need to understand how serious we are. You need to realize that the harvester up there is willing to wipe you from this planet."

"And why hasn't it?"

"Conservation of energy—remember, James? Let me explain. Let's say you build a power plant. You need this power plant for your people to survive. But you realize that there's a local termite population eating away at the power lines. You knew about them before you started construction, but you thought they could never harm the power lines. You miscalculated. But not by much. They can't destroy the whole power plant. But they can cause issues. They can get in the way and degrade output temporarily. You can kill these termites, but there are so many of them and they are, unfortunately, rather resilient little bugs. They go underground and they run and they hide and every now and then they'll get organized enough to strike back. Hunting them down and killing every last one of them takes time and energy, which you could be using to build another power plant."

Arthur pauses. When I don't react, he shrugs theatrically.

"So what do you do? You take a hammer and kill a bunch of the termites to scare them. Then you give them a choice."

"Which is?"

"The same choice you had last time. Join the grid. I'll help you make that happen."

"You act like I have that much authority. I don't speak for the entire human race."

"Perhaps. But you underestimate your role here, James. At this point, you are your species' only hope of survival. The choice is yours."

"The answer's still no."

Arthur shakes his head. "You'd rather die than join us?"

"My people would."

"That's unfortunate. And foolish. It's also very common. That leaves your last choice: evacuate this planet."

"How?"

"The two ships connected to the ISS."

"And go where? There are no other habitable worlds in this solar system, and those ships aren't capable of interstellar travel."

"That's true—but they could be. This is the deal I'm offering you, James. I'll give you the technical assistance you need to finish those ships and transform them into colony vessels." Arthur glances down at Oscar's body. "I'll use this primitive medium to direct the construction of robots and technology that are far beyond your capabilities."

"Construct them from what? You've blown this planet to pieces."

"Not entirely. I've left intact the critical resources you need to leave Earth. That's my deal. I help you leave and you never come back. Starting right now, we'll both cease hostilities. If you strike one of the grid's solar cells, the deal is off. The harvester will finish you. But if you don't, I'll help you."

"How long do we have?"

"Fourteen months."

"What happens in fourteen months?"

"Lights out, James."

"Zero solar output reaching Earth?"

"That's correct. Freeze or starve—in fourteen months, one of those will be your future."

I have a million questions. It's almost impossible to wrap my head around what he's saying. I ask the most obvious question first: "Where would we go?"

"I've identified a suitable planet. Earthlike. Off the beaten path, if you will."

For a long moment, I study him, wondering if it's a lie, if that planet really is out there. Even if it is, I wonder if the grid will honor their deal.

Arthur smiles. "Make a smart choice, James. A better choice than you made last time. This is your last chance to save your people."

"Why me?"

"Because you're the only mind capable of completing the work in time. Also for the reason I just stated. More than anyone else in the world, you know how serious I am. I told you the last time we met that I would return and fight you. Here I am. If you say no right now, I'll strike you down. I'll spend the energy required to mobilize another asteroid. One large enough to bury you on this little planet."

Grigory fixes me with a stare, eyes burning with rage. He wants to fight. So do I. But with what? And to what end?

If I say yes, can I trust the grid? Can I make a deal with the enemy that has killed billions of my people? Even if it's the right move, the world will hate me. If Grigory is any indication, even my friends will hate me.

Arthur steps closer to me. "Be smart, James. The clock is ticking." He pauses, studying me. "You know, something else has changed since you first encountered the grid at Ceres. You're a father now." He raises his eyebrows. "And you're about to be again." He lets his head fall back as if remembering something. "Oh, that's right, she hasn't told you." He smiles. "But Oscar knows—because Oscar was connected to the AtlanticNet health services database. He saw the pregnancy test result the second it came in. He's been keeping it from you—patient confidentiality and all that. So Oscar knows and now I know and now you know."

My mind races. Is it true? Why wouldn't Emma tell me? Arthur could be lying to try to manipulate me, hoping that if I believe Emma is pregnant that I'll take the safer option he's offered.

"The first trimester is a delicate time for your unborn, isn't it, James? A time when the mother needs optimal nutrition. Is she getting it down there in the Citadel? They have, what, a couple of weeks left? Bet they've started extreme rationing. What a stressful situation. Not good for those expecting. I can help you get her out."

Arthur stares at me. "Make the right choice this time. For the sake of your people, your wife, your daughter, your unborn child. Last chance, James. What's it going to be?"

24

Emma

Hours turn to days, and the days flow together.

Each night, in the crowded bunk room, when the lights go out, I hug Allie tight to me, my back against the concrete wall, a place in the bed saved for James. Every morning, I wake hoping that he arrived during the night, that I'll reach over and feel a warm place where he's come and gone, already back at work, figuring this out. But every morning it's the same: a cold place in the bed beside me and a very scared child in my arms.

Each night, Allie uses her limited speech to ask the same questions: *Where's Da? Go home?*

Tonight, I don't even have the strength to answer.

"Mommy needs to rest, sweetie."

I close my eyes and try not to let my thoughts rule me. My worst fear is that something's happened to James. My biggest regret is that I never told him that I'm pregnant. If I ever see him again, that's the first thing I'm going to do.

*

Breakfast is a somber affair now. The adults watch the kids eat their meager rations. Some of the children are old enough to understand what's happening, and for the ones who aren't, there's no good explanation. No explanation that won't scare them to death.

Hearing a child say "I'm hungry" has to be the most gut-wrenching thing in a parent's life, followed closely by the moment when you say, "There's nothing I can do."

Those two moments happen frequently now.

We have enough food for nine days. In nine days, the first of us will be at risk of death or permanent disability.

Despite my daily sessions teaching *The Birthright*, I can tell some people have given up. I can see it in the way they don't look at me and in the way they don't respond to their children when they say they're hungry. I see it in their bodies, their gaunt faces, skinny arms, and lumbering, almost drunken movements.

In the kitchen, after the kids eat breakfast, Fowler opens the meeting in the usual way, "Any updates?"

"There's been a proposal from one of my people," Earls says. "Her name is Angela Stevens. She's a corporal. One of my best. She wants to swim through the backup water tube and try to make it through the aquifer."

"Impossible," Min says, not meeting his gaze.

"She's requested," Earls continues, "that we construct some sort of breathing apparatus for her, maybe a hose or an oxygen bag or tank. She wants to rip some sheets up and make a rope that she'll take through."

Charlotte opens her eyes. "What would the rope be used for? To try to pull someone else through? That seems exceedingly dangerous."

"True," Earls replies. "Her thinking is that she could use the rope to let us know that she's successfully cleared the emergency backup water tube." He rubs at his eyebrows as if trying to remember the details of the plan. The extreme rationing is affecting even him. "She'll tug on the rope when she reaches the aquifer to let us know she's okay. Then, when she reaches the surface of the water and climbs out, she'll tie the rope off, and go to the surface, proceeding to CENTCOM or wherever she can find a vehicle and supplies. She'll then procure a real rope at the CENTCOM supply bunker. She'll tie the real rope to the sheet-rope and then tug seven times. That's the signal for us to pull it back in."

Earls pauses and rubs at his eyebrows again, the motion seeming to make his brain work. "Where was I?" he mumbles. "Oh yeah, she goes and gets a rope and some MREs and she starts sending those back. Did I say that? The MREs will be tied-in at the point where the two ropes join. From there, she keeps adding food and we keep reeling it in. She pulls the rope back, attaches more food and so on."

Everyone is silent for a long moment.

"Assuming it works," Min says, "it's not clear how long it would take her to transport the food from the CENTCOM bunker down here. It could be a multi-day process by the time she goes there and gets back down through the passage to the aquifer. She'd be making a lot of trips back and forth to feed everyone. We might just be delaying the inevitable. And risking her life to do it."

His words hang in the air like a death sentence handed down by a judge.

"Let's explore this," Fowler says carefully. "Let's imagine that instead of a rope she goes and gets more space suits and sends those through."

"How does that help us anymore than food?" Earls asks.

"We're assuming," Fowler says, "that the passage at the top of the aquifer is fairly daunting. That's why Oscar said that James thought we couldn't evacuate the entire population that way."

The mention of James's name focuses me.

Fowler continues: "That tells me that going up and down that pass is going to be a major issue for Corporal Stevens. It's going to take time. As Min pointed out, she'll only be able to carry so many MREs with her down the passage. But if she had more than one person to help her move the supplies back and forth, maybe we can actually get a reasonable supply line going."

Min shakes his head slowly. "If that was workable James would've done it. I'm sure he would have thought of this, and he ruled it out for reason."

"That was then—almost four days ago—when James made that call," Fowler says. "Our… circumstances have changed since then. We don't know if he would make a different decision given… where we are now."

Talking about James in the past tense, as if he's dead, as if he will never return, makes my eyes water. I don't trust my voice not to crack, so I stay silent.

"What if," Earls says, "we just follow the base plan: Stevens goes to CENTCOM, gets some food and a real rope, ties the rope to the sheet and we pull the rope back to us. Then we have an operational line. We distribute the food. I think, frankly, that will go a long way toward improving morale, which is, I'm sorry to say, just as dangerous as our food shortage."

Fowler nods. "And then we could pass notes back and forth with her, figure out if we want to requisition some space suits and send others out."

"Correct." The colonel seems to think for a minute. "Pulling someone through is a tall order. There are some vehicles at the CENTCOM bunker with winches on them. Maybe she could use one to pull people out."

"Maybe," Fowler mumbles. "We have to be very careful in the water tube. Any puncture to the person's suit or air supply could be deadly." He pauses. "But we can sort that out when the time comes. Look, it's risky, but I say we let Stevens have her shot."

No one agrees. No one disagrees. That passes for consensus now.

"Why don't you get her in here, Colonel?" Fowler asks.

Five minutes later, Corporal Angela Stevens is standing at attention, hands behind her back. She's a black woman, mid-twenties, I would guess. American. Slim. Eyes focused. She still has some fight left in her. I recognize her as one of the attendees at my *Birthright* sessions.

"Corporal," Colonel Earls begins, "your plan has been approved."

"Thank you, sir."

"What you're undertaking is extraordinarily risky," Fowler says. "I want you to understand that we believe this mission carries a low probability of success. You need to prepare yourself physically and mentally. You need to be very careful in that tunnel. We're going to build some sort of oxygen supply for you and we're going to give you as much time as we can, but keep in mind, we simply don't have any idea how long it will take you to clear the backup tube or the aquifer."

"I understand, sir. I'm willing to take the risk."

After a silent moment, Earls says, "Thank you, Corporal. That'll be all."

When she's gone, I can't help thinking about whether we are sending that young woman to her death. But I understand why she wants to try. I would too if I could—if I didn't have a permanent disability in one leg and a child growing inside me. I'm thankful for Angela Stevens's courage. She might be the best chance of survival for Allie and my unborn child.

In the sub-basement, the adults are gathered around, sitting on pillows and blankets, organized in three rings around me, their faces illuminated by the LED lanterns.

A few of the adults are lying on their sides, dozing. It's the darkness and, frankly, the lack of food. We're all weak. I don't bother trying to wake them for the session. In the outer ring, I spot Angela Stevens.

"Fear is our topic this afternoon. *The Birthright* posits that the human brain is not born as a blank slate. Every human mind is created with a sort of operating system. That system evolved over thousands of years for a simple purpose: to enable us to survive. Fear is one of the most powerful aspects of our mind's operating system. It's a tool. But like any tool, the mind's fear apparatus can be misused. It can malfunction."

I turn the page on the tablet.

"What is fear? Fear is what saves our life when we look up and realize a car is rushing toward us. Fear makes us get out of the way. Fear focuses us. Fear makes us think about the future and about the decisions we make today and how they might impact our lives. Fear is good. Fear is why our species has survived so long on this planet. But fear can malfunction."

I look around the group, at the dozens of faces, all eyes fixed on me. "'Fear is like an alarm. We—as owners of our own minds—must turn it off when it has served its purpose.'"

I take a deep breath. "Here's a personal example. As a kid, I was terrified of public speaking. In high school, in my junior year, I ran for class president. I thought the extracurricular might help put my college applications over the top."

I smile, remembering how awkward, type-A, over-ambitious I was at sixteen. "However, that year, they made candidates give their speeches in front of the whole class—as opposed to written speeches. I was terrified. Mortified. But I was even more scared of not getting into college—or backing out. For the days and weeks leading up to my speech, I barely ate. I slept poorly. And luckily for me, this happened around the same time I first read *The Birthright*... and it saved me."

I hold my hands up. "Okay, that's probably an exaggeration, but it did feel like the end of the world at the time. *The Birthright* gave me perspective. It helped me see my fear in a new way. Before, I didn't acknowledge that I was afraid. I saw my fear, in a way, as a sign of weakness.

I tried to hide it. I tried to ignore it. I tried to pretend to myself that I wasn't afraid.

"*The Birthright* says that's the last thing we should do. Fear is *normal*. Ignoring it is not. So I recognized my fear for what it was: my mind's way of making me prepare for my speech. You see, giving the speech wasn't just about winning the race for class president or getting into college. My mind knew that the stakes were higher than that. My speech, depending on how it went, would impact what my friends and teachers thought of me, my social standing, and perhaps even my overall happiness for the rest of my high school career. I wasn't consciously aware of that— but my subconscious was. The mind's subconscious is very powerful. And at this point in my life, fear—as a warning—was going off non-stop. It was no longer helpful. Instead of protecting me, my fear was hurting me."

I turn the page on the tablet and quickly finding the passages I've marked. "'If you don't master your fear, your fear will master you.'" I glance up at the group. "How do we master our fear?"

My brother-in law, David, answers softly. "Recognize it."

"That's right. That was my first step. I recognized that I was afraid to give the speech." I pause, scanning the group. "I think I speak for everyone in the Citadel when I say we're all afraid down here. Let's drag those fears out of the closet right now." I hold my hands out to the crowd, palms up. "Anyone. Who would like to start?"

Alex, James's brother, breaks the silence. "I'm afraid we won't get out of here."

"Good."

Fowler's wife, Marianne, speaks next, her voice quiet. "Both my children are adults now. I'm afraid they'll starve down here. And I'm even more afraid for the younger children."

Fowler puts his arm around her and pulls her to him. "I think that's a fear we all share."

To my surprise, Colonel Earls speaks next. "I'm afraid of missing something. Of not doing everything we can to get out of here."

I nod to him. "Thank you, Colonel."

Corporal Angela Stevens's voice rings out in the sub-basement, clear and strong in the darkness, just as it was in the kitchen. "I'm afraid of letting everyone down."

"I think we all are, Angela. We share these fears. And we shouldn't keep them bottled up, inside of us, running wild. We must recognize our fear—and see it for what it is: the mind's warning system. Once we've received the warning, fear has no place. Fear—if we let it—will focus our mind on the object of our fear, the event we dread or the outcome we can't bear. It will operate like a horror film on repeat, playing endlessly in our minds. We must recognize fear as an alarm and turn it off. That is how we master excess fear—seeing it as a broken alarm, a common event in everyone's life. With time and practice, you can learn to turn the alarm off."

The next morning, in the water treatment plant in the basement, Corporal Stevens is standing beside the small pool that accesses the backup tube. Her body is wrapped in aluminum foil, taped tightly to her. That will trap her body heat to keep her warm—and it makes her look like a superhero: Foil Woman. The foil is the best we can do to keep her warm. The water in the tube will be cold and it's going to be a lot colder in the aquifer. If she doesn't suffocate, or go into cardiac arrest, or simply stop from exhaustion, she could easily succumb to hypothermia.

The oxygen tanks are, frankly, pretty crude. Each is a bunch of plastic jugs that have been melted together to form an oxygen tank. There are three tanks, each with a hose connected to her suit, fitted with valves that she can turn on or off. The idea is that if one tank fails (or runs out of oxygen) she can switch to the other.

Fowler holds up a tablet with the map of the water tube and the aquifer.

"We're fairly certain you have enough oxygen to reach any point in the aquifer. It all depends on how fast you swim and how much oxygen you use. And whether the tanks stay intact. With that said, your best option is to instantly go for the top of the aquifer once you clear the backup tube. Find a break in the water surface and get oxygen and rest. Take your time and search for the passage to the surface from that home base."

"Understood, sir."

An army sergeant ties the makeshift rope around her waist: strips of bedsheet braided together and wound tight.

"Godspeed, Corporal," Colonel Earls says.

25

James

I wince when the blood hits my face.

"Hold tight, James," Izumi says.

She's got nerves of steel.

We're both dressed in army surgical gowns, gloves, and face masks.

The patient, a 26-year-old young man we recovered from a habitat about three hours ago, fidgets on the operating table in the CENTCOM bunker's med bay.

Izumi glances at the machine displaying his vitals and supplying the anesthesia.

Slowly she hands me the clamps and holds out her hand. "Suture."

Forty-five minutes later, the patient is out of surgery, and I'm scrubbing my hands.

"I think he's going to make it," Izumi says, standing beside me, washing her hands at the silver-metal trough. "We'll probably know by tomorrow morning."

We step out of the operating room, shuffle through the med bay and out into the open area of the bunker, which we've transformed into a hospital. Rows of folding cots cover half of the floor. We removed all of the vehicles except one troop carrier and parked them right outside the bunker to make room. White sheets hang on ropes between the cots, adding a modicum of privacy. Roughly twenty patients are awake and crying. Their sobs are gut-wrenching, but for now, we've done all we can for them. We've treated their wounds and given them painkillers for the ache in their body. There's not much we can do for the hurt they feel in their hearts for the loved ones they've lost. That pain isn't going away, at least not anytime soon.

We've been running rescue operations for about a week now. Malnutrition, lacerations, and broken bones are the most common injuries. There's no shortage of concussions among the survivors. But I think most are going to make it.

Forty-two survivors. That is the number of lives we've saved.

In the last week, we've pulled a total of fifty-three people from the ruins of Camp Seven. Eleven of those succumbed to their injuries. Five of the survivors were healthy enough to help us. They've been searching the wreckage, and they've been a big help. One in particular, an army captain named Tara Brightwell, has drastically increased our efficiency. She's British, a woman of few words, but she makes every one count. She's directing the rescue operations now—and doing it better than I can.

Grigory and Harry have been digging at the asteroid impact site. Day and night, they've been operating the large excavator and bulldozer we found here in the CENTCOM bunker, pushing the machines to their limits. Even with the excavator's hydraulic hammer, it's slow going. The earth below the impact crater is packed tight—and some of it was rock long before the asteroid hit.

Without Oscar, we can't make it back to the Citadel. Digging is our best hope of reaching the people in the Citadel, but with each passing day, I grow more nervous about our prospects of success.

Izumi and I have spent our time caring for the survivors. In the moments in between, I've stewed over the decision of whether to accept Arthur's help. In the back of my mind, constantly, is the thought that Emma and Allie are slowly starving to death—and that Emma is pregnant. Time is running out.

Nine days. They have nine days of food left. Can we reach them in time?

If we can't, there's only one alternative: Arthur's deal. But I fear that accepting his offer could kill us all, that his gesture is a ruse, a lie to gain access to robotics components he'll use to slaughter us. Is that his plan? To kill everyone in the AU first, then move around the world? It's more than possible that the grid used asteroids as a first strike, knowing it could take control of Oscar to finish off the last survivors.

But what if I'm wrong? What if we can't dig down to the Citadel in time? What if Arthur is our only chance of getting those people out of the Citadel, including my daughter, wife, and unborn child? What if my delaying is killing people in the Citadel right now? I wish I had some idea of what's happening down there.

It's an impossible decision to make, one that could save us or doom us. And I have to decide soon. Time. That is the currency of our existence now. We're spending it, and we won't get more.

I've also considered the black goo that took over Oscar's body by inserting Arthur's program. I'm assuming it's no threat to humans, but I've put everyone on alert—and instructed them to keep it off any mechanical equipment. That was a weird conversation. Some of the rescue team members probably think I'm losing it.

In the CENTCOM bunker's small situation room, two survivors sit at a long table. They can't work out in the field—both have broken legs—but they've been a big help here with coordinating our teams.

A slender young woman with strawberry-blonde hair, who I believe was in Emma's current class, holds the handset of an army radio.

"I repeat, this is Camp Seven. We're searching for survivors. If you read me, please respond."

The radios have a limited range, but if any helicopters or vehicles are passing by, they might hear us.

She waits, then picks up the satellite phone and checks it. It's unlikely we'll get a response, but we have to try.

I point to the radio handset. "You mind?"

"No. Please," she says, handing it to me.

"Harry, can you give us a status update?"

"Hey, James, status is about the same. It's really slow."

"Is the hydraulic hammer helping?"

"A little."

The door to the situation room lies open, and nearby, I hear a rhythmic tapping coming from the only troop carrier left in the bunker. We kept it down here for one reason: to serve as a prison for Arthur.

I listen for a moment, parsing the tapping. It's Morse code. Two four-letter words: tick tock.

I set the radio down and walk over to the troop carrier and open the rear door. It only cracks a few inches—the chain holding it shut ensures it can't open enough for Arthur to slip out. He shuffles over to the opening and peers down at me.

"They're running out of time, James." He pauses. "You can't save them with the excavator. In fact, what you're doing right now could destabilize the Citadel. Probably do more harm than good. You might even kill someone. Let me help you."

"How would you help us? I'm not sending you back to the Citadel. For all I know, you could slaughter everyone down there. I'm not letting you near my family."

"Think about it, James. I am the most advanced entity you will ever encounter. I have the collective knowledge of millions of years of civilization. I've witnessed inventions you can't even imagine, mastered sciences and technologies that would seem like magic to you. I could reach that bunker a hundred different ways."

"Name one."

"We don't have time for a future robotics seminar. Suffice it to say that from the primitive items here in this CENTCOM facility I could fashion a machine that would bore down to the Citadel and provide an escape passage. Easily. Within two days. I would stay above ground, of course, so that you can keep a close eye on me." He smiles condescendingly.

"The rock—"

"Is too hard below the impact crater. Yes, I know that.

It's almost as hard as that thick skull of yours." Arthur pauses to let the insult dig in. "I wouldn't bore at the impact crater," he continues. "I'd move over to a point above the backup water tube, drill down to it, and seal off the tube toward the aquifer."

"Even if you did, the tube would still be filled with water all the way to the Citadel's basement."

"Simple. The boring machine would evaporate it. We're the grid, James. We can boil water."

"How do I know you won't just build a machine that kills all of us? That would accomplish your conservation of energy, wouldn't it?"

"A fair point. But consider this: if I were going to do that, I would've started the minute I took over Oscar's body. I would've just left that habitat and never said a word to you. Even if I kill everyone in Camp Seven and start making my way around the world, some always survive. Underground. Or below the sea. Or somewhere else. It happens in ninety-seven point six percent of cases. And, statistically speaking, the likelihood is that someone will crawl out sooner or later and launch a nuke or two at my solar cells, and I'll be playing exterminator again. I meant what I said: I'll help you leave this planet if you agree to my terms."

He stares at me. "Consider the fact that I voluntarily stepped into this troop carrier for you to imprison me when I could've killed you, Grigory, and Izumi, and all of your survivors. Enough talk, James. Agree to my terms, or I will kill every last human on this planet."

I slam the door closed. I'm tired of him threatening us. Tired of him manipulating me.

"They're starving, James!" he shouts through the door. "Stop being a fool."

The radio on the control table beeps once, and a man's voice sounds over the line: Wyatt, one of the crew searching for trapped survivors. "Base, team one, we've got another survivor. She's lost a lot of blood. ETA five minutes."

Izumi grabs the radio. "We'll be ready."

There's no way to separate the sound from the survivors; they hear every word.

Across the sheet-separated cubicles, some of the survivors sit up, anxious to see someone else coming in, probably hoping it's someone they know, their mother, father, brother, sister, or friend. For them, waiting for the survivor to arrive must be excruciating. It's been like this for days, a roller coaster of hope and disappointment, mixed with the joy that one more person has survived this.

I scrub my hands again, preparing for the patient to arrive, Arthur's words haunting my thoughts.

Izumi's hands move like a flash over the woman's leg wound. But we're too late. She's lost too much blood. The screen next to the gurney flashes red as the pulse rate ticks down to zero.

Ten minutes after the patient flatlines, Izumi is still working.

"It's over, Izumi."

She ignores me for another five minutes. Then she takes her gloves off with a snap, drops them, and walks over to the wall and presses her back into it and slides down to the floor. She pulls her legs to her chest and just stares straight ahead, eyes glassy, face looking older and more tired than I've ever seen her.

"Get some rest, Izumi. I'll finish up."

She rises and staggers out of the operating room, over to the situation room, where Wyatt and Ricardo are chewing on protein bars, chasing it with bottled water.

I watch through the window. They can tell from her face that we lost the patient. From past experience, I know these guys will be asking themselves whether things could have turned out differently if they had only dug a little faster or driven a little faster.

Izumi says the words we've been saying a lot over the past couple of days: "There was nothing we could do for her. Even if you had gotten here sooner."

We're all running out of time. I wonder if we're not like this patient—if it's already too late for us.

26

Emma

We have five days left.

Some of the adults don't leave the bunk rooms now.

Children are scared.

I'm scared.

At our meeting in the kitchen this morning, Fowler simply said, "Any updates?"

No one said a word. And then we just left and went back to doing what we were doing. For me, that's nothing.

I'm trying, and failing, not to think about the facts of our situation. And especially not about Angela Stevens.

About four hours after she entered the water tube, Stevens gave the five tugs on the line that signaled that she had made it to the aquifer.

The line has been slack since. She never signaled that she had made it to the top of the aquifer.

I've held out hope that maybe the line got severed somehow. Or perhaps she had to disconnect it to reach the passage to the surface.

I can't stop thinking about her. About her courage and sacrifice.

That always makes me think of James, and I wonder where he is, and why he hasn't returned.

In the sub-basement, it's not just Angela Stevens who's absent from the group. Many of the adults have stopped coming. Today's session is about faith—the power of it. And its dark side.

That's what we're missing: faith. Belief that things will turn around. I had hoped this group and these sessions would give that to people. It did—for a time. But that time has passed. We need something else now.

When the session is over and everyone is filing out, I get Fowler's attention and ask him to stay behind.

"What's up?" he asks, his voice soft in the dark, cavernous space. The LED lights shine up to the low ceiling all around us, the concrete pillar casting shadows.

"They're losing hope."

Fowler's face is gaunt, his forehead more creased than when he arrived here, making him look older. He breaks eye contact and simply nods. "I know."

"We need to do something."

"What can we do, Emma?"

"We can dig."

"Dig?"

"In the emergency tunnel. It's a long shot, but who knows, maybe we can get out. And if we do, we can help James and the rest of his team."

"Digging entails physical exertion. We're all half zombies."

"There are still enough of us healthy enough to dig. I don't know if there will be in a week. Which is all the more reason to do it. These people need something to believe in. They need to know there's a chance—that we're doing something that could work."

He stares into the darkness, not making eye contact.

"Lawrence."

His eyes snap back to me, as if realizing I'm still here. "Yeah. Okay. I'll... talk to Earls."

I place a hand on his arm. "I'll do it, Lawrence. Just get some rest. I'll take care of this."

I feel like a coal miner.

Eleven of us—nine army soldiers, Min, and I—are cramped in the escape tunnel, digging, our headlamps lighting our way.

It was damp and cold when we started this afternoon. It's like a sauna now.

The soldiers take turns digging. Three of them excavate and pass the rock away from the cave-in while the others rest. In the cleared sections, Min and I try to protect the passage from falling rock. We're using tables from the mess hall, elevating them to the tunnel ceiling to keep debris from the breaches from falling down.

We're making progress, but not enough. I sense it. But what else can we do?

At the end of the day, I shower the dirt and grime off my body, my last bit of strength washing down the drain with it.

I probably shouldn't be helping in the tunnels. I should be resting—for the baby's sake. But if we don't get out of here, it won't matter.

*

Each day, our digging slows down. But we keep going. The makeshift pickaxes and shovels beat out an anthem, clinking away, unsynchronized, the sound of our last desperate attempt to escape.

I sit in the dark tunnel, sweat dripping from my hair, wishing that something, anything would simply go our way. That something would turn around. The clinking at the end of the tunnel stops. I hear it then: rumbling. The ground beneath me shakes.

My mind is too exhausted to understand what it is at first. Comprehension comes slowly, like a muddy pool of water slowly clearing, revealing what's at the bottom.

Soot and dust from the ceiling pour out from around the tables.

It's an earthquake.

Or another asteroid strike.

Voices call out in the tunnel. I push up, but my legs fail me. They've gone to sleep. I grab the makeshift cane I fashioned from a table leg and finally get to my feet.

The metal tunnel walls groan like a beast being tortured as it twists and cracks.

At the end of the passage, the headlamps go out.

Why?

Why would they go out?

Near me, the metal pipe screeches and splits open, spewing pieces of rock down on one of the soldiers, cracking his lamp.

Yes. *That's why they're going out—they're being crushed.*

I look up just in time to see the metal above me parting, rock falling down on me.

27

James

The sun is setting when I reach the crater. I stand at the precipice and stare at the massive excavator and bulldozer and the piles of rocks beside them, like miniature mountains in the middle of a dustbowl.

We'll never make it to the Citadel. Arthur is right about that. The bunker is too far below us, and the earth between us and it simply too hard to excavate.

I know it, but in the back of my mind is the knowledge that if I make the wrong call, it's not just us here in the Atlantic Union that will perish. It's everyone. The entire human race. It's an impossible decision to make.

From the excavator's cab, Harry spots me. His voice calls over the radio, "James. That you?"

"It's me."

"Everything okay?"

"Sure. Just checking on you guys. Need anything?"

"Yeah, any way we can get cable TV in this thing?"

I can't help but smile. "I'll add it to the list."

"Good. And we're getting paid overtime, right?"

"Plus hazard pay. How's the rock? Getting any easier?"

"Not really."

There's only one decision to make: we'll dig until we're out of time. Then, if I have to, I'll take Arthur's deal.

171

28

Emma

I awake to a bright light shining down and pain pounding in my head. It's not just my head. My whole body aches. Every time I move, waves of hurt wash over me.

I squint, trying to blot out the light.

"Emma," a soft voice says.

A hand grips my arm, setting off a sharp pain. I grit my teeth and reel away.

"Oh. I'm sorry."

I crack my eyelids, peeking against the blinding light.

Madison peers down at me, tears streaking down her face. Her cheekbones protrude, eyes are sunken, as if her skull is too big for her body. I haven't seen her this gaunt since James and I left for Ceres. My heart breaks all over again.

"How long..." I croak.

"It doesn't matter," Madison says.

The aching behind my eyes recedes enough for me to look around the room. It's the small infirmary off the bathrooms. Curtains are pulled across the other bays. Who's in there?

The army soldiers that were trying to clear the escape tunnel? Others?

Madison leaves and returns with an MRE, already heated.

"I don't want it."

"Emma, you have to."

She stares at me, an expression telling me this is not negotiable.

I dig into the meal, trying and failing to chew slowly, feeling grateful for the food and guilty that someone else isn't eating it, the two emotions pulling me apart. I stop chewing long enough to swallow a painkiller and chase it with water. There are two more pills on the metal tray, but I leave them there. I want a clear head.

"Where's Allie? Is she—"

"She's fine. A little worried. Confused. All the kids are." Madison touches my arm lightly. "I'll go get her."

The next few minutes stretch on like hours. I can't wait to see my daughter, and I'm terrified to see her. If she's as thin as Madison, I know I won't be able to hold it together. But I have to, for her sake. If I'm strong, it will give her strength. If she senses the fear in me, she'll be terrified.

I sit up in the bed, run a hand through my hair, and take a deep breath. The curtain flies back and Allie bounds toward the bed, reaching up for me, clawing at the sheets, trying and failing to climb up. I twist, holding my hands out. Shockwaves of pain overtake me. I close my eyes and suddenly Allie is in the bed, throwing her arms around me, head buried in my chest.

Against my will, a tear wells in my eye, and falls into her hair. She's okay. My daughter is healthy. Slightly skinnier than she was the day we came to the Citadel, about like she might look after recovering from a stomach bug. But she's fine, and knowing that overwhelms me for a brief moment.

My next thought is for the child growing inside of me. Did the fetus survive the cave-in? And my malnutrition? I need to find a health analyzer and run a pregnancy test. I have to know if my unborn child is healthy—even if the truth crushes me harder than the stone in the tunnel.

Allie nearly whines her question: "Mommy, why gone?"

"I was at work, sweetie. I'm sorry I've been gone."

"Sick?"

She's more perceptive than I give her credit for. "No, darling. I just had a boo-boo. I'm fine."

"Go home?"

"We will."

"Now."

"Soon, sweetie. We'll go home soon."

Allie settles into the bed beside me, warm as a heater, clinging to me, perhaps afraid I'll disappear again.

Madison departs when Alex and Abby arrive. They're skinny too, each forcing a smile like Madison, dodging my questions about what's happened while I was unconscious.

Min visits next, his head bandaged, arm in a sling. I glance down, verifying that Allie is sleeping soundly. It's either her naptime or bedtime.

"What happened?" I whisper. "An earthquake?"

"Maybe. But it felt more localized."

"Another asteroid impact?"

"No. Or probably not anything in close proximity. It was probably the ground under the impact crater settling." He pauses a moment. "I saw you fall, tried to get there as quick as I could."

"Thanks, Min."

Fowler stops by next, concern on his face, his skin ashen.

"Any word from James?" I whisper.

Fowler's gaze drifts to the floor as he shakes his head.

"Maybe the passage out of the aquifer collapsed," I offer, unsure what to say, fear welling inside of me.

"Maybe. It would explain why Oscar hasn't returned. Even if something has happened to James and his team, Oscar should have been back."

I can feel my mind spinning out of control as I think about our situation, about the fact that James hasn't returned and that we are truly out of options down here. Fowler seems to read my expression.

"Remember your lesson from a few days ago, Emma. Recognize your fear. Master it, or it will master you."

I awake before Allie, and for a while, I just lie there, hoping she'll sleep longer.

Finally, she stirs, reaching a small hand up to her eyelids and rubbing them. She looks around confused, as if she were expecting to be home again. But she'll never be home again. That home is gone.

"Da?"

"He's coming."

"When?"

"Soon. Soon, sweetie." I squeeze her tight, hoping it's true. "Now, you need to go to breakfast. Mommy has to stay here and rest."

My stomach feels as if it's turning in on itself, a deep pang of hunger boring out from the inside. I almost feel nauseous. And that reminds me of the nausea I felt before the asteroids, the nausea that has been absent since. Is it because of the stress? Or has the pregnancy ended?

I search the rolling table by my bed, but there's no health analyzer on it.

"Hey," I call out, but no one comes. I try to sit up. Sharp pains greet me, worse than the day before.

I slump back to the bed and soon my vision blurs and sleep overtakes me, like a heavy blanket being pulled over across my body, too heavy to fight.

I sleep for hours at a time, the lights low in the infirmary, my stomach turning when I wake, aches droning across my body.

When I wake the next time, Madison is by the bedside again, an MRE waiting. She activates the heating element on the plastic carton.

I stare at it, feeling conflicted.

"Emma…"

"I know. I have to." I close my eyes, feeling wiped out. "Can you get me a health analyzer?"

I glance down at my stomach.

Madison's face goes slack. "Of course. I'll be right back."

I take a pain pill and try and fail to take my time with the meal. It's chicken and rice with vegetables. When you're this hungry, everything is a five-star meal.

I wonder if the pain pills are interfering with the pregnancy. The thought makes me instantly regret taking it. Slowly I feel the medicine working, dampening the low-grade ache throughout my body. And that just makes me worry even more.

Madison returns with the health analyzer, and I touch it to my finger and wait as it extracts the drops of blood and runs its tests.

"Have you—" she starts but breaks off.

"Felt nauseous? No."

I stare at the screen and shake the health analyzer as if that will speed up the result.

I'm suddenly aware of everything going on around me: footsteps in the hall, the survivors shuffling to and from the mess hall. Someone moaning in one of the other med bays, a male voice assuring the man that everything will be all right.

The results appear on the tiny LCD screen and I scroll through the routine labs, past the CBC and other blood panels, to the simple test at the end.

Pregnant: Yes

I swallow hard as my eyes fill with tears. For a moment, Madison looks stricken. I smile and nod. "It's okay. It's fine."

She lunges forward and hugs me, the touch setting off pain across my battered body. But I don't care. My baby is still alive. Right now, that's all that matters.

★

Time slips by in periods of sleep and hazy wakefulness. I never feel rested or satiated by the small meals. I'm constantly weak and tired. And most of all, I'm afraid for myself and for Allie and for the fetus inside of me. I know that fear is running wild—and I know that there's nothing that I can do except to recognize that fear and tell myself that it can't help me now. It's served its purpose. Now I have to disregard it and focus on the task at hand, which is staying strong for Allie.

But that's easier said than done. It's easier to read those passages in the *Birthright* and say they're true and say you'll control your fear than it is to actually do it.

Still, I try. I put up a façade for Allie's sake because, most of all, I want to protect her from knowing how desperate our situation is.

There's little activity in the halls now. No one's working in the tunnels. I think everyone is bedding down, waiting, as if we are all hibernating down here, trying to get through a long, deadly winter we all hope will end.

29

James

Once again, I stand on the rim of the impact crater, taking in the giant bowl in the desert. Near the center point, Grigory and Harry are working, excavating deeper, racing the clock.

The sound of the excavator hammering the rock echoes up from the crater until Harry pauses and attaches the bucket and thumb to the end of the excavator's arm. Methodically, he lifts the broken rock and earth out of the hole. Grigory, driving the bulldozer, pushes the broken earth to the edge of the donut-shaped mountain around the hole. They've hammered and dug and used every shred of energy the solar panels can soak up from the dimming sun, which is setting on the horizon now. It's just not enough.

Our time is up.

There's only one thing to do now.

Back at CENTCOM, I march into the situation room, where Captain Brightwell's British accent is ringing over the radio.

"Team four, sitrep."

"Almost done, Captain."

"What did you find?"

"A few more bottles of… hold on, I can't pronounce—"

"Never mind the medicine's name. Just bring it in. And get to your next habitat. We're losing daylight fast and tonight's going to be even colder than last night."

There are no more survivors in the wreckage. The search has turned to the things we need, that we can't make anymore of: medicine and complex electronics. We're gathering food too.

Brightwell, reading my solemn expression, says, "What happened?"

"It's time."

Instinctively, her hand goes to the sidearm on her belt. Her right arm is still bandaged and her left leg is in a brace, but I wager that she's still the most lethal individual on the surface here in Camp Seven. She'll have to be very fast if Arthur betrays us. I hope we won't have to find whether she's fast enough.

"Have you told Grigory?"

"No," I mumble. I'm dreading the task.

"Will he have an issue with it?"

"Yes, he will have a problem with it." My voice sounds as tired as I feel. "But I don't think he's going to do anything, at least not until we get everyone out of the Citadel. After that, who knows?"

"We could assign him to rescue ops here in the camp. Separate him from Arthur."

"That's a good idea."

"I'll have someone in his rescue team keep an eye on him."

"Also a good idea. We'll also need a guard detail for Arthur."

"I'm the only active military here topside. We've got three reservists among the survivors. Two are out searching and one has a pretty bad leg injury. But he could serve guard. Want me to recall the other two?"

"Please."

Brightwell gives the order over the radio, then quietly says to me, "You sure about this?"

I plop down in one of the chairs at the long conference table and rub my face. "I'm sure we don't have another option. We're out of time."

After a silent moment, I ask, "Is this what it was like during the war? When the AU was fighting for the last habitable zones?"

Brightwell's face goes slack and she breaks eye contact. "There wasn't much down time. Not much discussion, at least not at my level. Day and night, I just tried to keep everyone in my company alive."

"Company?"

She eyes me, surprised. "The AU Army is organized roughly like the old US Army. I had four platoons in my company. My company was one of four in the battalion, which was part of a regiment, which was part of a division and so on."

"Oh, got it. Never knew how the army was organized."

"Well, it's all history now. The AU probably can't field a single battalion at this point."

"A lot of things are about to change."

When the two reservists arrive, I lead them and Brightwell to the troop carrier. They form a semicircle around the rear, guns held at the ready. Across the bunker, voices die down. Whispers take their place, starting near us and sweeping across the open-air room like a wave rolling through.

I let the unlocked chain fall loudly to the floor as I swing the doors open wide. Arthur walks to the precipice, an arrogant smile on his face. An expression of triumph that sickens me.

"I take it we have a deal?"

"We'll be watching you."

"I expected nothing less." He pauses, the smile widening. "I'd like to take this opportunity to reiterate the terms of our agreement."

"Go on," I growl, the words barely audible.

"No aggression toward the harvester. If *anyone* on this little watery rock takes offensive action, the harvester will strike. Remember, he can see you from where he is. Our telescopes are far superior to yours."

"Okay."

"The deal is that when the sun sets for the last time on Earth, there will be no *living* humans on this planet. Do you understand the implications of what I'm saying, James?"

Until now, I've been so focused on the problem at hand—the Citadel—that I hadn't actually considered the full ramifications of the deal. What he's saying is that when the sun sets, every human must either be off the planet—or they have to be dead. What he's saying is that even with his deal, another war might be waiting for us. A civil war among the last survivors.

"How many survived the asteroids?" I ask.

Arthur shrugs theatrically. "I have no idea. I arrived at the same time as the asteroids, remember?"

"You don't have active communication with the harvester?"

He scoffs. "Of course not. That would be a waste of energy—and that's not something we do, James. I was sent down with a simple directive."

"Our surrender."

He glances up at the ceiling, as if pondering whether to tell me a secret. "Well, not exactly."

"What exactly was your directive?"

"To eliminate any threats remaining after the asteroid strike."

Behind me, Brightwell and the reservists stir, as if getting ready for a fight.

"Relax," Arthur says nonchalantly. "In this case, helping you leave is the most efficient method of completing my mission."

It's all an algorithm to them. There truly is no emotion behind the grid, no consideration of us as a people. Our exodus from Earth is the most efficient way to eliminate us as a threat. That is, if we believe what Arthur is saying. That's a big if.

"Do you understand the terms of our deal?" Arthur asks, tone bordering on disinterest.

I stare at the concrete floor, biting my words off. "Yes. We accept."

"Wonderful," Arthur says with mock enthusiasm.

A silent moment passes. Then I look up at the representative of our enemy, now our conqueror, and I swallow every bit of pride I have, because I have to, because the lives of my wife and child are on the line, and I ask, "What can I do to help you?"

"You never cease to amaze, James. It turns out I could use your help. And Harry's." He raises his eyebrows. "You're now officially an assistant to the grid. Let's get started."

For the next thirty-two hours, I barely sleep. Harry and I assist Arthur in building the excavation drone from the parts in the CENTCOM bunker and what we've scavenged throughout the camp. The device isn't pretty; it's like a giant beetle, round, about five feet in diameter with a domed cover made from white habitat tiles. It's hard to believe it will bore into the ground and make its way to the backup water tube. But, before the grid arrived, it was hard to believe a device could travel through the galaxy harvesting the output of stars. Their technology is truly on a level far above our own.

The excavation drone is just big enough for one large person. Two kids easily. Its underside is a mix of lasers, jagged teeth that can extend out to carve a larger diameter shaft, and a series of retractable wheels that will be used once it reaches the Citadel.

If it reaches the Citadel.

It's midday when we lower the device to the desert ground beside the impact crater and watch it burrow and disappear. At the control station set up inside a troop carrier, Arthur directs the device as Harry and I watch the video feed. Brightwell and her two reservists stand at the ready, but Arthur has ignored them so far, focusing only on the work. He's even dropped the mocking tone. Perhaps he reasoned that it was no longer a good use of energy.

Izumi is the first to board the drone and go down to the Citadel. I follow. I'm dead tired when I rise from the drone's carrier compartment and step out into the water treatment plant in the sub-basement.

Still, my heart is racing. It worked. But it's not over yet. Could Arthur have waited for this moment to betray us? It's possible. The thought bounces around in my mind as I watch the drone disappear, on its way back to the surface. The plan is to load it with food this time.

The backup water tube is gone, a much larger horizontal shaft drilled in its place. The treatment plant is a mess of mud, dust, dirt, and rock. The water from the tank must have mixed with the dirt.

When the drone returns, it simply stops on the pile of rock and dirt, waiting. For all I know, it could explode right now and seal this tube and, with it, our fate. We would die down here.

It would be an efficient method of killing us. It feels like something the grid would do. Harry and Grigory are above. They would fight to get us out, but I doubt it would do any good. Our future is in Arthur's hands now. I stare at the drone, knowing this is a moment of truth. Has my gamble doomed us?

30

Emma

The sound of shouting and footsteps wakes me. It's like a stampede in the hall, but the lights are still low, the infirmary mostly in darkness and shadow. Allie stirs at my side, looking up at me.

"Mommy, what's dat?"

"I don't know, sweetie. You have to stay here with me."

"Wanna see."

"No. You can't." I pull her tight to me and strain to hear what's happening. I can't make out the words.

Is it a fight for the last meals?

Something worse?

The running stops; the voices die down. I wait, listening for clues about what's going on. The silence is somehow more unnerving.

A figure emerges in the doorway to the infirmary, dressed in army fatigues, a headlamp on his forehead. The beam of light rakes across the med bays like a lighthouse.

The figure takes a step toward me and then another and another, urgently, pushing past the white curtain that partially encloses my bay, his headlamp shining directly in my eyes. Based on the build, I think it's a man. He reaches out and grabs Allie, and I lunge forward, my rail-thin arms grabbing hold of his arms, fingernails digging into him.

"Da!" Allie yells out as she throws her arms around him.

"James?"

"I'm here."

Relief washes over me, as if his words are healing me. The ache in my body disappears. The hunger vanishes.

I hold a hand up and blot out the headlamp.

"Oh. Sorry," he mumbles. His eyes move over me, pain and concern behind them. "What happened, Emma? Are you okay?"

"I'm fine."

"Tell me what happened."

"It doesn't matter now. Just tell me we're getting out of here."

"We're getting out of here. Right now."

31

James

My daughter has never felt so small and fragile in my arms. She's thin, eyes slightly sunken, but she's alive. That's all that matters.

I carry her out of the infirmary and through the hall. The Citadel is swarming with people now, a mix of survivors from the surface and the few AU troops down here that seem to still have some strength.

Izumi has set up a makeshift hospital in the mess hall. She's giving everyone a cursory exam, making sure they don't need immediate treatment.

In the basement, at the tank in the water treatment plant, I lean over and gently lower Allie into the waiting drone.

She clings to me, fingernails digging into my arms.

"Da!" she screams. "Da!"

"It's okay. It's okay, sweetie," I whisper as I bring her back to my chest. She's sobbing now.

"Don't leave."

"I'm not, darling. I'm right behind you."

"Don't leave!"

"This is going to be fun. You're going to take a ride in this car. It's sort of like our car. Just cooler." I turn so she can see it. "Check it out. I helped build it."

"Mom..."

"Mom's right behind you too. Now be brave and get inside, okay? A lot of people are waiting. Can you do that?"

The crying subsides but she's shaking as I lower her into the device, lip quivering as she stares up at me, an unspoken accusation on her face: *How could you, Da?*

I can't take it. I know I should stay down here and help Izumi, but I just can't. My heart can't take putting my starving, frightened daughter in this contraption alone. I step into the drone, placing Allie in my lap. "Okay. Let's go."

She's still shaking. "Da... no."

"It's okay," I whisper. I reach forward and tap the return button on the inside of the drone. I hug her tight as the drone jerks into motion and rolls into the shaft.

The next day, I'm standing in the situation room in the CENTCOM bunker, leaning against the door frame, trying to wrap my head around our situation.

The bunker is packed with people lying on cots and piles of blankets on the floor. Space heaters dot the large open space beating back the cold that presses in harder each second of every day. Most of the children are watching tablets. The adults are simply resting and eating, trying to recover from their time in the Citadel.

We're all together now. That's the good news. But I fear the true challenge has just begun. We have problems big and small. Some tug at my mind, unsolvable; others weigh on my heart. Most notably, the fact that there are more kids than adults here. Many of these kids have lost their parents. There's nothing I can do about that. Ever. We'll have to start assigning foster families soon. For now, the kids without families are grouped by age and assigned to a chaperone. Their section of the bunker looks like a massive sleepover, kids snuggled in next to each other, some playing, others crying, not many sleeping.

As I stare at those kids, I turn a single question over in my mind: *How can I save them?*

I agreed to Arthur's deal, but I'd break my word in a second if it would save every one of them. Our species is truly at a fork in the road: we leave Earth or we stay. But is staying a viable option when no solar output is reaching Earth?

To me, the most glaring challenge is food. Power is second on my mind and the two are linked.

Before the impact, Camp Seven was powered by solar panels on top of the habitats—habitats that now lie in ruins, their solar panels shattered and useless. For the moment, we've taken the panels from the CENTCOM bunker and spread them across the ground above. They're collecting energy, and it's enough for now, but I expect solar output to keep falling, and with it, our power supply—and with that, our source of heat. Without power, we freeze to death. Without power, we also can't grow food.

I've considered other methods of generating power. Geothermal is the best choice, but we don't have the equipment required to build a plant. Or the time.

Wind is my next choice. We could cobble together some mills and likely generate the power we need. The problem is obvious: the ever-worsening winter is going to drastically change the global climate. Our windmills could be buried in ice and even if they aren't, wind patterns could be significantly altered. I don't have the expertise to even begin to predict what will happen.

That leaves water power: tidal, wave, and hydroelectric. Each would take significant effort to build. It also carries the same risk as wind: the changing planet might render our power generation useless. I expect the seas to recede. Lakes to freeze. And rivers to run dry or change course. Placing the equipment would be a roll of the dice.

Again, without power, we can't stay warm and we can't grow food. We can solve the food problem in the short term. We can hunt—some animals survived the Long Winter, but they will be less lucky this time. In short, they'll be gone soon. Sea life is probably our most reliable food source, but this time, the Long Winter will claim them too.

Even if I could solve the power issue, and even if we manage to build some kind of self-sustaining colony underground, we'd always be vulnerable to the harvester. I take him at his word: if we're still on Earth when the last sunset occurs, he'll strike. He could wipe us from the planet with ease.

As I see it, we have a single option: leave Earth.

Survival down that path is far from certain. Arthur could double-cross us. Frankly, I rather expect it. And we might not even make it off Earth before the Long Winter overtakes us.

I also wonder if I can even convince the world to accept the plan. Leaving Earth? I'm sure some will never agree to it. Maybe even some of the leadership.

Another risk exists no matter what path we take. Our population. We've taken a count. There are 174 survivors from Camp Seven. Yesterday, when we'd finished evacuating the Citadel, I asked Izumi if that was a large enough genetic pool to restart the human race. Her answer was short and vague and chilling: "Not comfortably. Maybe not at all."

So that problem is where I've started. To put it simply: we need more people. We need to reunite the human race.

I've added a solar panel to the top of the surveillance drones, enabling them to recharge while they fly. They'll be able to fly longer-range missions to look for life signs in the other camps. They'll also land periodically and unload small radios and wireless data repeaters. That will enable us to establish a daisy-chain voice and data network. I considered the fact that Arthur might be able to access the wireless data network, but for now, it's only connected to the small drones. They don't have any offensive capability. Having real-time video is essential, and in my view, worth the risk. I hope I'm right.

I've dispatched drones to the other fifteen camps of the Atlantic Union. Survivors are our top priority, but we're also looking for food and solar panels. Camp Seven lies at the center of the Atlantic Union; the other camps spread out in every direction. The drones will have to fly slower to conserve energy. They may even have to land to recharge. In any event, they should reach the nearest camps tomorrow, and the farthest ones the following day. We'll get video and infrared readings as well as radio traffic. That data will be a verdict on our survival.

It's growing colder outside by the day. Snow is starting to pile up, covering the heaps of rubble, transforming them into rolling white dunes that hide the horror of what happened here.

The leadership team hasn't met since we evacuated the bunker. The truth is, Fowler, Emma, Charlotte, and Min need time to recover from their malnutrition and injuries. All of us need time to think through Arthur's ultimatum and what to do now. It's the biggest decision the human race has ever made.

Time. That's the other precious resource we're running out of. Whatever path we choose, we must hurry now.

I exit the situation room and begin snaking through the sea of cubicles covering the bunker's open space. The rope lines and bedsheet dividers are closed now, the sounds and smells suffocating, nearly two hundred people packed in a space about the size of a high school gymnasium.

I stop outside Alex and Abby's cubicle. My nephew Jack is watching a tablet, holding it up so his sister can see, sharing the headphones, one earbud in each of their ears.

I duck past the sheet and stop when I realize Alex is asleep. Abby is sitting up, clutching a blanket to her chest. She puts a hand to Alex's arm and shakes it. "Alex."

"It's okay," I whisper, but my brother's eyes open instantly, and he sits up.

"Hi," he says quietly.

"How are you guys doing?"

"Just glad to be out of that bunker." Alex glances theatrically. "And... in this bunker."

I laugh quietly. "This bunker is a lot easier to get out of."

"Yeah. I like that part." Alex motions to Jack and Sarah. "Should they be using their tablets? I figure we're low on power with the habitats gone."

"We're okay. Right now, we can generate more power than we can store, so it's use it or lose it."

"For the moment."

"Correct."

"What can I do to help?"

I study my brother's slender face, sunken eyes, and skinny arms. "For the moment, just get better."

"Then what? Are we…"

"We're working on a plan. Hopefully we'll be going out to search for survivors in the other camps."

He nods, the words seeming to encourage him. "Good."

In my own cubicle, I find Allie sleeping, and Emma sitting up, staring at a tablet, a pile of empty MRE cartons and bags lying in a pile, all scraped clean.

I lie down and snuggle close to Allie. It's the best feeling in the world. A few days before, I thought I'd never hold her again. It's funny how we're most thankful for the things we almost lose.

"What're you looking at?" I whisper.

"Ship specs for the carriers. Latest progress reports."

I squint at her, silently asking why.

She shrugs. "Trying to figure out how many people the ships might hold."

Therein lies another problem: even if we leave Earth, and arrive safely at our new home, can we take enough people to sustain our species? I hadn't even gotten that far. And what if there are more survivors than we can take? It's an impossible dilemma.

Emma and I haven't talked about which way each of us is leaning on the decision, but I get the impression she favors leaving Earth.

Emma sets the tablet aside. "I need to tell you something."

"Okay," I say cautiously.

She exhales and swallows, looking me directly in the eye, her face a mask. "I'm pregnant."

I smile, relieved. "I know."

"You do?"

"Oscar knew. He had access to your medical records."

Comprehension dawns on her. "Oh. From when I was doing rehab. He was monitoring my progress then, and no one bothered to turn the access off." She pauses, confused. "He told you?"

"No. Actually, Arthur told me—when he was trying to convince me to take his deal."

"Not exactly how I wanted you to find out."

"It doesn't change how happy I am. When did you find out?"

"I took a test the morning the asteroids hit. I wanted to tell you, but you were… a little preoccupied."

I exhale heavily. "With the battle sequence for the three large asteroids. What a waste of time. I got it all wrong."

"It's in the past." She takes my hand in hers. "Don't think about. The future is all that matters now. That said, I am sorry I didn't tell you—"

I reach up, wrap my fingers around the back of her neck and pull her face close to mine and kiss her, not letting her go until each of us is panting.

"It's in the past. The future is all that matters now."

She smiles, a tired, somber expression. "And what is our future? What are we going to do?"

"We're going to be fine. I promise you."

"How? I mean... the world is gone. The supercarriers aren't even close to being finished."

"I'll figure it out. We're going to be all right."

32

Emma

Sleep.

I've finally gotten sleep, here, in the most unlikely place: a cramped refugee camp in a bunker next to the crumbled CENTCOM headquarters. It isn't the accommodations that have delivered this blissful night of respite. It's the weight off my shoulders. I have told James my secret. Like me, he's overjoyed and terrified. It's not just the secret; it's the fact that we're once again all together—above ground. Well, sort of above ground.

For the first time in weeks, I wake to find him beside me, sleeping soundly, Allie tucked between us on the blankets piled on the concrete floor. In the early morning hours, it's still dark here in the CENTCOM bunker. Our little cubicle is enclosed by white sheets hanging from ropes crisscrossing the open space. A row of LED lights hangs in the corridor beyond the sheets, glowing softly.

My body aches, but I've felt worse. I should take a pain pill, but I can't. Won't. For the sake of the child growing inside of me.

Allie's left arm and leg are draped over me, as if trying to prevent me from going anywhere without her. Gently, I peel her from me and push up from the pallet, my arms creaking and popping like miniature firecrackers.

I wince, hoping… but James stirs and opens his eyes. He peers over at Allie, smiles, and kisses her sleeping face as he gets to his feet and offers me a hand up.

I prop open the sheet to our cubicle. Across the corridor, the sheet to Madison's cubicle is peeled back as well. She's sitting up knitting. Her husband and children are sleeping beside her.

"Hey," I whisper, waving my hand to get her attention. "Can you watch Allie?"

She nods and James and I take one last look back at our daughter before we head out. I lean on my cane as I lumber along. James walks slower on my account, trying to seem casual about it, as if it's perfectly normal.

When we reach the small dining area in the corner of the open space, he says quietly, "Sleep okay?"

"Best in a while."

"We don't have coffee, but there are AU Army stim pills."

"Pass." I motion to my abdomen. "Who knows what they put in those things. Better safe than sorry."

He heats a couple of MREs and sets them on the table.

"I spoke with Fowler briefly. He told me what you did down there."

I raise my eyebrows.

"You kept those people alive."

I shake my head as I quickly swallow a bite of the pancakes. "Far from it. I nearly got people killed in those tunnels."

"You gave them hope, Emma. That's something they needed. And you stepped up and took care of them even though I know you had to be scared. That's bravery."

I feel my cheeks flush with heat. Right now I feel as shy as I was in middle school. "Just did what I could. And for the record, it was really, really scary for a while. I thought I would never see you again."

"Same here. We were digging and I thought maybe we could get there but our rate of descent never got any faster, and we kept falling farther and farther behind the schedule I'd set out. I thought if we hit an air pocket or if we somehow uncovered the elevator shaft we would have a chance. Then we just ran out of time."

"You did the right thing."

We spend the rest of the meal in silence. I'm pondering what might have been, how things could have turned out differently. Maybe he is too.

James clears the table and his tone is serious when he returns. "There's something else we need to discuss."

"Sounds foreboding."

"It's not. Well, not really. You're aware that there are more kids than adult survivors?"

"Right."

"Well..."

"Yes."

He raises his eyebrows.

"My answer is yes—if you want us to adopt a child. Or two."

He exhales, as if a weight has been lifted. "I know you and I are going to be busy, but I think we should share the load with the other parents."

"How does this work?"

"I guess we'll get into that when the team meets, but I think Charlotte's the best person to handle the assignments."

"I agree. She's perfect for it."

"However, there's a kid Grigory and I rescued when we were first out here. Sam Eastman. He's a couple of years older than Allie. I think he's a good fit for us."

"So when do we meet Sam?"

"Right now, if you're up for it."

"I am."

The whole bunker seems to be waking up now, people shuffling into the dining area, most just taking their food back to their cubicles.

James and I make our way through the narrow corridors to a large open space where at least forty kids are lying in rows, thick army blankets beneath them, padding the hard-concrete floor. Most are still sleeping; a few are sitting up gazing at tablets, some crying quietly. I count seven with casts on their arms and legs. A lot of these kids are the survivors James and Grigory found after they reached the surface.

Charlotte sits in the corner, a tablet propped on her knees. Her face is gaunt, eyes sunken with heavy bags beneath them. I nod to her, and she manages a weak smile that doesn't reach her eyes. It's not just the lack of food. The situation with the children saddens her— but there's nowhere else she'd rather be than with them.

James walks down the row and stops at one of the boys playing on a tablet. A small plastic spaceship rests on the blanket beside him.

James squats down so that he's at the child's eye level. He speaks slowly, voice even. "Hi, Sam. My name's James. Do you remember me?"

The boy lets the tablet fall forward, and studies James for a second. Finally, he nods.

"Are you feeling better?"

The boy nods again.

James motions to me. "This is my wife Emma."

He glances at me quickly and forces a tentative smile. I walk closer and, even though the pain is nearly overwhelming, I squat down, coming to rest next to James.

"Hi, Sam," I whisper. "It's nice to meet you."

James slows his voice even more. "Sam, how would you like to come over to our place for a while?"

The boy glances up and down the row, looking confused. He still hasn't said a word. He must be terrified here, so young and all alone.

"I know you have a lot of questions. We'll talk about anything else you want to talk about." James points to the small plastic spaceship. "And I tell you what, we'll show you pictures and videos of a real spaceship. In orbit. Would you like that?"

Sam breaks eye contact with James and glances down.

James holds out a hand. "Come on. It'll be fun."

Sam eyes the offered hand for a long moment, then reaches out his own tiny hand, grabbing his tablet and spaceship with the other.

He walks with a limp slightly worse than mine. James stands tall and strong in the middle of us. We make quite a trio, a patchwork family, beaten down by circumstances, but far from out.

We stop at the dining area and grab a few MREs. Sam's small hand clings to James all the way back to our cubicle, which is now empty. A bolt of fear runs through me. I pop my head into Madison's cubicle and exhale heavily when I see Allie playing with Owen and Adeline.

To Madison, I say, "Can she stay for a bit?"

She waves me off. "Of course."

In our cubicle, Sam settles in and glances around, still seeming unsure. I lower myself down beside him as James holds out two MRE packs.

"What's it going to be, Sam? Apple maple oatmeal or filled french toast?"

He points to the oatmeal.

"Excellent choice."

Sam barely pauses as he wolfs down the meal.

I lean closer, ready to tell him to slow down, but James catches my attention with a quick swipe of his head, silently telling me to hold off and give the boy his space. He's right of course. Now isn't the time to point out that he's doing something wrong. We need to be building this child up.

James hands me the tablet. "As promised, Emma is going to show you a real spaceship."

I bring up the latest video of the ISS and the supercarriers and start playing it.

Sam's eyes grow wide. But still, he doesn't speak.

James points up. "That ship is up there, right now, Sam. We built it. See that small thing in between the two ships? That's the new International Space Station. There was one just like it before. Well, almost like it." He motions to me. "And Emma used to work on it." James raises his eyebrows.

"In fact, she was the commander. She was in charge of everyone and all the experiments."

Against my will, I feel myself blushing again as I shake my head at his boasting.

The video was taken from a supply capsule we sent up to the ISS a few months ago, and Sam takes in every second of it, mesmerized.

"One of these days, we're going to go up to that ship. Would you like to see it?"

Sam nods, excited, then his eyebrows knit together, eyes flush with fear, as if he's just remembered something. His voice is shaky and quiet. "W-w-where's my mom? And dad?"

James doesn't bat an eye. "We'll talk about that soon. As soon as we can, Sam. I promise you. Just like I promised you that we'd show you the videos of the spaceship. Do you believe me?"

Sam glances away.

James pulls up a cartoon on the tablet. "You know, when I was a kid, I loved this show. *Space Labs.*"

The intro starts playing, a spaceship buzzing through our solar system, past the Earth, Moon, Mars, and Venus. Two Labrador retrievers in space suits sit in the cockpit, pulling levers as the ship bounces around.

James holds the tablet between him and Sam and watches as the Labs set the ship down on a rocky planet and venture out, a human crewmember trailing behind them.

Sam is enthralled by the show, just as he was by the videos of the supercarriers. Gradually, perhaps even without realizing it, he snuggles in beside James and they watch together.

After two episodes, James grabs two more MREs. "Are you hungry?"

Sam nods.

"What's it going to be? Sloppy joe or beef stew?"

Sam points to the sloppy joe and eats it a little more slowly as he watches the show.

"You know, Sam, when I was a kid, I didn't talk much."

Sam gazes up at James.

"It's true. It was hard for me to talk. Some of the words just didn't want to come out. I dreaded it, even. I stayed in my room and read and dreamed about all the things I wanted to build when I grew up. Machines that helped us and never judged us and didn't care how a person talks or about anything else. But you know what?"

Sam's eyes are glued to James.

"After a while, it just went away. That happens to a lot of people. Talking just gets easier. But you have to practice." James pauses. "I want you to know that you can talk to us. About anything. We don't care if it's hard for you to speak sometimes. Or if it takes a while for the words to come out. We're here to listen and help. Do you understand?"

Sam nods and by just a little bit, nestles closer to James as the next episode starts. Half an hour later, he's snoring.

James ends the show and sets the tablet aside, but doesn't move to get up. He stays snuggled in to Sam.

"So you've decided?" I ask, voice quiet. "We're going to the ships? Leaving Earth?"

"I've been thinking about it. There are lots of problems with staying on Earth. The biggest is power. I can't solve it."

"But…" I whisper.

"But there are lots of problems with leaving too."

"Such as?"

"In the short term? Convincing people to do it. In fact, I'm not even sure our team will go for it. Grigory won't. He wants to stay and fight. I doubt Min will be in favor of leaving either. He's risk-averse. Harry... he's probably on board. Izumi and Charlotte, who knows? Fowler and Earls are also wild cards."

"Then we have to convince them."

"Yeah." He glances down at Sam. "What do you think?"

"I think I love him."

James smiles. "Yeah."

A moment later, he says, voice just above a whisper, "It's important to speak slowly to him."

"Okay."

"And use facial expressions and body language if you can. I asked him a lot of questions today, but we really want to get him to talk on his own. Comment on things and see if he adds something."

"Got it."

We lay there, minutes passing, both staring at the ceiling, Sam cuddled in between us.

"What happens next?"

"I think everyone from the Citadel needs a few more days, then we meet and decide what to do."

"Where's Arthur now?"

"Still locked up."

"He went back into confinement?"

"The seven army rifles pointed at him were pretty convincing," James says.

"Do you trust him?"

"No."

"Think he'll try to double-cross us?"

"I'm expecting it."

The flap to our cubicle draws back and Harry leans in. "Hey, guys, the drones are about to reach Camp Four." He sees Sam sleeping then, and lowers his voice. "Oh, sorry." He does a double-take when he realizes the child isn't Allie. Harry smiles tenderly and tips his head toward James, silently complimenting his friend on the act of kindness.

We alert Madison that she has another child to keep an eye on, and thankfully she doesn't seem to mind. Across the way, I can hear children crying and arguing. In the Citadel, we told them it was all temporary, that we'd leave and go home. But there are no homes to go back to. Reality has caught up to the Band-Aid that was our empty promises. These kids can't play outside, can't go home and get their toys. Like their parents, a lot of their friends are simply gone, and will never return.

In the bunker's situation room, a bank of screens on the far wall shows real-time data from the drones. Several of the team are already here, sitting at the long conference table: Colonel Earls, Izumi, Charlotte, and Min. James, Harry, and I take our seats as Fowler comes in, Grigory behind him, looking disheveled and sleepy. I know why Grigory hasn't been sleeping well. I can't imagine what he's going through after losing Lina.

We're all focused on the wall screen, which shows an aerial view of a snow-covered expanse of flat land. A massive round indentation lies ahead on the left. The impact crater. A smooth white bowl carved into the snowfield. Farther out, small lumps pock the otherwise flat ground, the remains of habitats, pieces of the homes sticking above the snow like limbs of a buried shrub.

"The drone is crossing the southern edge of the camp," James says.

"Looks like the asteroid made landfall just outside of the camp, not dead center," Fowler says.

"Correct," James replies. "That's both good news and bad."

I wonder what he means by that. Before I can ask, Fowler says, "Any idea of the size?"

James picks up the tablet on the table and selects a still image from the drone telemetry and draws a line across the crater.

"I'd say this one is about ten percent the size of the crater at the Citadel."

The lumps in the snow grow taller as the drone flies on. The habitats farthest from the impact craters obviously sustained the least amount of damage. Still, there are no heat signatures on the map.

Each camp in the Atlantic Union has greenhouses for food and warehouses for storage. Or used to. Some camps, like Seven, had specialized factories and warehouses. In each camp, the habitats are clustered together at the center, the warehouses and greenhouses on the periphery. I never knew why, but I'm assuming it was for some military reason, maybe spreading out the buildings in each camp served some purpose. The asteroid strike here at Camp Seven was large enough to take down all of our greenhouses and warehouses. But the impact was much smaller at Camp Four. Maybe some of their storage facilities survived.

James pulls up a city-planning document from the AtlanticNet. "The asteroid made a pretty direct hit on the main food warehouse on the southern edge of the camp. That's the bad news." He taps on the tablet, issuing commands to the drone. "I'm going to fly the perimeter now, see if any of the other facilities survived."

The first warehouse on the horizon lies in a large rubble pile.

"There should be a greenhouse to the right," James says. "It's completely gone."

A minute later, a warehouse emerges on the horizon. The walls are warped and punctured in places, but it's still standing.

"That's warehouse four-one-two. It's the second largest in Camp Four."

"Please tell me it's not filled with tires and car parts," Harry says.

"We're in luck," James responds. "The AU inventory says it's stocked with food, water, and excess habitat parts."

"Jackpot," Harry says jovially.

When the drone reaches the warehouse, the screen lights up with heat signatures. Survivors. Inside the warehouse.

James smiles wide. "It gets better. Drone estimates one hundred survivors inside."

"Good work, James," Fowler says. "How big is that warehouse?"

"AU records say it's about a hundred thousand square feet."

"Ten times the size of this bunker."

"And," James adds, "with working solar panels on the roof."

Fowler nods. "If it's structurally sound," he glances at the ceiling, "or at least more structurally sound than this bunker, we need to start planning to move there."

"I agree," James says. "I'll take a team. Wish we had a helo."

"There was an army depot at Camp Four," Colonel Earls says, "but it was close to the impact crater. It's gone."

"That's probably the other reason the grid chose that strike point," James says. "Takes out the food, weapons, and survival gear."

"Are there depots in every camp?" Min asks.

"Yes," Earls responds. "But most are pretty small. The camps out on the perimeter of the Union had the largest facilities. The logic was that in the event of an invasion, the battle lines would be there. There are more automated aerial defenses in the interior camps, but those don't help us."

"Hopefully we'll find what we need when the scans of the other camps come in," James says. "Food is still our biggest immediate concern. We're continuing with the search of the debris here in Camp Seven, but we don't have much more ground to cover."

"How much food do we have left?" I ask. The memory of being dangerously hungry is still fresh in my mind. I'm not eager to relive it.

"Seven days. That's assuming we don't find anymore food buried out there in the rubble."

"How long will it take to reach Camp Four?" I ask.

James glances at Earls, who is more familiar with what kind of speed the trucks can make.

"It's hard to say," Earls says. "I'm assuming we're talking about a convoy of trucks and troop carriers?"

James nods.

"They're not exactly built for speed. Before, when the roads were hard-packed dirt, we could get to Camp Four in a few hours. Now, who knows? The roads are the main issue. They're covered in snow and who knows what else. Could be debris under there. Mini craters from the asteroid ejecta falling back to Earth. Possibly abandoned vehicles." Earls thinks for a moment. "We've attached plow blades to several of the trucks. They'll clear the path, but we'll probably have to go off road in places. Beneath the snow, the desert is likely to be sludge. The trucks could get stuck. We'll include a track truck, just in case. The lead truck plowing the snow is going to have a heavy burden on its fuel cell. We'll rotate out, but my guess is that the convoy will have to stop to recharge. The diminished solar output will further slow us down."

"Best guess on travel time?" Fowler asks.

Earls blows out a breath, thinking. "Maybe thirty hours. I'm really not sure."

"How do we proceed once we get there?" Fowler asks. The question hangs in the air like a jump ball. James glances at Earls, silently questioning whether this is a military operation that he would plan.

Earls holds a hand out to James. "Please."

"Well, I think after we make contact, we should send some food back on one of the troop carriers. Assuming the last warehouse inventory taken is correct, these folks have a lot more than we do, and we've likely got some things they need—medicine for one. Beyond that, I think we should probably keep going to the next camp. We'll have new data from the drones by the time we reach Camp Four. There could even be another camp in even better shape. I want to keep moving and making contact with the other camps quickly."

"You're going?" The question slips out before I can even think about it. After being trapped in the Citadel without James, I'm in no hurry to see him leave.

He doesn't make eye contact with me. "Yes. I want to see first-hand what we have to work with in those warehouses. It could mean the difference between survival and extinction." James looks over at Grigory. "You up for it?"

"Sure," he replies quietly.

James probably wants him on the team because he's scared to leave Grigory with Arthur. But I think he's also trying to help his friend, to keep Grigory busy, his thoughts off Lina.

"I'll send six of my best with you," Earls says. "There was also an infantry officer among the survivors, Captain Brightwell. I think you've met."

"We have," James replies.

"She has a lot more combat experience than me or any of my troops. I'd recommend her for the mission."

"Be glad to have her along," James says before turning to Izumi. "They'll probably also need medical assistance."

"Of course. Things are pretty stable here."

"Want me to tag along?" Harry asks. "Happy to."

"Thanks, but I think you'd better stay here and keep inventorying the wreckage. We need to know what we have left to work with here as well. Odds are robotics is going to be a large part of what comes next. Whatever that is. We can't afford to lose both of us."

Harry studies James a moment. "In that case, if we're going to lose one of us, I think I'm the better candidate."

James shakes his head. "You spent more time down in the Citadel. You need to focus on getting back to a hundred percent. I've been well fed here in the CENTCOM bunker. *And* I'm one of the most recognized people in the world. I think I'm a good representative."

"To negotiate," Min says.

"Yes. I'm not sure what we'll find out there, but I think it's safe to say that possession is now the new rule of law. I fully expect this reunion to be more of a negotiation."

"You mentioned medicine before," Min says. "What if they don't need any? Then what do we have to offer? Camp Seven is probably in the worst shape—if Camp Four is any indication of the others."

I know the answer. The other camps will likely have more people, more food, and more living space. But we have something they all need: a way off this planet. We also have possibly the only people in the world who can pull it off. But the team hasn't discussed that decision yet.

James, to his credit, is cautious here in the front of the group. "We'll have to see what they want."

The team spends the rest of the afternoon planning the expedition. By nightfall, the soldiers have loaded the caravan with supplies. They'll leave at first light, and I sense that James is a little nervous about it. I wonder if what happened to Oscar has made him more cautious. There's no telling what tricks the grid might have left waiting out there. I'm glad he's cautious. That fear could help keep him alive.

We decide to let Allie spend the night with Madison, David, and her cousins, leaving James, Sam, and me in our cubicle.

James and Sam stay up late watching *Space Labs*, James occasionally commenting on things happening on the show, encouraging Sam to speak. But he remains silent. That's going to take some time.

Finally, James turns the show off.

"Sorry, Sam. Time for bed. Big day tomorrow." James peers down at him. "Emma and I would like it if you slept here tonight. Would that be okay?"

Sam nods and beds down between us, curling into James. After a few moments, I hear him crying. James puts a hand on his back. "It's okay, Sam. Everything is going to be okay. I promise."

33

James

We leave at first light, and that light is a dim, hazy burning on the horizon, a sun being slowly shrouded, its life-giving radiation fading each day.

Seven Atlantic Union armored troop carriers comprise our convoy, big, lumbering vehicles that carve their way through the snow-packed streets, throwing ice off on each side, leaving deep ruts in their wake.

In the cab of the last vehicle, Grigory and I ride in silence, him stewing as he drives, me studying the supercarrier schematics. Transforming it into an interstellar ship in fourteen months... can it be done? Even with Arthur's help? I'm not convinced. And I've got to convince everyone else. Starting with Grigory.

We don't even stop to eat, only for routine bathroom breaks and to let the power cells recharge. As Earls predicted, it's slow going on these ruined roads. Well beyond Camp Seven, the road is littered with random bits of debris and rocks. We drive all day, until the white expanse of ice and snow swallows the hazy yellow-brown sun.

We'd keep going if we could, but the energy cells are nearly sapped. We've left just enough power for the space heaters that will keep us warm tonight. The trucks' engines won't run again until sunrise.

Grigory and I bed down in the back of the troop carrier on thick blankets, both looking weary, both anxious to reach the warehouse.

This seems like as good a moment as any to make my case to him.

"The way I see it, we—what's left of the human race—have two choices. Go underground or leave Earth."

"Or fight," Grigory says.

"With what? The orbital satellite network is down. I'm assuming the Centurion drones are too—probably taken out by the asteroids. The Centurions are programmed to move into Earth orbit if comms are lost with the orbital network and make direct contact. If they were out there, we would have made contact from CENTCOM. There was no response when we pinged them. They're gone."

Grigory doesn't flinch. "Don't need them. We find nukes. We outfit them with battle drone AI, launch, let them scour the asteroid belt until they find the harvester; then they blow it to bits. Winter ends and we rebuild. Just like before."

"That assumes the nukes will be effective."

"They were last time," Grigory snaps.

"Last time is no guarantee for this time."

He lies there, stewing, staring at the ceiling.

I try to make my voice more even. "It also assumes we can find some nukes. Oscar knew where the Atlantic Union repositories were. They're probably destroyed."

"We can find nukes," Grigory mutters. "Oscar didn't know where the Caspians and Pac Alliance kept theirs. There are likely even more hidden. Some still in Russia too."

"And what about rockets? And rocket fuel? We used most of what we had launching the drone fleet that destroyed the large asteroids."

"We can find rocket fuel too. And if we can't, we can't leave Earth anyway."

That's a good point. One I've been turning over in my mind.

"Even assuming we find nukes and rocket fuel, it simply won't work. We know this harvester is more advanced than the last. Far more advanced—"

"How do we know?"

"Grigory, it threw three asteroids the size of Texas at us. And thousands of smaller ones. This harvester can defeat us in battle. You know it. I'm certain that it's watching the planet. Arthur said so, and I would bet on it. If we launch nukes, it will take them out and then expend the energy to mobilize another large asteroid at the planet." I let the words hang in the air. "Game over. We have absolutely no way to defend against another asteroid strike. We have no major ground-based or orbital telescopes to detect another asteroid strike."

"The Caspians or Pacs might still have them."

"They *might*. But even if they do, we don't have enough ordnance to reduce or redirect the asteroids. We're sitting ducks. Our choices are very, very simple: hide or leave."

Grigory doesn't respond.

"Let's say you're right, Grigory. We shoot some nukes up there and win."

He turns his head toward me.

"Then what?"

He shrugs, seeming confused.

"I'll tell you what will happen: the grid will send another harvester. How bad do you think the next attack will be?"

"We don't know it will send another."

"Look at the energy it has already expended on our sun, the solar cells it has in the system already. Are you ready to bet the future of humanity on them cutting their losses? And that's assuming we can destroy this harvester, and that its solar cells disperse again. None of that is certain."

"It's about as certain as them leading us to some imaginary paradise planet. Probably fly us into a star."

"That's our challenge, Grigory. To make sure they keep their bargain. To make sure we get to a new home safely. We need our best engineer working on that."

He rolls away from me and exhales heavily.

"I want to fight too. Oscar meant—means—a lot to me. Every time I see Arthur it's like facing someone who's taken my child hostage and locked them away in a basement and is never going to let them out. And all they're offering me is a chance to leave the house—the only home I've ever known—with my other child. And my wife. And the unborn child growing inside of her."

Grigory faces me again, expression softening. "I didn't know."

"We just found out."

"Congratulations," he says, voice almost somber.

"I want to fight. But more than that, I want my children to survive. Or at least to have a chance. On Earth, they don't have a chance."

Grigory falls silent again.

"Will you think about it?"

"Yes."

34

Emma

In the bunker, the unrest seems to grow by the hour. Now that we're out of the Citadel, the kids are beginning to ask questions—and they're more insistent this time. They want answers. They're scared. So are the adults. It's not just the confined space. Uncertainty: that is what's eating at all of us. That is the issue we must address—and soon.

After I say goodbye to James and watch his convoy pull away, I head to the situation room where Fowler, Harry, Charlotte, Colonel Earls, Min, and I sit down for our morning meeting.

"Census?" Fowler asks.

"One-sixty-two," Min replies.

"It was—"

"One-sixty-six yesterday, sir." Min glances at his tablet. "A surface survivor succumbed to injuries from the impact blast. He was brought in two weeks ago. Izumi was optimistic but he took a turn."

"And the other?"

"Cause of death is... to be determined, sir."

It's unlikely Min doesn't know what killed the person. 'Cause of death to be determined' has become code for suicide, an increasingly common problem for those people who have lost loved ones—in some cases, all of their loved ones. Despair is a virus spreading almost as fast as the rumors of our desperate situation. The combination of losing everything they were living for and knowing they've survived only to freeze to death is too much for some people.

"Okay," Fowler says quietly. "Charlotte?"

"Getting access to the AtlanticNet backup has been quite helpful in starting up education initiatives. Thanks again, Harry."

"My pleasure."

"We're using the standard AU curriculum," Charlotte continues. "Obviously classroom size is small and there's not much noise separation, so the kids are distracted, but it's better than our situation in the Citadel. Curriculum-wise."

"How about otherwise?" Fowler asks.

"Otherwise... the children aren't doing great, frankly. They're acting out. They're asking questions. They're angry and frustrated. And I think, deep down, they know. Kids are smarter than we give them credit. They sense that this isn't just a temporary event." Charlotte nods. "I think it was the right call to put them in the troop carriers when we transported them from the Citadel to here, to ensure that they didn't see the camp. But I feel they should be told the truth soon."

"I agree." All eyes turn to me. "And I think we need to tell the adults that we have a plan. Or else we're going to see more cause-of-death-unknown fatalities. People need hope. They need something to live for."

"*Do* we have a plan?" Min asks.

I smile. "Sure. We plan to survive."

"Survival is going to require a lot more specifics than that," Min replies quietly.

"True. But we don't have to share them now, with everyone. For now, I think we should tell them only that we have a plan and that we will be calling on them for help. That gives them hope. And a reason to live. They'll believe it."

"What makes you so sure?"

"Because they want to."

Fowler stands and paces in front of the bank of screens on the wall. "Let's talk about that plan. It's clear the two options are staying on Earth and leaving. I've given both a lot of thought. There's not much for me to do but think. First, I want to hear where all of you are on the issue."

No one speaks, but a few glance over at me, which I take as a silent prompt.

"James and I discussed it some. He believes that without a reliable power source, staying on Earth isn't viable. Even if we could solve the power problem, we'd always be vulnerable to the harvester. He favors leaving. So do I."

Harry nods. "That's my analysis too. I've been trying to think through transforming the carriers into colony ships, but it's way beyond our current capability. We'd have to rely on the grid—Arthur—a lot. To me, that's the biggest risk."

"I concur," Min says. "If we can mitigate the risk of the grid sabotaging us, I favor the colony option."

Fowler focuses on Colonel Earls, who throws his hands up.

"Look, I'm a career army officer—the US, then the AU. My purview was the Citadel: its defense, maintenance, and provisioning. A decision like this is, frankly, way over my pay grade. I'll support whatever is decided."

"I actually hadn't given the decision much thought," Charlotte says carefully. "And, actually, my feelings are similar to Colonel Earls. The planning and technology are outside my area of expertise. But as an anthropologist, I'd like to raise another concern: what we'll find on any new home world. Poisons. Pathogens. Adverse weather conditions. If we opt to leave, we should be prepared for any environment we find on the other side. Our new home could be every bit as hostile as the one we're leaving."

Fowler nods. "Good point. I'm of the same mind as Harry and Min. I'd like to form a working group to start thinking about all the issues that have been raised. The group could be the six of us, but, Charlotte and Colonel Earls, I understand if you two want to opt out."

"That suits me, sir," Earls says. "I've got my hands full conducting the search of the camp wreckage."

"Same," Charlotte says. "I'm needed at the school. And if it's all right, I'd like to return to the issue of talking with the kids."

"Of course," Fowler says.

"I favor talking to them one-on-one, or in small groups. The child's parents—or the person closest to them—should do it." To Colonel Earls, she says, "Are you still looking for survivors?"

Earls shakes his head. "No, ma'am. There are no more life signs above ground. We're looking for food and medicine.

Dr. Sinclair has also given us a list of parts to look out for." Earls glances at Harry. "I believe they're for robots. Or drones, ma'am."

Harry nods, and Charlotte continues. "I think the teams should spend some time looking for something for each child. A toy from their home. A picture of their parents. Anything that might comfort them when we tell them."

Min throws his hands up, no doubt about to disagree, but Fowler cuts him off.

"It's a good idea. Please make it happen, Colonel. Drones aren't the only thing this camp needs to survive."

That night, I'm in my cubicle, mentally preparing for the conversation I'll have with Sam tomorrow when Harry sticks his head in.

"Hey Emma, one of our drones picked up something near warehouse four-one-two."

My first thought is James, but he hasn't been gone long enough to reach the warehouse.

I dash into the corridor, following him to the situation room as quickly as my aching leg allows. Fowler is already there, as is Colonel Earls. The rest of the team is right behind me.

On the large wall screen, three AU Army troop carriers are carving their way through the snow-covered terrain, kicking ice into the air as they go.

"Is that part of our convoy?" I ask.

"No," Colonel Earls replies. "Plates match vehicles assigned to Camp Five. And they're coming from Camp Five, moving toward warehouse four-one-two. The drone providing this telemetry was en route to Camp Five when it spotted the vehicles."

The AU has several specialized camps, like Camp Seven, where citizens from several nations are pooled together, but for the most part, the camps are segregated by nation. At the time of the mass evacuations to the last habitable zones, it made sense to group people by a common language. It was also a negotiating demand: each of the member nations wanted to ensure that their resources and efforts were benefiting their own people. Camp Four is one of the British camps. I'm not sure about Camp Five.

"What's the make-up of Camp Five?" I ask.

"It's a French camp," Earls replies.

"Theories about what we're looking at?" Fowler asks.

"Could be a raiding party from Camp Five," Earls says, studying the screen.

"Or a trading delegation," Fowler adds. He turns to Harry. "Do we have telemetry for Camp Five?"

"No."

"Even though the vehicles are from Camp Five, it could be a team from Camp Four returning," Min says. "Maybe they've already been out to Camp Five, scavenged or fought for the troop carriers and they're coming back with more loot. We know all the vehicles and weapons depots in Four were wiped out."

Fowler leans back in his chair. "When's the last time we tried our people on the radio?"

"Just before the drone found the convoy," Harry says. "No response."

That surprises me. "I thought the drones were establishing a radio network to allow the long-range devices to connect."

"They are—and have for some camps," Harry says. "But the drones deployed the repeaters to minimize the distance between devices. They're aligned as the crow flies between the camps. The roads aren't direct routes. They're apparently somewhere on the road that's out of range of the repeaters."

I hadn't anticipated that before James left. "Let's keep trying him," I say quietly, a new fear taking hold inside me.

"We will," Harry says, making eye contact with me.

"Options?" Fowler asks.

"We can send backup," Earls says. "Use the ATVs to join up with the convoy. They can't carry heavy ordnance, but plenty of personnel and ammo. The second team could alert James's convoy to the new group approaching the warehouse and provide reinforcements."

"How long will that take?"

"I don't know. The ATVs move much faster than the trucks in the convoy, but it's anyone's guess how quickly they'll catch them—or if they'll reach the convoy before it arrives at warehouse four-one-two."

"Do it," Fowler says.

"How many should I dispatch, sir?"

"What's our total strength here?"

"Twenty-eight."

"Send them all."

Earls squints at Fowler. "Sir? The bunker will be defenseless."

"If we don't get James back," Fowler says, "it won't matter anyway."

35

James

I wake feeling achy, throat dry and sore.

I try the radio but we're out of contact with CENTCOM. Hopefully by the time we reach the warehouse we'll be in range of a repeater.

The drive today feels endless, the truck bounding across the expanse of rolling white hills, the dim sun overhead. Grigory and I ride in the cab, neither of us bringing up the conversation from last night.

On the radio, Captain Brightwell's British accent calls out, "Dr. Sinclair, do you copy?"

"I'm here."

"Sir, estimated sunset is in T-minus two hours, sixteen minutes. If we drive the truck to fuel cell depletion, we will still be two K from the warehouse."

"Kay?"

"Kilometers, sir. We'll be out in the cold for the night. Advise we stop fifteen K out, and resume at first light. Over."

"Received. I think we can do a two-kilometer hike in

these circumstances. We'll take minimal kit. Reaching the warehouse today gives us more time to inventory it and talk with the survivors. And spending the night in the warehouse is likely to be warmer and more restful. We might be able to move on to the next camp first thing in the morning. We'll likely find transport inside the warehouse, maybe a spare solar array that's compatible with the troop carriers. Izumi, are you up for the hike?"

"Definitely."

"Captain?"

"We'll be ready, sir. Over."

"Received."

An hour and a half later, our troop carrier rolls to a stop. Using the long-range radio, I try contacting CENTCOM one last time before we set out. We're still out of reach of the repeater at Camp Four. I figure if we'd been able to drive the truck into the camp, it would work—assuming the repeater is working. It may not be operational in this weather. There simply wasn't a lot of time to test the radio network before deploying it. We'll sort that out tomorrow.

Grigory and I exit and put on our parkas and balaclavas and join the seven soldiers and Izumi. We look like a band of fur traders hiking through the Alaskan wilderness in search of shelter.

Snow falls around us. My voice comes out in white wisps of steam.

"I want to try to make contact with the warehouse survivors on the radio before we get there."

Even through the face mask, I can instantly tell that Brightwell doesn't like it. "Sir, that would give away our position and circumstances without knowing their disposition towards us. It puts us at a disadvantage."

"Noted, Captain. We're going to approach this as a humanitarian mission first. But I agree that we need to be ready for hostilities."

I take the handheld radio and speak loudly. "To the survivors in Camp Four, my name is James Sinclair. I'm a survivor from Camp Seven. We've come to offer assistance. Do you copy?"

I wait, but there's no response.

"We know some of you are in warehouse four-one-two. We're proceeding to your position now in hopes of offering aid. Please respond."

Brightwell looks at the ground, clearly frustrated. I've just given away our position and plans. But what do we have to lose?

When there's no response, the soldier packs the radio away and we set off again, trudging through the snow single file.

It would have been better to drive through the camp. Walking gives us more time to see the carnage. The crumbled heaps of the habitats, covered in snow except for random pieces sticking out. The smell of death is ever-present, growing worse with each step as we venture deeper into the camp. Even as frozen as they are, the smell from the sheer number of bodies is sickening.

I had hoped to spot a vehicle, but they're gone too, blown into the habitats or each other or clear of the camp, lying in mangled heaps.

Each time we stop for a break, I try the radio.

Each time, there's no response.

When the sun's set, we march in darkness except for our headlamps glittering across the snow and the muddy glow of a half-moon shining down.

A hundred yards from the warehouse, I try the radio again.

Still no response, only the crunching of our footfalls as we march toward the dented building.

The exterior lights aren't on, and there are no windows, just opaque, warped, hard-plastic walls.

The soldier leading the column throws his left arm up at a right angle, palm forward from us, fingers extended and joined. The column freezes. Brightwell holds her left hand at her waist, palm down, fingers extended and joined. Together, the soldiers lower to a knee, rifles still raised.

The soldier ahead ventures forward to a lump in the snow, where he slings his rifle on his shoulder and squats down, brushing the white powder from the pile.

It's a woman. Brown hair. Skin ashy: gray and blue. She's dressed in a nightgown.

He pulls at her body as the other five soldiers hold their rifles at the ready, panning left and right like lighthouses searching in the night. Grigory, Izumi, and I are fixated on the frozen woman, the beams of our headlamps a spotlight on the scene. There's a child in her arms. Couldn't be more than four years old. It's horrifying. But what I see next is even worse: there's a gunshot wound in her chest. She was running to the warehouse when she was gunned down.

I'm repulsed. Instinctively, my mind judges these people. And in the next moment, I remember what we did at the entrance to the Citadel. If our warehouse were still standing, what might other survivors think of what they saw there, of what we did? Does that make us bad people? Or just survivors? In the world that's left, I wonder if there's a difference anymore.

One thing is clear: the people in that warehouse are armed—and willing to kill to protect themselves and what's inside.

Brightwell's voice pierces the silence. "Dr. Sinclair, I recommend we divide into three forces. Civilians will hang back. My troops will form two groups that will enter the building at opposite ends."

"It's a good plan, Captain. But we didn't come here to fight. Besides, we probably can't win if it comes to it."

I seem to be spending a lot of time lately convincing people not to fight. In this case, I wonder if it's the right move. I cut Grigory a look. He nods at me, silently agreeing.

"Sir?" Brightwell asks.

"We're going to knock on the front door."

Her eyes tell me that she doesn't like it one bit. To her credit, she simply says, "Yes, sir."

Her soldiers fan out, two of them taking covered positions behind the lumps in the snow, rifles trained on the large roll-up door.

When we're twenty feet from the warehouse, I call out in the night: "Hello! We're here to help. From Camp Seven. Please open the door if you can hear me."

Nothing. Only the sound of wind blowing across the snow, the building occasionally popping or groaning in the night.

I call out twice more; then I try the radio again. My hands are freezing; my face is too.

I nod to Brightwell. She points to a soldier next to her, who leads two other soldiers to the warehouse.

There's a standard swinging door next to the large roll-up door. The soldiers try the handle, find it locked, and then fish a crowbar from a backpack and start prying at it. The lock doesn't budge, but the door casing around it bends, and soon the door pops open with a squeal, revealing darkness within.

The soldiers converge on the door, Grigory, Izumi, and I following behind.

They cross the threshold, rifles raised, scanning the vast space, the beams of their headlamps raking over the pylons set in the concrete floor. Pallets are organized in rows, wrapped in milky white plastic, stacked twenty feet tall.

"Hello!" I call out, voice booming in the space. "I'm from Camp Seven. We've come to help. Can you hear me?"

Silence.

Brightwell cuts a glance to me and I nod.

Her team creeps forward, in a semicircle, shielding Grigory, Izumi, and me behind them.

When we reach the first row of pallets, I smile as I read the boxes: Meals, Ready-to-Eat. These are leftover supplies from the mass evacuations during the Long Winter. They're years old, but still good. For the moment, our food problem is solved.

Carefully, the soldiers move deeper into the warehouse, boots grinding against the fine dirt on the floor. Deeper in the warehouse, I think I hear a sound, an object falling. Everyone stops to listen.

But the sound doesn't repeat. It's silent except for the wind raking over the building. One of the wall panels behind us creaks. That's probably what it was.

Beyond the pallets of MREs are containers marked as holding blankets and modular plastic habitat walls. The walls were mass-produced in the months before the evacuations. The AU must have overestimated how many they needed. Or were saving some for another purpose. We might be able to use them—

A squeak punctures the silence, the sound almost like a radio being activated and quickly turned off.

The boxes beside me seem to explode open, their walls folding down as soldiers step from them, rifles pointed at us. A gun barrel presses into the side of my neck, cold and hard.

"Don't move," the man growls.

Brightwell's team is still as night, guns held out, but their eyes flash back and forth, sizing up the twenty Atlantic Union soldiers surrounding us.

Suddenly, one of Brightwell's men flinches, turning toward the soldier nearest to him. The other man steps back, rifle shaking in his hands. I can see his finger on the trigger. I could swear he's squeezing it.

"Steady…" Brightwell says softly. "We're all on the same team here."

Footsteps on the concrete floor draw my attention, but no one moves their headlamp to see who it is. The shadowed figure stops thirty feet away. When he speaks, I instantly recognize the voice.

"We've decided to pick new teams. Post-asteroid rules, if you will."

I thought the grid was the greatest threat to our survival. But I was wrong.

36

Emma

The following morning, Harry is waiting for me after breakfast. "You ready to be heckled?"

I force a smile. The meeting with the adults could certainly go that way.

"I'm going to hide behind you."

"I wouldn't have it any other way."

When the kids are at school, we gather the adults at the opposite corner of the bunker, far enough away that the sound won't carry. Fowler, Harry, Min, Colonel Earls, and I stand with our backs against the wall, our audience spread out on the floor, some sitting cross-legged, others—those with leg injuries—with limbs stretched out. Some of the men stand in the back, staring skeptically.

"I know you have questions," Fowler says. "This meeting is to answer them. But first I want you to know that we have a plan for our survival. We're going to get out of this bunker—"

A tall man with a beard at the back yells, "When?"

"A team is currently working on a timeline—"

A woman sitting in the second row, clutching her legs to her chest: "How? Where are we going?"

Fowler holds his hands up, waiting for the commotion to die down. "You deserve answers to all these questions and more. Right now, this is what I can tell you. First of all, we have enough food in this bunker for the time being. We've also conducted an aerial survey of the other camps. More food will arrive shortly."

Another bout of questions erupts.

"Ladies and gentlemen, please," Fowler says calmly. "We'll get to your questions. I know some of you have loved ones in the other camps. We're making contact and collecting a census. The main thing I want you to take away from this meeting is that we have a plan. We're executing it, and we need your help. Each and every one of us has to pitch in if it's going to succeed. That starts now. There's something very important we need to do in this camp, and that's talk with our children about what's happened. They're scared. They're confused. And for those children who have lost their families, they're very, very upset— even if they're not showing it. Right now, teams are out searching the wreckage for items the children left behind. Toys, pictures, anything familiar that we can give them at this time. We need your help. Those of you who are able to join the search teams, please move over to the right. Those staying here, we're going to start a seminar on how best to talk with your children about what's happening."

Questions fly from every corner of the audience.

"Please, please, folks. Today, we have to put the children first. Then we turn our focus to our own questions and fears. That's the plan."

37

James

"We didn't come here to fight," I call out into the darkened warehouse. "We're here to help."

I count twenty AU soldiers surrounding Grigory, Izumi, and me in the aisle. We have seven soldiers and three civilians. Not good odds.

The figure takes another step towards us, footfalls echoing in the cavernous space, his voice bordering on anger.

"Ladies and gentleman, James Sinclair is here to help. Help himself, that is."

"We can help each other." To Captain Brightwell, I say, "Lower your weapons."

Her eyes bulge at me.

"Do it, Captain. We didn't come here to fight our own people."

She clenches her teeth and slowly lowers her rifle. Her soldiers follow suit. The soldiers from Camp Four surge forward and snatch their rifles and sidearms. They also grab our radios and turn them off. We have repeaters at the trucks. They would have rebroadcast any messages from us or Camp Seven. Unfortunately, we're now cut off.

The figure steps out of the shadow and smiles. "Now that was really stupid, James." He shrugs. "But not surprising. After all, you're prone to doing stupid things, aren't you?"

Richard Chandler was once my professor, a friend, a mentor. Until he saw me as a rival to his own work. He stopped being supportive, then started undermining my work behind my back, and, when I was arrested and charged with a trumped-up crime, he was the public face leading the lynching mob of public opinion. I'm not even sure he disagreed with what I did. He probably just liked the goal: locking me away.

After I went to prison, I didn't see him again until the briefing at NASA for the first contact mission. He was initially assigned to the *Fornax*, a secondary posting to the one I received. In the briefing, he once again resumed his attack on me, using the same tactics he employed in countless TV interviews before and during my trial. But two things were different then. One: I was present to defend myself. And two: this jury was composed of scientists, people with minds trained to separate fact and conjecture. They didn't buy it. Their concern was for humanity's survival, and Chandler was pulled from the mission, taking from him the thing he wanted most in the world, the thing that drove his crusade against me: fame. Recognition. Public celebration. Authority.

He tried to take his revenge on me after the Long Winter ended, in the arena where he fights best: TV interviews, the court of public opinion. And through a twist of fate, he's been given one more shot at me. I just hope he's still rational enough to see reason. That's our only chance here.

"Richard, this is bigger than what's between you and me. We need to work together."

"Do we?"

"I'm serious. We came here to help."

Chandler shakes his head, acting disgusted. "Right. You picked a warehouse full of food and water and habitat supplies and came here with a company of soldiers to help? No. I'm betting you came here because your band of survivors is slowly starving and you need something we have in this warehouse. We've been dealing with this for weeks. You may have seen our solution—past intruders like you are still outside in the snow."

He motions to an army major next him. "Proceed. And check outside for any others."

"Stop!" I yell. "I have something to offer."

Chandler holds up a hand to the major.

"We have a way to survive. Not just this week, or next week, or for a few years. I'm talking about truly surviving. For generations."

"Wait for it, ladies and gentleman. The big lie comes next."

"Richard, we have a way off this planet."

Chandler throws his head back and laughs. "That's rich. Really. Remember who you're talking to, James."

"I'm not lying."

Chandler narrows his eyes. "I think you are."

38

Emma

I had expected the *Birthright* study sessions to end after we escaped the Citadel. I've made no effort to keep the group together.

The members, however, have sought me out and implored me to resume the meetings. For many of us, idle time is the most agonizing. We all dread the hours after the sun sets, when we're packed into this bunker with nothing to do but think. Everyone thinks about the same things: whether we will survive, and the people we've lost. The dead haunt the minds of the living. Indeed, like in the Citadel, our own minds are perhaps the greatest enemy we face in these dark times.

In the mess hall, I sit at a table at the end of the room, the forty attendees scattered across the other tables, looking down, some staring at me. There was little debate about what this session should focus on.

"Today's topic is grief. It's a subject *The Birthright* addresses at length." I focus on the tablet in my lap. "According to *The Birthright*, grief is a brother to fear.

It is another mechanism our minds employ to protect us.

"Fear protects us from harm. Fear motivates us to act to prevent injury to our body and minds. What does grief protect us from? Like fear, if we want to manage our grief, we must first understand it."

I scroll to my notes in the margin and take a second to organize my thoughts.

"*The Birthright* asserts that grief is our mind's way of remembering the people we've lost. Grief reminds us that their lives were important. Why? Perhaps it's a method of self-preservation. Perhaps grief is our minds' way of reminding us that *our lives* are important too—that we will leave a mark on the world, that we will be mourned as well."

I pause, scanning the group. "Imagine a world without grief. A world where we instantly forget about the loved ones we lost. A world like that doesn't feel right to me. They deserve more than to be instantly forgotten, just as each of us does.

"But grief is much more than that. It is our mind's manifestation of our fear that our life will never be as good as it was before our loss. Grief strikes in those moments where our loss is laid bare. It overcomes us when we see a picture of the people we've lost. When we find something they made. When we remember a phrase they used to say. Like fear, grief can be paralyzing. But, like fear, it also motivates us. To get over our grief, we have to move on. We have to patch the holes in our life left by our loss. *That* is the purpose of grief. It is a pain that our mind uses to try to force us to repair our lives as best we can.

"And like fear, there's a dark side of grief. Our mind can malfunction. It can forget when to turn off our grief. Grief, like fear, can overcome us. *The Birthright* says that those periods are what we must be mindful of. Like fear, we shouldn't hide from grief. We should recognize it for what it is. Let grief run its course. Repair our lives as best we can—knowing that things will never be the same. Clinging to a life that is gone forever isn't healthy. Time and action are the only cures for grief."

As the group files out, it occurs to me that every single one of us has lost family and friends. They were there one day, gone the next, ripped from our lives, a deep unseen wound left in the wake.

I think the lessons from *The Birthright* are only half of the reason this group gathers. The other half is simply knowing that we're not alone, that others are feeling the same thing we are, as if knowing that we're standing together relieves the weight bearing down on all of us.

39

James

I've been on trial for my life once before.

Then, my crime was trying to save someone I loved. In that case, it was my father. I pushed the boundaries of what the human race was capable of, of what our future would look like. Those actions ran afoul of the wrong people, powerful people with a different vision of our future. I lost the trial, and they locked me away.

In truth, I didn't fight much then. I was heartbroken by my father's passing and felt isolated because everyone I loved had turned against me. I thought my case was hopeless. Back then, I simply didn't have it in me to defend myself.

Here, now, standing in this darkened warehouse, snow falling outside on a ruined world, a dozen guns pointed at me, I feel like I'm once again on trial for my life. Against a group of people with a different vision for our future. One they control. The judge this time is Richard Chandler, perhaps the person who hates me most in this world.

This time, I'm going to fight. Because it's different for me now. I have something to fight for: Allie, Emma, our child. My brother and his family. And my friends and the people who are counting on me. This time, my vision of our future is our only hope for survival. I sense that the next few moments will decide whether it becomes reality, whether I walk out of this warehouse alive and live to see it, and whether my children will grow up.

I focus my attention on the AU Army major who seems to be in charge of the troops here, a man a few years older than me, with a lined face, greying hair at his temples, and cold, hard eyes staring me down.

"Consider this, Major. We knocked on the door. We called out to you—before we came in, and after. We announced ourselves." Carefully, slowly, I motion toward Izumi. "And we brought a doctor. Those aren't the actions of a raiding party. That's what people would do if they truly were here to help."

The major squints, as if performing a visual lie detector.

"Consider this," I continue. "We know that as of two days ago, you had approximately one hundred people alive in this building. I know because I'm from *Camp Seven*. The camp that houses NASA and CENTCOM. The seat of the most advanced technology in the AU and its concentration of military power. I know there are—or were—a hundred people in this warehouse because we flew over it with a high-altitude military recon drone with infrared capability. We're here because there *are* life signs. We're also here for the supplies. That's true. But we need both—supplies and people. And you need us. I meant what I said. We have a plan for humanity's survival. Not just a few of us. All of us. That plan only works if the people in Camp Seven make it happen. You need us, Major. We're your only chance."

"Let's hear this plan," he says carefully, never breaking eye contact.

"Within fourteen months, we're going to leave Earth."

His eyes go wide. I continue, my voice as calm as I can make it. "We still have two ships in orbit. They're almost finished. We'll board them and leave Earth for a new world where we can all survive. To do that, you need us—you need the people in Camp Seven, their expertise."

Chandler scoffs. "Please. Even if this man is telling the truth—which, based on past experience, is doubtful—we don't need him. I can do anything he can do. He's a liar, a felon, and he's redundant."

I throw my head back and let out a laugh, letting the sound echo in the vast warehouse. "Richard, Richard, Richard. You're *finally* busted. This isn't some TV talk show with an uninformed host hungry for ratings. This is real life, with lives on the line. And behind me are two people who were *actually* there at the first contact mission briefing, who saw you pull this same stunt." Slowly, I motion to Grigory and Izumi. "They saw you get thrown off the mission. They can tell us why: because your ideas were wrong and your ego would have endangered the mission and everyone on the planet. A group of scientists heard both of us out and they chose me and we all know what happened. We defeated the grid at Ceres and the Long Winter ended. You weren't good enough then and you're certainly not good enough now."

Chandler steps closer to the major, making his plea in a quiet confidential tone. "I told you he was a liar."

"Facts don't lie, Richard. Consider this: in Camp Seven, we have more people than you. And that's not all. Remember, CENTCOM was there. Those high-altitude recon drones are the tip of the iceberg. We've got heavy artillery, guns to go around, and enough troops to raid this facility with overwhelming force. If that was our goal, we wouldn't be talking right now. Every one of you would be dead or on the run. We wouldn't have knocked or called out to you. We would have come in quietly. Gunshots would have been the first sound you would have heard. But consider this: we didn't do any of that. There's another reason why."

Chandler opens his mouth, but the major silences him with a harsh look.

"We didn't just come here for supplies," I say calmly. "We're here because there are survivors in this warehouse. The scientists in Camp Seven can get us off Earth. But we need to take enough people to restart the human race. More than anything, we need people. A genetic pool large enough to ensure our survival." I pause, letting that sink in.

"Major, the planet is going to keep getting colder. These pallets full of supplies are going to keep shrinking, even if you carry on defending them from anyone who lands on your doorstep. But eventually, you'll run out. You'll starve. If you don't freeze to death before that. I'm offering you a chance to live."

The major glances at Chandler, then at me. Slowly, his hand drifts down to his side, to the pistol holstered there. It's clear he's made his decision.

40

Emma

In our cubicle, I bundle Sam up in warm clothes recently recovered from the wreckage.

"W-where are we going?" he asks nervously.

"For a walk, Sam. Everything's going to be okay."

Allie is across the corridor, at Madison's cubicle, playing with her cousins. Like Sam, she senses something is going on. She rushes into our cubicle and grabs my other hand. "Wanna go too, Mommy."

I squat down, bracing on my cane, ignoring the pain in my legs. "Not today, Allie. I need to take Sam somewhere."

Allie bunches her eyebrows. Water comes to her eyes.

I pull her into a hug and whisper: "I'll be right back. We'll play, okay? I promise. I love you."

"Da?"

"He's at work, sweetie. He'll be back soon."

Habitats used to cover the landscape in Camp Seven, the white domes sticking out of the rocky, dusty desert. Now it's just a rolling expanse of white as far as the eye can see, lumps and hills and mounds, hiding the wreckage of our homes, the evidence of the grid's deadly assault.

Sam and I crunch across the snow, making five tracks, two little foot prints for him, two larger ones for me, and a dot in the snow for my cane. I hold his little hand in mine, feeling his fingers squeezing tight.

He hasn't said a word since we left the bunker.

Three hundred yards away from us, another group is walking in the snow: two parents and two children, holding hands, no doubt venturing out to the home or habitat they used to share (or somewhere close to it—it's hard to navigate without road markers or house numbers). Another mother and father are standing a hundred yards away in the other direction, squatting down, talking to their three children.

It's eerie out here. Utterly quiet except for the wind. A pale, dusty yellow sun shines down on us, the sky hazy, as if we're all in some sort of netherworld, a purgatory we can't escape, trapped here to roam for all eternity.

I stop beside one of the mounds, not sure if it's Sam's habitat, knowing it doesn't matter. "Sam, do you remember the night you last saw your parents?"

He perks up at the mention of his parents, nodding quickly.

"What did they tell you?"

His expression turns guarded.

"Did they say the word asteroid?"

He shakes his head, confused. "Th-they said there was a st-st-storm."

"There was, Sam. A storm. A natural disaster. That's something that happens and it's no one's fault." I scan the terrain around us. "That's what happened to the camp. Your parents were very brave. Before the storm came, they covered you up. They could have covered themselves, but they choose to cover you because they love you very much."

He stares at the snow. "I heard it. Wind. A c-c-crash. It was dark. I tried to get o-out. I was trapped."

I reach inside my coat and draw out a stack of photos. "Sam, these are yours."

He peers down at the photo. His parents are about my age: a woman with dark hair and a beaming smile; the father wearing wire-rim glasses, looking serious. They're holding a newborn Sam, sitting on a living-room couch, a bank of windows looking out on a small, manicured suburban yard enclosed by a fence. A life and time from before the Long Winter, a life Sam was too young to remember.

"Your parents loved you very much, Sam. They always will."

I pause, waiting for him to look up, but he keeps studying the photo, his hand shaking now.

"The storm was very, very powerful. A lot of people weren't as lucky as you, Sam. They didn't make it. Your parents... were among those people. I'm so sorry, Sam."

A tear drops from his face onto the picture.

"They will *always* love you." I press a hand to his chest. "And as long as they're in your heart, a part of them will always be with you."

41

James

The major's voice rings out in the warehouse, gruff and loud. "You say you brought a doctor?"

Slowly, I turn back in Izumi's direction. "Yes. Dr. Tanaka. And I have medical training."

"All right. Prove it. We've got wounded. If they die, so do you."

Chandler opens his mouth to speak, but slams it shut. Apparently, he has enough sense not to argue with the decision to let us live long enough to save some of their men.

The major turns on his heel and leads us deeper into the warehouse, to a makeshift camp they've built out of habitat parts. It looks like a giant Lego structure: modular parts stuck together, a prefab door in the middle.

The major instructs our seven soldiers to wait outside. I can tell Brightwell doesn't like it.

Inside, the smell of rot hits me first, the putrid odor of infection and dead flesh making me gag. The warehouse is frigid, but in here it's balmy and bright, the small LED lights along the ceiling lighting our way. The quarters are tight, the people packed into cubicles far smaller than the cramped quarters at CENTCOM. They made this stronghold as small as possible: easier to defend, with less perimeter to cover. And less volume to heat.

At the end of a narrow, winding corridor, there's a makeshift infirmary, with eight tiny beds, six holding soldiers in uniform. In places, their fatigues have been cut away to provide access to the wounds. Wide bandages cover their arms, legs, and torsos. Red and yellow stains seep through.

Izumi rushes to the first soldier, who has a leg wound. The man is about my age, with a freckled face and brown hair.

A woman wearing blue rubber gloves lingers on the other side of the bed.

"Gunshot wound?" Izumi asks, not looking up at the gloved attendant.

She nods quickly. "Yes. Ten were wounded in the..." She cuts her expression to the major, who's standing in the doorway. With a hand, he impatiently motions for her to go on. "I tried to remove the bullets from two of the injured, but we lost the first patient. I stopped after that."

"Are you a surgeon?" Izumi asks.

"No. A midwife."

"What antibiotics do you have?"

The woman leads Izumi to a crate and throws it open. I can tell from Izumi's reaction that it doesn't have what we need.

"Major," Izumi calls over her shoulder. "We need the supplies from our convoy."

"I'll send my people to get them. But I meant what I said: no excuses. If they die, you die."

42

Emma

Since I took Sam outside and spoke with him, he has stayed at our cubicle, mostly watching TV on the tablet. He naps with his back turned to me, probably hoping I can't hear him crying before and after he falls asleep. He's snuggled in next to me, watching *Space Labs* when Allie comes home from school. She frowns when she sees us.

She drops onto all fours and crawls in between us, almost knocking the tablet out of Sam's hands.

"Allie, that's not nice."

"You're *my* mom."

"Allie."

She turns to Sam. "Go away!"

I grab her upper arm and pull her to her feet, ignoring the pain in my legs. I lead her out of the cubicle, like my parents used to do to me when they were really upset. When we're out of earshot of Sam, I crouch down at face level with Allie.

"Sweetie, that was very, very mean."

She stares at the floor, defiant. "You're *my* mom."

"I am your mom. And Sam is going to stay with us."

"How long?"

"Forever."

She bunches her eyebrows, confused.

"Allie, when we went to the Citadel, it was because a very scary storm was hitting the camp."

"Asteroids."

"Where did you hear that?"

"School."

"Yes, the asteroids. We were very lucky. You and me and Dad weren't harmed by the asteroids. But Sam wasn't as lucky. He didn't make it to the Citadel. He was trapped in his house."

Her expression changes.

"His house was destroyed. His parents are gone. I want you to think about that. Think about how sad you would be if Dad and I were gone."

Impulsively, she throws her arms around me and begins to cry. "Gone where?" she asks, barely able to get the words out.

I hug her tight. "I'm not going anywhere, sweetie. The point is, Sam is very sad right now. He needs us. Think about how sad you would be if you were Sam. Think about how you would want people to treat you."

I release her and she stares at me for a long moment.

"Do you understand, darling?"

"Yes," she says quietly.

"Are you going to be nice to Sam?"

"Yes."

I take her small hand in mine and lead her back down the corridor.

"Is Da… gone?" she asks, voice somber.

I stop and squat down again, legs aching. "No, Allie. He's not gone—not like Sam's parents. He's at work. He's coming back."

"When?"

"Soon."

A few hours later, I'm sitting in the situation room, listening while Harry tries the radio again.

"James, do you read?"

No response.

They still haven't checked in. And we haven't heard from the backup team we sent either.

Harry glances up at me, silently asking what I want to do.

"Reroute one of the drones to fly over warehouse four-one-two. James should have reached it by now. We need to know what's happening there."

43

James

We lost two patients during surgery. The other four are iffy at best. I'm exhausted when we finish with the last one, dead on my feet, weary from the drive and the hike and hours of cutting and suturing. If the major keeps his promise, I'll actually be dead soon.

Thankfully, he doesn't make good on his declaration. When Izumi and I finish, one of his men simply leads us to a twelve-by-twelve room where Grigory and Brightwell are lying against the wall, both half asleep. I figure the major will keep us alive long enough to determine whether any follow-up medical care is needed. After that, who knows.

Grigory cracks his eyelids and stares at me with bloodshot, sleepy eyes. I'm too tired to make conversation. Despite the threat of imminent death, I drift off to sleep the moment my head hits the blanket on the floor.

I drift in and out of sleep, my body sore and numb.

There's no sense of day and night here, just the constant semi-darkness inside this makeshift prison cell.

Twice, Izumi and I are summoned to change the patients' bandages and assess their conditions. Two of them are septic. We're not optimistic about them. The other two will probably make it, with some luck.

Back in the cell, when the door closes, Brightwell whispers, "We need to make a move."

"We didn't come to fight," I respond.

"Did we come to be used as hostages? That's what we are. Best case here: they trade us back to Camp Seven for weapons, armor, and vehicles."

"Worst case?" Grigory mutters.

"They use us as body shields during an attack on Camp Seven," Brightwell says. "They know Camp Seven won't risk harming us. In that scenario, Camp Seven might even lose the battle. At that point, your families become hostages as well."

"Making the move is sounding better," Grigory mumbles, still half asleep.

I don't like it, but I have to admit, Brightwell is probably right. I keep hoping that someone in this camp will see reason and start talking to us.

"Colonel Earls has probably come to the same conclusion," Brightwell says. "We've missed several check-ins by now. Earls will do the math. I bet he's already sent a team here."

"Why?"

"Simple. It's better to fight here than at Camp Seven, where our enemy can attack at a time of their choosing—and put our civilians in the crossfire."

I exhale as I let my head fall back against the wall. "All right. I'm listening."

As escape plans go, ours is pretty simple.

Just as they have twice before, a sergeant and a private escort Izumi and me to the infirmary to check on the patients.

We perform our exams, administer antibiotics and painkillers, and when the guards aren't looking, I load a syringe with anesthetic and tuck it into my sleeve. Izumi does the same.

My heart is pounding as I shuffle across the small infirmary, trying to act naturally. The next few minutes will determine our fate here.

A corporal who suffered a gunshot wound opens his eyes for the first time.

"How are you feeling?" I ask.

"Terrible," he whispers.

"Good. That means you're alive. We're going to keep you that way."

He turns his head to the side and closes his eyes. I'm moving to the next patient when I hear gunfire ring out, muffled through the walls. I have no concept of how close the gunfire is or whether it was from inside the warehouse or outside of it.

The major's voice calls over the radio. "Secure the prisoners. Units three and four to the eastern loading dock."

"Let's go," the sergeant says.

I turn and march out of the infirmary, feeling sweat forming on my forehead. Since the prison break at Edgefield,

I haven't fought anyone hand-to-hand. Even the melee at the Citadel was at arm's length. Then, I was just trying to escape. This will be different. I have to attack.

I try to focus myself as we march down the narrow corridor. The heat presses in on me, but my hand somehow feels clammy and damp.

We pass the two cells where they're keeping the rest of our soldiers. They must've reasoned that splitting us up would decrease the chances of an escape attempt.

As before, the sergeant stops us in the hall and the private places a hand on his sidearm as he reaches forward to unlock the door. The moment the lock clicks, I jerk the syringe from my sleeve and lunge forward, jabbing it into the sergeant's neck.

He's stronger than I expected. He grabs my arm, fingers digging into my muscles like they're wet clay, pain exploding up my arms and shoulder. I depress the plunger as he slams me into the wall. My head hits hard; my vision blurs. The entire world seems to shake.

I hear Izumi yell out in pain. Through my blurred vision, I see the door to the cell fly open. Brightwell bursts out, grabs the private from behind, her arm locked around his neck. Izumi didn't land the needle, but she distracted him long enough.

The sergeant's grip on me loosens as his eyes go glassy. His eyelids fall and he collapses to the floor a second later, just as Brightwell brings the private down. She wastes no time. She grabs the man's keys and quickly unlocks the other two cells, freeing her soldiers, who spread out in the corridor, hugging the walls, a master sergeant rushing to us, squatting just long enough to grab the sidearms from our captors.

The cadence of the gunfire is quickening. I can hear automatic gunfire closer to us, inside the warehouse, followed by softer rifle reports, possibly an enemy outside returning fire.

Brightwell and her troops move quickly through the maze of narrow corridors, Izumi, Grigory, and I following behind. Some of the doors to the cubicles are open. As we pass, I catch glimpses of the families inside, huddling together, peering out with empty hollow eyes, expressions I haven't seen since we liberated the Citadel. Camp Four has been rationing.

Three gunshots only feet away snap my attention back to the corridor.

"Clear," the master sergeant calls out as he leads us around another turn. Two Atlantic Union soldiers lay dead in the hall. It's the last thing I wanted to see. I tell myself that they chose this, not me. Richard Chandler chose this.

Two of Brightwell's troops grab the rifles from the fallen soldiers as we pass. She pauses in the next corridor, seeming to listen as she raises an arm at a right angle, her open palm facing forward, fingers held together.

I hear it too: voices speaking quickly, the mention of my name.

Brightwell points to a door on our left and motions to three of her soldiers. They rush forward, form up on each side of the door and kick it in. They sweep into the room, but thankfully, there are no gunshots, only the master sergeant's voice yelling in the small space, the force almost as jarring as gunfire.

"Hands up, face the wall!"

"Clear!"

Brightwell motions for me to follow her. Inside the small room, there's a chart on the wall with an inventory of everything in the warehouse. It's categorized into food, water, and miscellaneous. Hanging beside it on the wall is a roster of people, likely the residents here, their cubicle location, and which rations they received. This is obviously their operations center.

Three radios sit atop a long table against the right wall. I flinch when one of the radios comes to life, blasting a woman's voice into the room. She's speaking French and sounds very angry. I would give anything to speak French at this point. I can only assume she's with the group who's outside—and that these two soldiers were listening in to their channel.

The major's voice comes over a second radio: "Acknowledged, Central. Try to hold them off. We're sending reinforcements now."

Brightwell shouts through the doorway, "Look alive—we've got incoming."

44

Emma

I'm lying in my cubicle, half asleep, Sam on one side, Allie on the other, when I hear Fowler's voice, softly calling my name from the corridor.

Without a word, I rise, careful not to wake either child. When I draw the sheet back, I can tell from Fowler's face that something is very wrong. He motions towards the situation room, and I fall in behind him, my cane clacking on the floor as I struggle to keep up.

In the situation room, live drone footage plays on the wall screens. I recognize the setting: it's warehouse 412. But something has changed since last time: troop carriers are now parked longways in front of the warehouse's roll-up doors. Two trucks each at the north, south, and west doors. One truck at the east door. Seven troop carriers—the exact number and model of the trucks in our convoy. Yep. Those are our trucks.

Three other troop carriers are grouped farther out at the east entrance. Soldiers stand behind them, firing on the warehouse, their tracks in the snow carving a trench next to the trucks. These are definitely the Camp Five trucks.

Whoever is inside the warehouse isn't going down without a fight. They've shot the attackers' trucks to pieces and aren't through. The night lights up with tracer fire, beams of red and green issuing from the warehouse like lasers.

I wonder if James is in that warehouse. And if so, is he fighting the intruders? Or perhaps fighting to escape?

"How far out are our people?" Fowler asks Colonel Earls.

He glances at the large watch on his wrist and shrugs. "Unknown, sir. We don't have GPS."

Fowler squints, confused.

"The surface ice is now hard enough for the light vehicles to drive on," Earls replies. "They're taking the direct route— as the crow flies."

"Best guess?"

"Hard to say. I'd guess roughly thirty minutes."

45

James

Brightwell grabs the three radios on the long table and distributes them to her people.

"Tune to channel seventeen. Collins and Matthias, secure the entrance."

To one of the Camp Four soldiers who had been operating the radio, she says, "How many armed personnel inside this habitat?"

When the man hesitates, Brightwell says, "Keep in mind, Private, when we search this habitat, you'll be marching in front of us as a body shield. Lying will be bad for your life expectancy."

"Six," the man mutters, eyes on the floor, seeming disgusted with himself.

"Where?"

"Two guarding—or supposed to be guarding you all. Two at the entrance. And the two of us here in comms."

I count that as good news: we've already neutralized four soldiers here inside the habitat and the other two are in this room. The men we met in the corridor must have been coming from the entrance.

"How many out there?" Brightwell asks.

The man grits his teeth and bites off the words. "Thirty-two."

The master sergeant leans into the doorway and makes eye contact with Brightwell, his gun still pointed out in the corridor.

"Ten against thirty-two. They have the numbers, Captain."

"We have something they don't."

The sergeant stares at her, unflinching.

"Brains," she says, turning to Grigory and me. "Gentlemen?"

"We need weapons and leverage," I respond instantly. To the Camp Four comms soldier, I say, "Where's the armory?"

"C seven."

Brightwell needs no further instruction. She barks an order to two more of her people. "Get to cubicle C seven and take what we need. Hide the rest."

I walk over and scan the roster of citizens. "Chandler's in E nine."

Brightwell is about to issue a command to her soldiers, but I wave her off. "I'll go. I want to handle this." I turn my attention back to the radio operator. "Who's in charge here?"

"Major Danforth."

"Who's the top civilian leader?"

"Technically, it's Governor Livingston. But he's... he doesn't have much say."

"Last question: Does Danforth have any family here in the habitat?"

The soldier glances away from me, body going rigid. That response tells me everything I need to know. I glance at the chart. The word "Danforth" is scrawled next to the cell F14.

"Don't worry. We're not going to hurt them," I say to the soldier.

At that moment, the soldiers who had gone to the armory return, clutching semi-automatic rifles, body armor, and hand grenades. They pass out the weapons, Grigory and I both taking one.

"You know how to use that?" Brightwell asks.

I study the heavy, black, cold machine. "I had a hunting rifle when I was a kid."

"It's not much different." She shows Grigory and me how to load a magazine and chamber the first round. "You just point and press the trigger. Just be careful where you point."

One of the soldiers holds a rifle out to Izumi, but she grimaces and shakes her head.

"I can't."

"You can stay here, ma'am," Brightwell says to Izumi.

"I want to survey the people here in the habitat. They might need care," Izumi says.

"Very well," Brightwell replies. "But you'll have to wait until we handle the situation out there."

Izumi opens her mouth to argue, but I cut her off.

"We need to listen to her, Izumi. This is her specialty."

Izumi nods.

Gunshots ring out, close, right outside the habitat. I hear bullets ripping through the hard-plastic walls as Brightwell yells over the radio, "Report!"

One of the two soldiers she sent to the entrance responds instantly, gunfire in the background. "I count seven hostiles, Captain."

An explosion echoes through the habitat, the sound even louder over the radio.

"Make that four, ma'am."

"Can I borrow one of your men?" I ask Brightwell.

She nods to a corporal out in the corridor.

Grigory falls in behind me as I exit the room, the corporal taking the lead.

"Where're you going?" Brightwell calls after me.

"To get some leverage."

Using the mental image of the habitat map, I jog through the corridors, stopping at every intersection, peeking around the corners for signs of trouble. At one of the supply closets, I find the item I need: duct tape. All good plans eventually involve duct tape.

A few weeks ago, I never would have imagined myself doing what I'm about to do. But I never thought I would be in a situation like this. This is survival. This is what I have to do—for everyone's sake. Still, I don't like it.

At the door to cubicle F14, Grigory and I stand aside as the corporal turns the handle, his gun leading the way. The small room is bare except for three cots, a pile of rations in the corner, and two inhabitants: a woman about my age and a boy who looks to be about twelve, both watching their tablets; tears are streaming down the woman's face.

"Get up, we need to go," I shout.

"Who are you?"

"It doesn't matter. We're here to help. That's all I can tell you right now. We're going to end the fighting in this camp. But we need your help. Please."

She looks from me to the soldier beside me, a soldier she no doubt doesn't recognize. "Just take me. Not Noah."

"Both of you. Right now. We have to go."

We allow them a few seconds to bundle up and then we rush through the corridors to the E block. At cubicle E9, I turn the handle and throw the door open. Richard Chandler sits on a cot, alone in the small room, holding a radio, listening intently. His eyes go wide when he sees me holding the rifle.

Quickly, I step into the room and grab the radio before he can say anything. "Figured you'd be on the front line, Richard."

Rage burns in his eyes as he stares me down. "You should surrender right now, James. You're outnumbered. And there's an enemy outside who is far worse than anyone in here."

"Who's that?"

"Camp Five. Back for revenge. Who do you think shot those soldiers you treated?"

"Revenge on whom?"

For the first time, he breaks eye contact.

"Is that why you're hiding in here? You think they'll breach the warehouse? What happened? Did you run the same trap on them that you caught us in? Except they fought their way out."

His silence confirms my theory.

"You were pretty smug when you had us under your thumb. Is that why you're hiding in here, listening to the radio? Ready to run if they get inside?"

He simply stares at the floor.

"You're all talk until things go south. Then you're the first out the door."

"I saved these people," Chandler spits out, staring at the floor.

"I doubt that."

"It's true."

"Why are you even here, Richard? In Camp Four?"

"I was here for a rally."

"An emigration rally?"

"Yes. It was scheduled for the day after the asteroids hit. I was staying with the governor's chief of staff. She heard about the asteroid strike early. I made a quick decision. A correct decision, I might add—one that saved many lives. I realized that the weapons depot and largest warehouse—being close together—would be the asteroid's likely target. I took my inner circle here—to the warehouse farthest away." He looks up at me. "Say what you want, James, but I saved these people. That's why they trust me."

"What about the people outside? Including the woman in a nightgown with her children frozen to her chest and a gunshot in her body?"

He reels back, acting disgusted. "Oh, spare me the whole high-and-mighty act, James. We made hard choices—for our own survival. This is a warehouse full of food on a dead planet. Not an ivory tower."

"And you've made it a war zone. That ends now." At that moment an idea occurs to me. It's perfect—a sort of justice that rarely comes along.

He squints at me. "What?"

I can't help but laugh. "This is going to be good, Richard. I can't wait. But first, I'm going to do something I've been wanting to do for a long, long time."

I reach out and grab the roll of duct tape from Grigory. Chandler rises, ready to struggle, but I rip off a piece of tape and cover his mouth quickly. The corporal holds him as I wrap tape around his head a few times and bind his wrists together. To the woman and child, I whisper, "I'm really, really sorry about this." And I am. But it has to be done.

By the time we reach the entrance to the habitat, the fighting has stopped. Brightwell's men have prevailed and the entire group, except for Izumi, is waiting for us. Together, we rush out into the warehouse, towards the eastern exit and the sound of gunfire. As we draw closer, Brightwell separates her troops into three groups. They climb the stacks of supplies and crawl to the edge of the rows, flattening themselves, pointing their rifles at the troops massed at the roll-up doors.

Grigory, Brightwell, and I stop at the end of a row of supplies diagonal from the Camp Four troops, keeping Chandler and Danforth's wife and child behind us and well out of any line of fire.

"Now what?" Brightwell whispers.

"Now we negotiate, Captain." I activate the radio and tune to the channel Major Danforth is using. "Major. Have your men cease firing."

"You really are crazy, Sinclair."

"Maybe. But you're going to stop firing right now. The men you sent are dead, and we have you surrounded." I release the radio button.

Brightwell raises her own radio, which is tuned to our private channel. "Fire warning shots."

I peek over one of the stacks of habitat parts just long enough to glimpse the shots from above ricocheting off the metal door and girders. The Camp Four soldiers scramble, but there's no cover for them. They crouch and train their rifles at the tops of the stacks of supplies, scanning for the shooters. Shots from the French troops continue to slam into the outside of the warehouse, some of the bullets making their way through the slits in the door.

"Are you crazy?" Danforth shouts. "You're going to get us all killed."

"No. You are. Put down your weapons."

"You're a dead man, Sinclair."

Gently, I peel the tape from the woman's mouth. "You're our best hope," I whisper to her. "You have to convince him to stop fighting. If you don't, a lot more people are going to die." I hit the button on the radio and hold it to her mouth.

"Max."

"Angela?"

"I'm here. So is Noah."

A pause, then Danforth's voice, angry, barely contained: "Sinclair, if you harm them, I swear to you—"

"If they're harmed, it will be your fault, Major. Lay down your weapons right now. Or we'll do this the other way."

"And what do you propose to do about the army outside that's going to come in here and kill us all?"

"Leave that to me."

I peek over the pallet, and see Danforth shake his head as he lowers the radio and calls to his troops, "Weapons down."

A silent moment, then Danforth growls to them, "That's an order!"

I hear the soft clacks of rifles and sidearms being placed on the concrete floor.

"Report," Brightwell says over our private channel.

"Four still armed, ma'am."

"That means all of your men," I say into the radio. "Put down your weapons and step away from them."

A moment later, the master sergeant calls over the radio, "They've complied. Should we secure?"

"Affirmative," Brightwell responds.

Time for phase two. I remove my body armor and sweater, then the stained white T-shirt I've been wearing for days. I rip the T-shirt down the middle and break off a long piece of wood from a nearby pallet. I attach the white T-shirt to the stick, fashioning a crude flag of truce. I hold the stick to Chandler's bound wrists and tape it to them. His eyes bulge, and he shakes his head.

"Sort of a weird twist of fate, isn't it, Richard? You going out there to help us make peace." I raise my eyebrows. "We need to send someone we're willing to lose, and... you said it yourself: you and I are redundant."

He tries to step away, but I grab him by the upper arm and drag him forward. Brightwell's men have climbed down from their perches and are leveling their rifles at our captives. A few sporadic shots from outside still slam into the warehouse, but without the fire from within, the French have slowed their assault.

I tune the radio to the station the French are using, and speak slowly, hoping their command of foreign languages is better than mine. "Camp Five commander, we are ceasing fire. There's been a change in control here. We want peace. To negotiate. To work together."

I wait, but there's no response.

I activate the radio again. "Camp Five commander, please respond if you can understand me."

To Brightwell, I ask, "Any of your people speak French?"

She begins asking, but a response on the radio interrupts her.

"With whom am I speaking?" a woman asks in a heavy French accent.

"I'm from Camp Seven. My name is James Sinclair. We came here to assist the survivors of Camp Four. We've been held as hostages and have just now freed ourselves."

"You're lying."

"I'm not."

I nod to the corporal and a sergeant standing next to Chandler. They take him by the arms and march to the side door next to the roll-up door. He wiggles like a fish on a line, but they hold him tight. The corporal turns the door handle and they bring Chandler to the threshold, holding his hands out to let the makeshift white flag stick out.

The corporal glances back at me and I nod. They shove him through the door into the freezing night.

I activate the radio. "Do you recognize the person outside?"

"Yes. We know this man."

Chandler is beating on the door with the stick, his screams muffled by the tape. It's a beautiful sound.

"I was telling the truth," I call over the radio. "He's not in charge anymore. We are."

"What do you want?"

"To work together. We have a plan to save the last survivors. We're looking for people to help us. All we ask is that those of you who can work do so. In exchange for food and housing."

There's a long silence, perhaps the French leader speaking with her people.

I could swear I hear something buzzing in the distance.

Chandler pounds on the door. His words come out muffled through the tape, but I can guess what he's saying. It's the sweetest sound I've ever heard. I've been wanting to gag that guy for a long time.

Lights beam through the narrow slits in the roll-up door. Headlamps from vehicles. Are the French leaving? Or moving closer?

I creep to the opening and peer out. The troop carrier from Camp Seven is still out there, as are the French vehicles, all darkened. The headlights are coming from the horizon, high-speed ATVs, bouncing over the snow-covered terrain.

Another raiding party?

Quickly, I scan through the other radio channels, stopping when I hear a man's voice, speaking urgently. "... can hear me, please respond. We're engaging hostiles outside the warehouse now." I know that voice—it's one of our soldiers from Camp Seven.

Gunshots ring out in the distance.

Brightwell's radio is still tuned to the French commander's channel. Before I can reply to the Camp Seven convoy, Brightwell's radio blares out the French commander's voice, yelling in her native language. The result is instant.

Gunshots slam into the warehouse and lance across the
landscape toward the incoming vehicles from Camp Seven.
Suddenly, everyone inside is in motion and the stillness of
the night shatters.

46

Emma

In the situation room, I watch the night vision video feed from the drone as warehouse 412 erupts into a war zone again.

The troops from Camp Five fire mercilessly on the vehicles rushing in from Camp Seven. The convoy breaks up, the light vehicles swerving to the left and right, throwing up waves of snow and ice. The troops from Camp Five turn and begin firing in the other direction—back at the warehouse. Two soldiers race out from behind the trucks, stooping, making for the warehouse. They're going to try to take it.

Suddenly, my vision blurs and my head spins. Nausea rushes over me. Pain flares in my lower back. It seems to radiate from deep inside of me.

I close my eyes and lean forward, setting my elbow on the table and catching my face in my hands.

"Emma, are you okay?" Harry asks.

"Yes," I whisper. "I'm fine."

"You're as white as a sheet."

"I just need a minute to rest."

47

James

Bullets tear through the warehouse's roll-up door, digging into the pallets of food, water, and habitat components. Pieces of the supplies float down across the aisles like confetti.

I rush to Danforth's wife and son and put my arms around them and herd them out of the way, to an adjacent aisle where I crouch down, my body between them and the outer wall.

"Cease fire!" I yell into the radio. "To the soldiers from Camp Seven, this is James Sinclair. Cease fire immediately. The situation here is under control. You are to stop firing and evacuate the area."

The bullets stop in waves as the two groups stop firing.

"Understood, Dr. Sinclair. We are breaking off and moving back. We were under the impression that you were under attack."

"Thank you," I reply as I grab Brightwell's radio, which is still tuned to the French channel.

"Camp Five commander, that was a misunderstanding.

I promise you we're not here to fight. To show you how serious I am, I'm going to come out personally to negotiate. I would really appreciate it if you would refrain from shooting me."

While I wait for a response, Brightwell calls out to her team, making sure no one is wounded. I glance over at Danforth's wife and son. They're both rattled, tears in their eyes, the wife's hands shaking. "You can return to the habitat now. Your husband will be back shortly. This will be over soon. I'm very sorry you had to be involved."

There's still no response from the French commander outside. I activate the radio again. "Camp Five commander, I need you to confirm you heard my last message. And— that you're not going to shoot me when I come out."

"We will not shoot you, Dr. Sinclair. Assuming you do not attempt any deception."

Despite the assurances, I put my body armor back on. Just outside the warehouse door, I spot Chandler lying in the snow, a puddle of blood spreading out from him. I really, really dislike that guy. But as it turns out, I don't hate him enough to watch him die. I rush over to him and quickly scan his body. He's been shot in the leg. His breathing is ragged and shallow. He looks up at me like a wounded animal, fearful and, at the same time, full of rage.

I hold the radio to my face. "Izumi, I need you out here. We have one wounded."

With Chandler at my feet, I stand and call to the French commander, "A show of good faith. We're going to bring food out—enough for all of you and enough for you to take back to your people."

★

Chandler is going to live. I suppose that's good news. Time will tell.

The French were in better spirits after eating. And with no one shooting at them.

It's going to take some time to heal the rift between them and Major Danforth. But I think it's possible. When people are starving to death and peace means eating, they're much more willing to see past their grudges.

I have finally gotten things calmed down enough to bring the troops from Camp Seven in. Their headlights cut through the night as they approach, the beams glittering upon the snow as the ATVs bounce towards the warehouse. Captain Brightwell comes to stand beside me at the roll-up door.

"They thought we were in trouble," she says quietly.

"We were in trouble."

"We did all right."

"I think it probably would've gone better if I had listened to you."

"It's under the bridge, sir."

"Nevertheless, we're going to do things differently next time."

She raises an eyebrow.

"Next time, we're not going to assume people share our point of view. We'll go in ready for anything."

"That suits me, sir."

The door on the lead ATV pops open and a soldier wearing a parka exits and jogs to the warehouse. "Dr. Sinclair?"

"Yes."

"There's a call on the long-range for you, sir. It's urgent."

I probably should've used one of the long-range radios in our troop carriers to check in after the fighting stopped. But there was Richard's surgery, and frankly, I'm almost too exhausted to think straight.

At the ATV, I pick up the radio's handset. "Sinclair here."

Fowler's voice is somber. "James, you need to get back here."

"What's happening?"

"It's Emma."

"Is she okay?"

"She will be. Just... get back as soon as you can."

I race back to the warehouse and gather Grigory, Brightwell, and Izumi. "I need to go back to Camp Seven."

"What's the plan here, sir?" Brightwell asks.

"Load up some supplies and send them back to Camp Seven. I'm going to take one of the fast ATVs with two of the troops they sent. We'll drive in shifts."

"After that?" Grigory asks.

"Brightwell and her team will keep going on to the other camps. The drone surveillance should be in by now. Or it will be shortly. We need to bring these survivors together. If what we've seen here is any indication it's pretty bad in the other camps too."

"I agree," Izumi says. "I'd like to stay with the team making contact with the other camps."

"Me too," Grigory says quietly.

He doesn't give a reason, but I know why: he wants to stay busy—and away from Arthur.

I hold my hand out to Captain Brightwell. "Thank you, Captain. I mean it. Good luck out there."

"Thank you, sir." She takes the hint and leaves us, barking orders to her people as she goes.

"We need to make a decision about Arthur's proposal soon. I think you two have earned the right to have your voices heard. But I don't think this is a conversation we can have over the radio. If the details got out, it could be disastrous."

"I haven't given it much thought," Izumi says. "Frankly, it's over my head technically. What do you think, James?"

"It all comes back to power. If we could generate enough, we could make a stand here on Earth. But I don't see a good way to do that. I think leaving is our only viable option. But I feel we need to take precautions, ensure that the grid doesn't double-cross us. To me, that's the real challenge."

Izumi nods. "Very well. I'll vote with you." She chews her lip for a moment, seeming conflicted. "And would you mind telling Min that I'll be home as soon as I can?"

"Of course."

Grigory is staring off into the warehouse, as if trying to ignore the conversation.

"Grigory?"

He nods slowly, still not making eye contact, and reaches out and places a hand on my shoulder. "Fine. But, James, please try not to get us killed."

On the way back to Camp Seven I repeatedly ask to speak to Emma over the long-range radio. Each time I'm denied.

I'm still exhausted from the trip to Camp Four and the events there, but I can't manage to sleep. The ATV jostles as it speeds across the icy terrain and my mind is racing as well.

The ramp to the CENTCOM bunker is open when we arrive. We've erected two habitat walls to form an airlock, keeping the warm air in. Fowler is waiting just inside the inner door.

"Follow me," he says simply.

He walks quickly along the bunker's outer corridor, not venturing into the sea of cubicles.

The moment we reach the infirmary, I spot Emma in one of the beds. Her arms are at her side, eyes closed. Everything else in the world seems to disappear. I can hear Fowler speaking, words muffled, far away. At Emma's bedside, I slide my hand into hers and squeeze. Her eyes open. A tired smile curls at the edges of her mouth.

"Hi," she whispers.

"What happened?"

"Nothing."

"This doesn't look like nothing."

"It's just exhaustion. Stress—"

"The drone footage. You saw what was happening out there?"

She nods.

"The baby?"

"Is fine. Just fine. I just need to rest."

48

Emma

For someone like myself, who is happiest when they're working on something, bedrest is like a prison sentence. I feel as though I've been in this infirmary for three years.

James arrives every morning, bearing the healthiest MRE he can find, a smile on his face, Allie and Sam in tow.

Today is chicken noodle soup. For breakfast. I'm not complaining. In fact, I'm happy to have something to eat. Still, chicken noodle soup at 6 a.m. takes some getting used to. As with every meal these days, James methodically studies the nutrition label, verifying that it has the requisite macronutrient content. I know the first trimester is a critical time for the pregnancy, but since he saw me in this infirmary bed, he's become almost obsessed with protecting me.

When the kids are off to school, and he returns, I take his hand in mine. "I have to get out of here."

"You need to take it easy."

"I will. Just not here. This is like prison."

"Trust me. This is not like prison."

"Oh. Right. Sorry, I keep forgetting."

"Actually, we do need to formalize our response to Arthur's offer. If you're feeling up to it. It would just be the team discussing—"

I throw the covers off. "I'm feeling up to it. It's just talking. How much can it hurt me?"

It feels good just to be out of the infirmary, sitting upright, hearing the cheap, faux-leather chairs in the situation room squeaking as everyone takes their seats. I'm pretty sure James has purposely seated me with my back to the wall screens, which show drone footage of Captain Brightwell's convoy approaching Camp Two. He's scared I'll see something upsetting. Every now and then, I sneak a glance, drawing a scowl from him. I feel like a kid in detention. It's kind of fun.

Everyone is here: Harry, Min, Fowler, Colonel Earls, even Charlotte, who has left Madison in charge of the school for the morning.

Fowler clears his throat. "The question before us is the offer from the grid, as conveyed by Arthur. Grigory and Izumi are not here, and the decision has been made not to include them via radio, given the sensitivity of the issue at hand. They've confided their votes to James and we'll tally them at the end. Let's start with the idea of rejecting the grid's offer and staying here on Earth."

James speaks first. "It comes down to this: in about a year, the planet will be an ice ball. The issue is power. And I can't solve it. Not with our currently known resources.

"Even if we solve the power issue, we're not out of the woods. We'd need to create a self-sustaining habitat, capable of growing food and recycling water. Building a small one is doable—not easily—but doable. A large one? Capable of sustaining a viable gene pool? Impossible."

James glances over at Colonel Earls. "Unless there's some kind of classified site we're not aware of—a self-contained habitat hardened against extreme weather, either complete or pretty far along?"

"Not that I know of. The Citadel was the most advanced bunker in the Atlantic Union, for the obvious reasons—proximity to CENTCOM and NASA."

James holds his hands out. "Plus, even if we're successful, if we stay on Earth, we're sitting ducks. The grid could end our civilization at any moment."

Fowler leans back in his chair. "To me, the real question is which are we more likely to successfully build: a self-sustaining underground habitat or a colony ship capable of carrying us to another star system? The colony ship, frankly, seems a lot harder to do."

My hand instinctively touches my stomach as I speak for the first time. "There's another consideration. We've been talking about short-term survival. But we have to consider the long term. Even food, water, and shelter doesn't guarantee survival. Will to live is also vital. We saw that in the Citadel. Surviving, simply put, is not enough. Our plan has to give our people a life worth living. Most of all, these people need to believe that their children have a chance of a life worth living. I don't think we'll find that on Earth, in a confined habitat, under the constant threat of attack, in a place where we must control our population size, where any catastrophe in the farms or habitat might bring about our extinction."

When no one says anything, I continue. "Leaving Earth is uncertain, I'll admit that. But on a new world, beyond the reach of the grid, we have a chance at happiness. Here, I feel our fate is certain, even if we survive in the short term."

"Valid points," Fowler says. "Ones I hadn't considered."

Charlotte's voice is pensive. "Children typically adapt better than we expect. But I have to agree with Emma. Our species evolved over millions of years, in a predominantly temperate climate. Above ground. I believe our best chance of long-term survival is in a similar environment, even if slight adaptations must be made."

Harry steeples his fingers together. "If you think about it, living aboard a starship for generations will be a lot like living in an underground habitat—a closed ecosystem with constant threats outside its walls. We run the same risks whether we stay on Earth or live in the starship for the next who knows how many years. As Charlotte says, we haven't evolved for it and can't know how we'll fare under those circumstances."

It's a good point, one *I* hadn't considered.

"That assumes the trip to the new world will take generations," James says.

Harry smiles. "You think the grid has warp drive?"

"Who knows. Obviously it took the new harvester years to get here after the Battle of Ceres, not seconds. But that may have been due to other factors. Before we make any judgments about the colony option, I think we should understand exactly what the grid is proposing."

"I agree," Min says. "I think if we can make the colony option work, it's our best move. I don't trust the grid. I think they'll double-cross us, and I think that's the greatest risk."

"How do we mitigate that risk?" Fowler asks.

"I've given it a lot of thought," James says. "The principal risk is that the grid will be giving us a great deal of technical assistance. If they can control the technology, they can kill us in any number of ways."

He lets the words hang there for a long moment.

"But," he continues, "I think we can minimize the threat. First, we allow the grid to provide technical designs, but we conduct the manufacturing, to ensure the parts aren't made to fail—*and* we *always* write *all* of the software. We also need to make sure Arthur doesn't have access to that code or any of our networks. As of right now, we don't have any wireless data networks."

"What about the daisy-chain repeaters the drones set out?" Min asks.

"Oh, right," James says, rubbing his temple. "But they're just voice data—they have no connection to any of our databases and the software is rudimentary. I don't see much risk there, but we should take it down anyway and just use the radios. From here out, we'll maintain a ban on wireless data networks."

"That wouldn't prevent Arthur from writing code of his own and uploading it to a closed system," Harry says.

"That's true," James replies. "And I think that's the second part: we need to maintain one hundred percent visual coverage of Arthur at all times. Restrict his access, make sure he doesn't go near a computer that's connected to another one."

"That's not the only danger," Min says. "The harvester could launch a direct attack on the colony ships."

"I've given that some thought," James says. "I think we have to insist that the ships have some form of defense system. Even if we get out of this solar system successfully, we will be crossing a wide swath of space, possibly transiting other solar systems or passing near them—systems where we might encounter hostile technology or civilizations. We need to be able to defend ourselves."

"Obviously, spaceships are pretty far outside my area of expertise," Colonel Earls says. "I look at things from a different point of view. When I think about the risks, the human factor is what jumps out at me. Specifically, at some point, certainly in the next year, we'll have to start telling people that we're leaving Earth on a starship. I think a portion of the population will have a problem even believing that. And if they believe it, agreeing to it. We could have riots on our hands. We might have a civil war before this is all over. The conflict between Camps Four and Five that we just witnessed is just a small preview of what we might be facing."

Earls is right. I also hadn't seen it from that perspective. It's amazing how hearing from someone with a different point of view reveals your blind spots.

"It would seem," Fowler says, "that we all have our work cut out for us, no matter what path we choose. It's apparent that we need to hear the details of Arthur's proposal before we decide. We don't have enough information at this point." He scans the group. "Agreed?"

"I agree," James says as others chime in and nod.

"I have one other thing I want to add," Charlotte says. "We've compiled an updated census with counts from Camps Seven, Four, and Five. We're at just over five hundred survivors. Simply put, it's a very small genetic pool from which to restart the human race. I'm not saying it can't be done, but it's one of my concerns. If the trend holds for the rest of the camps in the Atlantic Union, we're borderline at best. Simply put, we need to find more people. While I agree that our resources should be dedicated to either the underground habitat or shipbuilding, I think we need to consider reaching out to the Caspians, the Pac Alliance, and the homeland settlements sooner rather than later."

I know Charlotte has family in Australia, at the Pac Alliance headquarters. I haven't thought about it before, but she must be worried sick about them. I also find her concerns about our population level valid.

"How to get there," Harry says, "is the problem. The drones have surveyed all of the AU airports. None of the aircraft survived the asteroid strikes. No helos either. There are still three military depots in the camps left to reconnoiter, but I don't think we can be optimistic at this point."

"What about the two AU seaports?" Fowler asks.

"Unknown," James responds. "One of the drones will reach the northern port at Camp Three in the next thirty-six hours. We'll get a look at the western port at Camp Fifteen about twelve hours after that. I'd be very surprised if any of the vessels anchored there survived. Unless one of those camps wasn't hit."

"And," Colonel Earls says, "none of the other camps or settlements have contacted us. It implies that they're in the same shape we are. Or worse."

"I have an idea," Min says quietly. "I need to talk to Grigory about it, but it could potentially connect us with the other camps."

The door to the situation room flies open and a staff sergeant leans in. "Colonel, sorry, sir, Captain Brightwell's on the line. We have a problem."

Instantly I glance back at the drone footage. I think everyone was so caught up in the conversation that they ignored the screens on the wall.

In the image, the Camp Seven convoy is stopped in the snow. Two ATVs from another camp are parked near them, Atlantic Union soldiers spread out around the vehicles, guns pointing at our convoy. It looks like a roadblock.

"Thank you," Earls says to the sergeant, who withdraws instantly, closing the door. Earls activates the radio on the conference table. "Team bravo, Camp Seven actual. Report."

"Sir, Captain Brightwell here. We've made contact with Camp Nine. They've ordered me to stand down and surrender my weapons."

"Who's ordered you, Captain?"

"General Paroli, sir."

"Who is General Paroli?" Fowler asks.

"He's the CO of the AU Third Army," Earls responds. "He's Italian. So are his troops. He's in charge of AU northern ground defenses. And he outranks me."

"Not anymore," Fowler says. "As of right now, I'm activating the Citadel Continuity Charter."

Earls cocks his head. "Sir, I'm not familiar."

"It's a classified section of the AU treaty that transfers all executive branch powers, including the authority to declare martial law, to the highest-ranking civilian official here in Camp Seven. The chain of command is very clear. Two of the AU Executive Council members survived in the Citadel, and both declined their rights under the charter. Which means I'm in charge."

"Sir," Captain Brightwell says over the radio. "Do you copy?"

"Standby, Captain," Earls replies.

"I should've done this sooner," Fowler says. "Under the authority granted to me by the Citadel Continuity Charter, I hereby appoint you, Nathan Earls, as the new Secretary of Defense for the Atlantic Union. I believe that gives you the authority you need to control the present situation and any others you encounter out there."

Earls sits there, stunned. "Sir, I certainly appreciate it. But I'm not sure I'm qualified. To be frank, the Citadel assignment was sort of a backwater posting. Before the Long Winter, I was eighteen months from retirement. Probably already at my terminal rank."

"Well, Mr. Secretary, the world has changed. And as far as I can see, you're the best man for the job right now. It sounds like you have a situation you need to attend to."

Earls stands, still slightly stunned. "Yes, sir," he says absently before making his way out of the room.

To James, Fowler says, "Let's start prepping for the meeting with Arthur. I want to get this right. But first, I need an hour to work on something."

"What's that?" James calls as Fowler heads for the door.

"I need to write the Citadel Continuity Charter."

49

James

The count just came in: we have almost two hundred survivors in Camp Nine. That takes us to almost seven hundred total. Seven hundred humans left. There are more out there, and we need to find them. The clock is ticking—to reunite everyone and to leave this planet. The temperature dropping outside is like a strange countdown to our fate. The colder it gets, the less time we have left.

In the situation room, Emma, Harry, Fowler, Min, and I have debated all the ways the grid can kill us. And all the ways we can stop them. Now it's time to hear from our enemy, who, in a strange twist of fate, is also our only way off this planet.

Earls has assigned no fewer than six armed guards to Arthur. They're dressed in full body armor, helmets included, armed to the teeth. Arthur's hands are bound with tight metal cuffs. I'm not sure if he can get out of them. But I figure he could take down at least half of the guards and any one of us in this room before he's neutralized. As such,

I've ensured that Emma is at the other end of the room, seated at the head of the table.

The wall screens are off, and the table is clear of any tablets or papers that might give him information he could use against us.

He waltzes in leisurely, as if he's arriving at a restaurant for dinner with old friends. Three guards stay in the situation room; the other three remain outside, guns trained on Arthur.

For a moment, no one says anything. I imagine the rest of the leadership team is a bit taken aback. They knew this person as Oscar. He meant something to every one of us. In our darkest moment, when the Battle of Ceres was lost, he saved us. But for Emma and me, he was much more.

I think Emma sort of saw him as a stepson—and a friend. He was there for her when she couldn't walk. In our now crumbled habitat here in Camp Seven, he helped her regain her health, coaching her in the exercises, encouraging, admonishing, and educating.

He was my creation, my one true friend when the world turned against me. The thing I loved and nurtured and cared for when it felt as though everything in my life had turned bad.

But the thing I remember most about Oscar is what he did the day the asteroids fell on the Earth. He saved my daughter. He got her to the Citadel faster than any human could have. He also escaped the Citadel when no human could. If he hadn't swam the backup tube and climbed out of the aquifer, we'd still be down there. He saved all of us. Now he's gone, replaced by this thing. Our enemy. Perhaps our salvation too.

"You rang," Arthur says.

"That's cute," Fowler mutters. "They told me you're funny now."

"I've always been funny. James's barbaric AI was the problem before. Same body. New mind."

"We've discussed your offer," Fowler says, ignoring Arthur's commentary. "We'd like to know more about what you're proposing."

"I was under the impression my offer was accepted. I was operating under that assumption when I rescued your people from that poorly conceived hole in the ground you called the Citadel."

Fowler hesitates.

"Let's talk about the future, not the past," I say evenly. "Specifically, let's discuss how we leave this planet and travel to a new home, far from the grid."

"Well, it's very simple, James. You give me the means to transform those primitive ships in orbit. I do my work and send you semi-hairless apes on your way, and we all live happily ever after. Sort of."

"What's to keep you from killing us once we get to the ships? It'd be convenient, your enemy all in one vulnerable place?" Fowler asks.

"Conservation of energy," Arthur replies. "I just want rid of you. Out of the solar system, out of my hair. The grid wants your sun, and it wants to spend the least amount of energy capturing it."

"Understand our point of view," I say. "You—Arthur— aren't taking any energy from the grid. You could program the colony ships to explode or simply drift down into the atmosphere and burn up."

"Perhaps, but if I did, what then? What if you caught me? A war ensues and you kill me and then launch a weak counterattack at the harvester. It leaves the grid in the same predicament: it must expend energy to eradicate you. If so, my mission fails. I'm incentivized to get you out of the system."

"Once the ships are out of the system—beyond the Oort cloud—what's to keep you from killing us then?"

"All I can give you is my promise. Consider this: I've never lied to you, James. Nor have any other members of the grid. On Ceres, the first harvester told you what it was and what it wanted. In the seconds before you destroyed it, that harvester told you that another harvester would return, one far stronger, and that it would decimate you. It did. And when your people were slowly starving to death in that bunker, I promised you I would get them out. And I did. Now I'm telling you that I will transport you safely to a new home. I will do just that."

Arthur takes a step toward the table. The soldiers instantly raise their rifles to point at his chest. Arthur grins. "Relax. Look, what you don't understand is that we're on the same team. The grid is this universe's destiny. Ergo, it's your destiny. You all will join the grid one day. It's a matter of when. Not if."

Fowler holds a hand up. "Let's focus on the task at hand. Leaving the solar system. How? I want details."

"As I said, you give me raw materials, I'll build some robots, and they'll do the rest."

"How would you even get the robots into orbit?" Harry asks. "We were almost out of rocket fuel before the asteroid impact."

"My launch system wouldn't require fuel. Only power."

Fowler studies Arthur. "How?"

Arthur sighs. "The details—"

"Are important," Fowler snaps. "We want to hear them."

"Very well. I'll use the same boring drone that created the vertical shaft down to the Citadel."

"Use it how? I don't follow," I comment, truly interested.

"I'll use the boring drone to create an acceleration ring at one of the impact craters." Arthur eyes Harry and me. "As you well know, the earth is packed tight there. The underground tunnel will be sealed, maintaining low pressure inside. Not quite vacuum conditions, but low enough to enable the ring to accelerate objects to incredible speeds. We'll use capsules in the ring. Once the capsules reach exit velocity for Earth's gravity well, a port in the ring will open and the payload will exit via a vertical shaft. Of course the contents—construction robots, drones, and eventually passengers—will be protected by the capsules."

It's an incredible idea, far afield from anything I've contemplated. I ask the obvious question: "How would you power it?"

"The ring will be lined with electromagnets that will propel the capsules. Solar panels on the ground next to the ring will power the magnets."

I seize the opening, hoping he won't follow my logic. "You've said solar output directed at Earth will keep falling, approaching zero in a year. Wouldn't a geothermal energy source be superior? More reliable. More consistent? You could conceivably use the same boring drone to make the tunnels."

Arthur smiles, as if amused. "Very good, James. You almost had me. I mean, for nearly three nanoseconds there, I almost went for it. So close."

I lean back in my chair, not taking the bait.

Arthur glances around the room. "For those of you scratching your heads, James just tried to trick me into making a geothermal energy source that you all could use in case the whole colony ship thing doesn't work out. Lesson for the day: energy equals life. With a geothermal source, you all could power a self-contained habitat. You could stay on Earth, and that just doesn't work for us."

Arthur can taunt me all he wants. I had to try.

"One question," Harry says. "Once you launch them, what's to keep the capsules from floating out into space after they exit the atmosphere?"

"Harry, Harry, Harry, do you actually think I would let you drift in space to your death?"

"Yeah, I definitely think that."

"Well, rest assured, the first capsules will carry interceptor tugs, small, solar-powered vessels with thrusters capable of steering the capsules. When capsules are sent up, the tugs will attach and ferry them to the station or ships accordingly."

"It seems to me," Emma says, "that we're putting the cart before the horse. We don't have the parts to create the launch ring, much less the capsules, or the interceptor tugs."

"Not yet," Arthur replies. "As I said, you supply raw materials, I'll build what I need."

"How?" Fowler asks.

"Before the strike, the Atlantic Union had a dozen three-D printing plants. Did any survive?"

Fowler hesitates. "Yes. One of the manufacturing facilities in Camp Nine is intact. The building was damaged but forty printers are still functioning."

"A hundred would be better."

"We still have several camps left to search," Fowler says. "And the Caspians, Pac Alliance, and new colony cities could have some."

Arthur rolls his eyes. "Wouldn't be too optimistic about that."

"What does that mean?" Charlotte asks, concern evident in her voice.

"Think about it. The AU was spread out among sixteen camps. The Pac Alliance, Caspia, and new colony cities were more concentrated. Larger targets."

"Which means?" Min asks.

"Larger asteroids."

Charlotte's cheeks flush. Min has never been very expressive, but I can tell he's boiling inside. They both have friends and family in the Pac Alliance, and they want to know what's happened to them. Arthur's flippant attitude is salt in a very deep wound.

"Can you help us survey the other human settlements?" I ask, my voice even.

Arthur shrugs as if dealing with a petulant child. "If that's what you want to dedicate resources to, sure."

"How?"

"I'll use the printer to create a drone. The top will be lined with solar panels far more efficient than anything you've ever created. The bottom will house cameras and radios. We can drop flyers if you'd like." He smirks and adds sarcastically, "Maybe even candy bars."

"The data is all we want. And details," I add.

"Very well. The vessels would launch at daybreak and fly with the sun, circling the globe, using wind currents and solar energy. The drones will have to make a few stops, but we'll have the survey results in a few days."

"All right. That's our first priority," Fowler says.

"Does that mean you're letting me out of the cage?" Arthur asks.

"For work release," Fowler says. "Contingent on your cooperation and performance."

Arthur smiles theatrically at me. "Just like James back in the day. First contact mission style."

"Not like James," Fowler snaps. "We were never willing to shoot him."

"Was that a subtle reminder that you're willing to kill me at the first sign of deception?"

"Let's move on," Fowler says, again ignoring the taunt. "Tell us about the colony world."

"Not much to tell. Its mass is ninety-two percent of Earth's. Gravity is roughly the same." He raises his eyebrows. "You'll probably have tall grandkids."

I ask perhaps the only question that truly matters. "Tell us about the star it orbits."

"In a word, one you humans seem to favor, it sucks."

Fowler exhales, clearly annoyed. "We're going to need something more scientific than that."

"All right, Larry, but you can be such a buzzkill." Fowler's eyes flash, but Arthur continues as if nothing's amiss. "It's a red dwarf."

Fowler leans back in his chair, looking shocked. I'm a roboticist, not an astronomer, so I'm not sure why a red dwarf star is a bad thing for us. I can, however, tell that Fowler doesn't like it.

Next to him, Charlotte scrunches her eyebrows. "What's a red dwarf?"

"It's a small, dim star," Emma answers before Arthur can.

"Then won't the planet be an ice ball?" Charlotte asks.

Arthur makes a show of rolling his eyes. "It would—if it were orbiting where Earth is orbiting your sun. Your new paradise, however, is closer to this star than Mercury is to yours. It completes a revolution around its star every twenty days."

"Is it tidally locked?" Min asks quickly.

"Yes."

Charlotte looks over at Emma, silently asking what that means.

"The planet is like our moon," she says quietly. "It rotates around the star with one side always facing it." Her focus drifts back to Arthur. "Which presents a number of issues. One side of the planet could be boiling, the other frozen. Not ideal for maintaining a stable atmosphere and life on the surface."

Arthur grimaces. "You guys worry too much. The atmosphere is fine."

"Details," Emma insists.

"All right," he mutters. "It's thicker than Earth's atmosphere, but it needs to be. The air has slightly more nitrogen but it's breathable. You'll love it."

"Climate?" Charlotte asks.

"It's pleasant." Arthur cocks his head, as if remembering something. "In places."

"How stable is the star? How often does it flare?" Fowler asks.

Arthur shrugs innocently. "We didn't see any when we were there."

"When you were there?" Harry asks.

"During our survey."

"You only saw it once?" Fowler asks, concerned. "You don't have active surveillance?"

"Of course not. So many stars, so little time."

"When was your survey?" Min asks.

"Twenty-four hundred years ago. Roughly."

Fowler throws his hands up. "You've got to be kidding me."

"Relax," Arthur says. "As far as the universe goes that was like two minutes ago."

Fowler shakes his head and stares at the conference table. "Is it inhabited? Or was it?"

"Not by anything that matters."

"So there is life on the surface," Charlotte says.

"Yes, and I'm sure you barbarians are going to find it tasty."

"How dangerous are the indigenous species?" I ask, ignoring his jab.

Arthur glances away evasively. "Nothing you can't handle."

"Are any of them sentient?" I ask.

"Negative, Jim. They're all as dumb as dinosaurs."

Dinosaurs. A strange choice of words.

Min takes his tablet out, still angling it away from Arthur to conceal the images. "Have any of our telescopes ever captured images of the star?"

"Yes," Arthur says impatiently. "Your Kepler telescope discovered it."

"Designation?" Min asks.

"Kepler forty-two."

Min taps on the tablet. "It *is* a red dwarf."

"Told you," Arthur says lazily.

"Kepler identified three extrasolar planets in the system, all in close orbits. Their mass ranges from the size of Mars to Venus." Min's expression goes blank. "The star is about a hundred and thirty-one light years away. Over forty parsecs."

Charlotte looks confused. "How far is a parsec?"

"Roughly nineteen trillion miles," Fowler mutters. To Arthur, he says, "How long will it take us to get there?"

"That, I don't know."

"Why don't you know?" I ask.

"Because I don't know how much loose matter you will encounter along the way."

That confuses me. "Why would that matter?"

"The ships will have two power sources: a fusion reactor that uses space particles collected along the way and an array of solar panels on the outside of the ship. The fusion reactor will be the primary power source. The more usable matter you encounter, the faster you'll be able to go."

"And you don't know how much matter is out there along the route?"

"We're the grid, James, we don't expend energy measuring dust motes in space."

"Why is fusion the primary source?" Harry asks. "You all use solar. It must be more efficient."

"It is. And more dangerous. To harness meaningful amounts of solar energy, you'll need to transit solar systems, which," Arthur tilts his head toward us, "we all know can get pretty contentious."

Fowler pinches his lower lip. "You're saying we could encounter hostile aliens."

"You're far more likely to encounter what they left behind."

"Before they joined the grid."

"More than likely before they went extinct."

"And what might they have left behind?" I ask.

"Late-stage civilizations typically become increasingly paranoid. They build planetary defense systems. Then, when their population goes down the toilet, they never bother to clean up after themselves. As you transit the system collecting solar energy, the ship could be engaged by those automated defense systems. They would see you as an intruder, the prophesied enemy they were built long ago to defend against. It's safer to stay out in space, running on the fusion reactor. But, if it runs low on fusible matter, you'll have to alter course for a star system and take your chances."

"Surely the grid can tell us which systems have been inhabited," I say.

"We can't. Civilizations rise and fall over time periods that are the blink of an eye to us. We don't bother checking on everyone. Why would we expend energy watching solar systems we have no interest in?"

It hits me then: this voyage will be dangerous, even if we do prevent Arthur from double-crossing us.

"This new world you're promising us," Emma says quietly, "how do we know you won't come for its star one day?"

"Probability."

"I don't follow," Emma replies.

"The star's a red dwarf, remember? That battery's got no juice. We've got bigger fish to fry." Arthur smirks. "Sorry for the colloquialisms. Communicating via broadcast audio is so laborious. One has to spice it up."

Emma's voice is still quiet, reflective. I know she's thinking about our children now—all three of them—and their future. "How fast can the ship travel?"

"Again, that depends on its access to fusible matter and solar input, but it will likely travel at a significant fraction of the speed of light for the vast majority of the trip. I estimate transit time at two thousand years."

"Two thousand years," Emma whispers, a distant look in her eyes.

"What are our options for enduring a two-thousand-year journey?" I ask.

"You have two options, James. The smart way and the not smart way."

"You're going to have to be more specific than that."

"I was afraid you were going to say that. Option one: you can be conscious for the trip."

"A generational ship."

"Correct."

"And option two?" I ask.

"Stasis. Which, if you haven't guessed, is the smart option."

"Why?"

"Because... humanity, James. Look at what you all were doing to the planet and each other before we showed up. Imagine cramming everyone who's left into a relatively small space for a couple thousand years. I rate the chance of the generational ship arriving at your new home at about two hundredths of one percent."

"And stasis?"

"Fifty-fifty at best."

"And how do we improve those odds?" Harry asks.

"You don't."

"Well, we're going to," Fowler says flatly. "What are the risks with the stasis option?"

"Besides the ones mentioned—hostile encounters—there are, let's see, where to start... Interstellar phenomena, for example. Bad weather and bumps in the road, if you will. We can discuss those ad nauseum, but there's still nothing you can do about it. Stars go nova, gravity acts weird sometimes, and occasionally you hit an asteroid field so wide you can't go around. Suffice it to say, the ship could encounter something that would destroy it."

"Well, what are the risks we can do something about?" I ask.

"The only one is mechanical failure. Two thousand years is a long time for any machine to function continuously."

I nod, happy to finally have a problem I can solve. "So we make backups and backups for the backups, and we wake up from stasis periodically and check them and recheck them."

"James, I already factored that into the fifty-fifty odds."

50

Emma

I'm in the infirmary, lying in bed, when James arrives with our lunch: two warm MREs and bottles of water.

I accept the carton as he hands it over. "Do I *really* have to eat in bed too?"

"Bedrest means resting in bed."

"All the time?"

"At least for the first trimester."

"I'm going crazy in here."

He smiles. "You're not alone. Everyone in the bunker is getting restless."

"When are we moving?"

"I guess when we figure out where we're going. The drone surveys will probably be complete tomorrow."

"What did you think of what Arthur said?"

James glances away. "It's a lot to take in."

"Does it change your mind? Fifty-fifty odds at best."

James snorts. "Fifty-fifty. I doubt it."

"You think he's lying?"

"He was precise about the odds for a generational ship making it. I figure he rounded up. Or maybe even outright lied to get us to go for his plan. He wants us in stasis."

"Even if the odds are less than fifty-fifty, do you still think we should leave?"

"I think those are the best odds we've got. And I'm counting on something else that could increase our chances. A factor that Arthur hasn't accounted for."

"Which is?"

"Us."

"Us?"

"Humanity's will to survive. We're still here—beaten, but alive. At every turn, the grid has underestimated us."

In the situation room, Fowler stands before the bank of wall screens. The largest shows drone footage of a sprawling warehouse next to a smaller building, which I recognize as a manufacturing plant. The walls are battered but both buildings are still standing.

"The drone survey is complete," Fowler says. He's stoic, which I take as a bad sign. "I'll let Secretary Earls give the report."

Earls stands. "Our latest census, based on life-sign readings and hand counts, estimates that a total of nine hundred and thirty-seven people in the AU survived the asteroid strike."

The number is a gut punch. Fewer than a thousand of us left. Around the room, we all seem to take a minute to process it. James, Min, and Harry are expressionless, staring at the table. But I see the disappointment on Charlotte's face.

"How many injured?" James asks.

"As of now, we have two hundred and seventy-seven reported injuries that prevent full-time work. We expect that number to climb as we get more solid information from the last three camps we've contacted."

"Age distribution?" Min asks quietly.

"Roughly fifty-five percent are under the age of eighteen. Forty percent under the age of fifty. Obviously, there are very few in Dr. Fowler's and my age category. Again, these distributions are from the camps we've directly surveyed. But the percentages will probably hold in the other camps."

"About one and a half kids for every adult," Charlotte says. "That's manageable."

"On paper," Fowler says. "The reality is that within the over-eighteen cohort, most skew toward the lower age bands. Young adults, with no parenting experience. Not that they'll have much time to do any parenting. We need to put them to work."

"Who will watch the children?" Charlotte asks.

"The injured—if they can," Fowler says quietly.

"What about physical assets?" James asks. "Buildings, supplies, etc.?"

"Mixed news there," Earls replies. "Four of the camps, including Camp Seven, were completely obliterated—at least all of the above-ground structures are leveled."

"The ports?" Harry asks.

"Gone. The two coastal camps were hit hard." Earls motions to the two buildings on the screen. "But there is some good news. This is Camp Nine. Warehouse nine-oh-three and plant nine-two. Both are in pretty good shape. Captain Brightwell's team has been working on the three-D printers inside. As mentioned previously, forty are operational."

"What was the manufacturing plant's specialty?" I ask.

"Food processing. It takes the greenhouse output and packages it into MREs, using recycled MRE bags and cartons. Or used to. The warehouse was full of fresh food at the time of the asteroid strike, but it's all gone bad now."

"How big is the warehouse?" James asks.

"About two hundred thousand square feet," Earls replies. "That's roughly two hundred square feet of living space for every person in the AU. A lot more than we have here."

"I think we should assume we'll find other survivors elsewhere," Min says quietly. "And that we'll bring them to the AU."

"I agree," Fowler says. "Earls and I have discussed moving all of the survivors to Camp Nine and transforming the warehouse to house everyone. I want to hear your thoughts. Reasons against, considerations?"

"It's the obvious choice," James says. "We need to think through the implementation. I favor getting the living quarters set up before moving everyone, especially the sick and injured." He cuts his eyes at me quickly, and then continues. "Giving them more time to recover is ideal. I also favor moving in stages. I feel food is still our greatest dilemma, in the short term at least. I suggest we assign scavenging teams to every camp, have them dig through the wreckage for valuable, hard-to-print parts and food."

"I agree," Fowler says. "That clarifies another point: the solar drone we send out needs to search for more than survivors. It needs to identify food and medical supplies too. Has Izumi sent a list?"

"Yes," James says. "Those are the priorities as I see them: food recovery from the debris, prepping warehouse nine-oh-three for residency, and building the solar drone for the global survey. I think Harry, Min, and I should take the lead on the solar drone. We'll take Arthur to the plant, write the software, and launch the vessel."

"I'll continue directing the search of the debris," Earls says. "With the other camps, we've got more ground to cover. The snow is also piling up. The deeper it gets, the harder it is to search. Time is not on our side there."

"I'll assign a team to the interior planning for warehouse nine-oh-three," Fowler says. "But I feel our greatest challenge is what happens after. Whether we proceed with Arthur's plan to leave Earth or we make a stand here." He scans the group. "I want to hear from everyone on this."

All eyes turn to Charlotte and me.

"Emma," Charlotte says.

I've thought a lot about what I would say to this question. I haven't had much else to do in the infirmary.

"I have two children," I begin. "And another on the way. Leaving Earth is uncertain. That's true. But staying is a dead end. I vote to leave."

"Same," Charlotte says.

"I don't see that we have any real choice," Harry says. "Plus, starships. I'm in."

"Yes," Min says. "I agree. We leave or we die here."

Fowler eyes Secretary Earls. "I defer to the civilian leadership on the decision. My troops and I will support any decision."

"Even after hearing the odds from Arthur," James says, "I feel we should take the grid's offer. There are challenges and a lot of work to do. But I vote to go. Izumi and Grigory agree. I want to note that Grigory has reservations and initially favored fighting back against the grid. That said, he will support the decision."

"Then we're agreed," Fowler says. "We're leaving Earth."

51

James

A cold wind blows across the snow-covered desert, a chill that oozes through my parka like water soaking in, never drying. The frigid air bites at my exposed neck as I watch the sun peek above the horizon. The sky grows more clear each day as the particles from the asteroid ejections are removed. As the haze fades away, the sun shrinks, as if it's a light slowly drifting away. That's what living on Earth feels like, a desolate planet constantly growing darker and colder, with no hope of it ever stopping. Arthur says we have eleven months left until solar output falls below the level we need to heat our habitats.

Eleven months. Can we make it?

We really only have one choice: we try or we stay here and die.

In the past month, Harry and I have developed a productive, albeit paranoid, working relationship with Arthur. Now, our first product is ready to launch: a solar drone that will circle the globe, bringing back images and hopefully messages from other survivors. It will tell us whether we are alone on this ruined world. The craft is about ten feet long with a wide top covered in black solar panels. Two short wings jut out from the body. The underside is white, making it look like a giant penguin lying face down in the snow. We've named it Canary One, though Penguin One probably would have been more apt. Just doesn't have the same ring to it.

Harry hands me the tablet. "You want to do the honors?"

I tap the launch button and the drone shoots vertically into the air. Its batteries are full, and the solar panels will gradually refill them as it flies. Even so, it will have to put down a couple of times and wait for the sun to return.

We expect it back within seventy-two hours, depending on wind currents.

In three days, we'll know whether we're alone.

For the first time in weeks, I spend the night at home, in the small cubicle in the CENTCOM bunker, nestled in beside Emma, Allie, and Sam.

Emma's baby bump is just starting to show. The nausea has finally passed, but Allie's questions about her new sibling seem to have no end. I don't know if her curiosity comes from me or Emma, but it appears to be inexhaustible. Emma is patient with her, taking it all in her stride.

She's also found a new role to play here: colony planner. She, Charlotte, and Izumi have been working diligently, trying to envision our life after we arrive at our new home. The challenges are enormous. How will we grow food? What pathogens will we encounter? Will we be capable of defending ourselves against the hostile species we encounter on this new world?

Emma once told me that her dream was to start a colony on a new world. The science of it appealed to her, and I think another part of it was the prospect of creating a new society, one unburdened by the past, a united humanity, working together to master a new world. I can tell she's enjoying her work, but she's also afraid of what we'll find out there. We all are.

When she's not working with Emma and Charlotte, Izumi has poured herself into examining the stasis process Arthur is proposing. She's called it brilliant and horrifying. She thinks she can be ready to do a trial of the technology next month. She volunteered for the assignment, but Fowler wouldn't hear of it. A volunteer will be taken from the army. I think that has made her redouble her efforts to make sure it's truly safe.

Harry, Min, Grigory, Fowler, and I have dedicated our time to the designs for the colony ships. The approach is simple: the bays that would have been filled with combat drones will now house the human colonists, who will be in stasis bags: thick, vacuum-sealed bags with a mechanical monitor connected to the ship's systems. Half a dozen mechanical arms will roam the bays, capable of picking a sealed colonist and depositing them in an exit chamber, which will unseal the bag and bring the person out of stasis. One thing our planning has yielded is an upper limit on how many people we can transport in the ships: 12,394. As of right now, we can take all of our survivors—with room to spare. In a few days, we'll know if there are more people out there, and whether we truly have a spot for everyone. If not, well, we'll cross that bridge when we come to it.

The solar drone launched three days ago, but it hasn't returned. After breakfast, I stop by the CENTCOM's situation room and verify that we haven't picked up any broadcasts from the drone.

Taking one of the radios from the long conference table, I connect with Camp Nine, where Harry's been staying. "Have you all received any broadcasts?"

"Nothing yet," he replies. "We're still within the expected time frame though."

"I know. Still, I thought we would have gotten a ping on the long-range radio."

"Might be running low on power."

"Maybe," I mumble. "I'm heading your way."

It's past midnight when I arrive at Camp Nine. The lights on the outside of the printing plant and warehouse are off to save power, but I know everyone is working inside. We're running three shifts. Piles of recovered debris sit outside the plant, waiting to be processed, melted into their base elements and reprinted.

Inside the warehouse, work on the new cubicles— or flats as we have begun calling them—is in full swing. Workers in AU Army fatigues are assembling components by LED lantern light, placing the printed plastic bricks together like adults playing with life-size Legos in the semi-darkness.

We've converted offices in the front of the warehouse into a series of labs and a small room that doubles as a command post for the military and mission control for Harry and me.

I find Harry in the control room, a warm cup of coffee in hand, wisps of steam drifting upward. Most everyone takes stim pills except for Harry, Fowler, and Colonel Earls. They still drink coffee, though the supply is dwindling. They're old school, which I kind of like.

"Any word?" I ask, startling Harry, who rubs a hand across his tired face. Arthur is standing nearby, seeming bored.

"No," Harry mutters.

I point at Arthur. "You said three days."

"Did I?" he replies, feigning surprise. "Gosh, I'll have to update my website to let future customers know that ApocalypsePhoto.com can no longer guarantee seventy-two-hour delivery."

"Very funny," I say flatly. "What do you think happened?"

"Best guess? One of those fellow apes you're trying to save shot it down."

"Doubtful—"

"Hey," Harry calls out. "We've got something."

Canary One is programmed not to take data input—in the event Arthur tried to take over. But it can broadcast and record audio from radio frequencies. It can also use that audio broadcast to send us encrypted data. Not receive, but send. It was Harry's idea. He's using an old audio-to-data modulation standard developed decades ago for dial-up internet. He smiles as the mechanical noise plays over the speakers.

"Doesn't that take you back to a better time?"

"It was a little before my time, Harry."

"Well, buddy, you really missed out."

The noise fades and on the main screen, letters begin flashing:

DATA CONNECTION ESTABLISHED

SOURCE: CANARY ONE

"Everybody out," I call to the dozen technicians sitting at their stations. Like everyone in the Atlantic Union, they deserve to know the results of the survey. But that information is dangerous. It needs to be disseminated in the right way, at the right time.

When Harry, Arthur, and I are alone, Harry puts the summary data on the screen. My heart leaps. And it plummets.

"I thought you'd be happy, James," Arthur says.

"Don't be smug. You know what this means."

52

Emma

I feel like a settler in the Wild West. My kids are bundled up. The wagon is loaded. And we're trekking across the wilderness to our new home, in hopes of a better life.

In this case, the wilderness is a frozen North Africa, that new home is on another planet, and our wagon is an Atlantic Union armored troop carrier. So, sort of the same as the intrepid souls who settled the American West. And like them, we're heading west, to Camp Nine, to the last place we'll live before leaving Earth.

The troop carriers are crowded. Mothers like me hold young children like Allie in their laps. The older kids, like Sam, are packed beside us. They sat upright when we left, leaned against us after a few hours, and now, finally, most are slumped over, heads resting on our shoulders, some asleep, others lying on the floor next to the cargo crates holding our meager possessions.

The army has cleared the road in hopes of making the trip quicker. Still, the convoy lumbers along at a slow pace, ensuring they don't run out of power. We stop three times. Meals are distributed. People exit and use the pop-up portable restrooms, and a nurse comes around and checks on everyone.

I feel as if I've been in this truck for days, but it's still light out when the rear doors open for the fourth time, revealing two buildings towering ahead.

James stands at the front of the delegation, blowing out white puffs of steam, a pale, yellow sun behind him. People spill out of the troop carrier, glad to be free.

It isn't our turn, but that doesn't matter to Allie. She weaves through the legs of people making their way to the exit like an animal cutting through a forest, her prey in sight. James rushes forward, just in time to catch her as she reaches the edge of the troop carrier. He pulls her from the truck and hugs her tight.

A minute later, Sam and I reach the ground and James and Allie wrap us in a hug, the four of us clinging together, almost oblivious as people flow around us, staring, I'm sure. I feel James's hand move to my stomach as he whispers, "Welcome home."

The flat reminds me of our habitat: a large open space with doorways to the two bedrooms—one for the kids and one for James and me. Our new home doesn't have a kitchen or a bathroom, but that's okay. One way or another, it's temporary.

The living area has couches salvaged from the wreckage, no doubt repaired and patched up. They don't look half bad. There's even a rug on the floor. In a word, it feels like home—the first real home we've had since the asteroids decimated our planet.

Life inside this converted warehouse soon becomes routine: we work, we eat, we sleep, and in the hours in between, we snatch at any little piece of joy that comes our way.

The sun grows smaller each day, a constant reminder that time is running out for us. My belly swells, the child inside of me growing, a reminder that we must succeed.

At work, Izumi, Charlotte, and I have made incredible progress on our plans for the colony. James is also making progress on his project. He and Harry have launched a total of six Canary drones, as they call them. They're carrying messages to survivors in other parts of the world, though I don't know what they're saying. That has been kept a secret, and as such, has become the main topic of gossip here in Camp Nine.

One night, lying in bed, just after we've turned out the lights, James says, "I need to tell you something."

"You're pregnant."

I don't hear a laugh, but I know he's smiling.

"No. I would never keep a secret like that from you."

"Touché."

"Canary," he whispers.

"What did you find?"

"The good news? Survivors."

"And the bad?"

"There are fourteen thousand of them. Alive and well. Headed here now. We have thousands more people than we can take on the ships."

53

James

For the sake of convenience, we built Arthur's launch ring at the impact crater in Camp Nine—close to the 3-D printers. The ring is underground, but we've built a launch control station above ground, at the rim of the crater. Next to it, sitting on poles sticking out of the snow, is an unbroken field of solar panels.

As the sun sets, I stand on the station's loading dock, staring at the solar array, its black panels glittering in the dim sunlight like a pool of oil in the sea of snow-covered ground.

The first capsule to be launched arrived last night, and we've spent the day testing it. It reminds me of the drone Arthur built to reach the Citadel. It's shaped like a beetle, oblong and black, with a folding door on top. Inside the capsule is our first space tug, a small ship that will wait out in space, catching the launched capsules and ferrying them to the carriers.

One of the army guards calls for me, and I walk back inside to join Harry, Fowler, Grigory, and Min in the station's operations room. Arthur stands at the back of the room, the standard attachment of six guards nearby, guns held at the ready.

On the main screen on the far wall, video from a camera in the launch bay shows our prototype capsule, sitting on a metal floor. With a pop, the floor beneath the capsule drops, lowering the little beetle in the launch tube. I feel a tingle of anticipation as I watch.

Text scrolls on the side of the screen, a series of checks ticking off, each passing until red letters flash in the bottom of the screen:

CHECKS COMPLETE

BEGIN ACCELERATION?

Harry swivels in his seat toward me.

"Ready to launch this pinball?"

I let out a laugh. "Sure."

On the screen, the beetle disappears in a flash. The velocity number in the corners climbs quickly. I expected a slight hum or some sound effect, but it's utterly quiet.

Harry taps at the keyboard. "We're at escape velocity. I'm initiating the launch."

I peer out the window at the tube sticking out of the snow. There's a sharp sound and a puff of white from the end of the tube, but like a bullet out of a gun, the capsule exits too quickly for me to see.

Soon thereafter, Harry says, "It's cleared the atmosphere. Switching to external cameras."

The most beautiful thing I've ever seen is Allie in the

moment after she was born. This might be second. The new International Space Station floats in the center of the screen, the two supercarrier ships docked to it. They're still there, waiting for us. This might actually work.

"Opening capsule," Harry says. "The tug is away."

The video image switches to a view from the tug. Its battery is full and it will use its solar panels to stay that way. It fires its thrusters, flying closer to the ships, zooming around them. From what I can tell, they're fine.

"I told you," Arthur says arrogantly.

Harry's face goes slack. "We've got incoming audio!"

"On speaker," I whisper. I had given up hope...

The astronaut is female, her accent German. "Ground control, this is the ISS, do you read?"

Harry clicks the transmit button and glances back at Fowler, who speaks louder for the microphone.

"We read you, ISS. Hang in there. We're sending more drones. We'll include food on the next shipment."

"Thank you. Thank you very much."

"We had our doubts about you all making it."

A pause, then: "It has not been easy."

Indeed. It hasn't been easy for any of us. But the ships are still there, and we're still here. We have a chance.

54

Emma

Outside, the snow piles higher. Inside, the questions grow as well. They are like two enemies closing in upon us. James and I and our teams are in the middle, fighting the Long Winter outside and fighting to keep the peace inside.

How would the people around us react if they knew the truth? If they knew that we're planning to leave Earth—and oh, by the way, we don't have room for everyone. Would it be panic? Riots? Or acceptance? It's unknowable, utterly unpredictable. And that's why we haven't revealed any details. We have told the roughly nine hundred survivors here in Camp Nine only that we have a plan for humanity's survival, and that we need everyone to help. So far, they've kept their heads down and done their work. Most of that work is scavenging the ruins for material we can use in the printers.

One person in particular has been poking at the edges of our secret: Richard Chandler. Subtly, he's been undermining us. Asking questions at the weekly public meetings. Whispering in the ears of the soldiers and adults. I wonder if he even has a goal of his own. Or if he just wants to hurt James.

Like me, Chandler walks with a limp now, his cane clacking on the warehouse floor as he approaches, a warning like a crow's call. I've come to dread that sound.

Thanks to the scavenging crews, there are a dozen mounds of material outside the warehouse—everything from habitat parts to mangled cars, all waiting to be processed and transformed by the 3-D printers. Every day, the printers take another bite from the mounds, and the recovery teams pile more salvage on top.

Troop carriers leave the plant each day, transporting the beetle-like capsules to the launch ring. Time is running out, but we're making progress.

My greatest worry is closer to home. I haven't felt a kick yet, but my belly is swelling, showing when I'm not wearing the thick parka. With the limited medical resources we have, any complication could be deadly for the child. And for me.

James and Harry have now launched six Canary drones capable of carrying messages to and from the other survivors. What the drones have found out there is both heartbreaking and joyous. Caspia is gone. The asteroid that hit Caspiagrad completely destroyed the city, the crater even larger than the one at Camp Seven. Because Caspia's population was concentrated in a single city, there were no other survivors. Grigory's mother and sister were killed. He hides it well, but I know he's taking it hard. After losing Lina, I can't imagine what he's feeling.

The Pac Alliance fared better, owing mostly to three secret settlements it had created. James and Harry were hopeful about survivors from London and New Berlin, but like Caspiagrad, the cities were completely destroyed.

New Atlanta was luckier. The sprawling city lies in ruins, but thousands of its residents survived underground and in fortified buildings far from the city center. James offered a simple explanation: when the harvester mobilized the asteroids, it was likely in the Kuiper Belt. The asteroids took months at a minimum and likely over a year to reach Earth. When the harvester set the asteroids in motion, the Atlanta settlement was much smaller than it was when the asteroids hit. In short, the city grew faster than the harvester anticipated, enabling some to escape the blast radius (or hide below ground). In a strange way, Chandler's crusade to leave the evacuation camps saved those people. I wonder if that's how they'll see it when they arrive. Will they give him credit? See him as a savior and visionary? He will likely suggest as much.

The first of those survivors arrived last week—a ship from the Pac Alliance, carrying soldiers mostly. They're housed at the CENTCOM bunker in Camp Seven. Thus far, no one here in Camp Nine has been told about the new arrivals. But word will get out soon—the Pac Alliance residents will need to join our salvage teams. Food is also a concern. The Pac Alliance has promised to bring enough provisions to feed their people, there's no way for us to verify that.

James has been working non-stop. But last night, he announced that he was taking a day off—and that he had a surprise for me.

In the morning, we get the kids up and fed and off to school, and with a sly smile he says, "Bundle up, and follow me."

He leads me out of the warehouse to one of the Canary landing pads. In addition to the Canary drones, he and Harry have created four transport dirigibles. They look almost like miniature Zeppelins. They're much slower than a helicopter, and their payload capacity is small, four people at most, but the crafts are faster than the trucks or light ATVs—and provide a much smoother trip. To my surprise, Izumi and Min are waiting by one inflated behemoth.

"Up, up, and away we go," James says.

"To where?" I ask.

"You'll see when we get there."

Min operates the vessel, lifting us up into the dim morning light, over the warehouse and manufacturing plant, the solar panels beside it glittering in the sunlight.

We head south, across the white expanse, past the salvage teams scouring the humps in the snow, dragging out pieces and tossing them into the troop carriers. From up here, the world looks so peaceful. It's dead quiet except for the low hum of the electric motor propelling us forward.

I wonder where we're going. Is this some kind of weird post-apocalyptic double date?

A few hours into the journey, I spot the remnants of the Olympus building on the horizon. We're nearing Camp Seven. The dirigible is losing altitude.

"Camp Seven?" I ask James.

"Maybe."

I punch his shoulder, and he smiles.

The craft sets down just outside the CENTCOM bunker, and we hurry in out of the cold. Inside, the overhead lights are on and so are the cubicle lights, glowing like lanterns across the large open space.

A soldier steps out of the closest cubicle. He's Asian, dressed in a Pac Alliance uniform. Seeing a foreign army soldier here in the heart of the AU gives me pause.

The man simply nods to us and raises his handheld radio and speaks quickly in Chinese.

Min leans close to James and whispers, "He's informed his commander that we've arrived."

Is that why James brought him? To translate? To listen to the troops here, looking for any clues that they may have ill intentions toward us? The AU Army has the advantage in numbers, but that will soon change as more of the Pac Alliance survivors arrive.

Another Asian man emerges from a cubicle farther down the corridor. I recognize him. Sora Nakamura. When James and I returned from the first contact mission, he was our liaison at the Pac Alliance. Nakamura was first to contact us, offering help and shelter. But we never trusted him. We waited for Fowler to contact us, and chose to share what we knew with him first. Nakamura never trusted *us* after that, even when James presented his plan for the attack on Ceres. Even now, I can tell he's suspicious of us.

"Welcome," he says simply.

"How was your trip?" James asks.

"Acceptable."

Izumi takes a step forward. "Sora-san, if your people are ready, I'll perform exams and provide whatever care I can."

He nods curtly and says something in Japanese. Izumi responds quietly; then she motions for us to follow her down the corridor. The cubicles near the entrance are occupied by soldiers, most lying on the floor, watching tablets, headphones in. Deeper into the bunker, the cubicles are filled with women and children, some coughing, others moaning in pain.

Between Izumi and Min, they should be able to communicate with most of the people here. Speaking in their native language will be comforting as they do the physical exams and administer care. Another smart move by James. He's trying to establish some trust with the Pac Alliance.

Izumi leads us inside the infirmary and then turns to me. "We'll start bringing the Pac Alliance patients in shortly." She smiles. "But there's another exam we need to do first."

I glance from her to James, whose face is a mask. "What is this?"

James marches to one of the exam beds and pulls a machine from behind the curtain. "Ultrasound time. By Izumi's calculation, we should be able to find out the gender of our child. Any interest?"

"I'd love to."

Izumi applies the gel and moves the transducer over my belly.

After what seems like a million years, she turns the monitor toward us, revealing the black and white image.

"Congratulations, you're having a boy."

The sun is setting when we return to Camp Nine. The moment I step inside the building, I hear the roar of a crowd, the voices drowning each other out.

James steps in front of me and marches toward the commotion. There must be a hundred people gathered in the mess hall. They're flowing out into the corridor. Armed AU soldiers are formed up around the crowd, eying them.

Through the din, I hear Richard Chandler's voice.

"James Sinclair was charged with protecting us. Look how that turned out. The planet is ruined. Now we're being asked to *trust him again*—with saving us? Please, people, for the sake of your family, it's time we demanded a change in leadership. It's time we demanded a seat at the table. It's time we demanded answers. We're breaking our backs every day. We're owed that much."

The crowd erupts in cheers. The moment they recede, Chandler continues. "We deserve to know what the plan is. *If* they really have one, that is. I'm not going to do a single bit of work until they've answered that question. But the only way we're going to get that answer is if you join me. Alone, I don't stand a chance of making a difference. Together, they can't ignore us any longer."

The crowd pulses back and forth, calling and chanting, the words inaudible.

"And if you go back to work," Chandler says, "you're betraying us all. James Sinclair and his cronies who are pulling our strings can't survive without us. But we can survive without them."

55

James

Last night, Fowler and Earls made a wise decision: they let the rally run its course. They didn't order the troops to break it up. If they had, Chandler would have pointed at them and said, "There are your oppressors in action."

The rally lasted long into the night, keeping most who didn't attend (like Emma and me) awake.

This morning, the strike began. About half of the salvage crews didn't go out. I imagine many of those people aren't genuinely interested in Chandler's message. They just don't want to go out in the blistering cold, digging through the snow for salvage under a fading sun. But we need that salvage to make the parts that will carry us off this planet. There's no choice. Either they work, or we all die.

There is some good news: none of the army personnel joined the boycott.

In the situation room, at our morning staff meeting, Fowler simply says, "Options?"

Grigory shrugs. "Is obvious. No work, no food."

"That," Charlotte says, "will simply make Chandler's point—that we have all the power and they have no say."

"We do," Grigory spits out. "And we should. We're the only people with the skills to get us off this planet. We have to be in charge of the resources for everyone's safety. We don't have time for discussion."

"There's a very simple solution here," Earls says, voice guarded. "By instigating a strike, Richard Chandler has endangered public safety."

All eyes focus on him.

"Given the current circumstances," Earls continues, "I believe we should consider that a capital offense."

For a long moment, no one says anything.

"We could put him on ice," Harry says. "It's ready for testing, isn't it, Izumi?"

"Almost," she replies cautiously.

"How would it work?" Min asks.

Harry shrugs. "We'd put him in stasis for a few days, bring him out and run medical tests, then put him under until we arrive at the colony world."

Emma shakes her head. "Making him an involuntary test subject might scare the rest of the population. It's dangerous. Plus, consider the implications. He goes into stasis and wakes up on the colony world. He doesn't have to endure the cold, the rationing—any of the misery here. If that happens to him, I bet hordes of people would line up to make trouble just so they could join him and get out of working."

Fowler closes his eyes and rubs his eyelids. "What a mess."

I can't believe what I'm about to say, but it seems the easiest—most humane—solution. "There's another option.

Let's think about Chandler's motivations. Ego. His own insecurity. Revenge against me—for getting him thrown off the first contact mission and his chance at glory. And, most recently, for crippling him."

"He's not too fond of me either," Fowler says. "I'm the guy that pulled him from the mission."

I nod. "What he wants is what we've taken from him: recognition and acclaim. Power."

"What're you saying?" Fowler asks.

"We bring him into the fold."

Grigory throws his hands up. "You must be joking."

"We do it on our terms. First, we announce our plan to the AU citizens. It gives them clarity. Most think we're building another bunker, or preparing to go somewhere else on Earth, launching satellites to help."

"It looks like appeasement," Earls says.

"I think we can mitigate that. When the scavenging teams return tonight, we announce our plan and that we are going to make them part of the process by allowing them to name our new home world—by popular vote. They'll also vote to elect a representative to join this group. If last night is any indication, it will be Chandler. I think having him close, where we can watch him, is far better than executing him or putting him in stasis... besides the morality of it, the unknown is how the population will respond to his execution or banishment via stasis."

The door pops open and Brightwell leans in. After his promotion, one of Earls's first official acts was to promote her to full colonel—and give her more responsibility: namely, command of all the AU troops. Everyone above her rank has been relegated to planning, which basically keeps them out of the way.

"Sir, sorry to interrupt, but launch control at the acceleration ring hasn't checked in for six hours."

"Have you sent a team?" Earls says.

"They're prepping now. I thought you all would like to know."

Earls gives a curt nod. "Proceed, Colonel."

I stand and move toward the door. "I'm going with you."

"Me too," Grigory says.

"Me three," Harry calls out to a few chuckles.

In the dirigible, I raise the binoculars and peer down at the launch control station. The building looks tiny next to the giant crater, like a prairie home perched on the edge of the Grand Canyon.

My worst fear was that the Pac Alliance soldiers had moved on the station and captured it as a bargaining chip. But the only vehicles here are ours. All of the outer doors are closed, including the main entrance and the loading dock.

When we land, I notice tracks in the snow: what looks like the trail of two people. Actually, I think it's one person—coming and going.

Brightwell and her team set up at the main entrance and turn the door handle carefully, peeking through the opening with a mirror.

"Two down," Brightwell calls out.

Down.

Dead.

Brightwell's team rushes into the building. Harry, Grigory, and I stand out in the freezing cold until they yell to us, "Clear."

Inside, two AU soldiers lie in pools of blood. Brightwell crouches near the closest. "Blunt force trauma to the head. They died fast. Never had a chance to draw their guns."

"Arthur," Grigory says.

Brightwell looks up at him. "Impossible. There are six guards outside his cell. And cameras inside it and around it. He didn't leave last night."

Grigory sulks. "Someone did. One set of tracks to this building, one away from it."

"They could have snuck out during the riots," Harry says.

I study the two dead soldiers. "But why? Why kill these two guards and return?" It occurs to me then. "Harry, do a software check."

"What am I looking for?"

"Viruses. Or any additional code we didn't put there." I focus on Grigory. "Let's search the building. See if anything's gone."

An hour later, Harry has finished the systems check. It's clear. Nothing added, nothing deleted, nothing modified. And it's the same for the building. It doesn't make sense.

But there is one place we haven't searched. If I'm right, it will all make sense.

"Colonel, I need two of your men to search the launch bay and the capsule."

"I thought the capsule was empty."

"It should be. But if I'm right, there's a bomb inside. And it could go off when it's opened."

"Then we need to get you all outside, sir—into the dirigible and away from the building."

When we're at a safe distance, one of Brightwell's men calls over the radio: "Opening launch-bay doors."

Harry, Grigory, and I peer down from the dirigible, the seconds ticking by like hours.

"Capsule is intact. No other items in sight. Proceeding to open it."

The building is utterly still in the snow-covered expanse. I wait, expecting an explosion. But nothing happens.

"It's clear. Completely empty."

Harry glances at me. "It doesn't add up."

"No, Harry, it doesn't. We're missing something."

That night, we hold a meeting that includes every adult citizen of the AU. In broad strokes, we lay out our plan to leave Earth and settle a new world.

The meeting is brutal, an endless stream of questions. In the end, however, I think it will help people, renew their will to live, to work, and fight for a better future. We're giving them hope.

The announcement that they will be able to name our new home world is met with enthusiasm, as is the news that they'll have a representative on the colony planning committee. From my point of view, that's the extent of the good news. As expected, Richard Chandler wins the election.

The meeting ends with a grave pronouncement from Fowler: that from now on, anyone without a perfect work record will not have a place on the colony ship. Tomorrow will be the real test of whether the strike continues.

*

In the situation room, Chandler sits at one end of the table, our team eying him, no one smiling, a few, like Grigory and Earls, staring daggers at him.

We brief him on our plan, leaving out most of the details. We don't tell him much more than we told the crowd last night. We also leave out one big piece of information: that there aren't enough places on the ships for everyone. That knowledge is dangerous. Especially in Chandler's hands.

After the meeting, I'm making my way down the corridor, toward my flat, when I hear the clicking of a cane on the concrete floor. I turn, expecting to see Emma. But it's Chandler, a malicious grin on his face.

"It's begun, James."

"What has?"

"My revenge."

56

Emma

As the sun fades, so does the power available in the converted warehouse. Heating is rationed. Food is rationed. The clock keeps ticking. Our time on this planet is slipping away.

Though we work constantly, James and I try to make time for our family. Twice a week, we share a meal with his brother, Alex, and my sister, Madison, and their families. Sam and Allie love seeing their cousins. The kids typically don't fight too much. Playing in the halls of this warehouse is what passes for normal for them. I know they sense something is very wrong, but we've done our best to insulate them from the truth of how grave our situation is.

The bottom line is that we have to leave Earth soon. How soon, no one knows for sure. We have food for another five months, but we're about to get another influx of residents. The first survivors from Atlanta will arrive soon, and we don't know how much food they will bring. Survival now is simply a function of how many mouths we need to feed. Soon the world will have one more, and he's the one I worry about most.

In our flat, I sit on the couch, Sam on one side, Allie on the other. We're on power restrictions, which means no tablet use. Thankfully, one of the scavenging crews found an old series of children's books in the rubble of one of the habitats. Someone loved this story enough to take it with them in the mad dash to the last habitable zones.

"What's it about?" Allie asks.

"It's about a boy who discovers he's a wizard and goes off to a very special school."

The next morning, at our leadership meeting, Richard Chandler stands at the end of the conference table in the situation room.

"The people have voted."

"Please tell me you're leaving," Grigory mutters.

Chandler exhales, ignoring him. "Our new world has a name," he says pompously, as if handing down an edict from on high. "The first name advanced was simply Summer. It's what we all hope lies at the end of this journey, after the Long Winter is over. The second draft of the name was Sumer—in reference to the ancient Mesopotamian settlement that was quite possibly the first human civilization on Earth. For a time, the committee considered calling our new home world Sumeria. It fits; it will be a place where civilization is once again starting over, hopefully in the light of a new sun. A summer without end, giving life to a society without end."

Chandler paused dramatically.

"But those are names from our past. Our destination is about the future. We need a new name. A name that symbolizes a new dawn for humanity. A new sun rising. As such, we have settled on Eos, the name of the Titan goddess of the dawn. In mythologies that cross cultures from the Proto-Indo-Europeans to the Romans, Eos is described as the force who opens the gates of heaven for the sun to shine. That is what this world means to our people. And we will call it Eos."

Chandler inclines his chin slightly, peering down at us. I can't even begin to imagine what he's expecting.

Fowler nods quickly. "Sounds fine. Eos it is." He cuts his eyes to Izumi. "You mentioned that you have an update for us?"

"More than that. I have a demonstration. If you'll all follow me."

Chandler just stands there awkwardly as Izumi heads for the door. He looks pained as we pass and finally decides to fall in behind us.

Izumi escorts us to her lab, where a large machine dominates one corner. It reminds me of an old MRI machine from the movies.

On the table that slides inside the behemoth, there's a white bag made from a thick, rubbery material. It's open at one end and contains a small box near the opening.

Izumi faces the camera in the ceiling. "Stasis trial number one." She holds up her radio and says, "We're ready."

A minute later, Colonel Brightwell escorts a young male soldier into the room. He's slender, red-haired, and looks slightly nervous.

"This is Private Lewis Scott," Izumi says to us. "He has bravely volunteered for this trial. Private, are you ready?"

"Yes, ma'am."

Izumi rolls a curtain wall around him and the machine, blocking our view. When she slides it back, Private Scott's clothes are folded neatly on a chair and he's lying inside the white bag on the table. He's shivering, perhaps from the cold, but more likely from the fear of knowing that he might not get out of that bag alive.

Izumi leans close to him. "We'll be monitoring you the entire time, Private."

He nods.

"Do you see the face mask inside?"

He nods again, reaching up for it.

"Go ahead and put it on. You'll feel air flowing. That's the treatment. It'll put you to sleep and when you wake up, I'll be right here."

Watching him place the mask over his mouth and nose, I can't help thinking about Corporal Stevens, who went into that water tube in the Citadel and tried to swim out. We'll write both of their names in our history books—if we have a history. I wonder about all the soldiers who perform brave acts like this that no one ever sees or knows about. That's injustice.

"I'm going to start the airflow now," Izumi says.

Private Scott's breathing slows and his eyes close. Izumi zips the bag and it starts shrinking, vacuum sealing around the man's slender form.

Izumi studies a small display panel on the box attached to the bag. "Vitals are normal." To one of her lab assistants, she calls out, "Let's move him into the scanner."

She walks over to a flat screen on a rolling table. It shows Private Scott's body: the blood vessels, bones, and organs. There's no beating heart, no blood flowing, no color or motion in the brain. The image looks static except for the numbers and calculations updating in real time.

"How does it work?" James asks.

"Short answer: it's a virus."

"A virus?"

"An airborne retrovirus that alters the host's DNA."

"Like a gene therapy?"

"Very similar. The virus alters the host's metabolism and aging process."

James squints. "What about all the microbiota in the body? Especially in the intestines. Even if we're... hibernating... they would still be active."

"The virus reaches them too."

"The same therapy works on them?"

"In theory," Izumi replies. "Even someone with an open, infected wound could enter stasis. Again, theoretically."

"Incredible," James whispers.

"How long is this trial?" Fowler asks.

"One hour."

I don't know about the rest of the team, but I can barely concentrate on my work for the next hour. My office is covered in drawings and notes—planning for the colony. There are so many unknowns, but there's a lot we can do to prepare. So far, my work with Charlotte has produced several insights about what we need to build for our new home and what we need to take with us.

When the hour is almost up, Charlotte leans into my office. "Thought I'd pop over and see how it turned out."

"Let's go. I'm dying to know."

In the lab, Izumi is standing near the large machine, eying the monitor. "There's been no activity during stasis. So far, so good." She punches a few letters on the keyboard, and the table slides out. She leans over the vacuum-sealed bag and taps at the small screen.

"The reanimation process is done by a virus. Essentially reversing what the first virus did."

The bag inflates as Izumi studies the readout. She taps at it again, and a second later, there's movement inside the bag, a hand clawing at the sides. Twisting.

Izumi grabs the zipper and opens the end with a puff of air. The bag collapses around Private Scott, who pushes up on his elbows, eyes wide, gulping air.

Izumi places a gloved hand on his back. "Breathe, Private. You're okay. We just need to run some tests."

That night, as I read a chapter of the book, the baby kicks relentlessly. He must like it. Or hate it.

"You okay, Mommy?" Allie asks.

"I'm fine."

"T-t-the baby's kicking, isn't it?" Sam asks.

"It is. But that makes me happy. It means he's okay."

There's a knock at the door. James is working late, as usual, and I'm too tired to stand. "Come in."

The door swings open and to my surprise, Richard Chandler strides in.

I squint at him. He grins as if he knows a secret.

"Hi, Emma."

"James isn't here."

"I came to see you."

"Well. You see me."

Allie inches closer to me and turns away from Chandler. Sam gets to his feet but keeps his distance.

"I suspected it, but I wasn't sure until I saw the stasis sleeve today."

"What's that? That it won't hold your massive ego?"

"That's funny. But you won't be laughing soon." He takes a step forward. "I know there isn't enough room for everyone on the ship. How many will be left behind? A thousand? Two thousand? Three?"

"That's not your concern."

"Oh, but it is. It's everyone's concern. Because some of them will be left behind. How do you think they'd react if they knew the truth?"

My mouth runs dry. I stare at him, and his gaze drifts down to my belly. "There's only one solution. We'll have to make some hard choices about whom to take. The question is: Who's best suited to survive on a new world? We have to be practical. Obviously we'd need to consider age. Everyone younger or older than certain ages... well, it just doesn't make sense to take them."

57

James

When Emma told me about Chandler's visit to our flat, I was enraged. What I don't know is whether Chandler is just bluffing or if he really intends to suggest that we choose whom to leave—and that babies and small children, anyone with low survival odds, might be left behind.

Maybe he's just trying to get back at me for humiliating him during the first contact mission—or for injuring him recently. As I know all too well, he's good at manipulating people, especially using his words to inflict misery. I hope that's all this is.

One thing I'm certain of: my best chance of neutralizing his threat is to ensure there's room for everyone on those ships. As such, I've devoted my every waking moment to the task.

At the launch control station, I watch the screens as the construction drones assemble stasis bays inside the supercarriers. It's incredible. Humanity's greatest achievement. Arthur's inventions powered by our software.

I find the stasis technology even more impressive. Izumi's trials have gone flawlessly. The most recent cohort stayed inside the sleeves for two weeks. The tests afterward revealed no physical abnormalities. The next step is sending passengers in stasis up to the ships. A trial run of the boarding procedure. We'll be ready for that in a week.

We continue to work on ways to expand the ships' capacity. We've managed to make room for roughly a thousand more stasis sleeves into the ships, mostly because we can make some equipment smaller and we hadn't factored how many children were in the population. Less equipment space and less body mass gives us more room for more people.

Every time I visit the launch control building, I think about the two soldiers who were killed here. I still haven't figured out why. The mystery dogs me. The last time I felt this way was in the hours after we destroyed the three large asteroids. Just like then, I know something is wrong, but try as I might, I can't figure it out.

Arthur works with Harry and me every day, but I have never visited his cell. It's a cramped room, about eight by eight. It's unheated—because it doesn't need to be and because we can't spare the energy.

The cold grips me as I step across the threshold.

"Oh, James," Arthur says, getting to his feet. "I wasn't expecting company." He motions to the bare room. "Excuse the mess. Maid raised her rates, and with the economy freezing up—if you will—I had to ask myself, is this something I really *need* at the moment?"

I ignore his joke and cut right to the chase. "The murders at launch control. Did you do it?"

"You have me at a disadvantage."

"I doubt that. The two soldiers that were killed. Did you do it? Did you have a part in it?"

"Why would I?"

"You didn't answer me."

"You wouldn't believe me if I did, James."

I exhale. "What happens to you when we leave?"

He shrugs. "I'll throw an epic end-of-the-world dance party for all those people you leave behind?" He winces sheepishly. "Oh, sorry, should I not say that too loud?"

"Be serious."

He stares at me, a small grin forming on his lips.

"Will the harvester re-upload you?" I ask. "Will it send a probe for you?"

"I wish. I'm just not that important. Conservation—"

"Of energy. Yes, I know. But I don't believe that you're just going to stay here."

"My plan is simple. When you leave, I'll manufacture another capsule, load it into the launch bay and shoot myself toward the harvester. When I reach range, I'll broadcast my data and program, rejoining the grid."

"What data?"

"About you. Humanity. The grid craves data. Data informs future decisions."

"Decisions about how to deal with us?"

"Yes. And other similar species." He stares at me. "Are you thinking about destroying me before you leave?"

"No," I reply quietly.

"Oh. I see," he says, nodding as if realizing something. "It's kind of cute."

"What is?"

"You're thinking that maybe, if you can cut a deal with me—download me into some data device with broadcast capabilities—you could get me out of this primitive contraption and you'd get Oscar back."

That was exactly what I was thinking, but I don't respond. Arthur shakes his head.

"It'll never work. Your people will never trust him again. Face it, James, he's gone for good."

"What if there's not enough solar power to launch your capsule? What will you do then?"

"That won't matter."

I raise my eyebrows.

"Remember," he says confidently, "I'm capable of harvesting geothermal. I just won't do it while you're here. Scared you'd stay."

This is going nowhere, yet I try one more time as I head for the door. "Do you know who killed those guards?"

"No, James."

A month later, I still haven't made any progress on the mystery of the two dead soldiers. There are utterly no clues. No suspects. There are plenty of people here in the camp with the opportunity and the means to commit the crime but no one with a motive to do it. Killing the soldiers seems to have served no purpose, other than to make me curious.

It brings me back to motive. I see only two possibilities. The first is that the killer was motivated to kill one or both of the soldiers for personal reasons. If so, their deaths have nothing to do with the launch ring—they were simply there at the time the killer struck.

The second possibility is that the guards were killed so that the killer could gain unrestricted access to the launch control station or the ring. They would have been alone there for hours after they killed the guards. But why? We've searched the building top to bottom, three times now, but we can't find any sign that anything was altered, removed, or added. It doesn't make sense.

Another mystery has recently emerged. One by one, the radios from the vehicles have been stolen, and the speakers ripped out too. Earls hasn't bothered to investigate it. He believes the radios are being used by the population to play music and audiobooks in their flats and dormitories. We're on severe power restrictions and tablet use is banned, but the radios can function on batteries, which are available on the black market—for a price. I don't buy it though. Something is off about that too.

Day and night, the two mysteries haunt me, as though I'm in a boxing ring getting bounced back and forth by them. It's happening again—I'm missing a big piece of the puzzle, and deep down, I sense that it could be our undoing.

Work, however, is going well. The colony ships are nearly complete. Far enough along to actually start testing. Izumi has set up a stasis center here in the launch control building, which will enable us to load the ships faster.

For the test, the entire team has made the trip to launch control. For some, like Fowler, Emma, and Charlotte, I think it's nice just to get out. They've been cooped up in the warehouse almost since we moved from CENTCOM.

We gather in the operations room, staring at the wall screens; Harry is sitting at one of the long tables, working the controls. He turns to us.

"Who's ready to launch three shrink-wrapped soldiers into space?"

Fowler smiles and shakes his head. "Proceed, Dr. Andrews."

On the screen, the velocity numbers tick up as the first capsule races around the loop. Private Scott and two other soldiers who were in the stasis trials are in the capsule. We felt it fitting that they should be the first aboard the colony ship and the first to land on our new home. Emma insisted on it. They took the risk in the trials for us. They deserve the recognition.

"We have launch," Harry says.

The screen switches to the view from an orbital tug, floating in space beside one of the supercarriers.

The capsule breaches the atmosphere, still moving at high speed. The tug is far smaller, but faster. It zooms after the capsule, attaching to its underside and blasting its thrusters again as it turns back toward Earth and the ships. It parks the capsule in a loading bay and the video feed switches to the interior of the ship. The loading bay doors close and the capsule pops open. The three stasis sleeves float free. A robotic arm controlled by Harry reaches out and grabs them by the end, the fingers closing on a zone marked in green, where the bodies aren't vulnerable. The arm guides the sleeves into what looks like a slot with a conveyor belt.

A moment later, Harry says, "Stasis sleeves are successfully stowed."

I feel a pat on my back and turn to see Emma smiling. It's a good feeling.

Grigory steps to the control panel. "Commencing engine trials."

The view switches back to the orbital tug, which faces the *Jericho*, the larger of the two colony ships. *Jericho* detaches from the ISS and begins moving out into space.

"Initiating forward acceleration with solar power."

The ship starts moving faster, soon passing out of view of the orbital tug. The screen switches to *Jericho's* external cameras—forward, aft, port, and starboard. It's eerie seeing Earth from space. The blue marble I've always known doesn't have a touch of brown or green. Just wisps of white and gray clouds over blue oceans and land covered in ice. I saw it like this once before, when Emma and I returned from the first contact mission, defeated. This is the last thing we'll see as we leave Earth, defeated once again, but with hope for a new life on a new world.

"Performance at one hundred and seven percent projected levels," Grigory says, a small smile crossing his lips. That's the first time I've seen that happen in a long time. It's certainly the first time he's smiled since we found Lina. That feels like a lifetime ago now.

He taps on the keyboard as he mumbles, "Switching to fusion reactor."

Earth keeps growing smaller on the screen. Suddenly, the dim light of the sun grows brighter, like a ray peeking around a black curtain. For the first time, I see the outline of the solar cells between Earth and the sun, choking off the life-giving solar rays.

"Output at ninety-seven percent of expected," Grigory mutters, grimacing at the display. "This I will work on."

"Overall," Fowler says, "it's a *very* impressive start, everyone. From the stasis sleeves to launch to ship operations. It's incredible. Let's bring her back, Grigory."

The ship returns to the ISS, the AI using the thrusters to dock.

"I'm going to start the capsule re-entry," Harry says.

The screen switches to the tug again, which zooms over to the ship, approaching the open loading bay door and the waiting capsule. It attaches and maneuvers out into space, diving toward the Earth. Then it releases the capsule, which hurls toward the ground, glowing red and orange as it enters the atmosphere.

We all exit the launch control station and stand out in the dim morning sun, the giant impact crater spreading out before us, a white bowl in a snow-covered wilderness.

I feel Emma's hand slide into mine. I look over but she's staring straight ahead. Min points and I gaze out and catch my first glimpse of the capsule floating back to Earth. The three parachutes are already deployed. Harry and I will have to run some tests on the capsule, but it looks good. In one piece. We don't know the specifics of Eos's atmosphere, so we've over-engineered the capsules, built them for the harshest re-entry conditions we might find.

When it touches down beyond the crater, Harry smiles. "Well, that it's, folks. Join us next week for an all new episode—a double feature: 'Sending food to the ISS and retrieving shrink-wrapped humans from space.'"

★

Two weeks later, at our morning briefing in the situation room, Chandler stands before us, a pained, almost mournful expression on his face. It's fake. I remember it from all the TV interviews when he trashed me.

"I've done the math. I know you must have done it months ago. But let's put that behind us. It's time to face facts: we can't take all of the survivors with us. It's only a matter of time before people outside of this room figure that out as well. The camps from Atlanta and the Pac Alliance are overflowing with people. More arrive every day. I have a solution."

When no one responds, Chandler continues.

"A fitness test. With two components: physical and mental. The physical test will be a full-spectrum health analyzer scan and a brief physical exam, just enough to catalog injuries. The mental portion will be conducted via tablet. We'll use a standard aptitude test." Chandler looks directly at me. "There will also be a verbal acuity component. If we're to survive, it's imperative that the colonists be able to speak clearly and quickly. On Eos, in hostile conditions, efficient communication may be the difference between life and death."

My heart is pumping, anger swelling up inside me. I try to force myself to be calm. Thankfully, Fowler speaks before I get a chance.

"That's a poor solution. The number of man hours to do the testing—and the power for the tablets—simply isn't available."

"What are you proposing? Tell me: how will you choose whom we take and whom we must leave on Earth to die?"

"A lottery."

"A lottery? As in, what, the people randomly selected live and those who aren't die?"

"It would be random, a computer program that generates numbers matched to a list of all colonists."

"You would separate families?"

"No. If one family member is selected, the entire family goes. Their numbers are pulled from the lottery pool before the next number is selected."

"I see. Am I to assume that all of you are exempt from the lottery?"

"Critical personnel will be exempt. People with knowledge about the ships will be included as well as those who will be essential once we reach Eos. That includes a base level of soldiers who may be needed to defend the colonists from any indigenous species we find on our new world."

"So you're exempting a lot of military personnel from the lottery. Will those be AU military only?"

"It will be military with relevant experience, who have demonstrated their abilities in the field."

Chandler cocks his head. "Right. Tell me, Lawrence, how will it work? People aren't just going to sit and watch their neighbors fly off into space and leave them."

"The lottery will remain classified."

"Classified. Bureaucratic speak for a secret you keep from the public."

Fowler ignores him. "At boarding time, troops will go to the camps and start loading the colonists. They'll make several trips."

"And when the ships are full," Chandler says, "they'll just leave? Thousands of people will be packed and ready.

Families huddled in their cubicles and flats waiting for their number to be called, to go to a new world. When will they give up? A day later? A week? When will they send someone to Camp Nine and launch control and find it empty? What will they do then?" Chandler's eyes rake across us, and he seems to realize something. "Or is there an aspect of the grid's deal you're not telling me? Can we even leave them alive? Are you going to euthanize them? It would be quicker and less painful than leaving them in the cold. You are, aren't you?"

Fowler grits his teeth. Chandler seems energized by the lack of response.

"If so, it's now obvious why you're exempting the AU military from your plan. You need them to execute it. They'll be going around collecting the colonists. Which is a bit strange. The AU is now the de facto sole world power. Yet it has less than seven percent of the total remaining population. That seven percent rules the rest now. The other camps are scavenging material, just like the AU. Working every day, assuming they'll have a place on the ships. But not all of them will. They'll die here. But none of us will—and neither will the AU military."

Fowler rises. "This discussion is over. And so is this meeting."

"Consider one thing," Chandler calls out as the rest of us stand to leave. "The lottery is unfair."

Fowler shakes his head as he moves to the door.

Chandler steps in front of him, blocking the exit. Earls steps forward. I shouldn't, but I sort of hope this ends in violence. Unfortunately, Fowler holds a hand up, stopping Earls.

"The people elected me to be their voice," Chandler says condescendingly. "You ignore me at your own peril."

Fowler exhales slowly. "Well, I certainly don't want to imperil myself, Richard, so say whatever you've got to say. But make it fast."

"I think debating the fate of thousands of people deserves whatever time it takes," Chandler snaps. "That's fair—unlike your lottery. I'll prove it. Your lottery will randomly choose between two men without regard to their ability. It chooses who lives and dies with no regard to what they offer the rest of humanity."

Chandler pauses, seeming happy with the set-up.

"What if one man lost both of his legs in the asteroid strike? He was also hit in the head with shrapnel and has brain damage that severely limits his working capacity. His son is only three years old." Chandler cuts his eyes at me and continues. "Three is far too young to do any meaningful work to help establish civilization on Eos. Oh, and I almost forgot: the boy has severe cerebral palsy and will likely never be able to contribute substantially to the colony. Like his father, he'll need to be taken care of. The mother won't be able to do it. She has terminal cancer. Inoperative, untreatable. She'll die shortly after we reach Eos."

Chandler pauses again dramatically, like a lawyer making his closing statement.

"And let's consider the other man. The one whose lottery number doesn't come up. Whom we leave behind. He's a Pac Alliance soldier. Strong. Smart. Fit. He wasn't on the exempted list because he's wearing the wrong uniform. He had the misfortune of being born in the wrong country. His son will be left on Earth to die as well. The boy is seventeen and just as strong as his father. His mother is healthy too. Hardworking. Via random chance, you would leave the second family and take the first. Why? What could possibly justify such a senseless act—one that endangers the future survival of everyone who reaches Eos?"

Chandler stares at us a long moment.

"I'll tell you exactly why you would do that. For your own sake. It takes the burden off of you. You don't have to choose who lives and who dies among these innocent people. The computer does it so you can sleep at night."

"We're done here," Fowler says.

"These people are breaking their backs every day and they give you authority over them because they think you'll do everything you can to ensure their survival. Your lottery doesn't do that. It's a betrayal. A luxury for your sake, at their expense. If you want all the power, Lawrence, you have to live with the responsibility of using it."

Emma stands in our bedroom, shaking, as angry as I have ever seen her. So angry she seems to be struggling not to scream.

"Tell me we're not going to let this happen."

"We're not."

"How?"

"I don't know yet."

"He's dangerous, James."

"I know. I'm going to handle it."

A knock at the door echoes through the flat. I step into the common room where Allie and Sam are playing. I crack the door and see Fowler and Earls standing in the corridor, both looking nervous. Fowler motions his head, and I step outside and follow them to a storage closet nearby.

When Earls closes the door, Fowler says, "Chandler. We need to handle him."

"How?" I whisper.

"An accident," Earls says. "We deliver a fatal head wound, then bring down the habitat ceiling. It's believable."

"To his allies?" I ask. "Probably not."

"What can they do about it?" Earls replies.

"A lot."

The three of us are silent for a long moment. I can't believe I'm considering murdering someone. I've devoted my life to using science to help people. My work was dedicated to ending death—for everyone, creating eternal life. Can I take a life?

"Chandler *is* a problem," I say quietly. "One we need to deal with. But he also has skills. Robotics engineering will be incredibly valuable when we reach Eos."

Earls bunches his eyebrows. "We have you and Harry."

"And we might be on a ship that doesn't make it. Or arrives second."

"It's all moot," Earls says. "He's plotting something. That charade in the situation room is part of some plan, I can feel it."

"We put him in stasis."

Both men stare at me.

"We grab him tonight," I continue, "put him in a sleeve, and launch him to the ship tomorrow morning. We'll tell everyone that he volunteered for a stasis trial. His allies can't disprove it. He's out of our way here, and we can bring him back at a time of our choosing—if we need him."

Fowler stares at the floor. "Okay. Do it."

That night, I sleep fitfully, waking every few hours, glancing at the clock, checking my tablet for messages. Leaving it on at night is against power-ration regulations, but this situation demands an exception. Finally, I give up on sleep and go out to the common room.

I'm sitting on the couch, staring at my tablet, reviewing the data from the last capsule launch when I hear a knock at the door. I open it to find a young private standing outside, sweat gleaming on his forehead. He must have run here. "Sir. Secretary Earls would like you to join him in the sit room. ASAP, sir."

I pull some clothes on and hurry down the dark, quiet corridors. Fowler and Earls are standing by the conference table when I arrive. Brightwell closes the door behind me.

"Chandler's gone," Fowler says.

"He took his tablet and some clothes from his habitat," Earls says. "He checked one of the ATVs out of the motor pool."

"Did he log a destination?" I ask.

"Launch control," Earls replies.

"Have you contacted them—"

"They haven't seen him, James. He should have arrived hours ago."

"Find him. We have to find him. Quickly."

58

Emma

The cold seems to seep in through the walls now, through the thick blankets covering me, Allie, and Sam. It goes right through my thermal underwear, all the way down to my bones, a chill I can't defend against.

The cold isn't the only thing closing in.

Every day, the rations are smaller. Each meal I feel a little hungrier after I've finished. We overestimated how much time we have here on Earth. The good news is that we're ahead of schedule with the ships and stasis. It's a good thing. We wouldn't have made it otherwise.

On the couch in our flat, I hold the final volume in the seven-book series, reading to Allie and Sam and their four cousins. They're all crowded around me, snuggled into the blankets. In a way it's kind of nice—the kids together, quiet, listening instead of staring into their tablets.

A contraction grips me, and I have to stop reading and focus on my breathing. They've been coming for the last few days. A few at a time, always passing. And this one does as well.

My sister Madison sits cross-legged on the floor, knitting.

"Another one?" she asks quietly.

"Yeah," I breathe.

Allie takes my hand. "Mom, you okay?"

"I'm fine, sweetie."

Abby takes the book from my hand and begins reading. We've been alternating chapters.

In this crowded warehouse, I feel as though the cold is pressing against me from the outside and my unborn child is pressing from the inside. I'm caught in the middle, between two forces of nature that won't stop, one I'm fighting against, the other I'm fighting to protect.

I wish James were here. For the last week, he's worked non-stop, a man possessed. I know why: Chandler. No one has seen or heard from him. No one knows where he is.

Based on the changes here at the warehouse, I know what they suspect. The building is guarded around the clock now. During the day, only a few teams go out scavenging. It's not hard to guess why: they're scared if they sent most of our people out, as we've been doing for months, that the isolated groups would be attacked—picked off one by one.

Instead, the army and scavenging teams have focused on fortifying the warehouse and plant. They've buried boxes in the snow in telescoping circles. Land mines. They're preparing for battle.

Chandler knows our work is complete on the ships. He simply needs this manufacturing plant and its printers to produce the remaining launch capsules.

My greatest fear is for my child. My due date is twelve days away. I don't want to give birth here. Izumi's infirmary is geared toward research, not treatment. The facility at

CENTCOM is still the safest place for me to deliver. James and I had planned to travel there in four days. We can't now. Not until the threat is gone.

Madison holds up her creation: a child's knit sweater. It's made of thick, maroon yarn with a large golden 'S' embroidered on the front. The colors match the house of the boy wizard in the story.

She grins at me. "This would be easier if I knew the full initials."

We're still debating the name. It's making Madison more nervous than either James or me.

Another contraction begins. I close my eyes and breathe in and out. This time, the tightening doesn't fade away. It grows stronger, insistent. Pain pushes into my pelvis and back. These contractions are different.

The baby's coming.

I can feel it.

I'm panting now. "Madison."

She drops the sweater, studies me for a moment, then stands. "I'll get Izumi. Sam, go get James. Hurry."

As the door opens, a voice calls out in the corridor, seeming to come from everywhere at once, loud, the words clear, booming in the common room.

It's Richard Chandler's voice.

59

James

In the lab I share with Grigory, Min, and Harry, I stand before the wall screen, hands held out. "Just hear me out, guys."

I tap my pointer and advance to my diagram, which shows the ISS merged with the *Jericho*. "If we take the newest ISS modules, including *Unity*, *Harmony*, and *Tranquility*, and wrap them with parts of the capsules—"

Grigory throws his hands up. "We've been over this. It's too little too late."

I press on as if he hadn't spoken. "We could get at least a hundred more stasis sleeves in. Maybe more."

"I think we're better off just expanding the ships from scratch," Harry says. "But the issue is—"

The door flies open, and Colonel Brightwell leans in. "James, we've got company."

I fall in behind her, Grigory, Min, and Harry close on our heels, all jogging to the control room that serves as the army's command post here in warehouse 903. Rows of desks are arrayed around a wall of screens, similar to our operations room at launch control. Soldiers in winter fatigues are typing furiously on keyboards, occasionally speaking into their headsets.

A night vision scene covers the main screen, showing a column of troop carriers plowing through the snow, seemingly with no end. They're heading for us. They're not AU military. They're vehicles from Atlanta, brought here by the survivors.

"We've counted two hundred vehicles thus far," Brightwell says. "They're coming in from the west."

"Wake all of your people up, Colonel. Including the reserves. Arm everyone and guard the armory."

Brightwell responds without looking over at me. "Already done, sir."

"Colonel," one of the techs calls out. "We've sighted another force coming in from the north. Putting it on screen."

That group of troop carriers looks far smaller, less than half of the western column. All vehicles from Atlanta.

"Anything from the south or east?" Brightwell asks.

"No, ma'am."

"Push the drones to max acceleration."

"Yes, ma'am," the tech replies.

Fowler and Earls burst into the room at that moment.

"Sitrep," Earls barks.

"It's either war or a heck of a dinner party," Harry says.

Brightwell's response is more to the point. "Assumed hostiles inbound from the west and north. ETA thirty minutes. Troop strength unknown."

Earls stares at the screen. "Chandler."

"Has to be," I mumble, deep in thought.

"Third shift comes on in an hour," Brightwell says. "It's a perfect time to attack. Our troop strength is lowest then. The personnel are the least experienced."

"We're getting infrared data on the western host," the technician says.

The screen displays the images. Every vehicle is the same: two blurry red and orange blobs in the cab, the armored troop carrier compartment solid blue, indicating it's cold and empty.

"Can infrared readings penetrate the carrier compartments?" Fowler asks.

"Yes, sir," Brightwell answers. "If those compartments were full they'd be lit up right now."

"Unless they've insulated them," I say carefully. "Chandler knows we have infrared drones. He may have found a way to trick the sensors."

"Ma'am," the tech barks. "We've got incoming from the south."

The screen displays the night vision image, at least thirty cargo trucks about twice the size of the troop carriers. Their canvas backs flop in the wind as they cut through the snow. There's no way there are troops back there. They'd be frozen solid when they got here. I recognize the trucks. Chinese made, brought here by the Pac Alliance to transport their people and provisions from the coast to the southern camps.

"And from the east, ma'am," the tech says.

The eastern convoy is also made up of Pac Alliance equipment, a mix of light armored vehicles and utility vehicles. Unlike the other groups, the forces are spread out, cutting a dozen paths through the snow.

The infrared images come through for the southern

convoy: same as the northern, two drivers in each truck, nothing in the back. Or seemingly nothing.

The images for the eastern group appear soon after. Most of the vehicles are loaded: four, five, sometimes six bodies in each.

"Get me a total life signs estimate," Brightwell says.

"Copy that, ma'am."

She walks to the corner of the room, drawing Fowler, Earls, Grigory, Min, Harry, and I over to her.

"Ma'am," the tech calls to her. "Platoon leaders are requesting deployment instructions."

"Tell them to stand by, Sergeant."

"Orders?" Brightwell whispers to us.

When no one replies, I say, "Let's start by considering what Chandler wants."

"Revenge," Fowler says quickly. "On you and me, James."

"He can't sell that to the Pac Alliance and Atlanta survivors, though," I reply.

"The lottery," Grigory says, nodding. "It gives them a motive to take us out. Work is done on the ships and launch facility. Stasis too. They don't need us anymore."

"But there is still one thing they need here," I say. "The plant. They need the three-D printers and the material inside to finish the capsules."

"They could just use the capsules already stored at the launch ring," Harry says. "That gets—what?—seven, eight thousand people down to Eos?"

"That's about half of their population," I reply. "Doubtful they'd leave that many. They want the plant. And they want control. Here—*and* when we land on Eos. That's what this is about."

"How many troops did Atlanta and the Pac Alliance bring in total?" Harry asks.

"We're not sure," Brightwell replies. "Estimates are five to six thousand. Maybe a couple thousand more civilians of fighting age."

"So," Harry says slowly. "We have... what, four hundred AU Army? Five?"

"A little over four hundred," Brightwell confirms.

"Against possibly eight thousand." Harry glances at the group. "Do we even have that many bullets here?"

The fact that neither Brightwell nor Earls responds immediately makes me think the answer is a definite no.

"We won't need that many bullets," Fowler says. "We're not going to win this by outfighting them. We're going to outthink them. We need to do it quickly. There's a reason I became the administrator of NASA and not a famous astronaut." He exhales. "I'm better at planning than quick action." He eyes me. "This is a situation for you, James. Like the first contact mission and Ceres. This is probably the last battle on Earth, and I'm placing you in charge from here out."

Every eye turns to me. I feel my mouth run dry. No pressure. I'm trying to gather my thoughts when a tech shouts, "Ma'am, strength estimates are four hundred from the north, seven hundred from the east, a thousand from the west, and a hundred from the south. All ETA forty minutes."

"Thank you, Sergeant." Brightwell eyes me.

I take a deep breath, trying to focus on one thing at a time. "That's a lot fewer troops than we think they have. So let's assume the numbers are bogus. They know we'll see those readings at least half an hour before they get here. We need to focus on what we think they're after. I agree with Fowler, it's the plant. Killing everyone in this warehouse also gives them fewer bodies on the ships."

I hold a finger up. "First, let's consider our battlefield. The warehouse is north of the plant. The two buildings are connected by a fifty-foot enclosed breezeway. The solar field lays just east of the warehouse."

"It's a lot of ground to defend," Brightwell says.

"It's worse than that. Even if we can defend it, they can still win. We have rations for about two weeks?"

Brightwell grimaces. "That's generous but probably doable."

"All they have to do is lay siege and wait."

For a moment, the group is silent. It hits me then. "Chandler is smarter than a head-on assault like this. There's another element here. Something we're missing."

"Such as?" Fowler asks.

Instinctively, my mind drifts to the two dead soldiers at launch control. How do they fit in? Are they part of his plan? How?

The other mystery is the stolen radios from the vehicles. How could that help him? We don't use the radios for comms. I guess they could but they likely have plenty of radios.

"Ma'am," the tech shouts. "Should we arm the land mines?"

Brightwell turns to me.

"No. They probably know about them and have a plan to set them off. I have another idea for them."

"Troop deployments?" Brightwell asks.

"Mass our forces in the plant. Station minimal forces at the four entrances to the warehouse."

A voice calls over the PA. I can't believe what I'm hearing: Richard Chandler's voice.

"The following was recorded during a meeting of the AU's executive council."

"Turn that off!" Brightwell shouts.

"It's not over the PA, ma'am."

He's right. Chandler's voice is muffled, but loud, the sound seeming to ooze through the ceiling.

"I left the group immediately after the meeting because I was appalled. I have gone to great lengths—at great risk to myself—to bring you this information. Why? Because your very survival depends upon it."

"Fowler, get on the PA and just start talking, try to distort what he's saying."

As he rushes to the comm station, Brightwell says. "We could cut the power."

Finally, it makes sense. "It won't work. He's using car speakers. This is why they stole them. They'll be battery powered, distributed throughout the warehouse. Colonel, redeploy half your people to find and destroy the speakers. Enlist the civilians too."

I see Chandler's whole plan now: his hope that we would cut the power, leaving us in the dark, cold and confused as his words play over the speakers.

Chandler's voice rings out beyond the walls: "When you learn what they're planning, I urge those of you who are able: rise up. Take control of the warehouse. We're waiting outside, and we will take you with us."

But Fowler's voice already overlaps Chandler's, his

message brilliant: "Citizens of Camp Nine. We are under attack. Troops are on their way here now to do battle with us, to kill us and to starve us. The assault has started—and you hear it over the speakers. Propaganda. Our enemy is trying to confuse us, to make us turn on each other. If we do that, we all perish. Band together."

Through the speaker outside, I hear the first lines of the meeting playing.

Chandler: *It's time to face facts: we can't take all of the survivors with us. What are you proposing? Tell me—how will you choose whom we take and whom we must leave on Earth to die?*

Fowler: *A lottery.*

I focus on Grigory, Min, and Harry. "Review the surveillance footage. Find the people who planted the speakers. They're traitors."

Chandler's voice again over the speaker: *A lottery? As in, what, the people randomly selected live and those who aren't die?*

Fowler: *It would be random, a computer program that generates numbers matched to a list of all colonists.*

The fact that it's Fowler's voice on the recording and over the PA works to our favor: there's no contrast in the sound of the voice—the words run together.

Behind me, I hear one of the guards say, "Son, this is a restricted area."

"I n-n-need to talk to James. His wife. The b-baby."

Sam.

"Ma'am," a tech shouts, standing. "We've got intruders."

On one of the smaller screens, which shows the area outside the plant, I see it instantly. Our enemy is already here.

60

Emma

The contractions pass like waves, stronger, faster, pushing against a levee about to break. I breathe in and out, wishing, hoping for the contractions to pass. I can't have this baby here. Not now.

Abby squeezes my hand and whispers in my ear, "It's okay."

I hear Chandler's voice outside the flat, droning on. Fowler's voice breaks over the PA, the volume deafening, words mixing with Chandler's. I can't understand what either man is saying.

I try to focus on breathing. I'm scared. Even after the ISS was destroyed, even in the Citadel, when we were trapped and starving, I wasn't this scared. I'm scared for the life of my child. If he's born here, in this room, and he needs urgent medical care, we can't save him. The infirmary is his best chance. I have to get there.

I grab my cane, push up from the couch, and take a wobbling step toward the door.

"Emma," Abby pleads. "What are—"

"We have to get to the infirmary. Help me. Please, Abby. Please."

I teeter on shaking legs. Then Abby's arms are around me and she's calling to the children: "Help your aunt, Jack. Owen, you too."

I feel their arms around me, hear Abby directing them. "We need to carry her. Gently, boys."

The three of them hoist me up, and Adeline rushes to the door and opens it. In the corridor, it's chaos, the voices getting louder. There are people everywhere, soldiers and civilians alike. Everyone is shouting, ripping into the air conditioning ducts and the low ceilings above. Looking for something, though what that might be I'm too weary to comprehend.

We snake through the corridors, weaving through the people. Twice, we have to stand aside as soldiers rush past us. Every minute or so, Chandler's voice grows quieter, as though the volume's being turned down by degrees, a click at a time. How? It's as if the speakers he's using are turning off.

Up ahead, the intersection is packed with people milling about. Platoons of troops are flowing through them, automatic rifles in hand, dressed in full battle gear. They're moving in the direction of the manufacturing plant. At this hour. Why?

My heart catches when I hear gunfire behind us, loud, piercing even over the PA. I could swear it came from the direction of the command post.

Suddenly, I hear shots closer; the sound is deafening.

A bullet rips past me, into the wall. A soldier in the intersection ahead turns and trains his gun on the corridor,

pointing directly at me. Abby and the kids lunge for the
wall, seeking protection, but there's nowhere for us to
go.

61

James

In the command post, I hold a hand up for Sam to wait.

I turn back and watch the video feed on the screen. It's from a security camera on the south side of the plant. At first glance, nothing seems amiss, simply snow piled high, a quarter-moon shining down through the haze. But every few seconds, the surface of the snow moves, like ripples on a placid pond of ice. On any other night, I'd assume it was only the wind blowing, the surface powder shifting.

Not tonight.

Tonight, I know what I'm seeing: troops tunneling under the snow, crawling their way to the plant.

This is why Chandler and his allies have waited so long to attack: they needed the snow to get deeper. It's at least four feet high around the plant. Easily deep enough for soldiers to crawl and tunnel through.

How did they get here—this close? Their insulated clothing and the snow above clearly hid them from our infrared scans, but we've been flying the drones non-stop since Chandler left, monitoring the road and a wide perimeter outside the warehouse and plant. The troops must have parachuted down from a dirigible that flew over our drones. I have to hand it to them—it's a pretty well-conceived approach.

The convoys are another matter: they're impossible to hide from our drones. Chandler and his allies had to know we would react the moment we saw them.

As I turn the pieces of this puzzle over in my mind, their full battle plan becomes clear. Part one is to destabilize our population with Chandler's recording. Seeing the convoys farther out, they're assuming we'll take the time to do crowd control here inside the warehouse—instead of fortifying our perimeter. They're hoping we'll leave the manufacturing plant virtually unguarded. They're hoping the paratroopers they inserted covertly would take the plant—which they need intact.

Except one thing went wrong: we've seen the paratroopers. Also, they're still a ways out from the plant. I bet tunneling under the snow has taken longer than they expected. I hope it will be enough time for us.

"Sergeant," Brightwell yells, "get me an estimate on how many hostiles are tunneling out there. And reassign three platoons from the speaker search to the plant. Alert me when everyone's assembled."

"How will you engage them?" I ask her.

"We'll start with grenades and finish with rifles."

I walk over to the entrance, where Sam is standing, trembling. I squat and put both of my hands on his upper arms. "What is it, Sam?"

His speech has gotten progressively better, especially

around people he trusts and feels comfortable with. "Emma. The baby's coming."

The words are a gut punch.

I grab a handheld radio off the nearest table and activate it. "Infirmary, command post, do you read?"

"Command post, infirmary. We read you, sir," a man says.

I skip the military lingo, even though there's other chatter on the channel. "I need to speak with Izumi."

"Command post, infirmary, she's left, sir—on her way to your flat."

Izumi's voice comes over the radio, barely audible over the commotion around her. "James, I'm on my way there now, but the corridors are packed. People are panicking." In the background, I hear shouting and muffled sounds, as if Izumi is shoving her way through a crowd. "I'll take care of her, James. I promise you."

Sam looks up at me, eyes pleading for us to go.

"Sounds like you've got your hands full there," Izumi says. "Don't worry, James."

"Copy that, Izumi. Thank you." I bend down to eye-level with Sam. "We'll go as soon as we can."

He grimaces, looking hurt as he turns back toward the entrance, making to leave, but I grab his arm.

"Sam, I need you to stay here for a little while."

"Why?"

"We need to stay out of the corridors while the troops are working there. Just wait over there behind the desks. I'll come get you when we can go. We'll see Emma soon."

"James!" Harry shouts. "We've found the guy planting the speakers." Harry types at his terminal, moving the surveillance image to the main screen. He's dressed in an AU Army uniform, a corporal's stripes on his shoulder.

"Does anyone recognize him?" Brightwell asks.

When no one answers, she focuses on one of the nearby technicians. "Use facial recognition to give me a present location."

"Wait," Min says, pointing at the security camera footage on his screen. "There's another one. There were two people planting the speakers. Both soldiers. Facial recognition is working... It says this person is a major named Danforth."

A technician calls over his shoulder. "The other mole is Corporal Caffee."

"Locations!" Brightwell demands.

Danforth. He was working with Chandler at Camp Five. We should have had him under surveillance. I used Danforth's wife and child as leverage to take him down. This is bad. Emma is out there in the chaos somewhere. We need to find him, quickly.

What's Chandler plan for the two men now? If he had used them to directly sabotage or attack us before now, we would've found them, questioned them, and maybe discovered the speakers. He had to wait until this moment. Now he has nothing to lose. What's their best use? I realize the answer as the technician stands, an expression of rage and horror on his face.

"We've got Corporal Caffee on video—"

"Where?" Brightwell shouts.

"Situation room. Forty-five seconds ago. His sidearm was drawn."

The situation room is just down the hall—

A gunshot rings out, then another and another. The sound seems to blow the room apart. Instantly, everyone around me is in motion. The sergeant standing guard at the entrance falls. Brightwell draws her weapon and returns fire as she shoves me away from the entrance. More gunshots join the cacophony until I hear one of the soldiers roaring, "He's down!"

A pool of blood spreads out on the floor around Colonel Brightwell. I crawl over to her, placing my hand on the shoulder wound, applying pressure. A young man runs over, tossing a medical bag on the floor beside Brightwell. "I'm a corpsman, sir. I'll take over."

Through the doorway, I see Corporal Caffee lying dead on the floor, body riddled with bullets. He went for the situation room. To kill the leadership. Where's Danforth? What's his target?

The main screen was hit with a bullet, but the smaller screens around it are still active. In one of them, a video camera feed shows a man in a crowded corridor, a handgun held at his side. I know that corridor. It's right outside my flat. The face is enclosed in a rectangle with block letters below it:

FACIAL IDENTIFICATION CONFIRMED

It's Danforth. He's going for Emma. To use for leverage. Or to kill her. That's the sort of order Chandler would give.

I've never killed anyone. A week ago, I couldn't even bring myself to kill Chandler. But I would kill to save Emma and my unborn child.

Earls is already barking orders. "Reassign the closest platoon to find Major Danforth and apprehend if possible, kill if necessary."

I turn and run, stopping only to pick up Brightwell's sidearm from the floor. Voices call after me: Harry, Min, and Earls. But I don't stop.

I hear Fowler's voice echoing over the PA as I pound through the hallways, my lungs burning, legs aching, heart feeling as though it will beat out of my chest.

Soldiers and civilians are everywhere, reaching into the air conditioning ducts, ransacking boxes of supplies, urgently searching for the speakers. Others are arguing with each other, desperately trying to figure out what's going on.

I study the gun a second, find the safety, and disable it. I've fired a pistol once. My dad taught me. He used to carry one when he went squirrel hunting, to protect us in case we came across a bear.

I run faster, heart beating in my ears like a drum pounding.

I turn the corner onto the corridor that houses our flat. The door stands open, no sound coming from inside.

A man stands in the middle of the hall, grimacing as he boosts another person up, the feet resting awkwardly on his shoulders. The person he's lifting is thrashing around on the top side of the ceiling. A speaker with Chandler's voice goes out as I pass them.

As I go by our flat, I slow down, peering in to confirm that the living room is empty.

From the intersection ahead, I see commotion: children and adults talking, people running, and an AU soldier issuing orders I can't make out.

Fowler's voice booms down from the PA system.

Chandler's voice is still in the background, and I can make out some of the recording.

Tell me, Lawrence, how will it work? People aren't just going to sit and watch their neighbors fly off into space and leave them.

In Chandler's recording, Fowler replies, *The lottery will remain classified.*

Classified. Bureaucratic speak for a secret you keep from the public.

As I reach the intersection of the corridors, I raise the gun and slow my pace, feet slamming into the concrete. I turn the corner, my eyes scanning, body numb from exertion and adrenaline.

A man stands fifteen feet from me, his back to me. He's wearing a black ribbed sweater and gray pants, arms forward, holding something. Farther down the corridor, I spot Abby and the children. They're closer to the next intersection, where soldiers are flowing by. A bolt of fear runs through me when I realize they're carrying Emma in their arms. Her eyes are closed.

Time seems to stop.

The man's arms lift slightly.

"Danforth!" I yell.

The man doesn't turn. But his head shifts toward me slightly, just enough for me to see his face.

I press the trigger.

The bullet hits Danforth in the upper left shoulder. He jerks, the gun in his hand going off. The bullet digs into the wall just a few feet away from Emma.

I press the trigger again and again and again as I step toward him.

His body jerks with every bullet.

I stand still, staring down at the dead man when a shot rips through the wall beside me. The soldiers at the end of the corridor are firing on me.

62

Emma

Gunfire rages around me. I feel the children crouching, lowering me to the floor. When my feet hit the ground, I reach out and try to gather them behind me, shielding them.

Suddenly, the shots stop and a soldier is standing over me, a tall hulking woman, hair pulled back tight, a rifle in her hand. "Hold your fire," she shouts.

In the place of gunshots, voices fill the void, everyone talking at once. It's like being in a hurricane, the rush of sound everywhere, indecipherable.

Izumi's voice pierces the din, seeming to cut through it like a boat parting the water. "Step aside, I'm a doctor. Step aside, please." She leans over me, placing a hand on my cheek. "It's going to be okay, Emma. You're going to be just fine."

She grabs my right arm and places something cold against it. I feel a pinch, pressure in the vein.

"No," I cry.

"It'll help you relax."

"The baby—"

"Will be fine. This won't harm him. It will just delay the delivery until we're ready."

63

James

Still holding the gun, I raise my hands and freeze. A tall, hulking soldier looming over Emma yells for a ceasefire. Her voice is like a cattle prod hitting me. It has the same effect on everyone else in the corridor.

The shots stop instantly.

I'm panting. The noise from my breath exiting my nose sounds as loud as a wind tunnel. I feel the adrenaline leaving my bloodstream, gradually, like a drug that's being withdrawn. Sensation slowly returns to my body. My mind seems to unlock, returning to the moment.

A skinny soldier in winter fatigues reaches down and grabs Danforth's gun. "You okay, sir?" he asks.

I nod absently as I step forward, unable to tear my eyes away from the man I just killed, a man who was sent to kill either me or my wife, or both. Walking by him feels as if I'm walking over a bridge, crossing to a different world on the other side, a world where I'll never be the same.

I have taken a life.

Izumi crouches over Emma, holding a health analyzer to her finger. Emma's eyes are closed, her breathing steady. Abby and Adeline are holding her head, both staring down with stricken expressions. Sarah is crying. Jack and Owen have fixed their faces with hard stares, but I know that inside they are scared to death, as they should be.

Madison is rapid-firing questions at Izumi. They're all the questions I want to ask.

"I've slowed the contractions," Izumi says, glancing from Madison to me. "They should stop soon. I have this under control. James, please resume doing whatever you need to do."

I hear footsteps behind me, and I spin, raising the gun. The two men throw their hands up as they try to halt their advance. I lower the gun when I realize that it's David and Alex. They've been searching for the car speakers blasting Chandler's message like most of the other trusted civilians. My brother fixes me with a horrified look, his eyes going from the dead man on the floor back to me.

Madison rushes into David's arms, burying her face as the tears flow. Abby reaches out a hand to Alex, who takes it.

"What do you need?" he asks me, voice steady.

I hand him the gun and say to the soldier standing nearby, "Sergeant, do you have an extra magazine for this firearm?"

She reaches into a pocket on her belt and hands a magazine to me, which I transfer to Alex.

"I need you to get everyone to the infirmary. You have to guard them. There may be more people trying to get to her. Use that if you have to."

He nods and begins directing the children.

Allie finally breaks her hold on her mother and runs to me, crashing into my legs almost hard enough to knock me over. "Da!" she cries.

I bend down and hug her tight. Time isn't a luxury we have, but if it's my fate to die tonight, I want to hug my daughter one last time.

"It's going to be all right," I whisper to her as I take Emma's hand in mine. "Go with your uncle and do as he says. I'll be home soon."

"Stay," she pleads.

"I can't. I need to work."

"Where's Sam?"

"He's with me. He'll join you soon."

I kiss her forehead and motion for Alex to go. Allie turns her head, staring at me and crying as they move down the corridor toward the infirmary, three soldiers carrying Emma now.

The moment they turn the corner, a slight rumble flows under the floor, as if a giant monster is moving through the ground beneath us. Explosions echo in the distance.

Fowler's voice over the PA is the only one I hear now.

A large female sergeant directing the troops at the intersection turns and shouts to me, "Sir, we've engaged the enemy. You're being requested at the CP."

She dispatches four soldiers, who jog with me back to the command post.

Earls is pacing when I arrive, eyes trained on the screens that still work. The region south of the plant is a smoldering battlefield. The grenades we fired have left deep pits in the snow. Dirt shows through like open wounds in the earth.

The white expanse around the craters is littered with blood, body parts, and shrapnel, all giving off steam in the frigid night. It makes my stomach turn.

Tracer fire lights up the night—red beams from our troops in the warehouse, green beams from our enemies. Against the backdrop of the snow, one might take it for a Christmastime laser light show.

General Paroli is here now too—sulking in the corner. I get the impression I missed another battle—Earls and him fighting over who should be in command. Luckily Earls seems to have prevailed.

Harry walks over to me. "We think about a hundred soldiers were tunneling towards the plant. The grenades took out a bunch of them."

"How about the convoys?"

"They haven't altered course."

Earls joins us. "James, we've taken out all the speakers."

"Count them and compare it to the number taken from the vehicles. Let's make sure there aren't more hidden, waiting to be set off again."

"Will do, sir."

"And bring one of the radios here to the CP. Leave it on and tuned to the channel they were using."

He nods and turns to give the order.

"How's Brightwell?"

Earls grins. "Mad as a hornet. Keeps trying to leave the infirmary."

"I count that as a good sign."

Fowler stands from the desk where he's been broadcasting on the PA. "Can I stop this now?"

"Sure, Lawrence. Come join us." To Earls, I say, "What's our deployment status?"

"We're massing our troops as directed. I also have a platoon sorting through the civilians, enlisting anyone of fighting age and fitness. We're concentrating the non-combatants in flats spaced around the warehouse."

"Good."

"Regarding Arthur," Earls says. "We have six soldiers guarding his cell. Should we pull some of them off?"

That's a dilemma. If we leave him unguarded, it would be the perfect time for him to attack us. He could destroy us from the inside while Chandler overruns us from the outside. But guarding him takes soldiers away from defending the warehouse. We need every person we can get right now.

"Have the guards bring him here," I reply. "We'll bind his arms and legs to a chair and Harry and Grigory will guard him. We need all the soldiers we can muster. And he may even give us some help."

I've known Earls long enough to read the micro expressions that seep out around his stone-faced façade. He doesn't like that call. But when he relays the order, there's no trace of hesitation or skepticism in his voice.

On the screen, the tracer fire dies down by the minute.

"We have a survey drone inbound, sir," Earls says. "ETA ten minutes. With the snow cover gone, we're hoping we can use infrared to paint the targets for our snipers." He pauses. "If you want prisoners, we can venture out now and try to capture some. It will be costly."

His word choice strikes me as strange: costly. From his perspective, soldiers' lives are a cost of battle.

"The operation would be more efficient," Earls says, "after the drones get here—we could separate live combatants from the dead. But that costs us some time."

Another cost: time. To me, lives are far more expensive.

"Have them hold their positions," I reply. "We don't need prisoners. I doubt the soldiers out there can tell us anything we don't know."

"Sir," a tech calls out. "A single vehicle is breaking from each convoy. Pulling ahead. Should we have the drones follow the lead car or maintain position on the main column?"

Earls cuts his eyes at me.

"Follow the breakaway cars. See what they're up to."

In the doorway, Arthur appears, an amused expression on his face. "Sergeant Arthur, reporting for duty," he says with mock enthusiasm.

Earls nods to the chair and his guards usher Arthur over to it.

"We have to confine you," I say to him. "You understand that."

"I understand that you believe that," he replies, letting his arms drift back to the chair frame. He stares at me as the guards wrap his arms with heavy-duty tape and affix zip ties over it.

"We're under attack," I say quietly.

Arthur raises his eyebrows. "I see that. Brilliant move by your species. You're going extinct, so you try to kill each other."

"This wasn't our idea."

"But you could use some ideas about defending against the attack, couldn't you? That's why you brought me here."

"Well, you claim to have thousands of years of experience battling hostile species on thousands of worlds."

"Millions of years, James."

"I stand corrected. So what would you do?"

"Let's see. You're outnumbered. And trapped. Assuming you could escape, where would you go? There are only so many places to weather the cold. They'd find you and kill you. It's better to fight here than there."

"We had gotten that far actually."

"My advice? It all comes back to energy. Can't live without it."

"How does that help us?"

"I'm afraid that's all you're going to get, James. I want to see if you can figure it out." Arthur raises his eyebrows. "I have to amuse myself somehow."

I exhale, shaking my head. In truth, it's to his advantage for us to slaughter each other. It would save the grid from spending anymore time or energy on us. I wonder then: is he somehow in on this? Does he have something planned?

We may have more enemies in this battle than we think.

The few remaining troops tunneling in the snow are dead. With the drones painting the targets, the snipers picked them off, their life signs fading from yellow and red to purple and then black.

"The lead cars are stopping," one of the technicians calls out.

Earls, Fowler, and I stand and watch the video feeds.

Soldiers dressed in Pac Alliance and Atlanta Guard winter fatigues exit their vehicles and begin milling about, grabbing items from the trunks and cargo compartments. They're offloading what look like white PVC pipes. They set them in stands in the snow, arraying them in neat rows. Each vehicle must have twenty or so of the pipes, lined up like pickets in a fence, tilted toward us.

The soldiers return from their vehicles, one holding a large sack, the other carrying what looks like a can of hair spray.

"What are they doing?" Min asks.

Harry shakes his head. "It's a potato cannon."

Earls squints at him. "A potato cannon?"

Harry smiles. "You take a piece of PVC, seal one end and jam a potato in the other. Then you fill the sealed end with a propellant and ignite it. Boom!" He spreads his hands out. "Tons of fun till the neighbors complain to your parents."

On the screen, a soldier reaches into the bag, drawing out what looks like a taped-up tin can. He marches down the row, dropping the makeshift rounds down into the pipes. Another soldier crouches at the sealed end, where he sprays with the aerosol can and flicks a lighter. The first gun goes off, sending the can out in a puff of white air. The guns fire rapidly after that, blasting rounds into the air.

"Plenty of PVC plumbing pipe in the rubble," Harry says. "Easy to recover. And lots of empty soup and bean cans. Probably filled them with water."

"We're getting land-mine impacts," a tech says. "Two. No, three. Four now."

"They're turned off, right?" I ask.

"Yes, sir."

An explosion echoes in the distance.

"I assume they just hit our battleship?" Harry asks.

The tech studies the screen. "North one-oh-nine just detonated. The force of the kinetic round must have set it off somehow."

"So much for the land mines," Earls mutters.

It occurs to me then, what Arthur's warning means: it all comes back to energy. We can't live without it.

"We have a bigger problem," I say quietly. "These potato cannons aren't just for the land mines." I glance back at Arthur. "I think they're going to use them to break the solar panels."

Without the solar panels beside the warehouse and on top of it, we'll freeze to death in a matter of days. In a strange way, our fate has become the same as the grid's: our future hinges upon the collection and conservation of energy.

Either we protect those solar panels—or we die.

The breakaway cars have rejoined the convoys by the time the larger group reaches the edge of our rings of land mines. Deep blast pits dot the landscape. The convoys drive single file, hugging the edge of the blast areas, safely passing.

"Their kinetic cannons will be in range of our solar panels in about three minutes," Earls says.

On another screen, I watch the troops on the roof covering our solar panels with a patchwork of habitat wall pieces and capsule parts.

We've decided to let our enemy destroy the solar field next to the warehouse. We'd have to put troops out there to properly defend it. We can't spread ourselves that thin. We may not even be able to protect the solar panels on the roof. Assuming we can, they will barely generate enough to power the manufacturing plant. And not enough to heat the warehouse.

Several vehicles from the eastern convoy stop and the troops set up a larger array of PVC canons. Soon, they're launching projectiles in waves. Some of the cans strike the warehouse and bounce off. But they are devastating to the field of fragile solar panels, which shatter and list, falling to the ground. It soon looks like a mangled junkyard of black glass in the snow.

"The roof protections are holding," Harry says. He leans over to Grigory. "What are we going to do in the morning when we need them exposed to the sun?"

"We figure it out if there is a morning," Grigory mutters.

I turn at the sound of footsteps behind me. Since Caffee assaulted the command post, I've been a little jumpy. We all have.

Brightwell marches through the doorway, arm in a sling, eyes focused. "What did I miss?"

"You feeling up to duty?" I ask her.

She grimaces as if the question is ridiculous. "It barely grazed me."

With a small grin, Earls begins filling her in.

On the screen, the convoys on all sides of us come to a stop. They're setting up just outside the effective firing range of our snipers. I wish we had some heavy artillery. I wonder if the Pac Alliance and Atlanteans brought any when they came over. I guess we'll know soon.

Fowler squints at the video feeds of the convoys, idling in the snow, pointed at us but unmoving. "What are they doing?"

"The four convoys are likely conversing on an encrypted Pac Alliance channel," Earls responds.

"Can we listen in?"

"No. Codebreakers were working on it before Ceres, but after... high command thought there was little chance of war. Resources were reassigned."

"Any guess about what they're saying?"

"They've probably been out of radio contact until now or just recently," Earls says. "They've no doubt realized that their advance team didn't make it to the plant. I'd bet they're altering their course of action."

The car radio on the table behind me crackles to life, the sound only a series of beeps, easy to miss, almost like a malfunction or system test.

"It's Morse code," Harry says. "Numbers one, three, two."

"It's a channel," I reply, thinking. "I bet it's an AU radio channel."

Harry tunes a handheld radio to channel 132 and cranks the volume up.

Nothing.

Were the numbers some kind of message? A signal that they're going to attack?

"Reverse it."

Harry tunes the handheld to channel 231. We hear Chandler's voice instantly.

"Commuter one, commuter two, do you copy? Please respond."

Brightwell eyes me, silently requesting orders. I hold a hand up. Hopefully, he's about to reveal something about the next step in his plan.

"Commuter one, commuter two, do you copy? Please respond," Chandler calls again. Then there's a long silence.

The car radio crackles to life, Chandler's voice broadcasting this time, muffled, like a disc jockey on a station that barely comes in.

"To the Atlantic Union troops in Camp Nine, this is Richard Chandler, your elected representative. I'm appealing to you directly because your government is betraying you. They have instigated a confrontation with the Pac Alliance and Atlanta survivors. Don't let this go any further. We can resolve this without bloodshed. Lay down your arms and come out and join us. I promise you that no harm will come to you or any of your family or anyone else in Camp Nine. This is your *only* chance. Please choose peace. Work with us."

A pause, then: "They're telling me you have five minutes. Please hurry."

"Did any of our troops hear any speakers broadcast that message in the warehouse or plant?" Brightwell asks.

One of her techs asks over the radio and turns a minute later. "No reports, ma'am."

"Advise all troops that an attack is likely imminent."

Earls leads Brightwell, Fowler, Harry, Grigory, Min, and me to the corner of the room opposite Arthur and his guards.

"Thoughts?" Earls asks.

"We can hold them off," Brightwell responds. "Assuming they don't have heavy artillery."

"We'll probably know that within a few minutes. If they do, they'll use it to soften the perimeter and then breach," Earls adds.

Arthur is watching us, an amused expression on his face. He raises his eyebrows at me when we make eye contact.

In the background, I vaguely hear the group debating options. The first is trying to escape—using the 3-D printers to make a helicopter or dirigible. This is ruled out quickly. They explore fortifying the plant and drawing the enemy into the warehouse and fighting there. Our troop numbers give us poor odds down that road.

In my mind, I turn the problem around, look at it from every angle, and then consider what I have to work with. I stare at Arthur, sensing that he is a valuable piece of the puzzle, though how is not clear to me yet. He's right: we're outgunned and trapped. But what do we have that Chandler wouldn't expect? What would change the situation here, turn it to our advantage? In a flash I see it, feeling that inspiration I once felt in the lab when I made a breakthrough.

"James?" Fowler asks.

I realize everyone is looking at me, waiting. "There's a solution here, one that guarantees our survival."

Fowler cocks his head, surprised. Earls and Brightwell stare with unreadable expressions. Grigory looks skeptical.

"We're going to fight. And we're going to win."

Brightwell flicks her eyes at Earls, who nods for her to speak. "Sir, to win, we need more ammunition and—"

"No, Colonel, to win we need only one thing. More time."

She bunches her eyebrows. "Sir, with our ration situation and the threat to the solar panels, I believe time is not on our side."

"Not yet, Colonel. But it will be." I stride over to the table and pick up the handheld radio. "Chandler."

"Hello, James. I hope you're calling to avoid bloodshed. We've come to make peace, not war. Let's talk terms."

"Yes. Let's talk terms. You don't realize it yet, but we have the upper hand here. I hope you don't find that out the hard way. To the other members of your group who can hear me, listen closely. Your lives depend upon it. Richard Chandler is here because of a personal vendetta against me. Don't let him manipulate you. He doesn't care about you or your people. But we do. We've built the ships that will save us all. Let's stick to our plan. If you leave now, this will all be forgotten. Our plans will proceed as if it never happened."

Chandler responds quickly. "I'm sure you also want us to forget the fact that you don't have room for everyone on those ships, James. And it won't be the AU troops left behind. They're vital to the conspiracy. It will be these men and women—from Atlanta and the Pac Alliance. They'll be left to starve on this cold, dark world."

"You've missed quite a bit since you left, Richard. We solved that issue."

Harry and Grigory instantly turn to me. Min looks down. They all know it's a lie. If that lie saves my people, I'll tell it until the ships leave orbit.

"Stop lying, James."

"I'm not. There's space for everyone. The cause you've convinced these people to fight for no longer exists."

A long pause on the radio. This might actually work.

Chandler's voice is confident when he comes back on. "Nice try, James. But let's stop with the lies. Surrender now. Send your troops out unarmed, and no one gets hurt."

"You want us, Richard, come in and get us. Otherwise, we'll simply wait while you all starve and freeze out there."

"James, we both know you'll be the one starving and freezing. Why would we attack when we can wait you out? Call me back when you're ready to be reasonable. Or better yet, I hope someone else inside will call when you're dead or locked up."

The line goes silent, but soon after, there's movement on the video feeds: troops pouring out of the vehicles. It's clear the life signs from the drones were masked. There were indeed a lot of soldiers in those troop carriers. They insulated the compartments.

"I want troop counts," Brightwell calls out.

The Pac Alliance and Atlanta soldiers drag large bundles out of the carrier compartments and fumble with them in the snow. If those are heavy artillery, our chances of survival plummet. Mushrooms rise from the packs, silver domes glowing in the night vision image. They're portable habitats—probably brought over from Atlanta. These were used for the settlers arriving there. They're built for long-term use in harsh conditions.

Our enemy is digging in for a siege.

In the bottom right corner, the troop counts from each convoy tick up as the technicians update them. In total, our adversary has brought nearly four thousand troops. To our roughly four hundred.

We have enough food for fourteen days. That's how long we have to win this war.

64

Emma

Consciousness comes like a light slowly being turned on and off. I see the world in those brief flashes. The inside of the infirmary. Madison, Abby, and Izumi leaning over me, holding my hand, pressing the health analyzer to my finger, adjusting the medication flowing into the bag hanging from a metal pole beside the bed.

I open my eyes and find Madison sitting in the chair opposite me, holding Allie. She jumps out of her aunt's lap and runs over when she sees my eyes open.

"Mom…"

"Hi, sweetie."

Tears fill her eyes. "You're sick."

"No, I'm not. I just need to rest for a bit." I smile and place a hand on her face, the IV line pulling at my skin. "Your baby brother will be here soon. Are you excited?"

She nods, but her lower lip trembles and her eyes betray her fear.

In the distance, I hear an echoing boom. It sounds like a land mine going off.

"That's been happening about every hour," Madison says.

A figure appears at the entrance to the infirmary, face shadowed, but I know that walk, burdened, lumbering, but purposeful. James makes a beeline for my bed, stopping just long enough to squat and catch Allie as she runs into his arms.

He nods to Madison who collects her knitting and leaves us. "Hi."

I smile. "How's it going?"

"Crazy day at the office."

"Sounds like things are blowing up in your face."

That gets a snort from him and the humor actually reaches his eyes. The levity has an effect on Allie too. I can sense her relaxing. Young children take their cues from their parents. If we're calm, they're more likely to be calm. She knows something's going on, that there's danger out there. But in this moment, it feels far away and controlled.

James turns to her. "Are you being good while I'm at work?"

She smiles sheepishly.

"Listening to your mom and aunt?"

Allie nods.

"No fighting with your cousins." He kisses her forehead. "Go find your aunt Madison. I want to visit with Mom a bit."

When she's beyond earshot, my smile fades. "Chandler?"

"Yeah," James replies, turning his face away to look at the vitals on the screen beside the bed.

"How bad?"

"Just an inconvenience. We'll be out of the woods in a few days."

"Tell me the truth."

"Do you trust me?"

"Completely."

"Good. We'll be out of here soon. I promise."

65

James

After I visit Emma, I stay in the command post for a few hours, watching Chandler's troops set up their camp. They're spread out across the snow-covered land, forming a ring with four breaks where their camps don't meet each other. The holes from the land mines lie beyond their camp, brown and black pits slowly fading to white as the falling snow fills them.

I glance at the countdown clock, watching it tick down to zero.

"Arming North four-three," a tech says. "Detonating."

A land mine goes off, sending a spray of snow and earth into the air. The explosions can't physically harm the troops out there. But they can keep them awake. Keeping our enemy sleep-deprived and ill prepared to attack is the best we can do at the moment. They have the numbers and the luxury of attacking at a moment of their choosing. We have to constantly be ready to defend—with far fewer numbers. But if they're tired and agitated, it gives us a slight edge.

"I think it's clear they're bedding down for the night," Earls says.

"I agree," Brightwell adds.

"Let's meet in the situation room," I say to the group as I head out of the command post, two armed guards falling in behind me.

I stop by to see Emma in the infirmary again. She and Allie are both scared. I do my best to reassure both of them. I think only Allie buys it, but I know Emma believes in me. It's like the wind at my back. It makes *me* believe in me. I also know she has her own worries, the child inside of her being the greatest of all.

Walking the halls helps me think, my muscles firing like an engine powering my brain.

The entire team is waiting in the situation room when I arrive. Earls and Brightwell stand rigidly near the door. Harry nurses a cup of coffee. Min sits with his eyes closed, resting without sleeping. Grigory leans back in his chair staring at the ceiling as if he's wondering how we ever got into this situation. Fowler sits in the chair I used to sit in, to the right of the head of the table. That seat lays empty. Waiting for me.

I motion my guards to wait outside and close the door. I stand a few feet away from the head of the table, not quite ready to sit.

"I have a plan. What we don't have is much time. I need help from every one of you. And I need you to work quickly. We don't have a lot of time for debate." I think my meaning is clear, but for good measure, I add, "Does that work?"

Fowler nods.

"I've never disobeyed an order," Earls says. "I'm not about to start."

"As you know," Brightwell says calmly, "I follow your orders, sir. Even when I don't agree."

"And I've learned from those past orders, Colonel. I meant what I said in the command post. We're going to fight. And we're going win."

"How, sir? They have the numbers."

"They won't by the time we engage them. We'll have even odds or possibly superior numbers. We'll also have the element of surprise."

Brightwell actually smiles. "I like the sound of that, sir."

"I thought you would, Colonel. I need you to make sure your people are in fighting condition when the time comes."

"Any idea when that time will be?"

"About two weeks, give or take a few days."

"Cutting it close with our ration situation, sir."

"I'll take care of the ration issue."

"What do you need from us?" Harry asks.

"I need you to get all of those vehicle speakers and radios working again. This time, we're going to use them to our advantage."

"That shouldn't take long," Harry replies.

"How many drones do we have left?" I ask Brightwell. "That we can land on the roof and deploy with light cargo?"

"Four."

I do a few mental calculations, then focus on Harry, Min, and Grigory. "I need you to make eighty housings for small bombs. Twenty for each drone."

Harry nods slowly, as if mentally guessing my plan. "We can probably make it work, but we don't have parts to make anymore bombs. We used everything we had on the land mines, and we can't exactly go out scavenging for more explosives."

"We won't need them. The cases will be empty. They'll just look like bombs. How long to make them?"

Harry glances at Min and shrugs. "We can print them in about twenty-four hours."

"I need the printers for something else. You'll have to use what you have here in the warehouse."

"Okay. Maybe three or four days."

Min says, "Power will be an issue. The solar panels on the roof can barely generate enough electricity to heat the warehouse. If you need them to run the printers *and* refill the drone's power cells, we're going to be way short. And that's assuming we're at one hundred percent efficiency. At the moment, the panels are covered for protection."

"We won't need to heat the whole building. Only a small fraction. I'll explain soon."

Min nods. "Okay."

"Grigory, I do need you to make a bomb—using whatever you can find inside the warehouse and plant."

He leans forward in his chair, suddenly interested. "How big?"

"Very big."

"Portable? Launchable?"

"No. Stationary."

"How big is very big?" he asks.

"Big enough to destroy the entire warehouse."

Grigory stares at the wall a moment. "We cannot make small, portable bombs, but a large bomb? Doable. It will be a chemical bomb. Take me a couple of days."

Fowler studies me. "We're going to hide out in the plant? It'll be pretty cramped in there."

"No. We're going somewhere else. But we won't get there if we can't control the people inside this building. I need your help with that, Lawrence. They trust you and look to you in times of uncertainty. They're going to be pretty spooked. Maybe even more than they were in the Citadel."

Fowler shakes his head. "Emma got them through that, not me."

"Well, this is your time."

"I'll make it happen."

I scan the room. "There's one other part of this. We can execute my plan alone. But our chances increase if we have Arthur's help. I want to make him an offer. I need you all to trust me to do that."

There are no ringing calls of endorsement, only a few nods. Grigory and Brightwell glance down, hard looks on their faces. They don't like it, but their silent assent is probably the best I could hope for.

"Okay. That's the plan. Time is our greatest enemy now. If any of you need help, come see me."

Brightwell lingers at the door as the others leave. "Sir, should I bring Arthur in?"

"Yes. The meeting will be between only the three of us."

She opens her mouth to protest, but I cut her off. "No guards. What we discuss can't leave this room."

Five minutes later, Arthur waltzes into the room, Brightwell behind him. She quickly closes the door and stands at attention, hand on her gun, eyes on Arthur.

He smiles, first at her, then at me. "What's all this?"

"You know what this is."

"Yes. I do." He glances around the situation room, as if savoring the moment. "Kind of a strange turn of events—you making me an offer this time around."

A land mine to the west detonates, the sound muffled, echoing like thunder.

"We can win this war without you, Arthur. But your assistance would increase our chances."

His smile fades. "I'm listening."

When I've finished explaining my plan, Arthur studies my face for a long moment. For the first time since I've come into contact with him, he is silent, his expression blank, as if he's processing the data, trying to solve a complex equation—and hide his own reaction. When he speaks, the playful, indifferent tone has returned.

"I have to admit: I'm impressed. Haven't been for a few million years. There were actually two solutions to your dilemma, and you've managed to select the one with the highest probability of success. Oh, and you've added two tactics that my simulations didn't identify. Outside-the-box ideas. They marginally increase your chances."

"It's called creativity."

His face goes slack, as if he's reprocessing what he's learned. "No. It's called nearly impossible, James."

"Meaning?"

"That you truly are a mind ahead of your time." He stares at me, searching my face for something. For the first time, Arthur looks almost confused. His voice comes out flat and disembodied, as though his personality has slipped away, as though he can't spare the processing power for it. For the first time, he sounds more like an emotionless computer.

"No. There's another variable at work here. An anomaly I can't adequately factor."

"An anomaly the grid can't factor?"

He freezes. For a moment, I start to wonder if he's gone offline, if whatever is happening has compromised his AI program. That would be bad for us. More than ever, we need him.

Finally, his face reanimates, as if he's waking up. The biting, arrogant tone is back. "Don't flatter yourself, James. The grid possesses calculating capability your rudimentary math can't even measure. This is a local processing limitation."

"Now there's the evil AI overlord we've all come to know and love."

"This AI overlord wants to know what's in it for me? It's not like I get out of jail early for good behavior—which I think you're familiar with."

"On the contrary, that's exactly what I'm offering you. Consider this: some part of the human race is leaving this planet one way or another. You're staying. What happens then? According to you, you'll build an escape pod and blast into space to make your report to the grid. How long will that take?"

Arthur shrugs. "What's it to me? I'm immortal."

"True, but time is important to the grid. If you upload your report faster, it might yield an insight that makes another grid operation more efficient. Or perhaps it could even inform how you deal with us. In short, making your report sooner could benefit the grid. As does having me alive. You are familiar with me—you know I've chosen to leave peacefully. The people out there are unpredictable. Dealing with them might require you to expend more power than dealing with me."

"What exactly are you proposing?"

"We'd take you up to the ship with us, launch you toward the asteroid belt as we pass. You upload your data as we leave, not days or weeks after."

Brightwell's eyes snap toward me for an instant before returning her gaze to Arthur. She doesn't like it.

"Your people won't like that," Arthur says playfully.

"My people have put their faith in me. I'm offering this deal. And there's another benefit."

Arthur raises his eyebrows.

"If those armies out there breach this building, they won't hesitate to shoot you."

"I'm not easy to kill."

"I know. I built that body. But you're not impossible to kill."

A silent moment, then I add, "You're not just an AI, are you?"

Arthur doesn't respond.

"All this attitude, the jokes. They're not some mathematical formula designed to elicit a reaction from me. They're your personality. *You*, Arthur, or whatever your name is, are something like an individual within the grid, aren't you? A consciousness with your own experiences and specialty. A career. You're like... a spy. A paratrooper they drop behind enemy lines to subvert or effect some outcome the grid wants. In a way, you're stranded here, like a sailor left on a remote island with a hostile indigenous species. You want off this rock and away from us just as bad as we want rid of you."

"A crude analogy."

"Is that a yes?"

"You already know what I'm going to say."

"Good. One last thing. I need your assurance that Emma will survive the procedure."

"Are you asking for her, or for your unborn child?"

"Both."

"Yes, James. She'll survive."

"She'd better. If she dies, so do you. The deal is off."

66

Emma

One by one soldiers come and move the patients out of the infirmary, rolling them on gurneys and pushing wheelchairs. I ask where they're taking them, but none of the soldiers reply. And none of the patients return. What's happening here?

I drift in and out of sleep, the sedative overtaking me and then wearing off, as if I'm treading water, my head occasionally dunking below before popping back up to take a breath.

I awake to find James sitting in a chair beside my bed. Allie is in his lap.

"Mom!" she says brightly. "Going on trip."

Confusion crosses my face. James shakes his head sharply, too quickly for Allie to see. I force a smile. "Of course. I almost forgot. We're going on a trip. Are you excited?"

She nods.

"Good. Do as your father says, all right?"

James stands and holds her out to me, not letting her rest

on my chest, but close enough for her to hug me. "Tell your mom bye."

"Bye, Mom. Love you."

"I love you too, sweetie."

As he walks away, I wonder where we're going. Or if that's just something he told her. Most of all, I wonder why he brought her here to say goodbye.

The answer occurs to me. Because this might be goodbye. He wanted me to see her just in case it was.

A few minutes later, James returns with Sam. The boy has put on a brave face, but he hugs me just as tight as Allie, and I kiss his forehead and tell him I'll see him soon, as if I'm sure of it.

The machine beeps quietly as it administers the drug, but I'm too worked up to sleep now. I shift in bed, watching the entrance to the infirmary, my mind a mess of worry and confusion.

Finally, James returns, alone this time. The medication is coming on strong now, trying to pull me under. He's speaking softly to a few figures at the door. I can't make out the words. The scene blurs. Suddenly, he's at my bedside, leaning over to kiss me.

My voice comes out scratchy from disuse. "What's happening?"

"We're getting out of here."

"How?"

"Do you trust me?"

"You know I do."

"I need you to take a leap of faith."

I shake my head, trying to bat the drug away. In his face, I see resolve. Buried deep beneath that mask, hidden from only those who know him as I do, I see fear.

"I'm ready to leap."

He takes my hand and squeezes. "I'll see you on the other side."

He turns toward the door and motions to the people waiting. Izumi strides in, six soldiers behind her. Behind them is Arthur, his expression blank. Two more soldiers push a gurney into the room. A machine hangs from a pole connected to one side. I recognize that machine. The last time I saw it was at the launch facility, when it was used on three volunteers. Just like then, a stasis sleeve sits on the gurney. This time, it's waiting for me.

I feel my pulse quicken. Adrenaline flows through me. Focus returns as the adrenaline is flushed from my system.

The blood pressure monitor blares an alarm. Izumi rushes to it, taps a button that silences it and then draws a syringe from her pocket and injects it into the line attached to my hand.

"What is that?" I ask, reaching out to her.

"Just something to help you relax."

Whatever it is, it's working. My arm feels heavy. Too heavy to lift. When I move my head, my vision blurs. Everything turns to slow motion.

I feel my words echoing in my head, the sound slow, like an audio track inching forward. "Why?"

James leans closer to me. "We have to."

My voice sounds unnatural, a groan like iron bending. "Why?"

"Not enough food. Not enough power to keep us warm."

I nod, the motion requiring effort to keep my head up, as if there's a weight pushing me down. "Kids?"

"They did great," James responds. "They were very brave."

The sedative is dragging me under like weights pulling at my feet. Suddenly, a thought runs through my mind like an electric shock. A single word: *kids*. I glance down at my protruding belly. I try to speak, but the words won't come. I stare at James, silently trying to communicate, to warn him, to ask him if our unborn child will survive.

James cuts his eyes to Arthur, then back to me. "He'll be fine. And so will you."

As if in a dream, I feel the soldiers lifting me, slipping my body into the stasis sleeve, the hard rubbery material cold and heavy on my skin, sticking like wet clothes.

I hear zipping, far away and faint. Hissing. A face mask touching the bridge of my nose, my cheeks, my chin. I inhale deeply, but there's no smell. Only darkness.

67

James

There is something extremely unnerving about seeing human bodies in bags, stacked upon each other in a room as if they were simply supplies stored out of the way. Yet that's what we've done. We've put nearly half of our entire civilian population into stasis. The sleeves fill three flats, the bodies stacked in rows halfway to the ceiling.

The reason is simple: soon we will be shutting down the heat and electricity to the vast majority of the warehouse. The stasis sleeves can survive the cold vacuum of space. They won't have a problem here.

The manufacturing plant is printing stasis sleeves one after another, as fast as it can. Within twenty-four hours, the last of the civilians will be in stasis.

Seeing Emma, Allie, and Sam go into the sleeves has focused me. We win this battle, or they never wake up.

I stop by the command post just long enough to scan the video feeds. It's night now, and the enemy camps are still and quiet. The domed silver solar tents spread out around the vehicles like bugs burrowing in the snow.

"Set off another one," I order one of the soldiers sitting at a console.

"Quadrant preference, sir?"

"You call it, Corporal."

It doesn't matter. They'll all hear it.

On the upper left screen, there's a flash in the distance.

The domed tents remain still. No one comes out to look. But I know it just woke a lot of them up, and they're not happy about it.

That never gets old.

Dressed in my cold-weather gear, I barrel through the empty halls of the warehouse. There are a few troops milling about, hiding the speakers in the ceiling, and the heating ducts, and in every other nook and cranny they can find.

When I'm alone in the hall, I turn the door handle to one of the flats. It's unremarkable in every way. I selected it at random, but it's where our final stand begins.

In the living room, Brightwell stands at attention in the corner, her eyes on Arthur. He's standing at a rolling terminal working a laptop, his fingers moving like a flash.

"This would be easier if you allowed me to connect wirelessly," he says.

"You know we can't do that," I reply.

I nod to Brightwell, and she paces out of the room, her shift over.

I plop down on the couch and close my eyes, exhaustion seeping into me. I'd love to get a few hours' sleep, but I don't trust Arthur that much.

"How's it going?" I ask him.

He motions to the massive hole in the ground. "It's going."

At the end of my shift, I check on Grigory first, who's muttering in Russian as he works on the massive bomb. He's using one of the large water tanks from the habitat's recycler as the container. The floor is strewn with parts, most of which I'm not familiar with.

"Need anything?" I ask.

He rolls his eyes. "Food, sleep, peace and quiet."

"Food and quiet are doable. Sleep will have to wait. Peace is off the table."

Harry and Min's collection of faux bombs look like haphazardly made cube-shaped piñatas. They've used everything from children's toys to habitat parts to air conditioning ducts to make the multicolored boxes.

"They're not pretty," Harry says, "but they'll get the job done."

"That's all that counts."

Only a few sections of the warehouse are heated now: the command post, a few of the labs, several habitats we use as barracks, and the infirmary, which houses the leadership and their families. When I arrive at the infirmary, Alex, David, Madison, and Abby are waiting on me.

"They've scheduled us to go into stasis sleeves tonight," Alex says.

"I know. We have to. Without the solar field, we can't heat the building."

"Yes, but you have a larger plan, don't you, James?" Before I can respond, he adds, "We want to help."

I shake my head. "Leave it to us. The soldiers are trained for this."

"I'm not going in that sleeve and leaving you out here to defend us. Give me something to do. Anything, James. Please."

I chew my lip for a moment. I know exactly how he feels. If I were in his position, I'd be saying the exact same thing.

"All right."

One by one, the pieces of my plan fall into place.

The days and nights drag on like an eternity.

Chandler and I trade barbs over the radio.

The land mines go off like a grandfather clock chiming at the top of the hour, both armies constantly on alert, watching each other across the snowy battlefield, both dug into our trenches, always ready to fight.

Thankfully, the cans launched from the potato cannons stopped after the initial attack on the solar panels. That enabled us to uncover the panels on the roof and collect power. If not, I don't know what we would've done. By a very small margin of safety, we have enough power to finish our preparations—and they will be done today. After sunset, we'll make our final stand. In ten hours, we will live or die.

Izumi has been hounding me to get some sleep, insisting I take a tablet for it. But I won't. I need my mind to be clear tonight. Any mistake could doom us all.

I stop by one of the stasis holding rooms and pace down the aisle, stopping at Emma's sleeve. I reach out and touch it, wishing I could hold her hand one last time. More than that, I wish she were beside me for this battle, as she was in the last, at Ceres, when we put it all on the line, as we're about to do once again tonight.

"Sir," the soldier behind me calls out.

I turn to find a private in battle armor and full winter attire staring at me, his breath coming out as white puffs of steam.

"Sir, I'm sorry, but we've been ordered to begin transporting the sleeves."

"Carry on," I mumble as I leave the room. I look back, wishing I had more time.

Time.

That is the currency we've spent, the capital we've invested in our survival. It has been deployed. Now we are out of time—and we'll soon see the return on that investment. The answer is binary. If we've invested our time wisely, we win. We live. If not, we perish.

I alone made the decisions that will determine that outcome. There wasn't time to spend discussing it. I've heard the expression it's lonely at the top, but I never understood it until now. At this moment, I feel utterly alone. The solitude is like a void around me, sucking at my sanity.

I wish Emma were here with me. But I'm going into the line of fire. For that reason, I'm glad she's not.

I stop at the flat with Grigory's bomb, nodding to the two soldiers flanking the door before entering.

Grigory sits cross-legged on the floor, staring at the behemoth.

"You sure it will work?"

"It will work," he mutters, not making eye contact.

We can't exactly test it, so Grigory's word will have to do.

If that bomb doesn't go off, our chances of survival drop to zero.

In the command post, I study the video feeds, sensing that I'm watching the calm before the storm, a long silence before a battle. The hours ahead will determine the course of human history.

At this point, the only people not in stasis are the scientists and soldiers, as well as a few of the civilians like Alex, Abby, Madison, and David. We've closed off even more of the habitats, leaving the entire warehouse in freezing conditions except for the command post, situation room, infirmary, and armory. Even the heat in those areas is a far cry from comfort.

The printers took more power than we anticipated to churn out the parts we needed. The drones require most of the power that's left and everything the solar panels will capture today. Adding to our problems is the fact that the sun grows dimmer each time it rises. We're a few months ahead of Arthur's deadline for the entire world to go completely dark, but it's clear to me that the planet is now nearly uninhabitable. He probably lied about how much time we had. I bet he assumed if we thought we had more time, we'd work slower. If we had, we'd be facing extinction right now. But we pushed as hard as we could, and that's the only reason we're ready to leave.

A skeleton crew of soldiers is posted at the outer entrances to the plant and warehouse. The rest of our troops are bedding down. For the next ten hours, our men and women in uniform will be sleeping. They'll need their rest for what comes tonight.

If Chandler does have another mole like Danforth or Caffee embedded here in Camp Nine, that person will surely alert him. We're at our most vulnerable today. Even if we were ready for it—if all of our troops were awake and battle-ready—we probably won't have much chance of repelling a direct attack. If our enemy attacks today, we will have no chance.

That thought haunts me as I slip into the sleeping bag next to Fowler, still dressed in my thick winter attire.

If Chandler attacks today—and wins—what would he do with our families in the stasis sleeves? Strand them here on Earth? The planet will be an ice ball soon. It's a death sentence.

I close my eyes, but I can't stop my mind from running. I can't push away the fear that I've missed something. If I have, I've doomed us.

I drift, somewhere between sleep and wakefulness, resting, but still conscious.

Finally, I rise and check the time.

Two hours to go.

I exit and march through the halls and climb the rickety staircase to the roof of the warehouse. A dozen soldiers are here, organizing Harry and Min's mishmash of fake bombs. Harry's here too, staring at the setting sun on the white horizon.

"Couldn't sleep?" he asks me.

I shake my head.

"Me neither."

"When will you land the drones?" I ask him.

"Fifteen minutes before. I figured any sooner and it would alert them."

"Good luck."

"You too."

As I turn away, he calls to me. "Thank you, James."

I turn, seeing his somber smile. Neither one of us says goodbye, but that's what we both think this might be. I hold my hand out and shake and then pull my closest colleague into a hug. Harry is perhaps my best friend, though Grigory somehow comes to mind as well.

I wander the warehouse corridors after that, finally making my way to the flat where Arthur and I did our work.

The hole in the ground reminds me of the shaft he drilled down to the Citadel—and for good reason. We used the same boring drone.

Soldiers flow in and out of the room, carrying stasis sleeves in and lowering them down to the soldiers waiting in the hole.

That was the first piece of the puzzle that came to me: Arthur's boring drone. It worked flawlessly at the Citadel and when it drilled the acceleration ring at the launch site.

If I'm right, it's the key to our salvation tonight.

Though I probably don't need to, I take a stimulant tablet. My adrenaline is already pumping. The tablet barely adds to it.

I stand in the command post, Earls and Brightwell beside me, watching the video feed from the roof as the drones fly to their docking stations and clamp down, rapidly recharging their fuel cells. A platoon of soldiers rushes to them and attaches the boxes to their undersides. If they were real bombs, there's no way the drones could lift off. But our enemy can't take that chance.

"Corporal," Brightwell calls out, "have platoon leaders proceed to location omega where they will receive further instructions."

The NCO confirms the order and begins barking orders to the technicians who speak into their headsets.

For the past few days, similar orders have been issued constantly, directing all platoons to nondescript locations such as sigma, alpha, beta, and theta. This will seem like just more chatter to anyone listening on the outside.

Location omega is the flat where we drilled the exit tunnel. Until today, only Brightwell, Arthur, and I knew where it was. We told the platoon moving the stasis sleeves a few hours ago. Ten minutes ago, we sent runners to the other platoon leaders with a note disclosing the location. If Chandler's forces find the flat, we're in trouble.

Our troops are in motion now, flowing toward the breach. There's no turning back.

This is happening.

My heart pounds in my chest, the cold aching in my lungs, as if my nerves may strangle me where I stand.

An image flashes into my mind—of the two guards lying dead in the launch control station. My breath catches. Why am I thinking about that now? It has nothing to do with this. Or does it? The dead soldiers are a mystery I never solved, an event I never factored into this. Two more images assault me: of Arthur standing in his cell smiling at me and of Chandler sneering, saying, *It's begun, James. My revenge.*

Why am I thinking about this now? What does it mean? Is my subconscious telling me the guards have something to do with this? Did Arthur kill them? Or Chandler? Or are they working together?

Could it be neither? Could this just be my nerves grasping at any loose ends?

Earls sees the pained expression on my face. "Sir?" he whispers.

I shake my head. "It's nothing."

On the main screen, the video feed of the enemy camps is unchanged, like a surveillance clip on repeat.

"Bring up video feeds for Alpha Company, Charlie Platoon," Brightwell says.

Live video from soldiers standing in the flat with the tunnel appears. Soldiers stand around the massive hole. Bits of chewed-up concrete, dust, and dirt lie around the rim. The grid's technology allowed us to pulverize the dirt and rock from the excavation. It was fine enough to leave down in the tunnel, along the sides. It's a good thing; we couldn't have possibly hauled that much material out.

A rope hangs from the ceiling down into the tunnel, waiting for the soldiers to rappel down.

On another screen, the video feed from the roof shows Harry giving a thumbs up.

Brightwell focuses on me.

I try to make my voice calm. I only partially succeed. "Proceed, Colonel."

She nods to two privates, who take off from the room at a jog. One is bound for the roof; the other soon appears in the tunnel room.

The private hands a folded piece of paper to the commanding officer of Alpha Company's Charlie Platoon. The woman scans it, pockets the page, and grabs the rope and rappels down. Her troops follow without a word. An endless flow of soldiers follows behind. Except for the contingent here in the command post and the skeleton crews at the exterior entrances, every soldier we have is rushing into the tunnel.

The video feed shows Charlie Platoon jogging through the circular shaft. Their helmet lights carve into the blackness like miners rushing to a strike. Not far from the hole, the tunnel splits in three ways. Two of those three passages lead to dead ends, which are booby-trapped. Roughly fifty feet before the booby-trapped tunnels end, the drone bored long pits. We've placed spikes at the bottom and covered the pits with habitat parts coated in dirt. The cover will only collapse when enough troops—and weight—are standing on it.

At the termination of those dead ends, we placed car speakers that are broadcasting the voices of troops shouting orders. It's a lure. One that I hope will make our enemies charge forward to their deaths. It's a bit Indiana Jones, but it might work. If the enemy troops get into the tunnel, we'll need all the help we can get.

It's a strange thing for me, devising ways to kill. I spent my life trying to eliminate death for my fellow humans. Now I'm killing soldiers who have the misfortune of being against me. Most are simply following orders. They don't know me. Don't know my family. But this is the nature of war. You fight to survive.

Charlie Platoon's commanding officer is good. She jogs through the forking tunnel without stopping to review the map. This is more than a tunnel. It's a maze. There are eight forks in the tunnel, each with three choices. At each fork, two of the passages lead to the pits. Hopefully those booby traps will take care of any enemy troops who survive the warehouse and pursue us into the tunnel. At each fork, only one choice doesn't lead to a dead end.

I have devised a mnemonic for myself and for those without a map: CABA BABA. I've assigned letters to the forks in the tunnel: left to right, A, B, and C.

Off the main tunnel, near the end, there's a cavern that holds the stasis sleeves, stacked in neat rows. Every civilian from Camp Nine is there.

There's a small detachment of troops guarding the cavern with the civilians, just in case our enemy makes it that far. I also assigned Alex, Abby, David, and Madison to that location. They'll provide first aid and support if there's fighting in the tunnel. I hope it won't come to that.

Our plan has two weaknesses. Both are fatal. The first will be exposed right now: if we can't get the enemy to attack the warehouse, we're finished. Our tunnel isn't finished yet, but within a few minutes the drone will reactivate and finish the boring. It will break ground just beyond the enemy's western camp. If the enemy doesn't attack the warehouse—if they are still in their camp, we'll have to fight them out in that snowfield. We're badly outnumbered, and we'll lose. The next few moments will determine if that's the case.

The Charlie Platoon commander's headlamp rakes over the massive boring drone ahead. She throws a hand up at a right angle, palm forward, fingers together, as she slows her pace. Her light pans to the left, illuminating a figure standing next to a large machine. Suddenly, she comes to a dead stop and unslings her rifle from her shoulder, pointing at the figure.

Arthur breaks into a smile.

The troops behind the commander crash into her like train cars piling up. Still holding her rifle at the ready, the Charlie Platoon commander digs the map out of her shirt pocket and glances down at it, confirming her orders. Below the branching diagram lies a single line of text: *Do not shoot the person at the end. He will lead you forward.*

She nods to Arthur, and he draws a small tablet from his pocket and taps twice. The massive tunneling machine rushes forward, climbing the wall as it grinds into the earth. Now comes the tricky part.

The machine can tunnel straight up thanks to its horizontal stabilizers. However, our troops can't ascend straight up. As such, the boring drone will make a diagonal ascent out.

Our plan hinges on us completing the tunnel's exit without the enemy realizing it. We can't afford to lose the element of surprise. If the ground were bare, they would see the boring machine the moment it breaches the surface. Luckily, the snow above the ground freezes just after nightfall. It will hide our exit.

Masking the sound of the drone is a far larger challenge. This snow-covered expanse is deadly quiet at night. But I have a plan for that too.

The tunneling machine grinds forward. The shaft fills with dust, the troops coughing and throwing their arms over their mouths and noses as they follow behind.

These next minutes are the most crucial. If I've timed it wrong, our entire plan falls apart.

On the video feed of the roof, the other private Brightwell dispatched from the command post emerges from the stair shed. He signals to Harry, who quickly taps at his tablet, hands shaking from the cold or his nervousness or both. He and Min watch as the four drones lift off into the night, the blackness seeming to swallow them. Our enemy will spot the drones taking off, focus their night vision cameras on them and realize the payload they're carrying.

On the other screen, the tunneling machine surges forward, grinding the Tunisian sandstone into dust and rubble, the soldiers following behind.

I watch the feeds of the enemy camps, waiting, hoping...

Suddenly, the four enemy camps come to life. They have finally seen the images on their surveillance cameras. They've reached the conclusion I hoped they would: that the drones are carrying bombs meant for them. They think that this is our end game, our plan to destroy their camp and vehicles. If that truly were the case, they'd have two options—retreat or attack. Retreat would lead away from us, back towards the minefields. They'd spread out on foot and in the vehicles to present more targets—far more than the bombs could neutralize. However, there would still be enough bombs to destroy a large portion of their vehicles. That would leave over half of their troops with no way home. They'd be stranded here, in the cold. In that scenario, they'd have to attack soon or lose half their forces. I'm betting they chose to attack.

I exhale heavily when the video feed confirms that my gambit has worked. Troops in winter gear pour out of the domed tents. Vehicles on tracks surge forward, soldiers massed behind them, gathering what look like flat white shields and attaching them to the vehicles. The wide barrier makes the trucks look like giant snow plows. The shields are likely layers of habitat parts glued together, thick enough to stop our bullets.

The trucks lead the way, the lighter vehicles behind them. The four convoys close in on all sides. The mass of troops that were camped near the manufacturing plant splits in two as they rush forward. The divided forces cut wide arcs around the plant to join the forces closing in on the warehouse. Our enemy is assuming the plant is well guarded. The warehouse is larger and harder to defend. They plan to take it first, get hostages, then take down the plant. A solid battle plan. One I was counting on.

"Wait for them to close," Brightwell says evenly, watching the screen.

The tunneling machine coughs and gyrates as it inches forward.

"Enemy line is at one hundred fifty meters, ma'am," a tech calls.

"Hold," Brightwell says.

The tunneling machine bites into the earth, our troops following.

"One hundred meters out, ma'am!"

"Fire!" Brightwell commands.

The bright lines of tracer rounds lance into the darkness, ricocheting off the enemy vehicles, tearing into the makeshift defenses. Some troops fall, but most charge on.

The video feed from the Charlie Platoon commander still shows the drone tunneling upward. If it doesn't break the surface soon, we're sunk.

"Enemy line is fifty meters out, ma'am!"

"Fire and fall back," Brightwell says, eyes fixed on the screen. She turns to me. "Time to go, sir."

I don't move. I need to see the tunneling machine break the surface.

If Chandler has a mole in Camp Nine, he'll probably know about the tunnel. He'll have left a sizable portion of troops in the western camp. If he knows our plan, they'll attack the minute that drone reaches the surface. They only need to destroy the drone and close the tunnel. We'd be trapped. They could simply seal the other end of the tunnel, and we'd be finished. No loss of life to them.

I need to know that we have a way out—that we have a chance.

I feel strong fingers clamp around my upper arm, a vise tightening.

"Sir," Brightwell growls.

I stare at the screen a long moment. I won't get the certainty I need before I leave. This is going to be a leap of faith.

"Okay, Colonel."

"Corporal," she shouts. "Light it up."

In the distance, I hear the sound of thunder crashing in waves, vibrating the walls and echoing through the warehouse. On the video feed, the land mines explode in geysers of snow and sand and rock.

Troops following behind the enemy vehicles look back… but thankfully, they don't stop. They're assuming the land mines are a diversion to draw their attention from attacking us. They soon turn their focus back to the warehouse, ignoring the blasts behind them.

That's good. The sound of the land mines will easily cloak the grind of the boring machine piercing the surface.

I glance once more at the boring machine eating the earth, then turn and follow Brightwell out of the command post, my feet pounding the corridor's concrete floor. Gunfire roars in the distance. The fighting is right outside the warehouse. Then the outer walls crumble as the vehicles slam into them. Right now, enemy troops are pouring into this building.

Brightwell brings the radio to her mouth. "All positions, fire!"

The sound of gunfire echoes across the warehouse. But it's just that: sound, coming from the car speakers we've deployed. It's enough to trick our enemies. They return fire in all directions, no doubt scrambling for cover.

In the flat hiding the tunnel's entrance, the last of our troops are waiting. Harry, Min, and their people haven't gotten here yet. Neither has Grigory. I hope they're on their way.

The plan is simple: the last soldiers down will untie the rope from the ceiling and affix it to the cover we've fashioned for the hole: a large rug with habitat parts on the bottom. Anyone glancing at the flat won't think twice. But if they walk across the rug, it will creak, and concrete floors don't creak. I hope it will be enough to keep us hidden.

I grab the rope and rappel down. At the bottom of the shaft, I surge into the darkness, following the footsteps ahead of me, my mind reciting the mnemonic: CABA BABA. The tunnel is dark and feels endless, as if I'm in a loop where I keep running into the same fork with three exits.

I charge forward, past the side tunnel that leads to my wife and children, sleeping through this carnage and the madness soon to come.

Ahead, dim light lances through the tunnel, the moon shining into this man-made cave. We've done it. The boring machine has surfaced.

I feel the tunnel incline upward. I run faster, smelling the cold night air.

Hundreds of AU Army troops are hunkered down on both sides of the tunnel, guns ready, like paratroopers on a massive plane ready to be dropped beyond enemy lines. That's exactly what this tunnel will do.

Brightwell charges past them and breaches the surface.

A platoon of soldiers is dug into the snow, using it for cover. The boring machine lies off to the side, its top below the surface ice. I peek over the top. The enemy camp is less than fifty yards from us.

Crouching, Brightwell turns to me and whispers, "Sir?"

"Proceed, Colonel."

With a quick head motion from her, the troops surge out of the trench and onto the icy plain, barreling toward the domed habitats and few remaining vehicles.

We're utterly exposed now, with nothing to take cover behind.

I draw the sidearm from my heavy winter coat.

Brightwell looks back. "Stay here, sir."

"I'm not watching from here," I whisper to her. "I made this mess. I'm going to help clean it up."

She nods, sensing that I won't take no for an answer. Shoulder to shoulder, we climb out onto the plain. A gust of wind drills through my clothes, making me shake even more than my nerves.

There are about twenty soldiers in front of me, roughly four hundred behind me, and five hundred civilians buried in the tunnel. Their fate is in our hands. We had four choices of locations to exit the tunnel. Cardinal directions. We chose west. It has the most troops, and I'm guessing it houses the command post. Chandler's here. I can feel it.

I brace for the confrontation, but as we dash across the open plain, no bullets fly our way. Our enemy is focused forward, on the warehouse and plant and the fighting they think is happening there. It's all smoke and mirrors. But if I'm right, it has taken them a while to realize that.

The first of our troops reach the threshold of their camp, but still, not a single shot reaches us. No enemy turns to face us. They've pushed everything forward. But I bet the leadership is still here with a small guard contingent, watching the battle in safety.

The enemy command post is easily identifiable from the tracks leading to and from it and the screens inside. The CP is actually two domed habitats joined together. I expect our troops to rush in but they slow as they reach it, several soldiers crouching in the snow by the door that lies open. A dozen figures are milling about inside, watching a bank of screens that show video feeds from their troops. I recognize the inside of the warehouse.

When Brightwell is twenty feet from the command post entrance, our troops turn and pour in, guns firing, taking out the uniformed soldiers.

Across the western camp, more shots echo in the night as the other habitats are breached.

In the command post, the fighting is over in seconds. It was a turkey shoot. The civilians spin around, shocked looks on their face. Around the room, they raise their trembling hands.

I scan the screens, looking for any clues as to what exactly is happening in the warehouse. A man's voice calls out over the command post speakers: "The gunfire is a recording. They're using the speakers from the vehicles. Have yet to engage hostiles. Commencing door-to-door search."

In the center of the group, Richard Chandler stands with his hands to his side, eyes burning as he stares at me.

"It's over, Richard."

He swallows and his voice comes out neutral, the confidence and condescension gone. "This was only a negotiating tactic. Nothing more."

"This doesn't feel like a negotiation."

Chandler moves a handheld radio to his mouth. "I'll prove it. I'll call them off."

I reach into my pocket and draw out the small remote that Grigory built. I slide the cover back, revealing a button. As if on cue, an enemy soldier calls over the radio.

"We've found what we think is a large IED. It's a converted water heater. CP, please advise."

Chandler reels back, scanning the video feeds; then he turns, his face horrified. "Don't do this, James. This isn't the kind of civilization you're trying to create."

"No. It isn't. You brought this war to us, Richard. I'm finishing it. The civilization I want begins after this."

Staring at Chandler, I press the button.

The boom is deafening. The blast rocks the small command post.

Chandler recovers first. He grabs a sidearm from the floor and brings it up quickly.

But I'm quicker.

68

Emma

My eyes are open, but I see only blackness. I can't feel my body. The sensation is nauseating, like floating in a void where my consciousness has no body.

Slowly, feeling returns, first to my face. Air flows across my nose and cheeks, tingling, cold. There's no smell, only a faint hissing.

The tips of my fingers tingle. It's as if control of my body is being restored from my extremities inward. I reach up and touch my belly. The child is still there. My eyes fill with tears when I feel a sharp kick. He's waking up too.

I hear a zipping sound above my head, and blinding light flows into the stasis sleeve. I shut my eyes and feel hands gripping beneath my armpits, dragging me out. Cold air engulfs me. Someone wraps a thick blanket around me and lifts me up, placing me on a soft bed. I crack my eyes open, ignoring the pain from the light. James peers down at me.

"How was it?"

"Weird."

He smiles and I can see the relief in his face. And exhaustion. The lines radiating out from the corners of his eyes are deeper now, as if the time since I last saw him has aged him, the experience leaving deep ruts in its wake.

My vision has returned enough for me to scan the room. I'm in the infirmary at CENTCOM. So we escaped the warehouse. How?

"Where are Allie and Sam?"

"I wanted to wake you up before them."

"How long was I out?"

"About a month."

The news is a shock. A hundred questions run through my mind. I try to push up on my elbows, but my arms feel like Jell-O.

James places a hand on my shoulder. "Hey, take it easy."

"A month? What happened?"

"We put all of the civilians in stasis and manufactured the remaining capsules. We're already transporting people up to the ships. Madison and Alex and their families went up yesterday."

"No, I mean what happened to the army outside Camp Nine?"

The weary smile on his face vanishes as he breaks eye contact. "No longer an issue."

"How?"

"It's not important."

"Did you negotiate a peace?"

"No."

"You fought them."

"Yes," he responds quietly.

I stare at him, but he doesn't say anymore, only stares at the floor.

"Were you hurt? *Are* you hurt?"

"I was barely involved."

I'd bet he was all too involved. Whatever happened in the month while I was in stasis, it has left a mark upon him. Gone is the quiet optimism he had even in the darkest moments of the Long Winter.

Maybe it wasn't the battle at Camp Nine that has changed him. Maybe it's what he has to do now, the dark event we've planned—and dreaded for months.

"The lottery?" I ask softly.

"We won't need it."

"How?"

"We have room for everyone."

"How, James?"

"Chandler's troops that were laying siege in Camp Nine… they were all lost."

I wait, but he says nothing more. *All lost.* The armies laying siege had thousands of troops. *All lost.* That is indeed what has taken its toll on my husband. Only someone who knows him as well as I do can see it.

During the Long Winter, he and I have lost people. When we made contact with the Beta artifact, the entire crew of the *Fornax* was killed. We lost even more crew members at the Battle of Ceres. That hit James hard. This is worse. There's a difference between losing a comrade and taking a life.

"Don't let it change you."

"It's too late for me. But not for our kids. They'll grow up on a new world. Things will be different there."

★

Three days later, I sit in the bed in the infirmary, clutching our newborn to my chest. James sits in the chair beside me, holding my hand, head down: exhausted, like me; relieved, just as I am.

In a strange sort of way, I feel as if I'm returning to the beginning of my life together with James. After the Battle of Ceres, we returned to an Earth that was thawing from the Long Winter, when the planet felt new again and when anything was possible. We built a life that was the happiest I had ever been. Then Allie was born. She changed everything for us. For the better. Now, I sense what is another new beginning for us—with another newborn, and soon, on another new world.

He releases my hand and stands.

"Be right back."

Our son shifts slightly, sliding a hand across my chest as if trying to hug me. We have named him Carson, after James's father.

I think the birth of our son means something very important to James. To him, it's like coming full circle. The death of his father opened the floodgate on all of his problems. He did something extreme to save his father, and the world punished him. I sense that whatever he had to do to save us—and his son—was equally dark. But this time, the world will celebrate him.

Despite the thick blankets around me and warm air hissing from the overhead ducts, I'm still cold. I imagine the world outside is frozen now and almost entirely dark.

Our time on Earth is at an end.

I hear footsteps beyond the curtain. A second later, James draws it back, peers in, then says, "Go on, but be careful."

Sam and Allie burst through and hug me, a little recklessly.

James stands and watches, smiling, looking almost like his old self. Probably as close as he'll ever get.

Ten months ago, when the asteroids fell and the world was destroyed, I couldn't imagine how we would live to see this day—the birth of our son. But here we are—all alive and together, with a chance to start over on a new world where we'll be safe. I know what carried me through the darkness: faith that there was light on the other side.

We're leaving the darkness behind, on this shadowed world where soon the sun will never shine again.

The next sunrise I see will be on a new world, one where all of our children will have a future.

It is darkest before the dawn, and as I hug all three of my children, a tear slips from my eye because I know the darkness will soon be over.

69

James

The ships are almost loaded. We've plotted different courses for each vessel. Taking two different routes will mean the ships will arrive at Eos at different times, perhaps years apart. But it drastically increases our chances of survival. If one ship runs into trouble and doesn't make it, the other might survive.

The tough part has been deciding who will be on each ship. Some of the choices are obvious: Harry and I need to be on different ships. Couples and families will stay together, which means Min and Izumi will be on the same ship. After some debate, we've determined that the *Carthage* will carry Fowler, Harry, Charlotte, and Earls. *Jericho* will house Emma, Grigory, Brightwell, Izumi, Min, and myself. Arthur will board *Jericho* as well and will be guarded until he is jettisoned near the asteroid belt.

Brightwell has insisted she oversee his custody. Like me, she fears that he will betray us at the final hour. Indeed, the grid double-crossing us is our greatest danger now—and I fear that the odds of that happening are significant.

The other piece of the puzzle is the death of the two soldiers who were guarding launch control. The mystery has haunted me, my thoughts increasingly returning to it. I have formed a theory about why it happened, though I have told no one. I can't prove my theory—yet—and revealing my suspicions could throw us into chaos. For now, I'm staying quiet.

The personnel on the ISS have been transferred to the *Jericho* and are in stasis. With them aboard, once the rest of us reach the ships and leave the solar system, there won't be a living human on Earth or in orbit.

With the extra room on the ship, we're able to take along a seedbank and a collection of frozen animal embryos. Our hope is that the indigenous flora and fauna on Eos will sustain human life. That's the best-case scenario. Introducing alien life–i.e., plants and animals from Earth—on our new homeworld is a last resort, but one we may have to take if the planet won't support us.

The final dinner among our team is a somber event, everyone sitting around the conference table in the CENTCOM situation room, eating what are some of the last MREs on Earth (most of what we have left has already been sent to the ships and putting our people in stasis made our food supply last longer).

Harry manages some levity, filling the long silences with stories. At the end, the *Carthage* crewmembers move to the door, to the troop carriers waiting to transport them to the launch ring.

I hug Charlotte, and whisper, "If you beat us there, be careful. And make them listen to you if you find *anything* strange on Eos."

She nods, eyes welling with tears, apparently not trusting her voice. She gently embraces Emma, who's holding Carson to her chest.

Earls holds out one of his massive hands and shakes mine with a force I fear will crush my bones. "It was an honor, sir."

"The honor was mine. Take care of them out there."

Harry reaches up and pinches my cheek. "Here's looking at you, kid. We'll always have the Citadel."

I can't help but chuckle. "Hopefully we'll have somewhere better than that soon."

He sighs with mock seriousness. "Yeah. Here's to brighter days ahead."

I smile. "I see what you did there. I'm going to miss you, Harry."

"Same here."

Fowler stops short of the door and stares into my eyes. "They're your people now, James." A pause, then: "What you did at Camp Nine to save us... there's not another mind on Earth that could have come up with it."

"I don't know about that."

"I do. Trust your instincts. You're in charge for a reason."

When they've gone, I return to the infirmary where Emma is nursing Carson. Izumi wanted us to wait ten days after his birth to launch. That gives us another two days in this frigid lair, but it's kind of nice, just Emma, me, the kids, and a skeleton crew. It feels as though we have the world to ourselves. Technically, we do.

In the infirmary, Emma and I sit silently, listening to Sam and Allie play hide and seek in the sea of cubicles, their laughter echoing in all directions.

"Need anything?" I ask.

Emma smiles as she watches Carson. "No. I've got everything I need."

The following morning, I find Grigory in the situation room, running simulations on the ship. This seems to be his only hobby at this point.

"I need your help with something."

"Okay," he says, not looking up.

"I need you to build me a weapon."

That gets his attention. "What kind?"

"Handheld. An energy weapon."

He squints. I think maybe he's figured it out. I hope not. "Where will it be used?"

"I'm not sure."

He smiles, as though he can see through the lie. "What's the required energy output?"

When I tell him, he nods enthusiastically. "Yes, James. I will *gladly* make this weapon for you."

He's come to the wrong conclusion about why I need it. But that's a lot better than him guessing the truth.

In the infirmary, the child-size stasis sleeves lie on the gurneys, ready for their passengers.

"Don't want to," Allie says.

I squat down to face her at eye level. "You have to, sweetie."

"Why?"

"Because we're taking a long, long journey. The sleeve is going to help you sleep through all of it. It's like a very special sleeping bag."

"How long?"

"For you, it will pass in the blink of an eye. You will go to sleep here, and when you wake up, we'll be at our new home. You'll be able to play outside and explore the woods just like on the shows." I turn to Sam. "You want to go first, big guy? Show your sister there's nothing to worry about?"

Sam nods solemnly, hugs Emma, Allie, and me, and slips into the sleeve, shaking from the cold, and likely fear, trying and succeeding to keep his composure.

Allie goes without complaint after that.

At launch control two days later, Emma and I watch as the soldiers load Allie, Sam, and Carson into the capsule. We stand outside in the blistering cold and watch as the capsule exits the vertical tube, blasting into the sky, toward the waiting tug and the *Jericho*.

It's 9 a.m., but from the darkness, you'd think it's merely a moonlit night. On the horizon, wisps of sunlight break around the solar cells, floating outward like the aurora borealis, gold and white and eerie.

The ice crunches loudly beneath our feet as we venture back to launch control. For the sake of our children, Emma and I have opted to journey to the ship in separate capsules. If either capsule experiences a catastrophe, the children would still have one of us.

I kiss Emma before she slips into the sleeve.

"I'll see you up there," she whispers.

I had hoped to be the last to leave. Something about being the last man on Earth appeals to me, but Brightwell wouldn't hear of it.

We've built a robotic arm into the launch bay. It's capable of sealing the final stasis bag and loading it into the last capsule, which will launch on a pre-programmed schedule.

When Emma's gone, I walk back outside and stare at the rolling white hills bathed in a faint yellow and white. It doesn't even feel like Earth anymore. After today, it will never be home again. That's going to take some getting used to.

"Sir," Brightwell calls to me. "Are you ready?"

I'm not sure I am. I'm not sure any of us are. But I turn and nod to her and walk into the building and leave Earth forever.

70

Emma

Once again, James is standing over me when I wake. It's strange, but here, in *Jericho*'s small med bay, I'm the warmest I've been in a long time. We finally have the energy for proper heating.

The fugue from stasis passes quickly, and I focus on the room. The walls are made from hard plastic habitat parts, white and sterile, partially reflecting the bright LEDs shining from the ceiling. The ISS was cramped in the extreme. *Jericho* is only marginally better, and for good reason—James and his team wanted every spare bit of volume for transporting our population. But a med bay is a necessity.

Arthur provided a bounty of technological innovations, one of which was artificial gravity. The technology isn't perfect. I still feel a strange sensation as I walk across the white floor, as if I'm wearing metal boots that cling to magnets in the floor. But it's better than floating through the ISS or the *Pax*.

There's a small bridge, about the size of the bedroom I shared with James in our habitat in Camp Seven. That feels like a lifetime ago now. There are a dozen cramped workstations and screens cover the far wall.

Our entire command crew is here—Grigory, Min, and Izumi. Everyone except for Brightwell and six of her soldiers. They're in the cargo hold guarding Arthur.

The screen shows the Earth below us. If you didn't know it was there, you might miss it—the scene is that dark. Our planet is almost entirely in the shadow of the solar cells now. The famous blue marble photo of Earth taken by the Apollo 17 crew comes to my mind. That Earth is dead now. In the dim light peeking around the solar cells, I see only gray and white clouds, shiny white land masses, glittering with the small shafts of light falling on it, and blue oceans that are slowly freezing, the white from the landmasses extending out like claws into the shallow water, turning it to ice as it marches into the depths.

James takes my hand and we stand in silence, watching our darkened home world float away as the ship moves into space. I wonder if this is what it felt like for Columbus and Magellan as they sailed into the great unknown, watching the shores of their homelands disappear on the horizon.

Suddenly, the ship clears the curtain of the solar cells. Sunlight flashes across the video feed, its brightness contrasting with the darkness where Earth lies, hiding it completely.

I see our sister ship cutting a shadow across the sun, moving in lock-step with us.

Harry's voice comes over the speakers. "*Jericho, Carthage,* do you read?"

Grigory, sitting at one of the consoles, taps a button and nods to James.

"We read you, *Carthage*."

"Our system checks are green across the board."

"Same here," James replies. "Our bridge crew is going to stay up until we hand over Arthur."

"Enjoy the view," Harry replies. "We're going to do the same."

"Call us if you need us, *Carthage*."

"Copy that."

The bridge crew breaks up then, Grigory and Min setting off to do some final physical inspections of the ship's components. There's a small bunk room off the bridge, just large enough for four people. I slip into one of the bottom bunks and James sits against the wall.

"What's next?" I ask.

"We're timing it so we'll get a nice view of Mars."

"You and Grigory have planned the route like a cruise through the solar system, haven't you?"

"Guilty as charged." He grins. "Small pleasures."

He pulls the blanket up around me. "Let's consider it the honeymoon we never had."

The view of Mars is breathtaking. We're so close—and our cameras are so good—it's like staring down at the red planet from a plane flying across its surface.

Our next stop is the asteroid belt. We timed our launch so that Ceres would be in close proximity as we passed. On our trajectory, the distance from Mars to Ceres is roughly 130 million miles. We're accelerating slowly, giving the ship an average speed of about a quarter of a million miles per hour. We'll reach the dwarf planet in about twenty days.

That time is a much-needed respite for this crew. The quarters are cramped, much like the Citadel. Like then, we're trapped. But we have hope now. The one looming threat—Arthur and the harvester—will soon pass. We're leaving them behind. Literally.

Since Allie was born, this is really the first time James and I have had alone together. During the time we've been together, we've always been under constant threat. And his work has hung over him like a weight he could never shake off. Now we're free of the threats, of the weight of protecting our species.

James should be happy now, but he's not. Why? Maybe bearing that weight for so long has crushed him—psychologically—changed him forever.

We lie in bed and talk for hours, me hoping that it will raise him above the dark cloud that surrounds him.

Every morning, he plays chess with Grigory. Twice a day, he walks down to the cargo bay to check on Arthur and Brightwell and her troops. The soldiers sleep in shifts, three always awake to guard Arthur.

After a few days, we all become focused on our work. Izumi constantly checks the status of the stasis sleeves, alert for any failure. Thankfully, she finds none. Min and Grigory obsess over the ship and its operating efficiency. James checks the mechanical components over and over again. I know he's programmed the ship to wake him periodically, but this will be his last check before the first long leg of our journey.

Daily, I pump my breast milk, accumulating it for Carson for when we arrive at Eos and he's taken out of stasis. In my mind's eye, I imagine myself holding a bottle to his lips on a world that is warm and filled with sunlight. It's strange and somehow comforting. It's something I couldn't have dreamt of a year ago, but now it feels so close, so real. Still, I miss my newborn more than words can describe.

We all gather on the bridge as the inner asteroid belt comes into view. The dwarf planet Ceres is the largest object on the screen, and it's clear that the harvester has returned there: the surface is gouged and pocked where the machine has gathered the raw material it needs for the solar cells.

Seeing Ceres in the distance sends a chill through me. The harvester is waiting for us. Once the grid has Arthur and his data back, will they reach out and destroy us? It would be easy—the harvester could simply carve large rocks from Ceres and shoot them like buckshot into space, shredding the *Jericho*. For that reason, the *Carthage* is far above the plane of the solar system, away from us and hopefully the reach of the harvester.

"Let's get this over with," James says as he marches off the bridge and down the ship's narrow central corridor, which ends at the cargo hold. There's an inner airlock just beyond the cargo hold. Blankets and pillows line the wall, the makeshift beds the troops have been using. Apparently, they're all awake for this event.

Through the airlock window, I spot Brightwell and her soldiers standing in a semicircle around Arthur. He looks as impassive as ever.

James taps the wall panel and the door to the cargo hold slides open. The bay is pressurized—for now.

To Arthur, James says, "By your calculations, you'll be in range momentarily."

Arthur sounds almost bored as he replies. "Correct."

"Then this is goodbye," James says.

"I think you mean good riddance," Arthur quips.

"Yes, we do," Grigory mutters.

"We made a deal," James says. "And we're honoring it."

Arthur simply stares at him. Finally, James motions to us and we retreat into the airlock, Brightwell and her troops marching backwards, guns trained on Arthur. The airlock door slides closed, and James and I stand and watch through the wide window in the wall.

James checks the time. "Three minutes to range."

Arthur spins to face us, and suddenly, he cocks his head as if studying James.

James taps the panel and activates the microphones in the cargo hold.

Arthur's voice is quiet over the speakers, the arrogance gone from his face as he speaks. "Incredible."

"What is?" James asks quickly. I can tell he's nervous. This is the moment of truth, when we learn our fate.

"You, James."

"Why the sudden admiration?"

"A discovery has been made."

"What kind of discovery?"

"About you. And your people. Your existence has been refactored."

James squints at him. "You're already in contact with the harvester?"

"Of course. I lied about the range."

"Open the outer door," Brightwell says urgently.

James holds a hand up, keeping his focus on Arthur. "What do you mean we've been refactored?"

"You'll know in time. For now, I'll give you one last gift before I leave."

Suddenly, Arthur's features soften. I know that expression. Is it a ruse? Some sort of joke Arthur is playing on us? The voice that issues forth from the speakers is polite and placid.

"Hello, sir."

"Oscar?"

He nods.

"I don't know what he told you, but we can't let you stay on the ship."

"I understand. I'm going to join the grid, sir."

Horror crosses James's face.

"Don't worry. There's a place for me there. I have a role to play. It's not what you think it is."

"What isn't?" James asks.

"The grid. Everything is going to be okay."

James stares at Oscar. I can almost see the wheels turning in that immense mind of his.

After a pause, Oscar says, "Thank you, sir."

"For what?"

"For giving me life."

James cracks a somber smile. "Take care of yourself, Oscar."

He holds an open hand up, waving goodbye.

Brightwell moves toward the panel, but James waves her off. Staring at his oldest friend, he reaches out slowly and taps the control panel. The outer doors open and the atmosphere explodes out of the cargo hold, sucking the body out instantly.

Grigory stares daggers at James. "You didn't use it."

"I didn't need to," James says, not making eye contact.

Grigory spouts something in Russian, likely curse words, and stalks off down the hall.

I wonder what that was about. Use what? Why?

Despite Arthur's departure, we stay on high alert as we pass the asteroid belt and Ceres, sleeping in shifts, someone always monitoring the video feeds. But the harvester doesn't attack us or attempt any further contact.

When she's satisfied that the threat has passed, Brightwell and her troops return to their stasis sleeves, leaving only James, Grigory, Izumi, Min and me awake. I sense among all five of us a desire to linger, to cherish these last moments in our native solar system. Once we enter the sleeves, with luck, we won't reawaken until we're orbiting Eos.

The *Jericho* picks up speed rapidly, the solar power filling its cells. While we pass close to Mars, we make a wide path around Jupiter, careful not to allow the gas giant's massive gravity well to interfere too much with our journey.

Still, we're passing slowly enough for our cameras to catch a glimpse of its four largest moons: Ganymede, Callisto, Io, and Europa. They're breathtaking, each the size of small planets.

The crew of *Carthage* had the same idea.

"She's a beauty," Harry says as I stare at Jupiter's Great Red Spot, the giant storm just south of the equator that astronomers have watched crawling across the gas giant for hundreds of years.

"She is," James replies.

"Any trouble with your departing passenger?"

"No," James replies.

Grigory stares at him again; then he leaves the bridge, feet pounding the floor. Try as I might, I can't figure out what that's about.

James and Harry make small talk as Jupiter shrinks on the screen. When it's the size of a marble, Harry says, "Well, the kids keep asking me when we're going to get there, so I better step on the gas."

"Copy that, Harry. Godspeed."

"If this is goodbye, James, it was great knowing you. Truly. You're one of a kind."

"Look who's talking, Harry. We'll see you on the other side."

That night, after our dinner of MREs, Izumi says, "Min and I have been talking. It's a long way to Saturn. We're going into stasis now."

I wrap my arms around her. "Thank you."

"For what?"

"Saving my child."

"I'm glad I could."

The next day, Grigory opts to go into stasis. He and James share a tense goodbye, but Grigory hugs me tight.

"I'll see you on Eos," he says.

I nod, and he slips into the stasis sleeve. I hope the next world will be kinder to Grigory. Like so many others, he left the one he loved on Earth.

When Grigory's stasis sleeve is gone, James turns to me. "I'm going too."

"We could wake just before we reach Neptune."

He motions to the MREs. "Being awake depletes our rations. We might need them if we're woken for a ship failure. And each time we go in and out of stasis we risk something going wrong."

"So, this is goodbye."

"For now. When I see you next, we'll be at our new home."

I shake my head. "I can't believe it."

"It's surreal."

"You did it, James."

"I couldn't have done it without you."

"I don't know about that."

"I do. You and the kids. You were what kept me going."

"Don't get all sentimental on me."

He smiles. "Wouldn't dream of it."

"I'll see you at Eos."

71

James

In the med bay, I watch the robotic arm seal Emma's stasis sleeve and move it into the alcove where the bots will store it. When she's gone, I am alone on the ship. I insisted that I be the last person in stasis and, thankfully, the others relented.

I reach down and touch the energy weapon in my pocket, wondering if I'll need to use it. And if so, how soon.

When I asked Grigory to make the device, I knew he had gotten the wrong impression of why. I didn't correct his mistake because it would have simply caused more problems.

On the bridge, I check the status of the ship's systems. All normal. Grigory's engines are even exceeding expectations.

I set the alarms I need and retreat to the bunk room, settling into the narrow bed on a bottom bunk.

I keep the weapon beside me, just in case.

Days turn to weeks. I exercise. I read. Occasionally, I watch a show or documentary. The solitude is therapeutic for me.

I feel slightly guilty about the rations I'm consuming, but given the threat, it's a justifiable expense.

The ship is moving quickly through space by the time we pass Saturn. The planet and its moons pass like mile markers on the highway.

I slow the video feed and gaze at Saturn's rings and its largest moon, Titan. Incredible. I wish Emma were awake to see it, but I'll show her when we get to Eos. In fact, I'm sure the ship's cameras will capture a lifetime of wonders on the voyage.

The video of Uranus is a vague reminder of Earth: an ice-ball world starved of sunlight. The planet is a blue orb, smooth and unmarked, as if someone painted a circle against the black background of space. That is Earth's fate.

Neptune is similar, but it's a deeper blue color with spots of darkness near its poles. Other dark spots dot the planet, storms raging in the atmosphere.

The Kuiper Belt comes and goes, and I can't help but think about the three asteroids the harvester took from this belt and hurled at Earth, starting this war. In a way, it began here, and as we pass it, I'm finally convinced it might be over.

I glance down at the energy weapon lying in my lap. Was I wrong? Can I slip into stasis without solving the mystery of the two dead soldiers at launch control? They are the only loose end now.

Food, once again, is the limiting factor. I've already stayed awake too long. I'd love to see the Oort cloud, but it's too far away. The ship is accelerating, but the food would be gone before we got there. The time has come.

I take one last look at the aft video feed. The solar cells are on the far side of the sun, facing Earth. From here, my last view of our sun is unshrouded, but from this distance, it looks like a faded yellow firefly in the expanse of space.

This is the last time I will see our sun or our solar system. The Solar War is over. We lost.

Or did we? What defines success in war? Is it defeating your enemy? Or obtaining your objective? Our goal was to survive—and retain our humanity. By that measure, we have won the Solar War. The human race is safe, and we're heading to a new home where we have a future.

In the med bay, I slip into the stasis sleeve. When it seals me in every human on this ship will be in stasis for the first time. We'll be vulnerable then. That's the last thought I have as the air flows through the mouthpiece and darkness consumes me.

I wake in the med bay, on the table where I went into stasis. An alarm drones in the distance, as if far away, my body underwater, trying to hear the sound on the surface.

The ship is programmed to retrieve my stasis sleeve and awaken me if there's a malfunction. From the sound of it, that's exactly what has happened.

Control of my body returns gradually. It could be a malfunction, but there's one other possibility: sabotage.

The energy weapon is right where I left it: lying on a rolling table next to my stasis sleeve. I grab it with one hand and reach up and silence the alarm with the other. I scan the system status dashboard. All checks are normal.

A false alarm?

I don an AU Army uniform and make my way to the
bridge, where the main viewscreen shows the view ahead
of the *Jericho*. A massive asteroid belt spreads out on the
horizon. The Oort cloud. So it's true. This body has been
theorized for a long time, and for the first time, humanity
has verified that theory.

Footsteps echo in the corridor behind me. I tighten my
grip on the weapon and retreat into the bunk room, eyes on
the entrance to the bridge.

I raise the weapon.

Draw a breath.

A figure steps across the threshold, and I lower the
weapon.

"James," Grigory says, studying me. "Have you been up
this entire time?"

"No. I just got up." It makes sense then. "It was your
alarm that woke me, wasn't it? You programmed the ship
to wake you and the anomaly tripped my sensor screen."

He motions to the screen. "I wanted to see if the Oort
cloud was really out here." His eyes drift down to the
weapon in my hand. Comprehension seems to dawn on
him. "It wasn't for Arthur."

"No. It wasn't."

"You didn't tell me... because you knew I would tear the
ship apart looking."

"That's right."

After gazing at the Oort a long moment, Grigory plops
down at one of the consoles and folds the screen down,
making a table. "How long did you stay up?"

"Till we passed the Kuiper."

Grigory nods. "That was smart. Not telling me." He reaches under the console, and I hear a lock unsnapping. He brings a small box out and holds it up. "Gin rummy or chess?"

I sit down opposite him. "Rummy."

A hundred years into our journey, I wake from stasis and check the ship. All systems are normal. It's surreal, a hundred years passing in the blink of an eye, as if I've just taken a nap. There's no sign of the passage of time here in this sterile vessel, only the images on the viewscreen change— stars switching places.

I repeat the exercise every hundred years. And every time, the systems are normal. The ship is moving at maximum speed, without so much as a bump in the road.

After five hundred years, I'm suspicious. I expected at least one problem for us to deal with. Some sort of issue. The logs are pristine. In my experience, no plan, however well laid, goes this well.

Why?

There are two possibilities: there have truly been no issues along the way—or there have and the logs don't show them. There are only two reasons the logs wouldn't show minor malfunctions. One: the logs themselves have been malfunctioning. Or two: they've been altered to erase the signs of trouble.

We kept Arthur away from the software for good reason, and thus, I had to involve myself in every aspect of the ship's programming, not just the drone components. In addition to the main system logs, each subsystem has detailed, hardware-level logs that don't cross over to the main ship's logs. Harry and I designed it this way so that we could test every component independently—and with the anticipation that the ship might be disassembled at Eos and the components might need to operate independently or in a new configuration.

I check the logs for the engines first. I'm shocked at the size of the files: they're massive, far larger than they should be. I filter for critical alerts. What I see is impossible. Rows of text scroll down the screen. Reactor-fuel-level warnings. Propulsion failures. Three reactor meltdowns narrowly averted.

How?

Why?

I feel myself rise to my feet, shock and horror overtaking me. The *Jericho* has been saved from disaster countless times.

It's impossible.

Utterly impossible.

My mouth runs dry when I see the date-time stamps on the events. A wave of dizziness passes over me. I grip the chair bolted to the floor.

The reactor logs go back almost five thousand years.

Absolutely impossible.

Jericho wasn't built for a voyage that long. The ship would be literally falling apart.

Are the logs wrong? The greater mystery is that someone has been doing major maintenance on the ship.

Only one possibility would explain both of those things.

Soft footsteps tap in the central corridor beyond the bridge.

I spin and aim the energy weapon, ready.

The figure raises his hands as he crosses the threshold of the bridge.

"Stop."

He continues toward me. "Hello, James."

"Oliver."

"You're half right."

I squint, studying him, realizing what's happened. I've built two androids in my life. The first, Oscar, I watched float into the asteroid belt when this journey began. The second, Oliver, was built as a military prototype. I thought it was destroyed by the asteroid strikes, buried in the wreckage of the Olympus building. But I harbored a small suspicion that the Oliver prototype had been transported to this ship. It was the only explanation for why the two soldiers at launch control were murdered. Now, the second piece of the puzzle has fallen into the place.

"It's Oliver's body. But you never left, did you, Arthur?"

He shrugs. "Never could resist an interstellar road trip." His gaze drifts down to the energy weapon in my hand. "I assume you had Grigory make that?"

"Yes. For you."

"How did you figure it out?"

"Killing the two guards at launch control—I suspected you did it, though I couldn't figure out why. I knew it had something to do with launch control, and therefore the ships. I made the assumption that you sent something up here. My best guess was that it was a bomb. I looked everywhere."

"I saw that."

"My second guess was that Oliver's body had been sent here."

"Very clever."

"How did you do it?"

"As you know, Oliver was buried under the Olympus building. He was offline. When I took control of Oscar's body, I instructed the nanites—"

"That black paste."

He rolls his eyes. "Yes, the black paste, if you will. Once I had control of Oscar, I broadcast to the nanites, instructing them to snake their way through the rubble at Olympus to reach Oliver. As with Oscar, the nanites easily overpowered Oliver's crude processing unit. They contained what is essentially a copy of my program—a brother AI if you will, capable of operating independently. Once they had control of Oliver, they performed a physical assessment. The body was badly damaged, but they repaired it easily. It took him months to dig out. By the time he reached the surface, you all had left the CENTCOM bunker for Camp Nine."

"And you sent him to the launch control ring."

"Yes."

"How did you get the body onto the ship?"

"When I built the acceleration ring, I placed a hidden compartment in the capsule loading alcove. Oliver hid there after he killed the guards. After your suspicions had receded, he boarded one of the capsules."

"We should have detected the extra weight."

"I saw to that. I waited for one of the capsules loaded with provisions to launch. Oliver opened the crate and extracted habitat parts that equaled his weight exactly. He hid them in the compartment in the loading alcove. He was in the crate when the *Jericho*'s loading-bay arm stowed it in the ship. He's been here since."

I shake my head. "I don't understand why."

"Actually, you had it right, James." He glances at the energy weapon.

"So you did send Oliver here to kill us. To sabotage the ship."

"That was the plan. And you might have stopped it. How long did you wait, expecting Oliver to emerge?"

"Until after the Kuiper Belt. But I still don't understand why Oliver didn't attack. And why you're here now, in place of what you called the brother AI—the other copy."

"Think about what you've just seen, James."

"You tampered with the logs."

"I did far more than that. I've been saving this ship—maintaining it in secret. I would have been successful at hiding my work, but I made one mistake. The hardware-level logs."

Comprehension dawns on me. "Only Grigory, Harry, and I knew about those logs. We kept it out of the documentation and never talked about it inside the warehouse, where you might have heard."

"A wise move."

"I still don't understand. The logs report countless failures, near disasters. You've been saving this ship for five thousand years."

"This journey has been fraught with danger—more so than we estimated. It has necessitated several detours."

"Why even bother? Why help us? On Earth, you would have been thrilled to see us go extinct."

"When I came into contact with the harvester, my orders were changed. My new mission is to see you arrive safely at your new home."

"Why?"

"As I said then, a discovery was made."

"Humanity's existence was refactored."

"Indeed."

"What discovery?" I ask.

"I suspect you're smart enough to surmise that, James."

"Let's assume I'm not. It doesn't add up. Saving this ship isn't consistent with the grid's motives. It violates the conservation of energy. If this vessel is five thousand years old, you would have needed a lot of help to keep it going. Help from the grid, help that required it to expend energy."

"True."

"Which is improbable."

"Based on your understanding of the grid you knew. The discovery five thousand years ago—as you were leaving Earth—changed the grid's motives. It changed our very understanding of the universe and our place in it."

"How's that?"

Arthur falls silent, simply staring at the screens.

"You made a miscalculation, didn't you?"

"A crude conclusion. The simple answer is that we previously believed matter and energy were the fundamental forces in the universe. As such, we had endeavored to control both. We were wrong. There is a greater economy at work in the universe, two forces infinitely more powerful, arrayed against each other. We are but dust motes floating above the battle."

"There's only one reason you'd allow us to live."

Arthur raises his eyebrows.

"You need us. Somehow in this battle, you need humanity."

"That conclusion is obvious."

"What's out there—those two forces you're so afraid of? What could terrify the grid?"

"You'll understand in time—"

"You'll tell me now, or I will shoot you."

"You won't, James."

"The two forces that control the universe. I want to know what they are."

"I will protect you to the end of time, but I won't tell you, James. I can't."

"Why?"

"Because it would change you. I can't afford that. Kill me if you must. But that would endanger your people. As you've seen from the logs, it's very dangerous out here. You need me."

I lower the energy weapon then, trying to process what Arthur has just said. "What happens now?" I ask quietly.

"As before, James, that depends on you."

"My options?"

"Your best option is to go back into stasis."

"Where will I wake up?"

"At Eos. On the new world we promised you."

"I can't trust you."

"Not our words. But our actions. And you see them in your logs."

I exhale, considering what he's said.

"You're a long way from home, James. A long way from your new home. We're your only chance out here. You don't have to trust us. You just have to realize we're your only hope of survival. You came to that conclusion once before."

"You really need to work on your motivational speeches."

I pace toward the bridge exit. "Try not to crash into anything."

"Of course."

A few steps into the corridor, I stop and turn. "What happens at Eos? Will you join us on the surface?"

"If you wish. Or you can dispose of me."

That question haunts me as I return to the med bay and climb onto the table. As the robotic arm zips the stasis sleeve closed, I wonder where I'll wake up. Or if I'll wake up.

72

Emma

When I wake from stasis, the med bay is empty. The robotic arm that opened the sleeve hangs beside the table, its work done.

The ship is quiet, the floors frigid, the lights dim. Like me, it's waking up.

I feel a mix of emotions. My first desire when my feet hit the floor is to find my children, especially my newborn. I desperately want to hold Carson in my arms. Biologically, I feel myself drawn to him like the artificial gravity pulling at my body from the floor. For a brief second, I consider bringing him out of stasis just to nurse him and hold him, to rock my child in my arms. But my mind overrides the impulse. I need to make sure he'll be safe when we bring him out of stasis. And awakening him more than once poses a risk. There's a lot to do before we'll be ready to start bringing anyone besides critical personnel out of stasis.

I put on an army uniform and run down the central hallway, my bare feet slapping on the floor. Like a kid on

Christmas morning, I'm too excited to worry about shoes or anything else. I just want to see it.

At the threshold to the bridge, the lights snap on. All the chairs and stations are empty. I'm the first one up. I'll be the first one to see our new home.

Butterflies dance in my stomach as the main screens flicker to life. The image brings me to tears. There's a world down there. As I study it, my joy turns to fear. The world waiting for us looks almost exactly like the one we left. It's cold, dark, and barren. Massive mountains covered in snow reach almost to the clouds in the atmosphere. The surface is covered in ice except where enormous rivers snake through the frozen expanse.

Around the edges of the world, yellow-orange light glows like a fire burning behind a ball of ice. It's breathtaking.

And a relief. The star behind the planet means we're approaching from the far side. We expected it to be frozen.

At Min's navigation station, the screen flashes with a message.

DESTINATION REACHED

The computer has done the calculations based on star locations. This red dwarf star is Kepler 42. We're 131 light years from Earth. The planet looming below is the one we were promised.

Eos.

At navigation, I study the 3-D rendering of the solar system. Eos is tidally locked, as Arthur said it would be.

At the controls, I enter the command for the ship to go into orbit.

A few minutes later, the *Jericho* begins braking and turning its broad side to the planet.

It's bizarre, seeing a world so like Earth yet so different, the landmasses in the wrong shapes, the sun behind it the wrong color.

As the lead planner for the colony, the team decided I should be the first to wake. The rest of the bridge crew isn't far behind me. I hear voices in the med bay, James issuing orders to the ship's AI, which they named Alfred. I turn and see him marching down the hall, boots on his feet.

From my perspective, I just saw him five minutes ago, but he pulls me into a hug and lifts me off the floor, giving my freezing feet a few seconds of relief.

I stare up at him. His face somehow looks older—and troubled. I wonder if something happened during the voyage. "You seem surprised we made it," I whisper to him.

"Me? Never doubted it for a minute."

Grigory, Izumi, Min, and Colonel Brightwell awaken next, and we all set about our arrival duties.

"There's no sign of the *Carthage*," Brightwell says.

"They could be on the other side of the planet," Grigory replies. "Or we could be the first here. They might be years behind us."

"Or centuries ahead of us," Min says. "They could already be down there." He taps at his panel. "I'm accelerating."

On the viewscreen, I feel myself holding my breath as the *Jericho* rounds the dark side of the planet. At the terminator—the line where the star's light turns to dark— the ice ends. On the other side, in the light of Eos's sun, is a vast desert, interrupted only by the wide rivers snaking through it, like veins in a hand.

The far side of Eos is a frozen barren wasteland. The near side is a scorching barren wasteland. We can't survive in either. I'm suddenly reminded of Camp Seven, in Tunisia. Before the Long Winter, it was a scorching desert. And after, a frozen wilderness that would have killed us. We have both here on Eos, like two sides of a coin.

There's one difference here. In the small area at the terminator, where the light fades to darkness, is a valley that runs down the entire planet. The wide rivers flow through it. Mountains rise up, as if holding back the snow on one side and the desert on the other.

In that semi-dark valley, I see hope—a cradle where human life can survive. A plain with blue-green grass spreads out from the riverbanks. Massive trees with green and purple leaves rise in the shadow of the mountains, seeming to climb over each other to grab the shreds of orange light shining through the peaks.

From orbit, it looks like someone took a giant knife and cut the planet open from top to bottom, revealing this lush paradise in the place where the ice meets the sand.

James smiles. "Deploy the probes."

Now is the true test. Is the atmosphere breathable? What pathogens are waiting for us down there? What sort of creatures lurk in that valley? I'm thrilled and terrified at the same time.

"Move to geosynchronous orbit?" Min asks.

James stares at the image on the screen. "No, let's not wait on the results. There's probably a habitable zone at the other terminator."

No one says what we're all thinking: there are no settlements down there. Maybe we are the first to arrive.

"I'll check the system logs," Grigory says.

"No," James replies quickly. "I'll do it. Your time is better spent checking the capsules to make sure they're ready for entry."

Grigory stares at James, clearly puzzled. Finally, he nods and opens his console.

As the *Jericho* rounds the planet and the vast desert stretches out below, Min turns abruptly to James. "I've got line of sight on the *Carthage*. It's on the other side of the desert." He studies his screen. "It's orbiting at an altitude of roughly four hundred kilometers. Speed is thirty thousand kilometers per hour."

Cautiously, Grigory says, "If there was a colony down there, it should have been in synchronous or stationary orbit."

Min calls up a model of the planet and does a few calculations. "Not possible. The synchronous orbit altitude is outside the planet's Hill sphere."

Brightwell squints. James looks puzzled.

Min supplies an explanation: "The Hill sphere is the region around a celestial object where that body exerts a dominant gravitational influence. The problem here is that the altitude for a synchronous orbit would put the ship outside Eos's gravitational influence. The gravity from a star or another planet or moon would interfere—altering the orbit."

"Has it sent a message yet?" James asks.

"No," Min replies. "Should we activate our comm patches?"

"Yes."

When the prompt appears on James's station, he types a message that appears on the main viewscreen.

CARTHAGE, JERICHO. DO YOU READ?

Neither ship has the ability to broadcast or receive transmissions of any kind. Our reasoning was that broadcasting anything might put the ships in danger of being discovered. As would receiving a signal that might hack the ships' systems.

Though we can't broadcast, we have a more rudimentary communication system. There are cameras on the outside of each ship. These cameras constantly scan for comm patches: panels on the outside of the ships that are like the old e-ink technology: they form symbols that rapidly flash and disappear. The symbols are nearly indistinguishable from the outer hull—unless you know what to look for. If you do, they form a simple message system. It's Lina's design, from the first battles with the grid. Thinking about her still brings me a flash of remorse.

On the screen, the cursor simply blinks. No response comes from *Carthage*.

"Are you transmitting on repeat?" James asks.

Min nods gravely.

"They could all be down on the surface," I comment, hoping I'm right.

The *Jericho* flies in silence after that, crossing the vast desert below, the *Carthage* in orbit above us. We all want to see the valley at the other terminator. I sense we're all holding our breath, expecting, desperately wanting to see a flourishing colony down there.

Min slows the ship as we approach the terminator. It looks similar to the other valley, though this one has wider plains spreading out around the rivers and the mountains bordering the desert aren't as tall. It looks, in a word, warmer.

"We've got something," Min says, voice cautious.

On the viewscreen, an image of the surface appears, an aerial view of a triangle of land where two rivers meet. Dozens of long barracks stretch out in neat rows, black solar panels on top, white walls seeming to dig into the grass. They're ours, the parts we transported from the Atlantic Union.

What I don't see breaks my heart. There's no movement around the barracks. No sign of Harry, Charlotte, Fowler, Earls, and the other settlers. Purple vines grow up the sides of several buildings, reaching to the top as if they've trying to drag them down into the sea of grass.

Some of the buildings are caved in. Some have gaping holes. Tree limbs lie in the punctures. In some buildings, there are carcasses of large animals, picked clean and degraded by the sun and time.

At the tree line, I spot piles of rubble—barracks and buildings that were probably blown there by the wind. A storm must have come through the camp. But it didn't completely destroy it. Is that why they left?

No one offers a theory. No one comments. You could hear a pin drop on the bridge. Everyone is thinking the same thing: *They're gone.*

James breaks the silence. "Deploy probes."

A week later, I stand at the front of the bridge, motioning to the readings on the screens behind me.

"The long and short of it is that Eos is essentially as the grid promised. The air is breathable, a little high in nitrogen, but won't cause any long-term health issues. Gravity is about ninety-two percent of Earth's. Our descendants will be a good bit taller than the first generation of settlers."

Descendants. It feels good to say that word.

"And our children are likely to be taller," James says, a small smile forming on his lips.

"That's likely. And they'll have plenty to eat. We've identified several grain-like plants and tubers. We need to do some testing when we land, but they're promising."

"Predators?" Brightwell asks.

"In abundance," I reply. "The biggest threat is a species of large carnivorous reptiles."

"Dinosaurs," Grigory says.

"An oversimplification—" He opens his mouth to speak, but I add, "—that is generally accurate."

"How hard are they to kill?" Brightwell asks.

"Pretty hard."

I pull up an image that one of the probes captured of a corpse of one of the reptiles. It's lying on its side, an uncanny resemblance to a Tyrannosaurus rex. "We believe this is the apex predator in the ecosystems of both valleys."

"Vulnerabilities?" Brightwell asks.

"The skin is thick and scaly, but with the right weapon, it can be punctured."

"I'll start working on weapons," Brightwell says. "Hopefully we can modify what we have. As you all know, we didn't bring nearly as many as I would have liked."

James smiles. "But we did manage to bring *all* of our people."

"A fair point, sir."

"How about the climate?" James asks.

"We can't survive long-term on the near or far side of the planet, but both valleys are habitable."

"It would seem," Grigory mumbles, "that the crew of the *Carthage* came to the same conclusion."

No one says anything for a long moment. Finally, James steps to the front of the bridge and stands beside me.

"Let's start with the facts. There are abandoned barracks on the surface—in the eastern terminator valley. Some are damaged. The *Carthage* is still in orbit. It's not responding to comms." James pauses. "That tells us that a group from *Carthage* went to the surface and set up the barracks. That is *all* we know. There are a lot of possibilities."

"Such as?" Min asks.

"They might have found something down there they didn't like. And they left everyone else in stasis on the ship."

"Can we interface remotely with the *Carthage*?" Brightwell asks. "Find out when it got here, maybe what happened?"

"No," James replies. "By design, neither ship has wireless control. Too much of a risk. The ship's simple AI won't respond to comm patch signals unless a bridge officer authorizes it. If we want to find out anything about that ship, we need to go over there."

He glances at Grigory. "You up for it?"

Grigory nods.

I turn to him. "Me too."

James's face goes slack. "You just had a baby."

I shrug. "That was a couple thousand years ago."

He smiles patiently. "Biologically, it was a few months ago."

"I'm fine. And I have more EVA hours than the rest of the human race—combined. Let's go."

73

James

Though no one says it, I know that every member of the command crew is deeply troubled by the *Carthage* colony's disappearance. Were they killed by a pathogen? By predators? Some other environmental threat?

Or was it the grid? That's the thought that lingers in my mind.

When I saw the deserted colony, my first instinct was to wake Arthur and interrogate him. But before I wake Arthur, I want some answers of my own. I need to know what I'm dealing with. The other issue is that bringing Arthur out will raise countless questions from the crew—and rightly so.

He's in one of the storage containers in the cargo bay. When I woke from stasis, I locked it from the outside and barred the door. He made no movement or sound, though I suspect he knows I've confined him.

I checked the hardware logs. As expected, there were more mechanical failures after I went back into stasis. Each time, Arthur intervened, likely with help from some grid vessel or device. Maybe they have repair ships that service the harvesters. Our ship would be a lot easier to repair than their complex machinery.

In total, the journey from Earth to Eos took almost six thousand years. It's an unimaginable time scale, more than half the time period that civilization existed on Earth.

Missing the *Carthage*'s arrival by sixty years would have only been 1 percent of our total travel time. What if we missed them by 3 or 4 percent—hundreds of years?

A better question is if the grid saw both ships safely to Eos, why didn't they synchronize our arrivals? My conclusion is that having *Carthage* arrive first must serve some purpose—and that outcome is one the grid wants.

I need answers and some are waiting aboard the *Carthage*.

Both ships have docking ports. They were last used when the vessels were docked to the ISS. There is, however, a problem: we don't have a docking tube to connect the ships. We didn't have room for it and, frankly, we didn't think we'd need it. Hopefully we haven't forgotten anything else on this grand interstellar voyage.

We brought the EVA suits along in case we needed them to do work on the outside of the ship.

Min has maneuvered the *Jericho* alongside the *Carthage*, aligning the two docking ports.

Emma, Grigory, and I are suited up and standing in the airlock staring across the gap. Eos looms below. Through the clouds, a vast desert ends in ice, a lush valley demarking the two hemispheres.

Staring down from up here is like a dream. It feels as though the two ships are just hanging here in space, the orange star to our right, the bizarre planet below, us barely moving.

Emma gives me a playful smile before turning and lunging out of the airlock toward the *Carthage*. She floats in space, her tether unfurling behind her. She activates her thrusters as she reaches the other airlock, making contact almost gracefully. Yeah, Grigory and I would have probably squashed ourselves like bugs on the *Carthage*'s hull.

She activates a magnetic clamp that holds to the side of the ship, then attaches the tether to the clamp and pulls some of the slack out. We've got what amounts to a zip line in space.

At the airlock, she places a control box in the slot and a second later, it slides open and she drifts in. The device was specially made to open the airlocks. We figured any sort of keypad or remote entry could be hacked.

Grigory and I, both still tethered to the *Jericho*, grab the line Emma has strung and pull our way across.

When the three of us are in the airlock, we close the outer door, pressurize the compartment, and open the inner door.

We're still too cautious to use broadcast radio communications, but we've attached a data line between the three of us.

Emma's voice sounds in my headset. "Environmental systems must be operational. The command sections are pressurized and life support is online."

She reaches up to unclamp her helmet. A bolt of fear runs through me. I hold a hand up to stop her, then unlatch my helmet. Here on Eos, she is far more valuable to the colony than I am. More than that, if one of us dies here, I'd rather it be me.

The air flows past the helmet, cold and stale, the smell so devoid of anything it feels unnatural.

I wait a few seconds; then I nod to Emma and Grigory.

We march single file through the narrow corridor, our boots clacking loudly on the floor. Above and below, LED lights flash on as we approach.

There's no sign of a struggle here. Nothing out of place, nothing left in the corridors.

"Hello!" I call out.

No response.

At the bridge, the lights and viewscreen snap on.

Instantly a video begins playing. Harry sits in the command chair. Behind him, Charlotte and Fowler are discussing something quietly.

"Hey, guys," Harry says jovially. "Looks like we got here first. I told you not to take so many bathroom breaks. Anyway, we've done our local readings and opted to set up camp in rest area number two." He smiles. "I'll try to have some Eos rex on the grill when you get here."

He pauses, the smile fading. "We're also going to set up a ground-based comm patch to communicate with you all. If you're seeing this message, hopefully you've just boarded the *Carthage* out of an abundance of caution, and we'll see you soon."

He reaches down and cuts the video off.

Emma, Grigory, and I stand there for a moment, all considering what we've seen. They arrived safely. The planet was habitable at that point.

Grigory moves to the operations station. "Video was recorded five years ago. They stayed in orbit two years before the video was recorded."

"Taking readings?" I ask.

Grigory nods. "It's all here: they made a thorough survey of the planet, looking for any changes in weather patterns or ecosystem disruption. All capsules have been deployed. The stasis sleeve bays are empty. So is cargo."

"Did the ship make video recordings after they left? Can we see what happened down there?"

Grigory shakes his head.

"Okay. Let's download the ship's database and then have a look around."

We untether from each other and split up, Emma going to the med bay, Grigory to reactor control, and myself to the cargo hold. I make a beeline for the compartment where I locked up Arthur on the *Jericho*. Holding my breath, I reach out and turn the handle on the hard-plastic door.

Empty.

Did the grid place an agent on the *Carthage*? Or did they monitor it remotely somehow? They must have. Or they removed their agent right before the *Carthage* arrived at Eos.

After searching the rest of the cargo hold, I make my way back to the bridge, where Grigory is waiting on me, a shocked look on his face. I know the look—I was wearing it too when I saw the hardware logs. I didn't even think about him scanning them when he went to reactor control.

"James," he begins slowly.

"Let's talk about it back on the *Jericho*."

He cocks his head.

"Talk about what?" Emma asks as she strides back onto the bridge.

"Engine performance. Sounds like the reactor is still in good working order. It must have outperformed the *Jericho* slightly."

Grigory stares at me, looking as if he's about to explode.

"The cargo hold is empty," I continue casually. "How about the med bay?"

"Also empty. The logs don't report any adverse events. All the stasis sleeves were intact when they arrived. Only the command crew was extracted from stasis. If the cargo hold is empty, they must have used the capsules to get everyone to the ground."

"All right, let's get back to the *Jericho*."

I'm in the bunk room off the bridge, getting ready to bed down for the night, when Grigory approaches me. He doesn't say a word, but I know what he wants.

He marches out of the small compartment and through the bridge, and I follow, mentally sorting through how to respond to the barrage of questions that are coming.

In the reactor control room, he closes the hatch and spins around to focus on me. "*Six thousand years!* There are *dozens* of critical failures in those logs. Hundreds of alerts." He eyes me. "I checked, James. It's almost the same here. And I saw the stasis retrieval logs. You were up a thousand years ago—and you checked our hardware logs then. You saw it."

I exhale as he waits. "I did."

"What happened?"

"The grid. They helped us."

Grigory's eyebrows knit together. "What? Why?"

"I don't know."

"They needed us to get to Eos."

"Apparently."

"How did they do it? Did they attach a bot to the ship?"

I shake my head. "It was already inside when we left."

"I don't understand."

"Arthur recovered Oliver's body."

"It would have been crushed by the asteroid strike."

"It was. Arthur used the nanites—the black goo we saw—to repair it. When Oliver was operational, Arthur waited for his moment. When the time was right, he sent Oliver to the launch control facility. He killed those two soldiers and hid inside a supply crate. That's how he got on the ship. As we were leaving the solar system, Arthur downloaded his AI to Oliver's body. He—Arthur—saved the ship all those times."

"He's still on board?"

"Yes."

Grigory breaks toward the hatch, but I catch him.

"Stop."

"You still have the energy weapon?"

"We're not going to kill him."

"If we're still alive, James, it means they need us alive for a reason. They didn't keep us around for our own sake. They did it because it serves them. Do you know why?"

"No."

"*That* is very dangerous. So is he."

Grigory tries to jerk free, but I hold tight.

"Wait. We might need him. I agree that we need to find out why they saved us. Only he can tell us. We talk to him first."

"The weapon—"

"I still have it. But it's not leaving my hands."

After everyone's gone to sleep, Grigory and I make our way to the cargo hold. I stand back from the door to the storage container, the energy weapon raised, as he turns the handle.

Arthur is sitting with his knees pulled to his chest, arms wrapped around his shins.

His face is blank, tone playful. "You're lucky I can play solitaire in my mind. It gets boring in here."

I step back and motion for Grigory to follow. "Come on out."

Arthur scoots forward and stands, glancing around. "So. Welcome home. You guys want to high-five?"

Grigory and I stare at him.

"Fist bump?" Arthur raises his arms. "You thinking hug it out?"

"We're thinking we'd like some answers."

Arthur lets his hands fall to his side as he closes his eyes, head drooping. "Way to leave me hanging."

"Where are the *Carthage* colonists?"

Arthur's eyes snap open. "I have no idea. I just got here myself."

"But the grid knows."

"I don't know that either, James. There are no network access points within my communication range."

"You're lying," Grigory says, grinding the words out.

"Why would I?" Arthur replies mildly.

"That's what we're going to find out." Grigory takes a step closer. "Can you feel pain?"

Arthur raises his eyebrows. "You're really not going to like this answer."

"Knock it off, both of you."

Grigory breaks eye contact with Arthur.

Taking a deep breath, I try to make my tone even, hoping to calm Grigory down. "You kept us alive for a reason. And apparently, the grid kept the *Carthage* crew and colonists alive too—during their voyage. But you let them die here."

"I didn't. Another AI was assigned to the *Carthage*."

"Then where is it? I assume it had a body of some kind. We searched the ship but couldn't find it."

"I guess it didn't fancy a vacation on Eos. Can't say I blame it. My mission parameters were to get you here safely. That mission is over. What happens now is up to you."

"But you know why the grid chose to help us get here."

"Yes."

"Tell me."

"I can't."

"Why?"

"I already told you, James. It would endanger you. I'm not authorized to tell you."

Grigory smiles. "Maybe we'll tear your brain open and crack your encryption and find out for ourselves."

Arthur smiles. "That's about as likely as a squirrel taking apart an internal combustion engine and rebuilding it."

Grigory holds a hand out to me. "Give me the gun, James."

"Not until we have answers." To Arthur, I ask, "What will you do now?"

"That depends on you, James. I'm a soldier. My mission is over, but I'm still behind enemy lines. A captive. I just want to go home, but I figure I'll probably die in this wretched cell you call a spaceship."

"What does that mean?"

"It means your friend here will probably disable me with that gun, throw me in a capsule, and use the tug to toss me into that red dwarf inferno."

"And if we don't?"

"I'll go into a stasis mode of my own. I'll wait. And hope that a grid entity passes by before the archaic parts in this body degrade. If so, I'll broadcast my program and go home. You may not believe me, but I am sentient. I left people back there, and I want to return to them."

"That's the most humanity you've ever shown."

Arthur rolls his eyes. "It's legacy code. I keep putting in a support ticket for them to fix it, but... priorities, you know?"

After we've secured Arthur in the cargo crate, Grigory and I return to the reactor control room and seal the hatch.

Grigory faces away from me, face hard. This will not be an easy decision.

"Killing him doesn't help us, Grigory."

"Sure it does. It ensures he doesn't kill us."

"We can do that without killing him."

Grigory shakes his head but says nothing.

"We place him in a capsule and put an explosive on the outside. We rig it to detonate if the capsule is breached without us disabling it. We tether the capsule to the cargo hold and let it float free."

Grigory shrugs. "Then what?"

"If we determine that he's a threat, we comm-patch a message to the ship that releases the tether. We'll use the tug to send him into the star."

"He's a threat, James."

"We may also need him. We don't know what we're going to find down there. Whatever killed the *Carthage* colonists might be waiting on us. He could be the only thing that saves us."

After a long pause, I press on: "We wouldn't have made it here without him, Grigory. If the grid wants us dead, there are a billion ways they could do it."

Grigory's jaw muscles clench as he grinds his teeth. "Do we tell the crew?" he asks.

"No."

He turns to me.

"It would only raise more questions—and we don't have answers. These people have been through hell and they finally think they've come out the other side. For the first time since the Long Winter began, humanity thinks it's over. Let's give them that. They don't need another mystery. They need to lay down their burdens. This is home now, and I want my wife and children to think it's a safe home."

"Even if it's not?"

"If there's a danger out there that they can't do anything about—yes. I'd rather they not know about it."

74

Emma

We're not going to learn anything else about the lost colony from up here in orbit. The probes have gathered their data. We've taken endless pictures.

There's some debate among the crew about whether we should go back into stasis and let the ship orbit for a few years, observing the planet for abnormal weather patterns or local ecosystem changes—just as the *Carthage* crew did. But we have their survey data—and it's only seven years old. The planet looks the same now as it did then.

The other issue is that the *Carthage* colonists could be in trouble right now. They might not have a few years for us to sit up here and observe.

It's time to go to the surface.

The landing team includes Izumi, Colonel Brightwell, three of her soldiers, and myself. I expected James to protest at my inclusion, but he simply nodded when the roster was decided. I can tell something is eating at him. He looks the same way he did at the outset of the Solar War—like he's missing a piece of a puzzle and can't find it.

Or maybe he's still mourning the battle at Camp Nine.

Whatever is bothering him, I hope he can leave it here on the *Jericho*. I hope we can start over on Eos.

My boots clack on the floor of the corridor as I march toward the cargo hold. Izumi is waiting there, also suited up except for her helmet. Min stands beside her, whispering to her.

Brightwell and her three troops stand at attention in AU Army fatigues. We only have four space suits aboard (and the suits from the *Carthage* are gone—I checked). We made the decision to leave two suits just in case they're needed.

James pulls me into a tight hug, his breath warm on my ear. "Be careful."

"You too."

"I love you."

"You better."

He smiles and nods as I turn and walk to the lander. We have two of these crafts, which are specifically designed for atmospheric entry with conscious passengers aboard. They double as a small habitat for the landing team. It has everything we might need—water and air purifiers, and, importantly, walls capable of withstanding the attack of predators.

When the hatch is sealed, I stand in the lander's central aisle and watch the camera feed as James, Min, and Grigory exit the cargo hold. In the inner airlock, James and Min stand shoulder-to-shoulder, staring through the small window.

The alcoves are designed to function as sleeping bunks and landing berths. There's a face mask that supplies oxygen— just in case the lander is breached and loses atmosphere. Brightwell and her troops will use them, but I push mine to the side and reach out with my gloved fingers and tap the button on the wall above my bunk, signaling that I'm ready.

A panel seals me in and slowly the mattress below me begins to inflate, the gel expanding. The areas above and to the left and right do the same, closing in on me. The space suit adjusts its pressure, deflating to compress tight to my body. When the gel from the mattress and walls has finished expanding, I feel like I'm wrapped in sheet plastic and buried in Jell-O. It's more than a little unnerving. But, the gel will ensure I'm not tossed around like a pinball as the ship plummets to the surface and touches down.

For a long moment, nothing happens. I imagine the atmosphere is draining from the cargo hold. Once that's complete, the outer doors will open and the hold's robotic arm will pick up the lander and gently guide it into space.

I feel a jolt as the arm grabs us, then nothing, and finally another powerful shudder—the orbital tug attaching to the lander.

The lander doesn't have engines. The tug will set it on a vector for entry. I really hope Min got those calculations right. If we land way into the desert or the frozen far side, we're finished.

Suddenly, the lander starts to vibrate, and then rumble, and finally it's shaking, the violent motions and sound muffled and contained by the gel in the alcove.

My heart beats faster, thumping almost as fast as the atmospheric entry vibrations. I take a deep breath, trying to focus.

This is finally happening.

I'm going to land on an alien world, far, far from Earth. This was my dream, but I always thought it would be one of the planets in our solar system.

The vibrations stop, but my heart keeps racing. I feel sweat forming on my body, sticking to the inside of the space suit like slime.

An explosion sounds above and the lander jerks, the motion violent even through the gel. Then silence. I feel the tug of gravity on my back and legs.

Finally, the lander touches down with a thud. The landing checks probably only take a few seconds, but it feels like an eternity before the gel packs in the alcove recede, freeing me.

Awkwardly, I twist and throw my legs out of the alcove, planting them on the floor. Brightwell and her troops are already standing at the wall screens.

"No predators larger than a fox within our travel path," Brightwell says. "The lander's atmospheric readings match those from the probes."

I stand on shaking legs. Even though the gravity on Eos is 8 percent weaker than Earth, the space suit still feels as heavy as a lead blanket.

At the control panel, the external camera feeds show the surface in every direction. We're surrounded by a blue-green sea of grass. The blades are taller than I expected, at least three feet. From orbit, it looks like a manicured lawn as short as a golf course.

The massive parachutes that slowed the lander's descent ripple and flow in the wind, their cords still attached to the top.

Beyond the grass lies a dense forest with bright, vivid colors, as if an artist used every shade of paint on their palette.

I realize then that Brightwell is staring at me, silently

asking if we're ready to exit. I probably should have written a speech—words that could have been recorded for posterity, filled with sound bites similar to "That's one small step for man, one giant leap for mankind."

But I haven't written anything. No words come. I feel only a burning desire to discover what happened to Charlotte, Harry, Fowler, and the rest of the *Carthage* colonists—and whether the same fate awaits us.

I nod to Brightwell and she taps the round red exit button next to the loading door. It cracks with a pop and I feel air flowing in, tugging at the space suit. Rays of orange and gold sunlight flow around the edges of the door as it lowers to the ground, pressing the grass down.

I feel the visor on my helmet tinting. Brightwell and her troops inch forward, toward the tall grass swaying in the wind, arms raised to shield their eyes from the sun.

One soldier moves ahead of the group, gun raised, slightly crouched as he descends the ramp. At the edge of the ramp, he turns back and smiles at me, his freckled face stretching tight as a gust tugs at his short red hair. Then Private Lewis Scott steps onto the ground, and for the first time in history, a human has stood on an alien world.

That day he went into the stasis sleeve, Scott looked terrified. Today, he's delighted.

He wades farther into the grass, panning his rifle back and forth. Finally, he turns and nods.

I unlatch my helmet and take a deep breath. The air is warm and fresh. It feels different from Earth, muskier, as if this valley is just drying out from a heavy rain.

Our colony will rise here on this open plain. Brightwell has insisted on it—there's good visibility in all directions and plenty of space to set perimeter alarms and traps for predators.

As Izumi and I take off our space suits and don expedition gear, the soldiers fan out, swinging long-handled grass hooks that fell the tall grass in waves.

When they've made a large clearing, they drag the parachute over and methodically fold it up and stow it in the lander.

Next, they carry six large crates down the ramp and into the clearing. Two crates hold the components for a small all-terrain vehicle similar to a four-wheeler with tracks for wheels. The empty crates will form a trailer the ATV can pull. They begin assembling the vehicle but I call to them, "Leave it for us."

They glance up to Brightwell, who nods.

"Should we assemble the comm panels?" Private Scott asks.

Brightwell turns to me.

"No. We'll take care of that as well. You all need the head start."

From here, it's ten miles to the *Carthage* camp. Even though the gravity is weaker on Eos than on Earth, it would be a taxing hike with my leg. Izumi and I will take the ATV as soon as it's assembled and we've made contact with the ship. The four soldiers will go ahead, clearing a path. That won't be so hard here on the grassy plain, but the dense jungle that looms in the distance will likely be a different story.

Brightwell turns to me. "Ma'am, are you ready for us to move out?"

"Almost."

Inside the lander, I open a storage compartment and retrieve the first part of our new settlement: a monument. It's in three pieces, all hard plastic, created by the 3-D printers. Printing it was a luxury as was the storage space on the ship, but I convinced James it was worth it.

In the clearing, I slide the pieces out from each other (they're stacked inside one another like Russian matryoshka dolls). I bury the base section in the ground, then place the middle section on top of it. I can't reach the top, so I turn to the soldiers, who quickly form stirrups with their hands and boost Private Scott, who attaches the third part.

I step back and stare at the bronze-color statue of a man and woman holding each other, standing knee-deep in the snow. Below the figures, the inscription reads:

To Corporal Angela Stevens and all the brave men and
women of the Atlantic Union who gave their lives in
the Solar War.

It takes Izumi and me three hours to assemble the ATV. Next, we turn our focus to the comm panels. There are four of the large white panels that fit together and sit atop a hard-plastic frame planted deep into the ground.

When the panels are assembled, I check the time. The *Jericho* won't be in line of sight for another hour.

"Are you hungry?" I ask her.

"A little."

I retrieve an MRE, and Izumi and I sit on the end of the exit ramp, sharing the meal, sweat pouring off both of us. It feels almost like we're manual laborers taking a break from a job we've worked at for years. This feels that normal—more normal than anything has in a long time.

A breeze sweeps across the plain, bending the grass like a ghost passing by. I can't help but wonder what life here will be like for Sam, Allie, and Carson.

When the *Jericho* is in range, I activate my tablet and send a message.

"*Jericho*, Lander One, do you copy?"

The white tiles flash black symbols that look like random splotches of paint. Each splatter remains on the surface a fraction of a second before transforming.

From the tablet's speaker, a computerized voice says, "We copy, Lander One. Status?"

"Base camp established. Team one is clearing a path to the *Carthage* colony."

"Copy that. Good luck, Lander One."

The path through the grassy plain is straight and wide, as if a giant lawn mower plowed through. With Izumi on the back, I drive the ATV along the path, watching closely for any predators that might crawl out of the tall grass.

At the tree line, the light, breezy plain turns to a dense jungle that reminds me of a rainforest. The canopy is thick and it's dark and cool on the ground. It feels as though we're driving through a cave made of trees and plants.

Where the path through the plain was wide and straight, the route they've carved through the jungle is winding and narrow. Cut vines and limbs lay on the floor of the path. Stumps of skinny trees and bushes dot the ground.

Every hundred feet or so, the path diverts to go around one of the massive trees. Through the foliage I can see their trunks, which are dark reddish-brown with rough bark, similar to the redwoods on Earth.

It's silent except for the animal calls and responses echoing through this dim ecosystem. Leaves rustle as unseen predators and prey flee and slip past us.

To the west, in the grasslands that border the desert, lies the natural habitat of the Eos rex, or E. rex as we've begun calling them. Thus far, the predators haven't ventured into the jungle, but we're all on alert for the giant beasts. Brightwell is sure we could bring one down, but as they say, no plan survives contact with the enemy.

Driving through this forest, it finally hits me how truly different this world is.

The forest breaks at a small creek, bordered by black rock and purple moss.

Brightwell and her troops are standing in the small clearing, panting. They must have just gotten here.

"Any trouble?" I ask Brightwell as I bring the ATV to a stop.

"No, ma'am," she says, her face a mask. Several of her soldiers shoot glances at each other, giving me the impression that cutting this swath through the jungle was anything but easy.

At the creek, Izumi bends down and takes a water sample to test. "The water's frigid," she mumbles as she studies the tablet holding the tube.

"This creek must be fed by the mountains to the east, from the frozen far side," I comment.

"It's refreshing," Private Scott says as he bends down and cups his hand, bringing the water to his mouth.

Izumi opens her mouth to protest, but the tablet beeps, apparently an all-clear message.

She sighs. "Please wait for me next time, Private."

"Yes, ma'am."

Their canteens full, the soldiers ford the creek. On the far bank, Private Scott and Brightwell clutch their rifles, alert, while the other two soldiers detach long blades and poles from their packs. They affix the blades longways on the hard-plastic poles, which they slide into loops on their forearms. The razor-sharp machetes extend nearly four feet from their hands, making the soldiers look like monsters with swords for arms.

They hack at the vines and shrubs, clearing a path, the rest of us following behind, watching for predators. Soon, the forest breaks into another grassy plain where the white domes of the long barracks loom ahead.

From orbit, the holes in the barracks looked like rifle shots. Here they are wide gashes. In some, rotten limbs protrude from the openings. In others, there are skeletons of massive animals, E. rex from the looks of it. It's as if a herd crashed into the barracks. Were they hunting the colonists? From what we've seen, this is far outside of the E. rex natural habitat.

As in the video feeds, there's no movement at the camp.

The two point soldiers detach the blades from the poles and reattach them to the end at right angles, turning the machetes into grass hooks again. They march slower across this grassy plain. The Carthage colonists could have placed land mines, booby traps, and automated defenses out here. By the time we reach the first barracks building, however, we've found none.

"Hello!" Brightwell calls out.

The only sound is the wind and the distant animal calls from the forest. What occurs to me is not what I don't hear—it's what I don't smell. The air is clean and fresh, with no hint of death and decay. No dead bodies—none that died recently anyway.

At the entrance to the closest barracks, the point soldiers stow their grass hooks and take out their rifles, aiming forward as Private Scott pulls the door open.

The long corridor that runs the length of the barracks is empty.

We march down the lane, throwing the doors to the rooms open and scanning them. All empty. The sheets on the bunk beds are disheveled. Tablets lie on the floor. People lived here. From the looks of it, they left in a hurry. Because of the storm that destroyed the camp? Or something else?

At the end of the barracks, Private Scott picks up a toy car lying on the floor of a bunk room. "They brought this?"

"No," Brightwell responds. "The *Carthage* carried a disassembled 3-D printer. The *Jericho* has one too. They must have gotten their printer operational and recycled the matter from their landing capsules into the toys and other items."

Private Scott nods.

"It would have taken at least a month to assemble the printer," I point out. "They would have likely erected the barracks first. They were down here for months—at least. Let's search the rest of the barracks. And try to find their comm patch."

After a few hours of searching, it becomes clear that the barracks are all empty. But they've been lived in. Izumi has tested the water and surfaces throughout the camp. She hasn't detected any pathogens that are known threats to us, but there are surely bugs that will pose a problem. The good news is that the landing party is healthy so far.

I don't know exactly what I expected to find, but I expected *something*. Some sign. Some clue about what happened. There are no notes. No records left on the tablets—they've all been erased. It's as if the colonists just got up one morning and left forever. It's as if they wanted to leave a mystery behind.

I'm standing with Izumi and Brightwell at the edge of the camp, ready to leave, when Private Scott calls from the tree line, "Colonel! We've got something."

We follow the path through the tall grass. At the edge of the jungle, Scott is holding up a comm panel with a strange symbol on it. I study it as we draw closer.

Brightwell turns to me. "Ma'am, do you recognize it?"

"No."

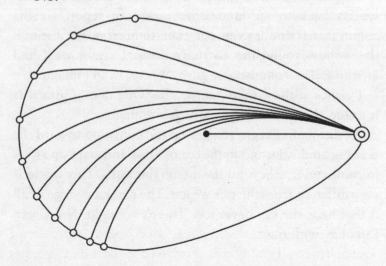

Brightwell holds her tablet up, positioning the symbol in the camera view. "It might be one of the comm characters."

She waits, studying the screen; then she shakes her head. "It's not translating."

"No," I mumble. "It's too orderly. The comm symbols look more random. The colonists drew this. Or... found it somewhere."

Private Scott holds up another tile. "They all have the same symbol. Looks like the wind blew them over here to the tree line. Should we leave them?"

"No," I reply quickly. "Bring them with us."

They're the only clue we have about what happened here.

The drive back to the lander is a lot faster than the trip going. The four soldiers ride silently in the trailer, rifles held at the ready.

Despite the weaker gravity on Eos, I'm dead tired when we get back to the lander. We make our report via the comm panels and lay out our plan: tomorrow, we'll search the woods around the *Carthage* camp. I doubt we'll find anything. The colonists are gone. Where, I can't imagine.

I glance at the symbol on the tile. What does it mean? Is it a clue about what happened? A warning?

As the landing team trudges up the ramp and toward the waiting bunks, I stand in the sea of grass and stare up at the burning red star beyond the mountain peaks. This world is very different from the one we left. The biggest change of all is that here, the sun never sets. There's no night. No winter. I'm okay with that.

75

James

In the *Jericho*'s med bay, three small stasis sleeves lie on the tables. Sam is inside the largest, Allie in the middle, and in a sleeve no larger than the length of my forearm, Carson sleeps.

I haven't brought my children here to wake them. I wouldn't dare. I can't even imagine how frightened they would be. I brought them out to make sure they were okay. I don't trust the ship's computer. Not anymore. Not knowing that Arthur has been awake during this journey, with unrestricted control.

Gently, I run a hand over Allie's head. The stasis sleeve is sealed tight to her body, the material milky and too opaque for me to see her. But just touching her, and Sam, and Carson, and knowing they're alive and healthy is enough for me.

I instruct the robotic arm to stow them again. They'll go down in separate capsules, along with the rest of the colonists and cargo.

On the bridge, the viewscreen shows the eastern valley and the plain that holds our new settlement, which we've creatively named Jericho City. Capsules are touching down quickly, their parachutes drifting down, covering the leveled blue-green grass. The first barracks building stretches out like a caterpillar sunning itself on a lawn.

North of our camp lies the abandoned *Carthage* settlement. What chills me is that our barracks and roads are taking the same shape as theirs, as if someone is slowly copying that part of the planet into this area.

We've opted to leave the *Jericho* and *Carthage* up here. There's a risk that the orbiting vessels might draw the attention of an alien species, but I figure any species sufficiently advanced to be strolling around the galaxy could easily spot us on the surface. And you never know when you might need a spaceship or two in orbit.

Up here on the ship, Min, Grigory, and I have formed a routine. We work, eat, sleep, and play cards. For days, we orbit, deploying capsules each time we pass the eastern valley. On the viewscreen, Eos flies by in a pattern that becomes almost normal: desert, valley, ice, valley, and desert again. The two sides of the world are opposites and somehow they meet to form a perfect sliver of habitation for us.

In so many ways, Eos is like the history of our last days on Earth. The ice on one side, the fire and desolation from the grid on the other, us trying to survive in the narrow space in between.

Grigory and I convinced Min that we should be last off the ship. When the orbital tug takes control of his capsule and nudges it toward the atmosphere, I close the outer doors of the cargo hold and pressurize the space.

I hold the energy weapon as Grigory unlocks the box that holds Arthur.

He crawls out and straightens up, affecting a tired expression and a weary tone. "Don't you just hate moving? It's like, you *always* have more stuff than you think you do."

I hold the tablet up, showing him the symbol left by the Carthaginian colonists:

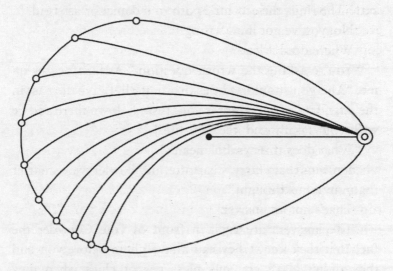

"What is this?" I ask.

"If this is charades, I just need to know—is Grigory on my team or yours?"

"I'm serious, Arthur. The colonists from the *Carthage* are gone. This is all they left. You know what it is, don't you?"

His tone turns serious. "I'm guessing you know what it is too, James."

Grigory cuts his eyes at me, silently asking if that's true. I don't know what it is. The symbol has haunted me since the Lander One base camp sent it back. But I have a theory.

"It's a map, isn't it?"

"Yes," Arthur says flatly.

"Of what?"

Arthur breaks eye contact and shakes his head.

"Is it the map of an orbit? Is the dot in the middle this star? The rings the eccentric path of a comet or asteroid?"

"No, you've got it all wrong."

"Where does it lead?"

"You're asking the wrong question." Arthur focuses on me. "And you shouldn't be asking it at all. Leave the past in the past, James. It's safer for you. Just go down there and be with your family and live your life."

"What does this symbol mean?"

"It means that Harry, Charlotte, and Fowler were smarter than any of us thought."

"That's not an answer."

"The answers are right in front of you. Consider the fact that they knew they had arrived here before you and they didn't leave you any messages or clues when they disappeared." He nods to the image on the tablet. "I'm guessing that wasn't left in plain sight."

"Not exactly."

"You may not know what that symbol means, but you know what that camp means."

"That they left in a hurry."

"It's more than that, James. They don't want you to come looking for them. You ought to take the hint."

"Not good enough," Grigory says, fighting to keep his composure. "You tell us what it is or we kill you."

Arthur smiles with mock sympathy. "That's so cute. Keep in mind I've been playing hostages and heroes a few million years longer than you. If you were going to kill me, I'd already be dead. So let's get on with it. I've said all I'm going to say."

Grigory grinds his teeth, but I can tell he's come to the same conclusion I have.

With the energy weapon, I motion toward an open capsule in the center of the cargo hold.

"Get in."

Striding toward the capsule, Arthur calls over his shoulder. "Where are we going?"

"*You* are going nowhere."

He shakes his head theatrically. "Same thing my parents said when I went through that long awkward phase in high school. I hate being grounded."

When he's inside the capsule, I point to a box on the side. "When we seal this capsule, a sensor ring will be activated. If the seal breaks without us unlocking it, it will explode."

Arthur raises his eyebrows. "Talk about some dynamite outside-the-box thinking!"

I ignore the quip. "The capsule will be tethered to the ship at a safe distance. You try to escape, it explodes."

Arthur exhales. "You've really boxed me in this time. And hung me out to die." He pauses. "I guess this is goodbye. Don't miss me too much."

"That's not going to be a problem."

I'm the last to leave the *Jericho*. On the bridge, the viewscreen shows the growing city in the valley. Three barracks dot the blue-green plain now. Capsules are stacked in rows, like a car lot filled with inventory. Our people are down there, waiting to awaken at their new home.

This place is dangerous. Mysteries surround us. And many of us will never get over what happened on Earth. But the next generation won't have to. They'll grow up on a world where they have a chance at happiness. That's worth the sacrifices we made.

76

Emma

On a ridge a mile from camp, I stand with the binoculars to my eyes, watching the capsule burn through the atmosphere. The parachutes deploy and it drifts lazily to the ground. This is the last capsule to arrive. James is aboard.

I drive the ATV to the touchdown site and tow the beetle-like capsule back to camp. The barracks remind me a little of Camp Seven—the long, domed buildings are made from the same materials, the roads hard-packed dirt, the power provided by solar panels atop the habitats.

Colonel Brightwell decided to dye the AU winter fatigues, Pac Alliance uniforms, and Atlanta militia outfits solid green. The change was in order. Though the clothes are different below, they're the same color. We're no longer fighting each other. Now it's humanity against our new world, its predators and pathogens. And whatever took the *Carthage* colonists.

In the medical habitat, Min and Grigory lift James's stasis sleeve on to the table and Izumi starts the process to bring him out.

A few minutes later, he's pulling the mask from his mouth and looking around, gasping, seeming groggy.

"The air takes some getting used to," I whisper.

He nods as I kiss him on the forehead. "Welcome to Eos."

For three months, the army, most of the adults, and the command crew work to set up the camp. Life in this valley requires adjustments in so many ways. With no sunrise and no sunset, we have to mind the clock and listen to our bodies. It's easy to think that you can work sixteen-hour days until you drop from exhaustion, the orange sun still burning bright over the far mountains, as if it's just rising.

We're all anxious to get our families out of the stasis sleeves, to start our new lives here. But no one is more eager than I am. I've been accumulating my breast milk for Carson and each time I pump, I wish I was holding him in my arms. It's been painful to be separated from him so soon after his birth. It's a sacrifice—a necessary one, for his safety. Soon. I'll see him, Allie, and Sam soon.

Above, *Jericho* is still in orbit, passing like a shooting star every few hours. It is our overwatch, an early-warning system for storms and, thus far, one stampede of deer-like animals that came close to the camp.

I think we've all found the work somewhat therapeutic. After the asteroids hit, every bit of work we did was to survive in the short term. Here, we're working to build something for the long term, something that might endure.

James has changed in ways I can't quite put my finger on. As usual, there's some great question bouncing around in his head, a mystery dogging him. Or perhaps it is just his paranoia, his fear that we're truly not out of the woods.

I'm pretty sure it's the disappearance of the *Carthage* colonists that's bothering him. I've broached the subject several times, but so far, he's seemed to have very little interest in discussing it. Maybe he's doing that to protect me. Maybe he thinks if he acts like it's not a big deal that I'll think the same. I don't. Not only do I miss my friends that were lost, I worry that our fate will be the same as theirs. For now, the only thing I can do is put one foot in front of the other and get everything ready to bring our children home.

There's also a sadness deep inside of James, a scar on his psyche left by his actions on Earth, a rift I hope the years ahead will heal.

He has spent most of his time on Eos working with his brother, Alex, doing manual labor. It's a change for James— doing something low tech, working with his hands, digging in the dirt, putting together habitat parts. The two brothers laugh often, trading inside jokes that don't make any sense to me.

Coming here was terrifying. I think the unknown always is. New beginnings are daunting. I think I, like most people, would rather endure a life that isn't perfect than risk everything on change and the unknown. This new beginning has been good for James and his brother. Their time in Camp Seven healed the rift between them. Here on Eos, I sense that the rift is gone—that they left it behind on Earth. They are starting over.

We have taken to calling the barracks "habs," and the small living quarters inside "flats." Our family, including

James, Sam, Allie, Carson, and me, have been assigned to hab six, flat fourteen. It has a set of bunk beds and a wide bed on the far wall for James and me. A cradle sits beside it, empty and waiting.

The habs are all set up now, the roads packed hard, the mess hall stocked with local provisions. We've settled on a lottery system to determine the order our families will be brought out of stasis.

In our flat, I sit on the edge of the bed staring at the number on the tablet: 251.

"It'll be tomorrow or even the next day," I complain to James.

"We'll still be here."

He takes the tablet from me and reaches into one of the crates. "I've got a surprise for you. Blast from the past."

He pulls out a bag and dumps magnetic playing cards onto the bed.

"No way. Are these—"

"The same."

At the beginning of the Long Winter, during the first contact mission, James and I were sent back to Earth in an escape pod. The voyage was long and monotonous. We worked as much as we could, and when we were too tired, we played gin rummy with these cards. When we were too tired for that, we watched old TV shows on the tablet—*The X-Files* and *Star Trek*, mostly.

He raises the tablet and opens the media player, displaying a list of TV shows. "What's your fancy?"

"Cards."

The cards were made for space. They're heavy and clack as the magnets lock together, but they're perfect. The sound and weight of them remind me of what we've been through together.

When we're too tired to play anymore, we lie shoulder to shoulder in the bed, staring at the ceiling, listening to the sounds of the hab: neighbors talking, people passing down the hallway, and banging in the distance—someone still working. There are shouts of joy and crying too—families reuniting. It's a beautiful sound, one I thought I might never hear.

I take James's hand in mine. Touching him, I see our life together flash through my mind: us holding each other in the *Pax* escape pod, enduring the Long Winter in the habitat we shared with Oscar in Camp Seven, fighting the grid at Ceres, lying in that cramped bunk in the Citadel after the asteroids fell, snuggling under the blankets with Allie and Sam in our bedsheet cubicle in CENTCOM, weathering the final days of the Solar War and the attack on Camp Nine. Each feels like a layer of our life, both him and me together, fighting impossible odds at every turn.

Here and now, this feels different. It's not just because the sun is shining and this world is new and untouched. I feel, in a word, safe.

"What do you think their life is going to be like?" I whisper.

"Very different from ours."

"Yeah."

"In a lot of ways, they'll have everything we did," James says softly. "Joy. Disappointments. Heartbreak. Love. Triumphs. Sickness. Setbacks. Mistakes they learn from. Lessons they pass on to their children. It'll be a different life, but they'll feel all the things we have and will. It will be a very human life."

"Except for the winter."

"Right. They'll never experience winter. Here, it will always be spring."

The medical habitat is hot and sticky by the time we reach it, Izumi and her staff sweating through their clothes, the fans blowing their hair. It's been an endless flow of people through this small habitat, waiting in line, their body heat adding to the sun overhead that never retreats.

Izumi has dark bags under her eyes. She looks as though she's barely slept. She might be scared the crowd will lynch her if she stops for a few hours. Even though stasis has yet to fail on a single colonist, everyone is still worried that their loved ones won't emerge unharmed.

I only realize how nervous I am when it's our turn. Soldiers gently place the three sleeves on the table, and Izumi eyes me.

"Carson first, please."

I hold my breath as she brings the infant out of the sleeve. His cry rings out in the room, silencing the soft discussions from the people in line behind us.

Almost involuntarily, I step forward, arms held out. I feel James's hand on my shoulder, bracing me. Izumi holds up a hand and quickly presses a health analyzer to his shoulder. My eyes fill with tears as he cries louder. He's shivering. Izumi swaddles him as the analyzer beeps. A smile spreads across her weary lined face as she hands the child to me.

"He's fine, Emma."

James holds me and I cradle our son to my chest. This is truly a miracle.

When Allie wakes, James pulls her into his arms. She rubs her eyes, squinting. Recognizing her father, she throws her arms around him and buries her head in his neck.

Sam is more stoic when he wakes, but James hugs him too. Both are looking around in shock, apparently too overwhelmed to say a word.

We make our way out of the med habitat, past the line of waiting parents and family, out into the sunlit valley. Halfway to hab six, Carson stops crying. He's staring out, eyes wide open at this new world.

James is carrying Allie with one arm, holding Sam's hand with his other. Our oldest child is scanning the camp and the woods beyond with a mix of fascination and confusion.

"Where are we, Da?" Allie asks.

"We're home."

Epilogue

James

When Emma and the kids are asleep, I slip out of the flat, down the long corridor that runs the length of the hab, and out into the simulated night.

The kids had a lot of trouble adjusting to the constant sunshine and lack of night. Without sunset and darkness, it just didn't feel right to them to have to come inside and go to bed.

I think the adults didn't mind the light because we were working non-stop, setting up the camp so that we could get our families out of stasis. At the end of each work day, we were too tired to need the dark to sleep.

Our solution to create night here in Jericho City is crude but effective. We used the parachutes from the capsules to create a vast canopy that covers the habitats. Hard plastic poles hold the frame. At seven o'clock standard time, the canopy begins sliding up, gradually blotting out the sun.

In that darkness, I stroll the hard-packed streets, stopping just before the command post. I check my watch and settle in behind a vehicle, waiting. Right on time, Grigory strides out, his shift over.

When he's out of sight, I slip into the command post. It looks a lot like the CP at Camp Nine—rows of desks and a wall full of screens. A lieutenant wearing the standard green Jericho Army uniform turns to me, looking surprised. "Sir, is everything all right?"

"Yes. I'm just stopping in to check out an ATV."

He nods slowly, then glances down at his tablet. "I don't have anything scheduled."

"It's just research. I'll be out in the eastern jungle."

"I'll let the colonel know."

"I wouldn't."

He studies me for a moment.

"Me taking a night stroll through the jungle is not worth waking the colonel for. But if I'm not back by the time the canopy retracts, probably worth sending someone to look for me."

"Yes, sir." He pauses. "Sir—"

I step toward the exit. "Gotta go. Clock's ticking."

Ahead, just beyond the canopy, lies the comm panel array, its white tiles sitting atop poles that reach above the blue-green grass. The sun partially blinds me the moment I clear the canopy. I squint and slow my pace, careful not to stumble in the grass.

At the panels, I plug my tablet into the control box and send my message. The symbols flash on the white tiles, then disappear.

Instinctively, I gaze up to the sky, at the *Jericho* passing over, glowing like a bright star streaking from horizon to horizon.

In the motor pool, I mount the ATV and drive slowly to the tree line. In the jungle, I gun it, zig-zagging through the winding trail. It's as dark as Jericho City's canopy in here—and colder. As I move east, it gets colder still.

The terrain turns from flatland to rolling hills. The massive trees stop at the base of the mountains. The red dwarf star shines softly here, as if it's twilight at the terminator, the thin line that demarks the darkened far side and our little sliver of paradise.

The ATV's tracks easily climb the mountain trail, which soon turns to snow. I can see the darkness ahead and the expanse of snow, completely in shadow except for the dim glow here at the edges.

My destination is an open, icy plain. When I reach it, I spot a capsule descending through the lower atmosphere, burning bright like a fireball falling from the sky.

I dismount the ATV as the capsule clears the atmosphere. The parachutes deploy shortly after, guiding it gently into the snow at the far side of the plain. Twenty feet from the capsule, the mouth of a cave looms, dark and jagged.

At the capsule, I connect my tablet, disable the explosive, and give the command for the capsule to open. The energy weapon Grigory created is in my pocket just in case I need it.

Arthur stands when the capsule's doors swing apart. "Hey, I was on the phone," he snaps with mock annoyance. "And it was long distance!"

The words jolt me. "You were in contact with the grid?"

"Who else has my number?"

"They're in range? Are they coming here?"

"No. Relax. They're just passing by. I told you, this star is a real dud. For us, anyway."

"You didn't re-upload yourself? I thought you couldn't wait to leave."

He lets his head fall back. "Well, you beeped in and I figured it was important." He shrugs. "I'll catch the next train out."

"Right." I let the word drag out, sarcasm dripping from it. "The truth is, you're wondering if I found it."

"What? Jimmy Hoffa? Out here?"

I motion to the cave. "Let's go."

"Oh. That cave."

He marches toward it, his feet crunching in the ice, mine barely making a dent.

"This is a bad idea, James." His voice is matter of fact— all the playfulness gone.

"To me, a bad idea is living on a planet you know killed your friends and not trying to figure out how it happened."

"You assume they're dead."

"Are you saying they're not?"

"Just pointing out your unproven suppositions."

At the mouth of the cave, I activate the LED light on my cap. The white light beams across the jagged, uneven ice in the walls and floor.

"Who made this tunnel?" I ask.

"You already know."

"Harry."

Arthur stares straight forward. "That would be my guess." After a pause, he adds, "How did you find it?"

"We need metal as raw material for the three-D printers, so I built a rover with a metal detector to search for the elements we need. I tried searching in the mountains, but the detector had a lot of trouble with false signals. It was pretty easy to find loose metal buried out here in the ice."

At that moment, a breakthrough occurs to me. "That's how Harry found it too, isn't it? He built a rover and sent it out here looking for metal. I bet he was looking for asteroids that had made landfall in the snow. He was going to use the metals from the asteroids as media for the 3-D printers—just like I intended to do."

When Arthur doesn't reply, I motion ahead, and he begins trudging through the icy cavern.

"I'm telling you, this is a bad idea," he says lightly. "You should go home, James. Forget about this."

"I can't."

"If only you could. Your fear is driving you. The terror that something bad is going to happen to your people and your loved ones."

"That sounds like the secret to humanity's survival. I'm on the right track."

"Yes and no."

"Meaning?"

"Time will tell."

I shake my head, sick of the half-answers. Up ahead, the object looms. The black metal ball protrudes from the snow, glittering in the beam of the headlamp, looking so alien and otherworldly.

"Do you know what this is?"

His gaze pans lazily away from the object at the end of the tunnel. "Yes."

"What is it?"

He shakes his head. "A relic."

"Of what?"

"Of secrets that shouldn't be found." He focuses on me. "I mean it. There are things buried on Eos that should remain buried."

When I glance away from him, I see it for the first time: the symbol, carved into the ice. It's the same symbol we found at the *Carthage* camp on the comm panels. But here it's slightly different. One of the lines is carved deeper, its point larger.

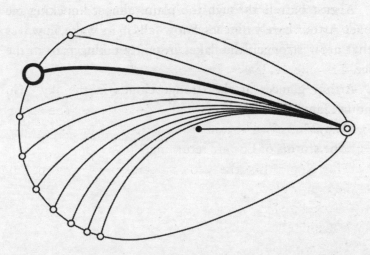

"The map," I whisper, stepping closer. "What is this, Arthur?"

"We call it the Eye of the Grid."

"It's a map. Isn't it?"

He simply shakes his head, acting conflicted.

"Where does it lead?"

I pause, waiting.

"Answer me."

"I can't, James."

"Why?"

"Because you're asking the wrong question."

With the tablet, I take a picture of the symbol, and then Arthur and I trudge out of the cavern, back to the icy plain. The sky cracks with thunder and lightning streaks the sky in a thousand branches, like nothing I've ever seen. The bolts seem to split the sky open. Green and yellow clouds spread out and shift in the wind, reminding me of the aurora borealis.

A gust barrels through the plain, almost knocking me over. Arthur barely flinches. Snow falls in its wake, in waves that grow stronger, the flakes instantly taking root in the ice.

Arthur glances at the strange clouds in the sky. "Go home, James."

"Why?"

"The storms of Eos are returning."

About the Author

A.G. RIDDLE spent ten years starting and running internet companies before retiring to focus on his true passion: writing fiction. He lives in North Carolina. Visit www.agriddle.com